STAINED
Light

Also by Naomi Foyle
Seoul Survivors

The Gaia Chronicles
Astra
Rook Song
The Blood of the Hoopoe

STAINED
Light

NAOMI FOYLE

Book Four of The Gaia Chronicles

Jo Fletcher
BOOKS

The moral right of Naomi Foyle to be identified as the author of this work has been asserted in accordance with the Copyright, Designs and Patents Act, 1988.

A CIP catalogue record for this book is available from the British Library.

PB ISBN 978 1 78206 927 0
EBOOK ISBN 978 1 78429 966 8

10 9 8 7 6 5 4 3 2 1

Typeset by Jouve (UK), Milton Keynes
Printed and bound in Great Britain by Clays Ltd, Elcograf S.p.A.

for Brenda Davis and Ripley

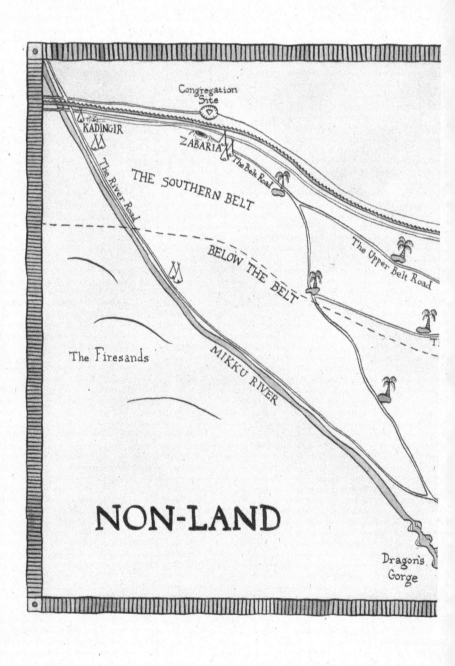

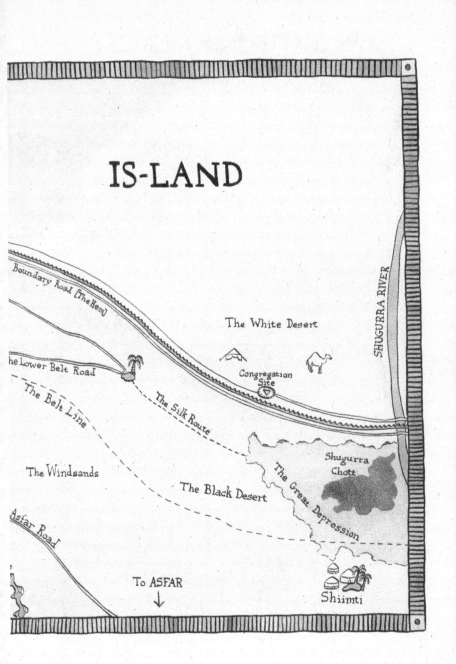

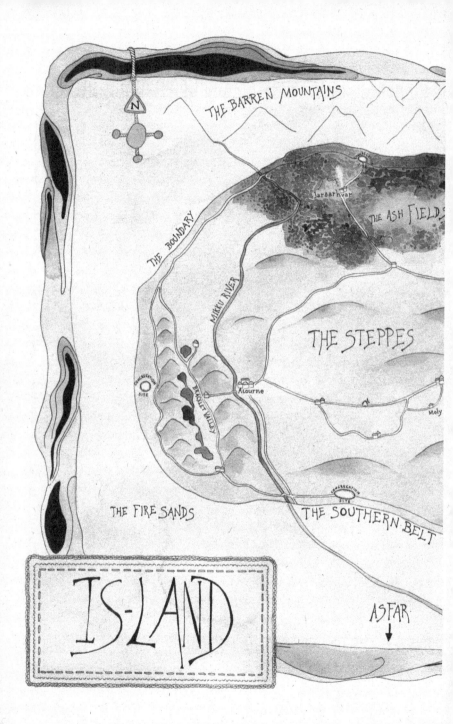

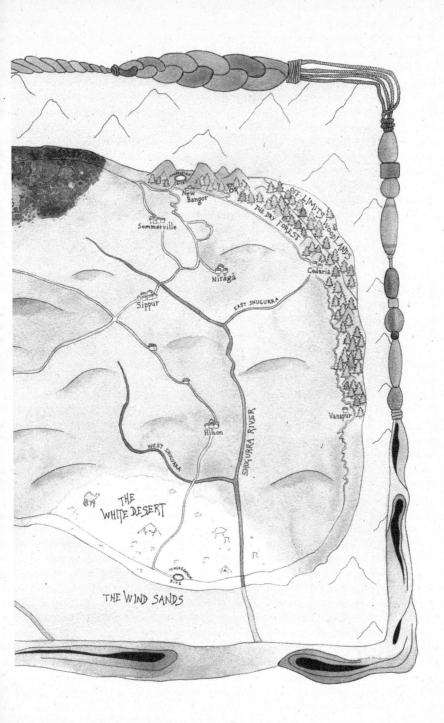

Dramatis Personae

IS-LAND

The Ashfields

Astra Ordott	Political prisoner; Oracle
Cora Pollen	Political prisoner; friend of Astra's Birth-Code mother, Eya, and niece of Astra's Shelter mother, Hokma Blesser [both deceased]
Charm	Political prisoner
Rosetta	Political prisoner
Pallas	Political prisoner
Fern	Political prisoner
Sunflower	Political prisoner
Lichena	Prison guard
Bircha	Prison guard

Atourne: capital city of Is-Land, home to the National Wheel Meet and its various Ministries, chief among them the Is-Land Ministry of Border Defence [IMBOD]

Superintendent Dr Samrod Blesserson	Code Scientist; Hokma Blesser's brother; Member of IMBOD's secret Vision Council

Chief Convenor
  Stamen Magmason
	Head of National Wheel Meet;
	  Head of the Vision Council

Deputy Convenor
  Riverine Farshordott
	Deputy Head of National
	  Wheel Meet; Member of
	  the Vision Council

Crystal Wyrdott	Wheel Meet Chief Minister of Spiritual Development
Justice Blade Stonewayson	Prosecuting Judge in the Ministry of Penitence
Harald Silverstreamson	National Prosecutor in Stonewayson's office

Bracelet Valley ~ Yggdrasila

Freki Yggdrasiladott	Child (pre-Sec Gen), twin to Ggeri
Ggeri Yggdrasilason	Child (pre-Sec Gen), twin to Freki
Sif Yggdrasiladott	Code Shelter mother to Freki and Ggeri; partner to Vili
Vili Yggdrasilason	Code Shelter father to Freki and Ggeri; partner to Sif
Fasta Yggdrasiladott	Birth Shelter mother to Freki and Ggeri
Esfadur Yggdrasilason	Community Elder; Code Shelter father to Eya
Brana Yggdrasiladott	Community Elder; Birth-Code Shelter mother to Eya

Eya Yggdrasiladott	Birth-Code daughter to Esfadur and
	  Brana; Birth-Code mother to Astra
	  and Halja [deceased]

Halja Yggdrasiladott	Birth-Code daughter to Eya; Sec Gen

Bracelet Valley ~ Springhill Retreat

Chief Superintendent Clay Odinson	Director of Springhill Retreat; Former Head of the Non-Land IMBOD Barracks
Tulip Hiltondott	Wheel Meet Minister of Penitence
Ahn Orson	Celebrity bio-architect; Hokma's ex-partner

The Dry Forest

Klor Grunerdeson	Astra's Shelter father; Code worker
Nimma	Astra's Shelter mother; Craft worker
Sheba	Klor and Nimma's Code daughter [deceased]
Peat	Astra's Shelter brother; former Sec Gen [see Shiimti]
Yoki	Astra's Shelter brother; Sec Gen
Meem	Astra's Shelter sister; Sec Gen
Congruence	Ahn's partner, a relationship begun secretly and illegal in her teens; non-Sec Gen

NON-LAND

Occupied Zabaria

Lilutu	CONC worker; YAC activist; AKA Tira Gúnida
Anunit	Mother; Former sex worker in Pithar
Girin	Son of Anunit
Bud	IMBOD communications officer
Neperdu	Sex worker [deceased]

Shiimti

Peat Orson	Former Sec Gen Constable; Astra Ordott's Shelter brother
Bartol	YAC Trainer and Warrior
Dr Tapputu	Physician; former CONC medic in Kadingir
Zizi Kataru	Astra Ordott's Code father [deceased]
The Zardusht	The High Healer of Shiimti
Ñeštug	Dream Voyage Guide

The Non-Land All Action Revolutionary Commandos (NAARC)

Enki Arakkia	NAARC Commander
Muzi Bargadala	Shepherd and Forager; Astra Ordott's husband
Ñizal	NAARC Commander
Sulima	NAARC Commander; married to Enki

ASFAR

The Mujaddid	Ruler of Asfar
Colonel Akira Thames	CONC Envoy; Former CONC Compound Director in Kadingir
Tibir Ögüt	Billionaire and secret patron of NAARC

The Non-Land Alliance (N-LA) [Non-Land Government-in-Exile]

Una Dayyani	Lead Convenor
Marti	Personal Assistant to Una Dayyani

| Artakhshathra | Chief Researcher |
| Tahazu Rabu | Chief of Police |

The Youth Action Collective (YAC) [Non-Land resistance group, allied to N-LA]

Ninti	Speaker and Warrior, Voice of YAC in N-LA
Malku	Speaker and Warrior, Voice of YAC in N-LA
Tiamet	Singular
Simiya	Singular
Asar	Singular
Sepsu	Asar's Carer

Muzi Bargadala's Family

Habat Bargadala	Daughter-in-law of Uttu, widow of Kingu
Nanshe Emeeš	Daughter-in-law of Uttu, widow of Gibil
Geshti Bargadala	Daughter of Kingu and Habat
Hadis Bargadala	Daughter of Kingu and Habat
Suen Emeeš	Son of Gibil and Nanshe
Esañ	Husband of Geshti
Ahmad	Husband of Hadis
Mordi Bargadala	Infant son of Geshti and Esañ
Uttu Dúrkiñar	Elderwoman; grandmother of Muzi [deceased]
Kingu Dúrkiñar	Eldest son of Uttu [deceased]
Gibil Dúrkiñar	Second son of Uttu [deceased]

AMAZIGIA

Jasper Sonovason   Astra's lawyer
Calendula Goldstone   Cora Pollen's lawyer

NEUROPA

Photon Augenblick   Blogger; Former CONC Mobile
                          Medical Unit Medic

NUAFRICA

Rudo Acadie   CONC Officer; Former Mobile
                          Medical Unit Medic

NEW ZONIA

Sandrine Moses   CONC Officer; Former Mobile
                          Medical Unit Supply Coordinator

The biggest threat to life on Earth is human beings. You are the parasite that threatens to kill the host. Humans made a secret pact with one of the Oldest powers of all, Metal; with Metal's help you proliferated, polluted, exhausted ancient energies, forced chain reactions, destroyed the fundamental balance of this planet. Finally, the rest of the Old Ones roared in anger against you . . . When oceans rose to drown your cities, temperatures soared to scorch your fields, clouds gathered to blot out the sun, many humans did at last realise the error of your ways. But already, the most brutal among you are re-forging your species' pact with Metal, and if the rest of the Old Ones convulse again, this time only a few rodents and insects will survive. Remember, Astra, Metal is not wild and free and loving like the wind or the sunshine or water. Metal is hidden, inert, ambitious, jealous and cunning. But it is also part of your bodies, your minds and your souls. Humans are composed of everything that exists: that is the secret of your own enormous power. In you mingle molten droplets of gold, copper, lead, iron; the birth and death howls of all living creatures; salt and sweet waters; trickles of sand from the canyons; swirls of dust from the stars. In this awareness of your universal nature lies your redemption . . .

Istar to Astra Ordott, RE 87

'That which is hateful to you, do not do to your fellow. That is the whole Torah; the rest is the explanation; go and learn.'

Hillel the Elder (110 BCE – 10 CE)

'Do not let the kingdom of heaven become a desert within you. Do not be proud because of the light that brings enlightenment. Rather, act towards yourselves as I also acted towards you: I put myself under a curse for you, that you might be saved.'

Jesus in *The Secret Book of James* (8:14–15)

'And of His signs is this: He created for you companions from yourselves that you might find rest in them, and He ordained between you Love and Mercy. In this indeed are signs for people who reflect.'

The Message of the Qur'an (Surah 30:21)

'Alone, she will fly to the ashlands and bury herself in the earth. When she arises the placeless ones shall be in all places, and all places shall sing glad hymns of welcome and of [word missing].'

The Prophecy
[Fragments from cuneiform tablets c. 3250 BCE]

THE VERNAL EQUINOX
21.03.99

Acid Green

Misted Silver
Sour Gold
Misted Silver
Sour Gold
Misted Silver

Shadow Blue

Acid Green

Bracelet Valley

'*Whaaor.*' Breaking the first rule of the willow tree hideout – silence during active surveillance – Ggeri plopped back down behind the cedar log, the spyglasses clutched to his chest. Crouching beside him in the dirt, Freki stifled a giggle. Ggeri's face changed expression so often his nickname in Yggdrasila was Little Windwolf. Right now, his eyes bulging like grapes and his lips puckered with shock, her twin looked like a catfish: one of the giant, bug-eyed bottom feeders that hoovered dead fish off the muddy bed of Lake Asgard, keeping the water clean for the manatees and freshwater dolphins. He was even the right colour – the light filtering through the spring branches had turned his skin a blotched, clammy green.

'See, I *told* you,' she hissed – she had made the rule and could ignore it if she liked. Plus, it was clear Ggeri had forfeited the rest of his turn with the spyglasses. She wrested them from his grip and crept, stealthy as a snake, up to the top of the log.

Shady and fragrant with cedar and soil, the space she and Ggeri had created beneath the willow tree was a secret chamber, a hidden playroom, but its jewellery boxes of scarlet ladybirds and turquoise caterpillars, its world-record-tall twig tower and the *hnefetafl* board they had scored in the earth with a stone were all just silly kids' toys compared to this new game. Leaning in close to the lacy curtain of willow leaves, Freki trained the glasses into the mossy heart of the glade, scanning the broad trunks and spreading branches of the oaks until the sunlit shapes of the man and the woman filled her vision.

The man was the same man as the other day. He was tall and thin, with a cloud of fuzzy white hair like a dandelion clock. When she fiddled with the focus, she could see his eyes rolling back inside his head and his mouth twisting like he was a llama trying not to sneeze. He looked a lot like a llama, actually, his woolly chest and legs gilded gold in the late-afternoon sun. He wasn't all hairy, though; when he bent down to shake the woman's shoulders, she could see a shiny round bald patch on the top of his head, as if someone *had* sneezed and blown some of his dandelion seeds away. The woman was a different woman. She was small like the one before, with the same glowing bronze skin, but she had long, straight black hair and, instead of crouching like a dog in the grass, she was kneeling in front of the man, her head at his hips. Through the spyglasses, Freki could see clearly that her head was bobbing up and down on his Gaia plough. You'd never see dogs doing that! She inched her elbows forwards and shifted her belly up the log for a better view.

Ggeri lunged for her arm and pulled her back down beside him, scraping her wrist against the cedar bark and making her knock over the twig tower. She rubbed her arm and glared at him. 'Look what you made me do.'

'They'll see the glass shining, stupid!' he scoffed.

'No, they won't. They're *busy.*'

'Yeah, until the sun hits the glass and sends a blast of light to blind him in one eye and—'

'*Shhh!*' She bared her teeth and stuck out her tongue like a dagger. Yggdrasila didn't call her Little Firewolf for nothing.

Ggeri puffed his cheeks out hard with air, flared his nostrils and crossed his eyes, but followed her orders at last. *She* was in charge here. She had found the glade, tracking a trail of deer spoor one afternoon when Ggeri was in the Warrior Hall watching the Sec Gens practise their judo moves. Ggeri couldn't wait to have his

Security Serum shot and take his place on the mat. He wanted to lose his puppy fat and earn Black Belts in judo, karate and tae-kwondo, and be ready to pulverise any Non-Lander and international troops that might try to invade Is-Land after the Hudna was over. But that was because Ggeri played too many Tablette games. Now that the Boundary had been clad it was impossible to breach, every-one said so, and the Sec Gens were just-in-case. Who wanted to be super-strong just-in-case? Freki liked it when Oma Fasta blew kisses into her tummy and called her roly-poly, and watching the Sec Gens was boring. The older children could throw their judo instructor across the gym, but where was the fun in watching them do that over and over again? Even their parents found it boring, she could tell. They looked up and clapped, but most of them were read-ing on their Tablettes in the stands.

What was happening in the glade was a million times more exciting. Yesterday and the day before, out playing on her own, she had discovered what happened here in the afternoons. Today she had sneaked a pair of birding binoculars from Oma Sif's desk and, swearing Ggeri to secrecy on their twin bond, had tempted him out to the woods to help her build the willow tree hideout. He'd wanted to know why, of course, but she had only said it would be worth it. Now she had been proved right. Just like she had promised, this was way better than watching the Sec Gens; better, even, than watching the community dogs mate. She slung the spyglasses strap around her neck, rose up on her knees again and peered back out at the glade.

'It's *my* turn now.' Ggeri bobbed up beside her, but she elbowed him away. The man was digging his fingers into the woman's long black hair, his eyes were closed now but his mouth was stretched wide open and drool was coming out of it. She snickered again. The man made funnier faces than Ggeri. That must be why you weren't allowed to watch adults mating, in case you burst out laughing when they were trying to boss you around later on.

Then, in a single movement that nearly gave Freki a crick in her neck, the man whipped the woman's head away from his groin, pulled a stick out of his hipbelt and brandished it high. A willow branch was in the way, but Freki fingered it aside and through the glasses she could see the stick was big and jagged and made of silver metal. It flashed in the sun like a lightning bolt.

'What's he—' Ggeri pressed closer to her. It was as if they were glued together with sweat and dirt, unable to stop watching, barely able to breathe. The man shouted but Freki couldn't make out the words. Then his arm plunged down and he stabbed the woman in the chest with the lightning stick.

Freki and Ggeri's gasps were lost in the flutter of birds flying up from the trees. Jerking and flailing, the woman fell to the ground.

Run! Run away! Freki silently screamed. Ggeri was tugging at the spyglasses but she kept them jammed to her eyes. The woman just kept wriggling and writhing and arching her back, her hair falling in a black wing over the grass. The man was panting and his pale face was all red. He raised his arm again, holding the lightning stick high, like a storm god in one of Oma Fasta's Tablette stories. He jabbed the woman again, and again her body convulsed, her arm knocking something beside her – a pink hydropac – and sending it tumbling over the grass. With a sudden blurred arc, the man kicked her in the ribs. It was warm in the hideout, sticky and warm, but Freki was as cold as ice. She let Ggeri take the glasses and squeezed her eyes shut. There was a roaring in her ears, like a storm in the forest. *Why wasn't the woman fighting back?*

Ggeri leaned close and spoke into her ear. 'She's not *grown up* yet, Freki.' He gulped, as if he was about to cry. 'She's just a girl. I dunno, Year Eight or Nine?'

Heat blazed in her chest. That was *so* stupid. Adults weren't allowed to Gaia play with girls, not even Year Twelves.

'No, she isn't.' She glared at her twin. 'She's just short.'

'She's a girl, Freki. Her hydropac has got Gaia World characters on it. This is bad.' Ggeri held his stomach, as if he felt sick. 'I want to go home.'

She grabbed the spyglasses back and peered again at the pink hydropac lying in the grass. Was that Acorn's green hat, or just a pattern? It was hard to tell. And grown-up women could be small. Then the woman let out a high, weird shriek and her fist hit the pac again, getting caught in the straps and flipping it over. With a hot, acid spurt, Freki's stomach turned with it.

There on the bag were the familiar, friendly, big-stitched outlines of Acorn and Seedling – Year *Seven* characters – smiling their goofy smiles at the girl as she lay twitching beside them in the grass, her hips rocking up towards the man. For she was a girl, there was no denying it: the way she was lying now, Freki could see that her breasts were just starting to bud. And her cries were the whimpering cries of a child.

Freki wanted to run down into the glade, grab rocks and big sticks and throw them at the man, dash the lightning bolt out of his hand. But she couldn't move. She just stared and stared until her eyes felt hard as marbles. The girl was slender, dainty as a fairy dancer, but she kept on taking the kicks, rolling her body as if begging the man to kick her everywhere. And he did. He kicked her in the *head*. Tears boiled up in Freki's eyes.

Ggeri yanked her back down into the dirt. 'We have to go and tell someone. Quick, while they're still here.'

Battling back sobs, she kneaded the earth, barely feeling its moist peatyness, cool and dark between her fingers. 'No,' she blubbered. 'We can't.'

The tears burning down her cheeks now, she dug her fingers into the bark of the cedar log. The reddish-brown bits crumbled over the *hnefetafl* board drawn in the dirt, and she scuffed the game out with her heel, gouging a hole in the ground and scattering the pebble pieces amongst the wreckage of the twig tower. Over in the glade, the girl shrieked. The girl who could be kicked and punched and struck by lightning without getting hurt. The unbreakable girl.

Ggeri pulled his sandals on and tossed Freki's against her legs. 'Don't be stupid. Of course we can. We can tell Oma Sif and Oma

Fasta and Apa Vili, and they'll tell Apa Esfadur and he'll tell Major Brockbankson.'

'Major Brockbankson won't help us!' Freki rubbed her swollen eyes dry. 'He's in IMBOD and IMBOD won't *care* because IMBOD *made* her, Ggeri.'

'What?' He recoiled. 'No, they didn't.'

'Yes, they did.' Freki threw a fistful of dirt down between them. 'She's a *Sec Gen*. Isn't she? That's why they make Sec Gens so strong, even the fairy dancers. Don't you see? It's so that grown-ups can kick them and hit them as hard as they like.'

'No, it isn't!' Ggeri's whisper foamed with outrage but her words had hit home: fear rippled in the air between them.

'It *is*.' She overpowered her brother's doubtful gaze with her fiercest Firewolf stare.

Ggeri's lower lip wobbled. 'She looks like Bluebell.'

She leaned close and pressed her forehead against his. As their breaths mingled and their knees touched, at last she felt it: their twin bond pulsing between them. Her teachers said that when they became Sec Gens they would feel a deep bond with their entire generation, but she didn't need to run in a murmuration with a hundred other children. For all his bossiness and stupidity, all Freki needed was Ggeri; all she wanted to do was spend her life squabbling, playing and prowling through the forest with her womb brother, like the wolf cubs they'd been named for.

She looked into his big, black eyes, all doubled and floaty and swimming with sadness. 'We have to run away,' she whispered. 'Run away to Lake Asgard and hide in the woods.'

'We can't do that!' Ggeri pulled back, kicking the rest of the twig tower into the hole she had dug with her heel. But the twin bond still connected them, bound them together as if they shared the same heart.

'Yes, we can.' She hooked her finger into his elbow. 'We're the wolf cubs. We can live on nuts and berries and wild mushrooms and salad leaves, and sleep in a cave where no one can find us.'

'I don't know . . .'

He trailed off. It was as quiet as the bottom of a lake in the glade. A muddy, poisoned lake that an army of catfish couldn't clean. Freki took one last peek over the log. The man had stopped shouting. He was on his knees now, straddling the girl's body, staring at her face and doing something to himself that Freki didn't want to watch. She stuffed the spyglasses into her hipbelt, then dropped onto all fours and crawled out from under the willow, back into the forest. Ggeri crept with her, on hands and knees through the dirt and roots and softly crackling twigs and leaves, until they were far enough away from the glade to stand up and run, run as one being, safe in the breath of the forest.

At last they reached the sweet chestnut stand and the thatched roofs of Yggdrasila came into sight between the trees. Freki stood in front of Ggeri and, panting, blocked his way.

'We can't tell anyone, Ggeri. *Promise.*'

He folded his arms and pouted, but didn't argue. She stepped closer, chest-to-chest.

'We *have* to run away.' She pointed with an earth-black finger back at the glade. 'That's what's going to happen to *us* if we have the Security Serum shot.'

Misted Silver

The Ashfields

She was naked in the sun, her body cradled in a hollow of tall grass, her limbs wrapped around a smooth, lean, endless young man, his arms enfolding her, his embrace somehow uniting her with the clean blue sky above. She could smell the man: he smelled of wild honey and mountain sage. His face was a dazzle of sunshine, but beneath her fingertips his spine was a road home; clasped in her palm, the stump of his right wrist was a staff to lean on; planted on her neck and her face, his kisses were soft steps to heaven. 'Are you ready?' Muzi whispered in a language she'd forgotten she knew. 'Are you ready, Astra?'

'Yes,' she murmured, closing her eyes, her vision shading to red. 'Yes.'

Muzi thrust his groin against hers. She awoke with a gasp, to darkness and the stink of shit. Her hand flew down her body, over the steel shield of her tankini breastplate, to the steel crotch of her girdle. Tears pricking her eyes, Muzi's mouth still wet on hers, she thumped her hips against the bed mat. As she tipped into orgasm, the cell flooded with light. A harsh white glare burnt into her brain, ice-cold air blasted down from the ceiling vent, and, in a great spasm of beating wings, scissoring beaks and flashing eyes, the giant wallscreen opposite the bed exploded into vigilance.

'Penitent AO202,' Vultura hissed. 'You have engaged in Gaia play. Ten marks have been deducted from your Privilege Account.'

The last traces of the dream vanished. Astra pulled the sheet up over her goose-pimpled flesh and its steel cage. 'Fuck you, Vultura,' she muttered.

'Penitent AO202.' The avatar's hooded eyes bored into her, two acid-yellow pinpricks in a cratered grey face. 'You have spoken before six a.m. An Impertinence Penalty has been deducted from your Privilege Account.'

She lay curled up beneath the sheet, shivering and rubbing her arms. The light dimmed to a spectral glow and Vultura resettled into brooding watchfulness, a huge, hunched, black silhouette against a granular grey background. Vultura was not sleeping – Vultura never slept – but the avatar's eyes were half-closed again, its massive bald head still, the only movement on the wallscreen the remorseless progress of the clock. 21.3.99 · 05:42:15 . . . 16 . . . 17 . . . The seconds flickered like insects and the minutes crawled like snails: over one hundred and eighteen to drag by before breakfast. Nine more of freezing-cold air to endure.

But she had bested the girdle. She had peaked, right under Vultura's black beak. As the last tremors of triumph and pleasure flushed through her veins, Astra willed herself back to sleep, back to her oasis with Muzi.

It was no use. She was cold, the tankini breastplate and girdle cut into her flesh, her loose upper-left molar nagged at her jaw and the sheet was scant protection against the stink in the cell. Running on the spot was the best response to the ceiling vent, but if she got out of bed she'd be punished again. Her teeth chattering so hard she feared the rotting one would crumble, she rolled onto her back, the most comfortable position the chastity shackles allowed. It was nearly morning: a new day soon to be welcomed. But as the grey dawn light seeped into her cell through the frosted window, and the brickwork vaults and cameras above her came into focus, another, deeper darkness washed over her.

Being in jail was like being swallowed by a whale. A dead, frozen whale with a twenty-four-hour surveillance system implanted in its guts. And why was she still clinging to dreams of Muzi? In twelve years in jail, although her lawyer secretly communicated regularly with his family, she had never received a message from him, not a single, smuggled word. As the creeping morning sunlight etched the limits of her world, absence, the complete absence of everyone and everything she loved, scraped her hollow again. If it weren't for her medication and the Old Ones, she'd be just like the self-harmers: trading in razor blades, cutting her wrists, her throat if she could.

If you choose to merge with Istar you will suffer – but your suffering will have meaning.

The words rose up from the core of her being. Hokma's words, first soulspoken in that other stone cave more than a decade ago. Astra had repeated them so many times over the years, if they'd been a scrubbing brush they would have worn away the walls of her cell. With them came a glow of resolve, a light to repel the darkness welling up from within her. She waited. She was good at waiting. At last, the air vent closed and then, eight minutes later, the clock finally leapt over the threshold to 21.3.99 · 06:00:00.

'Astra Ordott!' she declared, out loud, but not quite loud enough to incur another burst of cold air, or to disturb Charm in the next cell.

Vultura's eyes snapped open and the domed head began its warning swivel, not scanning the cell – the cameras did that – but reminding her that she was being watched.

As if she ever forgot that. She shook her fist at the camera above the toilet. 'Fuck you, Vultura. I have chosen to endure this ordeal. Not just cold and loneliness, fucking chains and fucked-up guards. I have chosen to wage an emotional war with myself. For a reason!'

As if on command, a strong beam of sunlight poured across the cell to light up the shelves beside the door: metal shelves crammed to bursting with rows and rows of paper, that archaic technology, sheaves and files and bundles of news articles, case notes and letters, all, thanks to Jasper's persistent defence of her rights, stamped APPROVED by the prison censor, their edges gilded by the dawn. *Yes.* Let Vultura stare: Sun was on her side, sending light through the darkness, to recharge and sustain her, to renew the failed promise of her existence. She sat up. What was she doing, lolling around in bed? Today was a *Visitors' Day*. Jasper was coming. Her lawyer, travelling all the way from Amazigia to bring news of her campaigns, documents for her files, defiant reminders of her reasons for choosing to live in this Gaia-forsaken hole. She had work to do, hours of work. Thank *frack* she had woken early.

06:02:18. She scrambled out of her bunk to the sink, took her head pills and brushed her teeth, flinching as the bristles frisked the rotting molar. Then she squatted over the blocked toilet and urinated through the grille in the tankini girdle. As she was hosing herself down, her bowels shifted. She pressed a button on the wall, the back of the girdle slid open and Vultura's eyes began to flash. She defecated, cleaned herself as quickly as possible and waited for the girdle to close.

It didn't. Sometimes this happened to tempt you to Gaia play with yourself. She clapped her hands on top of her head. The squat was good for her thighs.

At last the girdle shut. Vultura's eyes resumed their default acrid smoulder. Astra stood in the small oblong of floor space between bed, narrow desk, shelves, door, toilet and sink. Facing the cloudy window above the bed, feet alive on the cold stone, she opened her arms wide. Vultura was watching from the wallscreen, the giant head swinging back and forth, but Vultura couldn't stop her worshipping. She was a human being and she had a right to worship her gods. *Sun*, she petitioned silently. *Great Globe of Fire. Please infuse me with your power.*

Even at noon on a summer's day, kneeling on the bed with her face pressed to the window, she could barely see anything through the frosted glass. The best view she ever got was a dark smudge of what she knew was a lavascape, and above it a fuzzy white sky. But she had a right to natural light and she never took it for granted. As the sunbeam flowed into the cell, Astra lifted her face, invited a gentle wealth of photons to tiptoe over her lashes, dance on her cheeks, cascade down her body. The light polished the tankini, but it also sheened her skin until she exuded a honey-gold aura to repel Vultura's gaze, the stink from the toilet, any shit the day might throw at her. As the cell steadily brightened, stealing the gleam from Vultura's eyes, she did her morning yoga: sun salutations, Warrior One, Warrior Two, Warrior Three. Corpse pose.

Afterwards, she lay on the bed, observing her breath. Yoga prepared her for visitations from the Old Ones, and even if the Old Ones didn't come, the exercise and meditation were a good use of time. Time, not an endless ladder of numbers, but a healer who brewed bitter herbs, the doctor she must never perceive as her enemy. Hokma had said that. Hokma, whose presence she hadn't felt since . . . The memory clouded her mind, trailed by a pale, hopeful thought.

Old Ones, she soulspoke. *Jasper is coming today. I would be grateful for a message for my people. And if You don't mind*, she added, *I have a question for You.*

Istarastra.

Istarastra: the name the Old Ones called her when they expected her to be solemn and wise, to accept all the hard, impersonal truths of the universe. The sibilant cellular transmission sent a nervy quiver running down from her scalp to her toes. She raised her arms behind her head and braced them against the wall.

Earth. Thank you for coming.

Earth sniffed, setting all the hairs on her body erect. *It smells good in your den. And you taste . . . like the desert.*

She was never quite sure if the Old Ones understood that she was in prison. Perhaps they had soulspoken to so many cloistered mystics over the millennia the distinction was not clear to them. And probably a blocked-up toilet would smell delicious to Earth.

Thank you. I drank long of Sun.

One day you shall swim again in Sun's heat. That day has not yet come!

Earth's roar jerked through her and her arms began to ache. She was prepared for it now, but soulspeaking with Earth was nothing like she'd imagined it would be. Earth was no nurturing mother deity, more like an irate Abrahamic god.

You ask Me for a new message, Earth rumbled. *I have an old message, an old message from all of the Old Ones. Today Earth, Air, Fire and Water send your people the same message as always, but for one crucial difference: today it comes as a final warning. Today, Istarastra, you must tell the Creatures of Clay that the Old Ones have run out of patience. Your miserable species has one year left: one year in which to end your vain romance with Metal or perish.*

The bed rattled, her brain wobbled like a sack of jelly in her head and a spark of fear ignited in her stomach. *Perish? Already? But I'm only just starting to get Your messages out to the right people—*

Hah! Earth scoffed, a sensation rather like having one's kidneys scrubbed with sandpaper. *The right people are irrelevant, Child. It is the* wrong *people who should be heeding the Old Ones. The wrong people who are digging more mines, plundering the planet for rare-earths metals, copper, iron and tin, creating sink holes and swamps, toxic lakes, erosion that scatters the soil to the winds. The wrong people who are building more bombs, courting war and disaster. The wrong people who are proliferating, year on year, in thrall to Metal, a renegade force that seeks ever to attain dominion over the family of elements, desires only to disrupt the balance of the universe. I tell you again, Child: the Old Ones searched for billions of light-years to find this planet and garland it with every beauteous form of life, and We will not allow Metal to transform it into a barren rock, populated only by robots and devil worms. The Creatures of Clay may hold life in contempt. We do not!*

She winced. *I know. I know mining and weapon-making are happening, and they shouldn't be. We should have learned more from the Dark Times. But we did give up fossil fuels, Earth. And we banned war, for a hundred years. To keep making positive changes we just need a bit more time—*

Yes, you gave up gobbling black gold. Earth's sneer made her skin crawl and an unsavoury taste rise in the back of her throat.

After you raised the global temperature four degrees and cratered the continents with nuclear strikes; after the seas rose and devoured your cities; after famines and disease consumed entire nations; after a generation of survivors endured two decades of sunless skies; after human beings nearly made yourselves and every other species on the planet extinct – at last you put your heads together and decided to give up burning oil and take a little breather from war! For a brief moment, it appeared you had learned from your mistakes, but that moment has passed like the fart of a camel. For the Creatures of Clay are akin to cracked jugs: you do not hold the waters of wisdom long. Again you witless infants drool at the feet of Metal. Even you are still using Tablette technology to send Our messages to the world. And look at that barbaric contraption you're wearing! How do you expect humanity to break its lustful bond with Metal if even you are cladding your sexual organs in steel?

I'm sorry, she grovelled. But I told you before, I'm stuck in here. The authorities make me wear this stupid outfit. I can't travel or give talks. And it's the humans who are still using Tablettes that we most urgently need to reach.

Reach them, then! Reach them all. Today, Istarastra, you will tell your woeful species that it has one year within which to cure its fascination with Metal and return to a state of equilibrium with the Old Ones. By the next Vernal Equinox, humans must forbid all metal mining, abandon their Tablettes and destroy all their weapons, or they will incur the ultimate wrath of the Old Ones. If you do not obey Us, Water will rise again, Earth convulse, Air roar and Fire rage, and this time We will show no mercy: We will smash every last one of you like badly thrown pots!

As abruptly as it had started, the bed stopped shaking. Every joint in Astra's body throbbed, her breastplate was practically sawing her right arm off and her head felt perpendicular to her neck. Altogether, a cheerful start to the conversation. If you could call being bombarded with clods of hot lava a conversation. All these pains were just a gentle tickle, though, compared to the tension mounting in her stomach. A year to break the bond with Metal was an impossible demand.

Thank you, Earth. That is a powerful message. As she'd learned to do the hard way, Astra paid obeisance before attempting to negotiate. Earth was by far the most demanding of the Old Ones. Fire was volatile yet inspiring, Water emotional and often compassionate, Air logical and sometimes uplifting; Earth, though, was dogmatic and only very rarely nurturing. It hadn't always been this way, apparently: the depletion of the planet's topsoil, Water had told her, had made Earth increasingly stone-hearted. But though stubborn and unsympathetic, the Old One was not entirely immune to reason. *I could not agree more,* Astra humbly persisted, *that humanity is in great danger of repeating the worst mistakes of our past. For the last twelve years, I've urged people to do all the things You and the other Old Ones demand. And with the greatest respect, Earth, I do think people are listening. I am helping Jasper to prepare a legal case that has the potential to result in an international ban on rare-earths mining. Plus, a year today marks the end of the Hudna. Barring minor skirmishes and a few small chronic hot spots, on the Vernal Equinox Regeneration Era 100 humanity will have successfully achieved a century of peace, an unprecedented extended ceasefire between nations. Everywhere people are calling on their leaders to make this ceasefire permanent by embracing a programme of universal disarmament in which all nations will surrender their weapons of war to our international government. I believe therefore that we have a strong chance of meeting two of your demands. Giving up Tablettes by next year will be hard, though. Perhaps impossible. We need to be able to communicate with each other and we don't have a viable replacement technology yet.*

Then find one! Isn't that what Air has been telling you for years?

We are *trying. But it's difficult. Perhaps . . .* She had asked this before, but it was worth another try. *Perhaps You might be able to tell me something that could help?*

Earth snorted, a not entirely unpleasant experience for Astra, some-what akin to a quick loofah rub-down. *Humans can communicate with the stars. But you're obsessed with talking to each other! Empty vessels, the lot of you. Empty vessels you would rather stuff with rubbish than illuminate with stardust. Such a waste of good clay. Frankly, the sooner you all stop breeding, the better.*

Grumbling was a good sign: Earth was calming down, might be willing to haggle. *Earth?* She adopted a flattering tone.

Earth belched, nearly cracking one of Astra's ribs. *Yes?*

Is the infertility epidemic a warning from the Old Ones?

Don't blame Us for that. Tell your fellow humans you are punishing yourselves! Your sterility is a symptom of your abuse of Our good nature.

She let the tremors subside before starting to wheedle. *Is a year's deadline necessary, then? Couldn't you, perhaps, please, give us fifty years to break the bond with Metal? If humanity can't learn to respect the planet by then, maybe we'll just die out on our own.*

You have had fifty years. You have had one hundred years, one hundred thousand years. If the Creatures of Clay do not heed Our final warning within one more revolution around the sun, the Old Ones will rise again and devour you all, down to the last stillborn child!

The bed rattled so hard she couldn't stop it thudding against the wall. Earth yawned. *Was that your question?*

She hesitated. Earth wouldn't budge now. She'd have to talk to Water or Air about granting an extension, or accepting an interim result. Water was empathic, Air reasonable: either might be flexible. *No* . . . She paused, fighting off a sudden sense of futility. But she had to ask. *I was wondering if You could ask Hokma to visit?* I *haven't felt her presence for nearly eighteen months now. Before, she used to come at least once a year.*

Earth sighed and her body warmed, as if immersed in the steam from an enormous underground hot pool. *Time means little to those who dwell in the tunnels. She's probably lost track of it. Or is busy. As you should be.*

Her stomach clenched. *But couldn't you try to find her—*

No! And you should not be thinking of her. Today you must give Jasper Our message. Jasper, Earth purred. *Such a sensible name. What a shame it belongs to a cracked pot. Tell him one year, Istarastra, one year. Tell them all.*

With a final seismic spasm, Earth departed. Astra lay still, letting the heat of the Old One drain away and blinking back tears. Today was supposed to be a good day, a day when a host of smashed promises might be mended, mended like broken bowls with pure silver light. Instead it had brought a mortal threat to humanity, and a deeper sense of emptiness where Hokma was supposed to be. She opened her eyes. The scent from the toilet had ripened in the morning's warmth and behind Vultura's looming head the wallscreen glowed a dull warning orange, signalling she was under active observation by the guards in their office. Perhaps one year left of human life wasn't such a bad bargain after all . . .

'CRAW CRAW CRAW.'

She winced and squinted as the wallscreen lit up, for the second time that morning bleaching the cell a blinding white. 'Penitents.' The avatar's beaky jaw snapped open and shut and its hunched shoulders heaved. 'It is seven a.m. Today is the Vernal Equinox, the beginning of spring and a time in which to rebalance one's conscience. Today is also a Visitors' Day. Unless you are receiving a visitor, you will remain in your cell until noon, reflecting on your crimes and asking forgiveness from Gaia.'

The wallscreen dimmed. Astra sat up and rubbed her face, got the blood flowing. She couldn't let misery master her. She wasn't the only lonely person in this prison. But, though Earth might not think so, she was one of the busiest. Perched on the edge of the bed, she flipped up her Tablette from the front plate of her girdle.

PENITENT AO202.
YOUR PRIVILEGE ACCOUNT IS IN AMBER STATUS.
BY ORDER OF THE GOVERNOR
OF ASHFIELDS MAXIMUM SECURITY PENITENTIARY
AND IN ACCORDANCE WITH THE POLICIES OF
THE IS-LAND MINISTRY OF PENITENCE
WITH THE EXCEPTION OF LEGAL DOCUMENTS
YOU MAY NOT READ OR WRITE UNTIL 28.03.99

Soulspeech was ingrained in her cells, word-for-word, as it arrived, but in case anything should happen to her she wrote all the Old Ones' messages down. Thanks to Jasper, IMBOD had been forced to acknowledge these texts as legal documents: their international reception was evidence of her status as a political prisoner. She tapped on the icon, transcribed Earth's ultimatum and logged the document into the prison censor's queue, where it would be vetted for any mention of Muzi and his family and then forwarded to Jasper in advance of their meeting. She pushed the Tablette back down into the girdle with a satisfying snap and a surge of determination. Jasper was going to be updating her on the rare-earths mining case. Even if Water or Air couldn't grant an extension, if she could meet at least one of Earth's demands by next year, that would surely be cause for renegotiation of the ultimatum.

07:03:35. Around her, the wing was waking up. Next door, Charm was singing a bluesy tune; across the hall, someone banged a riff with their fists on a door. A lightness filled her chest. It *was* a good day: a Vernal Equinox, a day of equilibrium Vultura could not be allowed to own. She thought about Jasper. He would be waking up now, washing and shaving and getting ready for his morning run. Soon he would be pounding a path through the lava field, stopping only to flick out crumbs of basalt from his trainers, looking forward to steaming in the hotel's mineral hot springs before breakfast, fruit salad followed by scrambled alt-eggs and chives on rye bread, all washed down with strong, freshly ground coffee. He hadn't wanted to tell her about his tourist pleasures in the ashfields in case it made her envious, but Astra had insisted. She *liked* imagining him enjoying his morning. Knowing he was doing those things because he was visiting her made her part of the landscape; a pock-marked rock in the austere lava plains she could not see but knew stretched around the prison for hours and hours. Jasper brought that forbidden horizon close: described the lichen and the moss, the geysers and waterfalls, even did a passable imitation of wild horses whinnying in the mist.

As if looking into the far distance, she stared at the sunlit window. An image from the dream flashed against the opaque glass. A mop of dark hair against a turquoise sky . . . a sun-dazzled face. Her breath caught in her chest. So much was forbidden her, but she would never stop yearning for everything she was denied. *Never.* Jasper also brought the possibility of news of Muzi, or even – she tried, but could not push the hope down – a message from him, a sign that Muzi still considered himself . . . well, if not her husband, at least her friend and ally.

She fingered the edge of her Tablette. Her feelings about Muzi, while no longer raw, were still turbulent, painful, unsettling. That, she had gradually accepted, was the nature of love. If sex, with its hot urges and tender ecstasies, enabled *Homo sapiens* to biologically evolve, love, with its emotional ordeals, breaking people down to rebuild them anew, existed in order to fuel the spiritual evolution of the species. All the poets said so. If she wasn't being punished for peaking this morning, she could read a love poem, something in the ebook anthology of pre-Abrahamic spiritual verse Jasper had finally forced the censors to allow her three years ago, after her father died. Zizi had created a more comprehensive anthology for her, *Nights Beyond Measure*, back in Shiimti before she turned herself in. She hadn't been allowed to keep it: Abrahamist poems, however antique, were considered subversive material. The replacement poems, though, were now off-limits for a week.

And Earth was right: she had work to do. She got up, crossed the cell to her shelves, pulled out a fat red file and hauled it back to bed.

The Council of New Continents [CONC]
International Court of Environmental Justice
CASE 6291AX
*The People of Zabaria vs the Is-Land Rare-Earths Mining
Corporation [IREMCO]*

She had read the witness statements dozens of times but they never failed to anger, move and motivate her. She turned first to the testimony of a woman who had given birth to a child with no head and no skin, next to the account of a woman forced into sex work with the mine managers who had then killed her newborn infant, dashing the boy's head to a pulp against a rock. These women had been lucky: they had escaped from Zabaria during IMBOD's violent takeover of the Non-Lander mining town. Is-Land's Ministry of Border Defence hadn't been defending the nation's borders at all; rather, with miraculous speed, it had extended them, building a four-metre-high wall that cupped out from the Boundary to annex Zabaria and cut off the town from the world. CONC made noises, of course, but no one had done anything concrete about that Gaian monstrosity. Who knew what was going on behind it now?

'Penitents,' Vultura squawked, interrupting her thoughts. 'In honour of the Vernal Equinox, I will be broadcasting an educational film at eight a.m., *Gaian Achievements in Veganism*. Failure to watch this film will result in five marks being deducted from your Privilege Account.'

'Oh, shut up,' she muttered as the flap at the bottom of the door clattered open and a tray of porridge and half-spilled tea slid into the cell. The porridge was cold glue, leftovers from yesterday. She ate methodically, then set the tray on the floor and returned to the file, revisiting the agony of the men, women and children of Zabaria, people now living on a pittance as refugees in Asfar, waiting patiently for her lawyers to deliver justice for their suffering. The now-familiar tales never lost their power to shock. She stared at photographs of a rare-earths tailing pond, a toxic pool of black sludge spreading over the scrublands east of Zabaria, a stain that grew larger every year.

She set the file aside on her bed. Earth was right. This could not go on any longer. Outrage mounting in her chest, her mind began to hurtle towards the vision of the future that had kept her sane and on course for twelve long years. She had chosen to live in this tomb, a secretary-slave to the Old Ones, because embracing martyrdom was the most effective way for her to fight – not only for humanity and the planet, but also for justice for Non-Land. If Jasper's team could win this case, CONC might finally decide to ban rare-earths mining – or at least wrest control of the industry from nation states and private corporations. In either case, then surely Zabaria would be freed.

More than that, she also needed CONC to make the Hudna permanent, outlawing war in favour of diplomatic and economic sanctions and initiating a process of universal disarmament. Then Earth would let humanity live on, and perhaps the Boundary would fall and all the exiled Non-Landers would finally be able to return to their ancestral home to help build the new nation of One-Land.

She couldn't say 'One-Land' aloud in prison; like the word 'Muzi', it would bring immediate punishment. She picked up the file again and stroked the cover. The IREMCO trial was coming up. Even if her vision of a united Is-Land and Non-Land was never realised, even if, a year from now, the Old Ones rose and devoured humanity down to the last child, her life need not be wasted.

Savagely, she turned to the page of biographies and photos of the Board of Directors, the men and women who ran the Is-Land Rare-Earths Mining Corporation. There, above a bulging paragraph of credentials, honours and awards, he was: the esteemed IMBOD Superintendent Dr Samrod Blesserson, a leading Code Scientist responsible for the development of the Security Serum and, quite impossibly, her Shelter uncle. For Samrod had done nothing to protect her, but had only ever exposed her to the elements; offered her up to harm to save his own skin. His heavy-jowled, impassive, bespectacled face was contoured like Hokma's but devoid of all of his sister's kindness, wisdom or joy. Instead, arrogance and greed twisted his mouth and deadened his gaze.

She would wipe that contemptuous smirk off his face. For now, she blotted it out with her thumb.

'Your day of reckoning is coming, Samrod Blesserson,' she whispered. 'I'm going to *get* you, if it's the last thing I do.'

Sour Gold

Occupied Zabaria

'Do you think the car's safe here?' Lil checked over her shoulder. The cucumber salesman didn't look bothered – she was a good metre from his cart – but she'd pulled up in front of a kebab stand and the vendor might object to her crowding his frontage. In some districts of the Non-Quarter that could result in a keyed paint-job, four flat tyres, or an empty gutter where her car used to be. She tried to peer around Roshanak to catch the man's eye, but the Singular's tall red-robed frame and four arms – outstretched on a raised knee, idly burrowing up a sleeve, crooked against the window, twirling a lank strand of hair – filled the view.

'The neighbourhood council on this street is run by three knife-tongued grannies.' Roshanak sniffed. 'No one's going to steal your old rust-bucket, don't worry.' With delicate precision, the Singular peeled a scab from their upper-right wrist, dropped the congealed crust between the seats, licked a fingertip of their lower-left hand and pressed it to the scarlet sore. 'Can we settle up now, please?'

Provocation or minor first-aid crisis, she ignored Roshanak's welling wound. 'I *said* I'd pay you to take me to Anunit's apartment. We're not there yet.'

Roshanak pushed the lock of hair behind an ear and flicked the window with a chipped blue nail, indicating a narrow stairwell behind the kebab stand. 'The old yellow building, second floor. Do you want me to hold your hand up the stairs?'

She craned again at the kebab seller. Barricaded behind a tray of magenta pickles and emerald lettuce, slicing a strip off a grey cone of alt-meat, he didn't appear to even notice the CONC vehicle straddling the kerb. Out on the street, no eagle-eyed grannies were in evidence, but neither were any resentful-looking slouching young men. A scraggle of boys who should have been in school were playing football with a wodge of cardboard and tape, kicking it over the rutted road and up against a faded mural, a pastel vision of the steppes roughly slapped on a wall between a coffee kiosk and a school supplies stall. Behind the car, a woman in a brown headscarf was preparing for battle with the cucumber vendor, squeezing and discarding his no doubt withered produce; and directly ahead, an old man sitting on an upturned bucket, his face riven with fissures, was clicking prayer beads in a dusty haze of morning light. A more hedonistic sun-worshipper, a mangy cat, lay sprawled on a window ledge scratching its fleas, as unconcerned as the rest of the residents by the slogan on the wall beneath it – 'One-Land or Die', freshly sprayed in bright-red letters, and as yet undiscovered by IMBOD patrols.

She gazed up at the building above the cat. A shadow moved away from a window and a grimy curtain twitched. She turned the engine off. 'Wait for me here. I need you to mind the car.'

Roshanak rolled their kohl-framed eyes. 'Your dune buggy days are so o-ver, hun. I *told* you already: no one here wants a joyride on a CONC *donkey*. Look, I gotta *go*. It's time to pay up, Lil.'

They held out a palm. The Singular's four forearms were polka-dotted with needle marks and their nose dripped constantly like a sick sheep's. But their cheekbones still cut a regal half-profile, and when Roshanak's husky voice trembled with bravado, something squirmed inside Lil.

'I *told* you,' she muttered. 'Don't call me Lil.'

'All right. It's time to pay up, *Tira*.'

She hesitated. Though she and Roshanak went back a good decade, they were hardly old friends. They were barely former colleagues, and

Roshanak had wandered a long way since down the path of deceit and self-interest. They'd met again at the morpheus recovery meetings Lil facilitated; the Singular was romancing a woman in recovery and was a disruptive presence, using the meetings like a theatre to declaim to a captive audience that love was the greatest addiction of all. Roshanak had immediately recognised Lil, but it had taken them three meetings to decide to talk to her, and three more to trust Lil enough to agree to ask around in the Non-Quarter for Anunit's address. Though trust was a rather large word for the dubious emotional exchange they had embarked upon. Whatever paltry sum Lil gave Roshanak in exchange for their help, the Singular, she was sure, was going to head down one of the Non-Quarter's dark alleyways to immediately trade it for morpheus. Tira could be sacked for that.

But she *had* promised.

'I'll give you half now. Half later. *If* she's there.'

'That's not *fair*. What if she moved? That's not my fault, is it?'

'What's not fair,' she hissed, 'is you demanding money for this in the first place. I'm doing it for *Tiamet*.'

Roshanak's eyes flashed. 'Me too, Lil. But I'm the one sticking my neck out. I've only got one of those. And you're the one with the cushy CONC job. Look at you, in your frumpy blue shirt and world government car.' The corners of their purple-stained mouth turned down and their voice stuck a hurt note. 'It won't make any difference to *you* if I end up crawling back to the Welcome Tent.'

'Oh frack, Roshanak.' But emotional blackmail was far preferable to the other kind. Ignoring the use of her name, Lil took the bag of gold beads from the pocket of her trousers and counted out three. 'Take these. Come back to the morpheus clinic next week, and if this is Anunit's place, I'll give you the rest. Even if she's moved.'

Roshanak bared blackened teeth, snatched the beads and stuffed them down their brassiere. 'Shame about the uniform, but otherwise you're looking good, Lil.' They batted their falsies. 'I always thought putting on a bit of weight would suit you.'

She flexed her fingers, clawed the air. 'Meeeow!'

The Singular's shredded lips curled into a smirk. For a moment, laughter sparked between them. 'Otherwise you haven't changed a bit. Still the "helpmeet of harpies", hey babes?'

Outside, the cucumber customer sailed by, her bag full. Lil flinched. '*Please* don't talk about me like that here. Or anywhere!'

'Oh, don't be such a jitterbug. It's just us in here, chatting about the old days. I get that pirate radio sometimes. *One-Land.*' Roshanak splayed their hands into four starbursts. '*Ooh ooh ooh. YAC Attack.*'

Roshanak had once had a good voice. It was tarry and cracked now, but hit the high note like a distant bullseye and gave the last phrase a breathy, almost sultry, finish. Lil felt another twinge of discomfort, mingled with something like sadness. 'Those days are over, Roshanak. I'm just trying to help one person at a time now.'

'Yeah, that's all any of us can do, ain't it the truth?' The Singular traced a finger down the window, then tossed their hair and rattled at the door handle. 'Well, don't forget, sweetie, I've helped *you*.'

'I won't, Roshanak. Thank you.' Lil released the lock and with a big fat air-kiss, Roshanak slid out into the street, leaving the door half-open.

Lil reached over, shut the door and watched Roshanak, sure enough, glance up and down the street then dart into an alley. She stepped out of the car herself, into the smell of fried alt-meat, the shrieking babble of children and a brown cloud of grit: not road dust, but dirt floating down from the sky. Coughing, she brushed off her sleeves, shook her hair and peered up. On the second-floor balcony, a woman was beating a carpet with impressive but worrying vigour. The rusted railings looked about to swing down over the kebab stand. Above them the crumbling sandstone building sagged under the weight of concrete extensions, solar panels, wet sheets and blankets, wind vanes and a snakes' nest of electricity cables. On the third floor, two children waved at her over a grey cindercrete wall, then disappeared. Anger flared in her chest.

Zabaria had more than enough room to spread out: from the roof of their building, those kids could see halfway across the scrublands. But IMBOD's new wall had squeezed the town's Non-Lander residents into the smallest of four unequal new quarters, forcing Occupied Zabaria to grow dangerously upwards since Lil and Roshanak had shared a tent here ten years ago. This brickwork didn't look too bad, but buildings collapsed in the Non-Quarter every other month or burnt down in electrical fires. Just last week a five-storey building not far from here had buried twenty-three people, including seven children.

'Kebab, Kebab!' the seller cried. 'Best kebab in Old Zabaria!'

'Maybe later.' She smiled at the man and stepped round his stand, avoiding a puddle of dried mud and rotting veg. As she moved into the shade, her work Tablette buzzed against her hip.

She had clocked out. Her line manager shouldn't be bothering her. Was it Roshanak? She pulled out the Tablette and checked the screen.

Happy Equinox, Tiger Tira! When you coming round? I'm a bull elephant for u, babe!

Bud. They had plans for this evening. She muted the phone and entered the stairwell, checking the walls for cracks and bulges. It was her afternoon off and for once she wasn't going to spend it polishing Bud's horn.

Misted Silver

The Ashfields

'Orrrrrrrr-*dott*.' Her name drilled into the cell, punctuated by the bang of a fist on metal. Astra jolted upright and gawked at the screenwall clock. 10:14:23. No! She leapt up, sending her breakfast tray flying, and jammed her feet into her sandals.

'Penitent AO202,' Vultura croaked. 'It is ten-fifteen. Prepare to meet your visitor.'

She knelt in front of the door and stuck her arms through the meal slot into the corridor.

'*Humble!*' screeched Vultura.

Astra bowed her head until her nose touched the floor. Calloused hands roughly clicked cuffs around her wrists. She retracted her arms, hopped back to the bunk and stood, blear-eyed in the harsh light of the screenwall, as the bolt slid open with a violent *grawk*.

'Is-Land Forever!' Lichena stepped into the cell and gave a Gaia salute, fist from chest.

'Is-Land Forever,' she muttered, returning the salute as best she could with cuffed hands. Not doing so was grounds for a twenty-mark Privilege Account deduction. And if any guard would enforce that petty rule, Lichena would. Scrawny, vicious, her ripped muscles weltered with rune tattoos, the guard was a nasty piece of work. Right now, her bitten nails were scratching at her hipbelt, her nose twitching like a rat's – a rat with an allergy to everything Astra touched.

'Smells like *shit* in here.'

There was no point telling Lichena that was because the toilet was backed up, or in asking for it to be plunged while she was with Jasper. If she did that, the toilet would erupt in a fountain of sewage the next time she flushed it. Earth might like the stink in the cell; Astra was not so keen on it that she wanted shit all over her bed. She stood impassively, staring over the guard's shoulder at the open door and probing her loose molar with her tongue.

'What did I say?' Lichena's eyes were flint chips in a bony mask. She jabbed her discipline stick at Astra's chest.

Despite the morning's yoga and meditation, Earth's visit and all Hokma's advice over the years on how to stay calm in the face of the guards, Astra's bladder loosened. The diss-stick was only supposed to be deployed if the guards felt physically threatened, but somehow whenever Lichena used it, Vultura malfunctioned. The pain of being prodded was crippling. She could take it, had taken it, many times – but not now. *Not now, please.* She couldn't spend her precious time with Jasper gasping, sweating buckets, trying and failing not to vomit.

'You said it smells like shit in here,' she repeated tightly.

'Oh, is that right?' The smirk appeared, the one that always accompanied Lichena's famous trick questions. 'And what kind of shit would that be?'

You couldn't give a clever answer. It was best to play it clueless, let Lichena prove you wrong. She took a stab at it. 'My shit?'

'*Traitor's* shit.' The smirk disappeared in a tonsil-quivering rat-shriek, the guard's spittle spraying Astra's face as the diss-stick grazed her chin. She concentrated on immobilising her features as Lichena ranted on: 'Traitor's shit stinks worse than Non-Land shit! What does it stink worse than? What? *What?*'

'C'mon, Lichena, we ain't got all day.'

The fat guard, Bircha, stuck her head in the cell. *Thank you.* Bircha was a brute in her own right, but at least she stuck to enforcing the rules, didn't make them up as she went along like Lichena.

The woman wrinkled her nose. 'Gaia's knockers. Pongs in here, dunnit?'

'We was just saying.' Lichena's gnawed fingers scuffled at her hip-belt, pulled out a latex glove. 'C'mon, Ordott.' The guard snapped the glove down over her wrist. '*Mouth!*'

It was standard security procedure, useless to resist. She dropped her jaw, let Lichena shine a torch down her throat into her bowels, tried not to inhale – Lichena's sighs of satisfaction smelled of mouldy teabags. Finished with her inspection of Astra's oesopha-gus, the guard tucked the torch back into her hipbelt and dangled a small key in front of Astra's face. 'Time for your *favourite* part of Visitors' Day, Ordott.' She grinned, showing off thin, shiny inci-sors. 'You know the drill.'

Astra's stomach contracted. This shouldn't be happening. But it was, again. As it did every time this happened, her body screamed, *I have rights.* And it did, CONC-mandated rights: the right to sunlight, filtered through the frosted prison window and directly on her skin for an hour a day in the yard; the right to exercise; the right to three nutritious meals and two litres of drinking water a day; and though under current Gaian law prisoners in a maximum-security jail were not permitted sexual pleasure, or contact with plants and animals, her body had the right, above all, to physical integrity, not to be violated except under conditions of reasonable suspicion of an infringement of prison rules.

'You can't do this, Lichena. I haven't been anywhere or seen any-one. I've had the girdle on round-the-clock.'

'Uh-uh, Ordott. Vultura says you was up early, fiddling and flop-ping around under the sheets in the dark. Then you took an extra-long time cleaning yourself. All on a Visitors' Day. Doesn't look good.'

'The belt wouldn't close. I had my hands in the air the whole time!'

'You wiped, baby. Only takes a second to fiddle the clit. Now obey a direct order or with Bircha as my witness I'll revoke all your privileges for a month.'

The difference between a right and a privilege varied from country to country. Privileges at Ashfields Max included eating hot food, reading approved ebooks and a heavily censored digest of Is-Land news, writing poems, stories and journal entries on one's Tablette, watching films and other entertainments, working in the sewing room, spending earnings in the prison shop and being seated at a table with other people at collective mealtimes. Depending on the status of one's Privilege Account, everything that made prison bearable could be suspended in a second. A week with no privileges was about as much as she could bear. A month was nearly unendurable.

'Vultura!' She addressed the wallscreen, pointed at Lichena. 'I want this security check recorded for my lawyer.'

10:17:12. 10:17:13. Vultura's drooping eyelids slowly closed. The guard brandished the diss-stick. 'Time for Vultura's morning nap, Ordott. Now turn around and *bend over.*'

Sometimes Astra resisted Lichena's assaults. It always went badly for her when she did. Today she had to convey Earth's message to Jasper and prepare a campaign strategy for the year ahead, perhaps the last year of human life on the planet. She could not afford to be diss-sticked. Her face flaring, she obeyed, spreading her cheeks and gritting her teeth as the guard unlocked the belt, probed and dug, pinched and squeezed, pulled and rubbed and humped her hips, emitting mock groans of pleasure to Bircha's laughter from the doorway. *Your body is a garment your soul chooses to wear for a time,* Hokma had taught her. *No matter how they rend it, the guards cannot even touch the soul within.* It was true, she knew. Yet no matter how she tried to slip out of her flesh when Lichena came to claw it, her body, like a heavy robe in a stream, pulled her back down into the mud.

10:24:23. At last she was standing straight again, flushed with anger, disgust and shameful arousal, avoiding the guards' eyes. Lichena peeled off the glove and tossed it onto the bunk. Astra ignored the provocation, focused on shearing those last seven minutes out of her life and stuffing them into a bulging ragbag marked 'past suffering'. The ordeal was over. It was time to go.

But Lichena was lazily slapping the diss-stick against her palm.

'You know what I think, Bircha?' she mused. 'I think Astra Crazydott's afraid we won't be giving her manky old Gaia garden any special 'tention any more. I think she thinks that when all her visitors are ghosts made outta light and smoke and invisible bits of fluff, we're gonna stop worrying about security around here. But she don't have to worry, does she, Bircha?'

'Oh no, girl.' Bircha belly-laughed. 'We're gonna keep on keepin' a real close watch on that skinny Non-Lander-shagging arse of yours.'

Visits from ghosts? Did they mean the Old Ones? They were talking in riddles to rile her. They did that sometimes, like two drunk witches. 'I'm sorry.' She regained what she could of her dignity. 'I don't know what you mean.'

'What?' Lichena snickered. 'Didn't little Miss Press Release read the official announcement? Doesn't she know this is the last time she's going to see that fat boyfriend of hers?'

She tensed. 'What announcement? And Jasper's not my boyfriend, he's my lawyer. You can't stop me seeing him.'

'Don't get so het up! Vultura explained it all in the Daily Missive, didn't she, Bircha? Guess you missed it. You can still see yer lover-lawyer, but he's not coming, shall we say, in the flesh again.'

If they meant to torment her, they were succeeding. A chill tore through her. Were they saying that Jasper was dead? A dissident Gaian who'd left Is-Land to work for the Council of New Continents at its global headquarters in Amazigia, Jasper took a Zeppelin twice a year to Is-Land, then travelled from Atourne to the ashfields, protected by two CONC officers with sonic guns. So far, he'd never been ambushed, but there was always a first time. Or there could have been an accident: the road to the prison was cut narrowly into a steep cliff above a rapid river. Would a rockfall have been cause for an official announcement?

'Why?' She glared at Lichena. 'Was there a problem on the road?'

''Fraid not. Shame there won't be one more chance for that sweaty maggot to fall into a ravine.'

'Then what—'

Lichena laughed. 'Don't she look cute when she doesn't know what's going on?'

'C'mon, Ordott,' Bircha drawled from the door. 'Prisoners are supposed to listen to Vultura, read their emails, keep up to speed with what's going on around here.'

'I was up early meditating. Then I had a nap,' she explained with haughty dignity.

'Ooo, poor baby missed the movie, too, did she?' Lichena pressed the diss-stick up against Astra's chin. 'That's another ten marks off your Priv Account.'

'Aw, don't keep her in suspense, Lichena,' Bircha said. 'We gotta get going here.'

Lichena lowered the diss-stick and leaned in close. 'The Wheel Meet announced it today at nine-thirty, Ordott,' she hissed. 'From next month no one's getting no more guests in person. Is-Land prisons are investing in fancy hi-tech boxes, and all your visitors will be . . . well . . . I heard they'll look like vacuum-bag dust.'

Oh. She understood at last. They were talking about ion chambers – the long-running CONC campaign to bring all prisons and neurohospices in Is-Land up to international standards by installing the sophisticated holographic communication devices for visits. There'd been a ruling, and she'd missed it.

But CONC hadn't intended the ion chambers to replace flesh visits. She stood, awash with confusion and prickling with fear. Was it true, was this the last time she would see Jasper in person?

'Yeah, I know.' Lichena cackled. 'Far too good for the likes of you. But don't worry.' She poked the diss-stick between Astra's legs. 'You'll still get frisked when yer frisky. Spot checks. Before and after dinner. That's what I said at the staff meeting, didn't I, Bircha?'

'You did.' The big guard chuckled. 'Got a star for that recom-
mendation, far as I recall.'

'It is ten-thirty a.m.' Vultura's eyes flew open and her beak
snapped like shears. 'Penitent AO202 must be transported *now* to
the Visitors' Hall.'

Lichena jabbed her with the dead end of the stick, then stuffed
it back into its holster. 'You're making us late, Nutpotdott. Now
move.'

It was happening. Never mind Earth's ultimatum and refusal to
help her with Hokma; never mind the guards' abuse or the alarming, puzzling news: the morning light had promised a good Visitors'
Day. First, though, she had to get downstairs without being diss-
sticked, slapped, punched or kicked. All of which were still distinct
possibilities. Because there, blazing beside Bircha in the dim corridor, was Cora. Scrawny, defiant Cora Pollen, with her wild grey
hair and broken nose, her wiry limbs and arthritic hands, and eyes
that burnt like pale grey lasers through the bullshit of Ashfields
Max. Cora, the daughter of Hokma's older Code sister Paloma,
who after Paloma's death had become Hokma's accomplice in treason; technically Astra's Shelter cousin, but more than that her Elder
and self-appointed guardian of her family's great maternal tradition
of dissent. After thirteen years of imprisonment Cora looked a decade older than her fifty-four years, yet even with her wrists cuffed
behind her back, her body shrivelling inside her battered tankini,
the woman was still an incandescent powerhouse of contempt for
IMBOD and its minions. Cora spat on the argument that slovenly
Bircha and rancorous Lichena were ill-educated, brainwashed victims of Is-Land and should be treated with patience and compassion.
Tiny as she was, Cora Pollen thought nothing of provoking the
guards to extremes of mindless violence.

Please don't, Astra willed.

But Astra's will had never so much as left a scratch on Cora's.
'As-*tra*!' Cora cried.

'Shut *up*.' Bircha grabbed Cora's winter twig of an arm. Not hard enough to break it – the guard had been disciplined for doing that before – but her cousin would have the bruise for a week.

Not that Cora cared. Her eyes glinted, grey sparks in the hall. Astra straightened her shoulders. 'Cor-*ra*,' she dutifully shouted in reply.

Lichena nearly yanked her arm out of its socket. But the touch-paper was lit. 'As-*tra*. As-*tra*.' The bellow of Charm's powerful lungs filled the hall, joined by the banging of fists on metal and, from the cell opposite, Rosetta's glassy soprano. 'Cor-*ra*. Cor-*ra*. As-*tra*, As-*tra*.' All along the corridor, prisoners pitched in. No one shouted 'One-Land' any more after what had happened to Fern, but the Traitors' Chorus was a Visitors' Day ritual her comrades never missed.

Cora threw back her head and yodelled. The cries ceased. 'Hu-man *guests*,' she shouted. 'No ghost spies.'

Bircha punched her – in the gut, right on the seam between her breastplate and girdle. Cora grunted and doubled over, but the breath had been knocked out of her too late: the new chant had already been taken up by a dozen women, screeching, whooping and drumming on their doors.

'HU-MAN GUESTS. NO GHOST SPIES. HU-MAN GUESTS. NO GHOST SPIES.'

A protest already. The guard's hand was a vice screwed to her elbow, propelling her down the dark stone corridor, but rebellion was in the air, in the shaking of metal doors, the clattering of tray flaps, voices raised in jubilant defiance. Lichena kicked at a door; behind Astra, Bircha shouted, 'I got your number, Hiltondott,' but nothing could stifle the commotion. As Cora had explained so long ago: 'If you're going to be diss-sticked for nothing, you might as well be diss-sticked for *something*.'

They reached the elevator at the end of the hall. Lichena pressed her palm against the key panel, then pushed Astra into the box and manhandled her around. Now Cora was in front of her, her stick-like arm still clenched in Bircha's meaty grip, her head high, her coarse cloud of hair nearly teasing Astra's nose. As the elevator doors slid shut, far back in the corridor, a voice cried, '*Isssss-tar!*'

Her heart skipped a beat.

'Oh, *Istar*,' Lichena hissed in her ear as the elevator descended. 'Heard any big, scary voices lately? Don't worry, we can always put you back in the neurohospice if they're troubling you.'

'Astra Ordott is a political prisoner and she stays on this wing,' Cora barked.

'Who asked you?' Lichena kicked Cora's calf.

Cora's knee buckled and Bircha hauled her upright again. 'Still don't know why we let *this one* out of her hole in the ground,' the fat guard growled. 'Cheap 'n' easy, wells are.'

Lichena cackled. 'I reckon once the Hudna's done and dusted and IMBOD can fight fair at last, these two'll be getting *well-looked after!*'

Astra raged silently at the physical abuse, but the threats were little more than old jokes. During her first two years of imprisonment, the thought of being returned to a neurohospice or transferred to a Traitors' Well had terrified her, eaten away at her resolve, jolted her awake in the night to ask herself, *What have I done? Maybe I am mad.* But her lawyers had struck a hard deal with IMBOD. She had given herself up in exchange for twenty-three Non-Land hostages, including Muzi's family, volunteering to serve all their sentences consecutively, on three conditions: that she was never placed in solitary confinement or deprived of her medication, and was represented by Cora Pollen's lawyers. Jasper and Calendula, leading lights in CONC's campaign for international prison reform, had ensured she and Cora would serve their sentences in Ashfields Maximum Security Penitentiary and monitored her situation like hawks. Three years ago, CONC had even forced IMBOD to sign the global agreement to abolish solitary confinement. Life was hard in Ashfields Max, locked up in the chastity tankini and deprived of the sight of the landscape, but it could be a lot worse. She had rights. Rights that could not be violated for long without severe repercussions for Is-Land at the highest diplomatic and economic levels.

Chief among them was the right to protest. The cries of the women on Traitors' Wing still ringing in her ears, she watched Cora Pollen step like a crooked heron out of the elevator; leading the way to what would *not*, if Is-Land's most infamous political prisoners could help it, be their last ever in-the-flesh meetings with their lawyers.

Sour Gold

Occupied Zabaria

The woman on the second-floor walkway was small and round with worn cheeks and greying hair. She appeared to be waiting for Lil, the wicker carpet beater tucked beneath her armpit, and a small girl clinging to her skirts. As her head was uncovered, Lil took a guess and greeted her in Somarian.

'Good morning.' She flashed her Tablette, displaying her CONC ID. 'My name is Tira Gúnida. I'm looking for a woman my records show lives in one of these apartments. Her first name is Anunit. Can you direct me to her residence?'

A gaggle of children appeared from a door at the end of the walkway. The woman flapped the carpet beater at them and they ducked back inside. She clasped the little girl closer to her side and regarded Lil with large, watery eyes.

'Who was that . . . creature you brought with you?'

Lil tensed. Zabaria was full of people from all over the gender and alt-body spectrums. Somarians were notoriously conservative, she knew, but hadn't this woman at least learned how to be polite about her neighbours? Now was not the time for a re-education session, though. She smiled brightly. 'That person was just a community-service user who gave me directions.'

The woman's forehead puckered with worry. 'What services does it use? Our children play in the streets. We don't want any trouble here.'

Lil winced again, but kept her tone calm and unoffended. 'I can't divulge any confidential information, ma'am, but I can assure you that my client has never to my knowledge hurt any children. *They'* – she stressed Roshanak's preferred pronoun – 'are a gentle person. I would never bring anyone violent here, I promise.'

The woman's wary expression relaxed into softer creases and she released the child, who ran full pelt down the walkway to join her playmates. The woman gave a brief smile, fleetingly revealing the apple-cheeked girl still ghosting her withered skin. 'You speak very good Somarian.'

'I'm half-Somarian. From Kadingir.' Which was only half-true, but being a Non-Lander in the pay of the world government that had caused this stinking mess in Zabaria was already a mark against her. Divulging that she was part-Gaian, born in Is-Land, would destroy any chance of trust-building. 'I moved to Zabaria before the annexation,' she added, which *was* true, though missed a lot out. 'Before I got this job, I used to work in the mine. Now I'm trying to help people get benefits they're entitled to. CONC owes Anunit some back payments. Is she home, do you know?'

'You used to work in the mine?' The offhand approach had worked. A tone of awed curiosity had crept into the woman's voice.

'For a couple of years. The skin rash has healed now.' She peeled up a sleeve to reveal the scars, then tugged it back down to her wrist.

The woman hesitated, worry needling her forehead again. 'Anunit didn't say anything about back payments.'

A breakthrough. Lil hid her mounting excitement. 'She wouldn't know about them. There was a problem with the system. She was never told she was eligible.'

The woman's eyes shone like two watery brown suns. 'Am I owed anything? Kaliga Engu. My husband is Eeron Singa. We both worked in the mine for twenty years. Can you check the system?'

Lil's stomach twinged as she swiped at her Tablette. 'No. I'm sorry. Anunit's the only person in this neighbourhood I have to find. Like I said, there was a glitch in the system, and I'm not exactly sure which apartment is hers.'

The woman reached over and tugged her sleeve, her eyes flooded with desperate hope. 'Please. Come and meet my husband. He's had the cough for four years. Every morning I have to wash the sheets and the pillowcase. Aren't there any back payments for that?'

'I'm sorry, no.' Oh frack it. Lil reached into her jacket and drew out a gold bead. 'But in my department, we have a special discretionary fund. For cases of particular hardship.'

The woman glanced at it, but stepped away, to the door. 'Just come and meet him. Have a glass of mint tea.'

'I'm sorry. I'm not a social worker,' she lied. 'I'm just from accounts.' Her mind whirred. Who could she ask to come and not tell their line manager she had been here first? Ahmad. He was always keen to help a mine-worker. 'But I can send a social worker if you like.'

It wasn't much of a promise, but it seemed to appease that terrible hope. Kaliga took the bead and fingered it in her palm as Lil made a note of the names.

'I really hoped to find Anunit today,' she lamented. 'If I don't locate her soon, the money will be written off back into the general accounts.'

Kaliga slipped the bead into her apron pocket. 'Anunit lived there.' She pointed at the nearest drab grey door, then, as if shaking off a sparrow that might have landed on her hand, twisted her palm to the air. 'But she left three years ago, after her mother died. She didn't even say goodbye. Just packed up and vanished overnight with the boy.'

It was as if an ocean of sun had spilled over the balcony, and then drained away into dusk. But Lil just squinted at the door, swiped the Tablette screen again and made a note of the number.

'That's a pity. So you don't know where she went?'

Kaliga stared at Lil, took a step towards her. The woman's eyes were large enough to drown in. 'You remember Zabaria before the occupation?' she whispered.

Occupation. Remember. Dangerous words. Lil moved to the railing, lightly rested a hand on the peeling iron and looked out over the

narrow chasm of the street. In the chink between the opposite buildings, she could just see it: the Boundary extension, the towering grey
wall the Gaians had curved around Zabaria, clamping the town to
their fortified border. 'I was a teenager. Life was hard, but looking
back it seems . . . like paradise. Barbecuing lizards out in the scrublands. Driving to Kadingir for parties.' She jerked her chin towards a
dark tier of mismatched balconies, in the general direction of the
Gaian quarter. 'Before those *frackers* turned this place into a prison.'

Kaliga moved closer. Lil caught a sickly whiff of rose water.
'People were different then. We used to talk more. We didn't have
to worry about . . . you know.' She gave Lil another searching look.

This time, Lil held her gaze. 'CONC doesn't collaborate with
the police. I know there's not enough of us here, but we're totally
independent of the Gaians and the *traitors* who work with them.'

There was a long pause, then, at last, Kaliga began to speak. 'She
used to tell me everything. We were girls together. I saw her . . .' The
woman patted her chest. 'You know. Her thing. When she was
little, everyone thought she was just birthmarked. Then it started to
grow, and we knew she was one of *them*. But not like the one you
came with. Her thing was hidden. She could have stayed here,
maybe even got married. But her father grew sick, and her mother
sent her away . . . to work.' She clearly knew the kind of work
Anunit had done; her expression clouded as she struggled with
the memory. 'Did you know her father had the cough, too?'

'No, I didn't know. I'm sorry,' Lil murmured.

'Anunit came home to look after him. Right at the start of the
occupation. She came back with her baby. A totally normal little boy.
It made her father so happy. Her mother was angry because Anunit
was unmarried, but she was sick, too, by then, needed Anunit to do
the shopping and cleaning. Her father died, oh,' Kaliga's brow furrowed, 'five or six years ago. Then her mother got the cough, too, took
to her bed. Anunit ran the household then. But she'd changed. So
secretive, she was. Religious, too. She wasn't Karkish, but she started
wearing the *niqab*. I asked her why, and she said the boy's father was

Karkish and she'd heard that he had died. I guess grief affects some people like that. When the boy started school, she went back to work at the mine. I told her don't be stupid, think of your son, but she said she needed the money to send him to school, and the *niqab* would protect her lungs. Two years later, she started coughing, too.' Kaliga's lips pursed. 'And all the time she was owed *back payments*.'

'Yes. That's right.' Down on the street, a queue had formed for the kebab seller. Lil kept her voice low. 'Her payments relate to the child's father's death. It's been an inexcusable delay, I know. But we want to make it right. Are you sure you don't know where to find her?'

'I told you – she didn't even say goodbye.' Her eyes swam with reproach, then a troubled veil descended over Kaliga's face and she turned away and studied the sheets on the opposite balcony.

The smell of alt-kebab rising up from the street was starting to turn Lil's stomach. 'There's no one else who might know?' She tried to keep her frustration from infecting her voice. 'It's a considerable sum. Enough to put the boy through college.'

Kaliga picked at a piece of loose paint on the railing. Then she placed her carpet beater against the balustrade and pulled out her Tablette. She made a call, then another, spoke rapidly. *Yes, yes... No, I know... but I'm telling you... No, there's nothing for you... Think of the boy.*

She hung up. 'Her brother says last he heard she was living in the market. He doesn't know where exactly, and she might have moved since.' She slipped the Tablette back into her apron. ' "Small families are a big mistake," that's a true proverb. Do you have children?'

'Not yet.' Lil's smile felt as rusted as the balcony. She wanted to throttle the woman, to scream. The market was huge, a warren of cramped apartments and alleys where Anunit in her *niqab* would be almost impossible to find. She'd come so far. How could the trail dry up here?

'Take my advice. Have six or none at all.' Kaliga pursed her lips. 'You could ask at the market for the music teacher. His name is Todo. The boy's good at drumming, so Todo said. All that bashing drove us mad, but she wouldn't hear a word against it.'

It was as if the small, round woman had waved her carpet beater and the whole neighbourhood had turned to gold. Everything gleamed. 'I'll go there straight away,' Lil said. 'Thank you, Kaliga, thank you.' She patted her heart, inclined her head. 'I'll send someone to interview your husband as soon as I can.'

She bolted back down the stairs, fumbling for her keys. 'Kebab! Kebab!' The seller shouted as she dashed past him. And pulled up short. In the carpet dust on the windscreen, a finger had written *Istar Forever* and drawn a wonky five-pointed star. The YAC star.

She checked the street. The old man was soaking up the sun like a lizard; the children were trying to get their ball of cardboard down from the roof of the coffee kiosk.

'Did you see who drew that?' she asked the kebab seller, pointing at the windscreen.

He shrugged. 'Your friend came back. Didn't buy a kebab.'

Did Roshanak want to get them both arrested? 'They're not my friend,' she insisted, as if the man were an IMBOD officer. 'They gave me directions, that's all.'

'Directions to the best kebab stand in Old Zabaria.' He grinned.

She wasn't hungry. But Bud would be later. She bought a greasy pocket of alt-meat, salad and pickle, lashed with garlic and hot pepper sauce, and thrust it in her bag. Back in the car she turned the wipers on. As the graffiti disappeared her good mood returned. *Drumming.* She pattered her fingers on the dashboard. Anunit had given him drumming lessons. She revved up and drove off, dancing inside.

Misted Silver

The Ashfields

'Astra. So good to see you.' Rotund, balding, stretch-marked and irrepressible, Jasper Sonovason half-rose, bobbed and nodded, and plumped himself back down in his metal chair.

She blinked. There was only one small wallscreen in the Visitor Room, but the strip lighting in the ceiling was an eye-scalding white. 'Great to see *you*, Jasper.' Touching was forbidden. Beaming, she sat down at the table and let Lichena remove the Tablette from her girdle. The guard stashed the device in her hipbelt, then locked Astra's cuffs to a metal ring bolted onto the tabletop, making a noisy show of testing the shackles in the process. Astra couldn't care less. She just wanted to stare inanely at Jasper. Middle-aged, of middling height, with black-furred man-boobs and paunch, his bald patch tonsured by anarchic curls, his face as crumpled as an old toffee bag, her lawyer's dishevelled appearance, she had come to learn, belied the warmth and stamina of a mother bear. This, possibly her last unmediated sight of him until she didn't know when, was unexpectedly precious. There he was, a pen tucked behind his ear, fingering a dog-eared file folder, a slim stash of notes and news stories he'd gathered like wildflowers especially for her.

Not being allowed his own Tablette during his visits, Jasper had invested in a watch. He glanced pointedly at it and then at Lichena. '*If* you are done, may I please begin my private consultation with my client?'

'Private' was not exactly accurate. For 'security reasons', IMBOD was allowed to film their meetings, the small wallscreen positioned right behind Astra's head, ostensibly blocking Jasper's face from view so neither could be lip-read. Still, though, despite Lichena's removal of her Tablette, their conversation was being monitored, subject, like all her communications in, into and out of the jail, to IMBOD's contorted and contested interpretations of international law. By CONC mandate, Astra had the right to unlimited (except by Server malfunction) Voice Calls with her lawyer. CONC protections allowed for considerable variation, however, and under IMBOD prison rules, Astra was not allowed to email anyone, even Jasper, and only had the right to write to and receive letters, Tablette Talk Calls and visits from residents of Is-Land. With the exception of Zizi, her Code father, international communications had been forbidden her. Most restrictively of all, she was not even permitted to speak about Muzi and his family who, as the relatives of two men executed on false charges of espionage, were deemed enemies of Is-Land. Somehow IMBOD lawyers had convinced a CONC judge that updates from her lawyer on Muzi's whereabouts and well-being could be considered forms of communication from him; and that it was reasonable to fear that Jasper might be tempted to pass on any thoughts Astra might express to him about her husband or in-laws, even if she had not expressly couched these thoughts as a message. The rule stood, and any attempt to break it would result in the immediate and indefinite suspension of all her prison privileges. Mics embedded in the walls were programmed to recognise a list of any forbidden or suspicious words; anything to do with Muzi or his family would trigger Lichena's return, the end of the visit and the start of a long, cruel period of deprivation.

To get around this, she and Jasper used a code they'd devised before Astra was incarcerated; so far, it appeared to be working, though she knew it was possible that IMBOD had cracked it years ago and were just waiting for Muzi to try and contact her before pouncing. Aware that Vultura was most likely illegally recording everything they said, she and Jasper were also careful never to refer to any Non-Lander IMBOD might want to hunt down and hurt. Still, lawyer-client privilege applied. Apart from any mention of Muzi, nothing they discussed on Jasper's visits could be used against her in a court of law. They spoke relatively freely, Jasper updating her about the wider world and helping plot her various campaigns. Just the sight of him gave her a sense of victory over the guards.

Not that Lichena noticed. 'Ain't the cleanest bunny on the block, this one,' the guard sneered. 'I guess you must be glad this is the last time you have to smell her.'

'*She* smells fine, guard.' Jasper peered at Lichena's armband. 'That's right. Seven eight two.' He opened the file folder, took the pen from behind his ear and noted the number on the top paper.

Lichena curled her upper lip. 'Oh, so Traitor Gaians like the stink of shit? I heard some of those top-line ion boxes have a smell function. Seeing as Ordott's such an *international celebrity*, maybe we could order one of those for you?'

Without waiting for an answer, she left, tapping her diss-stick against the door frame.

'That woman is a rabid jackass.' Jasper crumpled the sheet of paper into a ball and threw it at the closed door. Astra giggled. 'So.' He pulled out her copy of the agenda and slapped it down in front of her. 'Item One: the news.'

Item One was usually the latest message from the Old Ones, but emergencies, like the time Astra had come in with a black eye and a burnt arm from a diss-stick beating, took precedence. She inched to the edge of her seat. 'IMBOD can't do this. The ion chambers are supposed to be used in addition to flesh visits, not instead of them. We have to fight this decision, Jasper. I need you to put pressure on IMBOD in Amazigia. I haven't been able to talk to Cora yet, but the politicals are protesting already. I know she'll be telling Calendula the same thing.'

'Aha. There it is.' Her lawyer riffled through the papers, whistled under his breath, pulled out a blue sheet. Suddenly, she knew why he was ignoring her.

'You don't want to come to Is-Land any more,' she stated flatly. Of course he didn't. A Gaian dissident, now a permanent resident of Amazigia, Jasper was about as popular in Is-Land as she was. His biannual visits to her put him in personal danger and cost a fair chunk of the *pro bono* firm's budget on security, as well as a working week of his time. He didn't have to come: they could Voice Talk any time they liked. But he and Calendula visited in person twice a year because they knew that otherwise Astra and Cora would have no visitors at all.

He set the blue sheet to one side. 'That's not it, Astra. Of course not. But Calendula and I have talked it through. We have to pick our battles, and we've decided this Wheel Meet move is a compromise we're best off accepting.'

'*What?*' She stared at him in horror. Jasper liked a bit of cut and thrust, she knew, and was no stranger to devil's advocacy, but this was an unbelievable concession to IMBOD's regime.

'Let me remind you that the ion chamber technology has advantages.' He counted off the reasons on his thumb and stubby fingers. 'One: the communications experience is not just next-best to flesh contact but better in some ways – the ion bath is good for your health. Two: prisoners, especially those in remote jails, are likely to get visitors who would otherwise never come to see them. Here at Ashfields Max, few prisoners get a visitor more than once or twice a year. And, three, best of all' – grinning like a psychotic clown, he ducked right and cocked a look at the camera in the wall behind her – 'CONC ion chamber connections are unhackable, so when we're in one we can't be overheard.'

'I know all that.' She glowered with exasperation. 'I've been in an ion chamber, in Kadingir, remember? I was totally behind the CONC campaign. But we can't let IMBOD hijack it. Think, Jasper! Gaians hate ion chambers. The manufacturers boycotted Is-Land for years. So why would IMBOD suddenly not only agree to roll out a deluxe hi-tech communications experience for murderers and animal abusers, but make it mandatory?'

Jasper drummed a jazz riff on the table with his thumbs. 'Things have changed since you used the chamber, Astra. The company's been sold and the new owners are gagging to do business with Gaians. IMBOD says it's a compassionate measure that will increase contact time with loved ones and improve security. It's true that Is-Land's minimum-security prisons are rife with Tablette and drug smuggling. That's another advantage of ion chamber visits, Astra. No more cavity searches.'

She flushed, but now was not the time to report on Lichena. 'IMBOD showing compassion for political prisoners and neuro-hospice patients?' she scoffed. 'C'mon, Jasper! The guards make up any excuse to probe me, you know that. And do you really believe IMBOD would do me any favours? They've got hackers all over this tech: CONC specs or not, they're going to be bugging the visits, of course they are. Worse than that: it'll be like getting a MRI scan every time we meet. They could monitor my physical health, target my diet . . .' An even more awful possibility occurred to her. 'Jasper. IMBOD could make a *hologram* of me and use it to transmit false messages from the Old Ones.'

She went cold just thinking about it. Jasper, however, remained unfazed. 'Probably all the Is-Lander visits will be bugged, sure. But believe me, security-wise, CONC's chambers are state of the art. They can detect any surveillance device installed at your end, and they also wipe out any digital trace of the interaction the instant after it occurs. There are significant implications to this, Astra.' He lifted an eyebrow, one of his best courtroom tricks. 'Communicating in a CONC ion chamber, we can finally bypass all the outrageous restrictions on your freedom of speech and association.'

He was referring to the prohibition on communicating with or about Muzi. It was a risky statement, but general enough to fall just this side of acceptable. She shook her head. 'I don't trust IMBOD, Jasper.'

'Trust *me*, then. For once, the wheels of justice aren't grinding you into the ground, Astra. It's a decision that's been taken for broader reasons, and this time you're going to come out on top. Here, Photon's analysis came in just before I entered the jail: take a look.'

He slid the blue sheet of paper under her nose, a printout of an article from *Is-Land Watch*, a dissident website no Gaian in Is-Land was able to access. But Jasper had fought long and hard to establish her right to read all material relevant to her case, except that which mentioned Muzi and his family. Before taking in the headline, though, she soaked up Photon's picture. His shock of white hair was thinning, and a pair of wire-framed glasses perched on his nose, but his eyes still shone with her friend's gentle brilliance and constant devotion to her cause. Her other former colleagues in Kadingir, Rudo and Sandrine, were still with CONC – Rudo, Jasper had told her, had been promoted to Head of Child Services in Eastern NuAfrica, and Sandrine was in Amazigia, still working for Major Thames, now Non-Land Special Rapporteur Colonel Thames; but, frustrated by CONC's diplomatic restrictions, Photon had left eight years ago to dedicate himself to serving the Non-Land resistance through activist journalism. She read the article slowly: Photon's Inglish had massively improved, but hers had rusted like a trowel left out all winter in the rain.

Victory in Is-Land Jails? CONC and N-LA Celebrate, But Questions Remain
by Photon Augenblick

A MASSIVE WIN FOR HUMAN RIGHTS?

Human rights workers are celebrating the long-awaited latest step in Is-Land prison reform: the decision to install ion chambers in all the country's prisons and neurohospices. But the CONC campaign to improve visiting rates at Is-Land's archaic jails is not the full-on success Is-Land Watchers were hoping for. Although the technology has the capacity to host visitors from all over the world, the IMBOD ruling currently allows only lawyers and Is-Land residents to use the newly installed ion chambers – and as soon as ion chamber inter-actions are introduced, The Is-Land Ministry of Penitence intends to ban *all* physical visits. Nevertheless, following the Wheel Meet's agreement three years ago to eliminate soli-tary confinement, the new policy is another demonstration of Is-Land's increasing vulnerability to international pressure. Among *Is-Land Watch*ers, it raises hopes that the hermit nation will soon be forced to open its borders and welcome home its original inhabitants.

ISTARS TOGETHER: UNA DAYYANI TO VISIT ASTRA ORDOTT

Speaking from Amazigia, Non-Land Alliance Lead Con-venor Una Dayyani reacted with optimism, saying, 'The Non-Land Alliance congratulates our Gaian counterparts on today's progressive decision. Prison reform is a key dimen-sion of N-LA's vision of One-Land, a democratic, law-abiding country where Non-Landers and Is-Landers can live together in peace.' Known to her compatriots as Um Kadingir, the mother of her people, and hailed by many as Istar Reborn, an earthly incarnation of the matron deity of her displaced populace, Dayyani also responded in her capacity as spirit-ual leader, adding, 'I remind the world of the Prophecy of Istar. "Alone she will fly to the ashlands and bury herself in the earth," the Prophecy states. "When she arises the place-less ones shall be in all places, and all places shall sing glad hymns of welcome." In the twelve years since my lonely flight from Kadingir, I have lived in exile, surrounded by the dunes of Asfar, while my long-suffering "Sister Istar", Astra Ordott, has been incarcerated in the ashfields of Is-Land. Held under conditions that cause grave concern for her men-tal and physical health, she has nevertheless all this time

bravely communicated to the world her urgent messages
of vital ecological importance. When I am able to make
an ion chamber visit to Astra, and our visions are united,
then surely Istar will have risen and, as the Prophecy pre-
dicts, the Boundary will fall and my people will be welcomed
home!'

She looked at Jasper, hiked an eyebrow. 'Sister Istar? And '*lonely
flight*'? She had her family and the entire N-LA police force with
her!'

'Be nice, Astra. She's giving you press.'

'She's questioning my sanity!'

'You're competition, sweets. Though frankly she does have the
lion's share of the Istar following at the moment. A visit from
Dayyani would do wonders for your Old Ones' appeals.'

She grunted. '*And* she's misquoted the Prophecy again. She *never*
mentions the missing word.'

The Prophecy was incomplete. Written on a fragment of an Old
World cuneiform tablet, it actually ended "glad hymns of welcome
and of . . ." Researching it back in Non-Land before she gave herself
up to IMBOD, Astra had learned that, given Istar's dual nature as
the goddess of the morning and evening star, some scholars believed
the missing word could be 'vengeance', or even 'war'. When she'd
asked Istar about it, though, the goddess had told Astra not to pursue the question, that the Prophecy was powerful precisely because
it was ambiguous: people could read their own visions into it. That
was true, but it irked her to see Dayyani truncate and sugarcoat
Istar's revelation. For one thing, it was wrong to suggest that the
Boundary would fall simply as the result of a meeting between two
famous figureheads: the rising of Istar energy was a collective
experience and if mishandled could result in terrible violence in the
region, violence that could overflow into the world. And, at a deeper
level, it was wrong to use the Prophecy to advance a political agenda,
even one Astra agreed with. The Prophecy didn't *predict* anything:

in its evocation of death and rebirth, male and female leadership, individual sacrifice and universal consciousness, it simply honoured how life *was*. How life had to be lived if human beings were to survive, let alone fulfil their potential on Earth.

Not that Jasper cared. They'd had this conversation many times, and he always failed to appreciate the finer points of ancient scriptural analysis. 'Yeah, I know,' he said. 'But "glad hymns" sounds pretty positive, doesn't it? And if we're not fighting for a happy ending, why are we even bothering? I know she's a big buzzy queen bee, Astra, but as long as Dayyani's still acknowledging you as an ally, your freedom will have to figure in any eventual peace deal.'

'I've told you before,' she muttered. 'My freedom's not important.'

'It is to me,' Jasper said quietly. *'I've* told *you* before. I'm going to get you out of this hellhole if it's the last thing I do.'

She glanced up, met his eyes, then lowered her head and read on.

Dayyani is in Amazigia this week to speak in defence of CONC Commitment 1899A, her long-fought amendment to Commitment 1899, *The Right of Reinstatement Act*. It remains to be seen if the indefatigable political powerhouse has succeeded in turning the vote, but she claims to have already convinced a majority of Human Diversity representatives and enough National Ambassadors to agree to make the Council of New Continents liable for the *entire* thirty-billion New Shell compensation bill for property lost and physical and psychological suffering endured as a result of the creation of Is-Land.

Even if Dayyani wins the vote, insiders believe Is-Land will continue to refuse to co-operate with the other demands of the original Act – also known informally as the 'One-Land Commitment'. But with a sudden increase in Non-Lander wealth and continuing economic decline in Is-Land, the Wheel Meet, the Gaian nation's ruling council, may be forced to capitulate to outside pressure.

Is-Land has never recovered from the humiliating diplomatic defeat of the overwhelming CONC vote to condemn the 'Security Generation' warrior force experiment and ban the 'Security Serum' as a weapon of war; and the sanctions imposed after the Gaians' rejection of the original C1899 are biting hard. Once CONC's lavishly overfunded darling, now a pariah state, Is-Land defiantly claims it is on target to meet its goal of complete economic self-sufficiency by RE 110, but sources close to the Is-Land Ministry of Border Defence – which effectively runs the country since Wheel Meet Chief Convenor Stamen Magmason declared a State of Emergency ten years ago – acknowledge that the isolationist country is still struggling to pay the extortionate costs of its controversial security projects, the Boundary Wall cladding and the vilified Sec Gens programme.

The Is-Land economy is under threat not only from the trade embargo which restricts Gaian exports, but also from the steady rise of innovative Asfarian biotech and metaphysical engineering companies, which are overtaking traditional Gaian dominance, and from the rise of anti-government forces at home as Magmason contends with the New Purist social movement sweeping the country.

IMBOD must, at all costs, avoid further CONC economic sanctions.

While those who continue to fight for a just settlement of Is-Land's long-running conflict with Non-Land take heart from today's concession, the world watches to see if Dayyani can summon a landslide that will, if not topple the Boundary, at least cause a crack in the cladding.

She frowned. 'I'm not sure that's such good news about the amendment.'

'C'mon, Astra.' They'd had this argument before too, but Jasper indulged her. 'I know it's hard to hope, but this really *is* a slice of the good stuff. IMBOD was never going to cough up its half, and frankly the whole mess was totally CONC's fuck-up in the first place. They ought to pay, and once they do, Is-Land's whole argument that they can't afford to honour the Right of Reinstatement collapses like the house of soggy cards it is.'

'Yeah, and then IMBOD moves to a war footing, endangering any chance of post-Hudna peace. And besides, *Is-Land* could have made peace and reparations with Non-Land decades ago. Why should struggling countries halfway around the world have to help bail us out? I'm with Enki Arakkia on that one.'

'Relax, Astra.' Jasper stretched. 'The IMBOD war machine is out of commission. There hasn't been a Sec Gen sighted beyond the Hem for eight years now. Any violence in the Southern Belt these days is coming from your old mates. Enki Arakkia, frankly, should be rounded up and shot.' He grinned. 'With a pea-shooter, of course.'

She pushed the paper back. 'Arakkia's not my friend. And IMBOD's not to be trusted, Jasper, ever. Photon says, in fact, that the new measure is open to abuse and needs further analysis.'

Jasper refiled the article. 'Photon's not a lawyer. Calendula and I agree that the new measure's not perfect, but it's a big improvement on the status quo. We've got other cases to fight; we'll monitor IMBOD, of course, but we can't afford to push this one hard right now.'

'But—' Her voice broke. 'I won't get to see you properly any more.'

Jasper slid his furry hand across the table until their fingertips were nearly touching. 'I'm not abandoning you, Astra. If anything, we'll be able to meet more often than we do now. Okay, time's tight, let's move on. Item Two: Earth's message.'

She gave up. She'd have to talk to Cora about it later. Jasper read Earth's message back to her. Word perfect. The prison censor must be new.

'So. Humanity has a year left to ban mining, abandon our Tablettes and destroy all our weapons, or the Old Ones will rise up and devour our stillborn infants.' Jasper tsked. As much as Earth liked his name, he liked Earth's bombast, and she was expecting him to crack a joke. But he didn't. He exhaled heavily. 'Frack, Astra. I was afraid this might happen.'

'It doesn't have to,' she reassured him. 'I can probably get Water and Air to give us an extension. But the Old Ones are running out of patience. We've got to meet one of Earth's demands at least. And maybe we can pull two birds out of the same hat. If we win our case against IREMCO *soon*, we could use the victory to strengthen the campaign for universal disarmament.' He tried to speak, but she rattled on. 'Rare-earths are vital to weapons systems manufacture, so if on the back of an IREMCO triumph we could tack on a mining-ban clause to the Hudna vote, we would really show Earth we're serious. If someone somewhere makes progress on replacement Tablette tech by then, we've got a super-strong case for being granted more time on the planet.'

'Woah.' He raised a plump palm. 'Hold on to your horses, Astra. IREMCO is Item Four. Look, I don't mean the scenario is bad news. I mean the *message* is. People are tired of apocalyptic ultimatums. No one believes 'em any more. If I put this threat out there, you're guaranteed to lose ten times more followers than you'll gain.'

Sometimes Jasper did that: lifted a big paw and slapped her down like a cub. But twice in a row? And over the Old Ones? She glared at him. 'There's nothing I can do about that. I'm just the messenger.'

'Well, maybe you can send Earth some feedback from me. Normally I charge five hundred New Shells an hour for that, but for Earth *pro bono*. Give us a carrot, Earth! Something to inspire us. Humanity's done with the doom and gloom!'

'Jasper.' She scowled. 'Earth doesn't take notes from cracked pots. Just deliver the message, okay?'

'Of course, Istarastra.' He doffed an imaginary cap. 'Via all the usual channels. Now, scooting on to Item Three: reaction to the Old Ones' last message.'

She sank back in her chair, as far as the chains would allow. Jasper, it was clear, didn't believe Earth's threat. Sometimes she wondered if Jasper believed in the Old Ones at all. Twelve years ago, when they were still settling terms with IMBOD, he had asked if she wanted a psychiatrist on her legal team. *I'm not crazy*, she'd roared, and he'd never brought up the subject again. Watching him now, refiling Earth's message, humming under his breath, she felt all the excitement of the morning drain out of her. Jasper did his job, transmitted the messages, even expressed affection for the Old Ones and their quirks, but maybe he really thought, as even Cora and Charm did, that they were just hallucinations, figments of Astra's neurohospiced mind.

She hopped off that train of thought. It didn't matter what Jasper believed, as long as the messages got out there. Hope bubbled up in her. The last message before Earth's ultimatum had been from Water: a beautiful, lyrical plea, imploring humans to cleanse their souls, live simply on the Earth and let their Tablettes and weapons rust in the rain. It had made her cry. Surely it had affected other people, too.

Jasper tsked again. 'YAC Attack set this one to music. "Simplicity Song" they called it. Nice tune – if you call me sometime, I'll play it for you. The track was a hit in Asfar, as usual. Elsewhere, it didn't *exactly* go viral, but it's still attracting clicks, to an end result of . . . oh,' he grimaced, 'a minuscule drop in international Tablette sales and Server usage. Statistically insignificant, I'm afraid.'

'It's to be expected,' she shot back. 'Until a viable metal-free global communications technology is developed, we can't expect people to relinquish their Tablettes.'

'So far, metal-free Talk-tech remains filed under "pipe dream", along with the perpetual motion machine.'

'So far. What about Is-Land? Has "Simplicity Song" made any impact here?'

It was risky, but she asked every time. In an Amazigian court of international law, Jasper had won her the right to release the Old Ones' messages to the world media, but though IMBOD had been forced to obey the CONC judge's ruling, the Gaians had jurisdiction over their own internal security and still refused to broadcast her warnings within Is-Land. It infuriated her. The Old Ones didn't care about international conflicts; They were only concerned with the health of the planet. And in any case, Earth, Water, Air and Fire were the original Gaians: Is-Landers ought to be able to hear what They said. Some, at least, wanted to: as they'd agreed before she'd been taken into custody, Jasper sent the Old Ones' messages by Owleon to the entire Is-Land dissident network.

'There's nothing in the Gaian media about it, but inevitably some people will be aware of the messages.' His stock reply, as disappointing as always. Top Gaian Code Scientists were receiving the Old Ones' messages. Why weren't they responding? 'Now.' Jasper flicked through his papers as she fumed, and placed one on top of Photon's article. 'Item Four: the IREMCO case. You will be delighted to learn that the case has been delayed again.'

'*Again?*' She frowned at the notification. No new date had been set. 'We've been waiting years. And we need to close the mine down before Earth's deadline!'

He cracked his knuckles. 'Unfortunately, due to the small matter of, oh, a dramatic global rise in infertility, for the time being the international courts are fully booked.'

'What's the infertility crisis got to do with the courts? No one's discovered the cause: there can't be any damages cases yet.'

He raised a podgy forefinger. 'No, but CONC investigations into the food supply chain have exposed a helluva lot of cases of corruption and agricultural malpractice. A couple of Gaian companies are up on big charges.'

'Babies are being born no problem in *Is-Land*,' she pointed out. 'Who cares about some desk jockey making a few extra bucks on currency exchange or adulterating trail mix? You should be looking for evidence that IMBOD is conducting a secret campaign to exterminate all meat-eaters!'

She was on fire, but yet again he was a damp blanket. 'And deprioritise the IREMCO case? I've only got so many hours in the day. And Astra, Is-Land isn't the only vegan nation in the world. Southern Himalaya is still popping out the sprogs.'

'Southern Himalaya doesn't have a wall around it, or an army of biologically engineered cannibals, or a pathological hatred of the outside world.'

'The latest research suggests some kind of livestock virus is responsible for the late miscarriages and low sperm count meat-eaters have been experiencing.'

'And IMBOD can't produce a virus?' Her head began to throb. It happened like this: not often, but in lightning flashes when she was most worked up, as if under the pressure of anger and frustration the Old Ones' messages stored in her cells spurted an answer straight into her brain. 'It's all *related*,' she blurted. 'IREMCO and the virus. From birth defects to infertility is not a big jump. Tell your team to heed the message from Earth. Read it again, Jasper – *Tell the humans they are punishing themselves. Your sterility is a symptom of your abuse of Our good nature.* Rare-earths mining is the biggest abuse we're committing against Earth right now. So we need to look for evidence of IREMCO scientists doing tests on mine-workers: any tests at all related to pregnancy, sperm count or miscarriage.' She had spoken in such a great rush she felt dizzy. 'Sorry, that probably didn't make sense. What I mean is—'

But Jasper cut her off. 'Astra, I know as well as you do there's nothing those bastards wouldn't do. But I can't risk a countersuit. Get a team of CONC lawyers making Is-Land or IREMCO their secret prime suspect in global genocide and quite the hue and cry will be raised from yon Gaians. Conspiracy, discrimination, gross abuse of CONC funds. We could be barred, or bankrupted, at the very least tied up for years in the courts. We've got plenty of evidence against IREMCO and I don't want to prejudice that trial by dragging conspiracy theories into it. Which brings us to Item Five: your Is-Land National Memory Archive access request final appeal. About which there are two bits of excellent news.' He drummed a brisk ta-da on the table. 'First up, we have a date!'

She slumped back in her seat. 'When?'

Jasper pouted. 'Not excited?'

She shrugged. 'I guess.'

She should be pleased, she knew. Nine years ago, CONC lawyers pressing for Gaian prison reform had exposed the fact that political prisoners in Is-Land were often subjected to Memory Pacification Treatment and the files extracted from the probes stored at INMA – an institution ostensibly dedicated to preserving Is-Land's history in the form of memories donated by national heroes and community leaders. The news had electrified Astra at the time. If Hokma's final memories were in the archive, they might help prove that she, arrested on charges of treason for sending Code secrets to Non-Land by Owleon, had not died of a stroke in her cell as reported, but had been killed – most likely on the orders of her brother, in collusion with her former Gaia partner, the celebrity bio-architect Ahn Orson. Both men would have been desperate to avoid Hokma revealing to the court that Samrod had helped her protect Astra from the Security Serum, a secret Ahn had discovered, and kept, in Astra's teens. Hokma, in her visits to Astra, had always refused to answer questions about her death, saying only that it didn't matter how she'd died, nothing could bring her back, and Astra should forgive her family and focus on healing the planet. But, driven by her desire to see Samrod Blesserson fall, Astra had instructed Jasper to file a request to access Hokma's files. Even though she was *persona non grata* in Is-Land, as Hokma's only Shelter child she had a slim legal case for access. Four years later, her request had been rejected on the grounds of national security, and three years ago, her first appeal had been denied. Yes, she ought to be excited. But Earth's visit this morning had deflated her; she'd much rather have Hokma's living presence in her cell than access to some grainy files from which all incriminating evidence had probably been erased.

Jasper named the date: early autumn. *'And'* – he rubbed his palms together as if to set the air on fire – 'looking at the Justices' schedule, you've got a fifty-fifty chance of getting *Stonewayson*.'

'Stonewayson?' The name sounded familiar.

'Justice Blade Stonewayson. One of the leading New Purists. You remember – his recent ruling that restaurants have the right to require people to wear clothes nearly rocked the Wheel Meet off its spindle.'

Oh yeah. Him. Stonewayson was a rebel. But the New Purists were hardly on her side. 'No way-son. They'll appoint the other judge. And anyway, the New Purists are just cranks, Jasper. They claim to stand for Gaia but they've never responded to the Old Ones' messages. They mainly just care about getting Gaians' minds off sex and back onto working hard, like the Pioneers.'

'Don't be so sure. The man's got it in for the whole Wheel Meet upper echelon and he hasn't been disbarred or pushed into the River Mikku yet. We don't know what's going on behind closed doors. I'm telling you, Astra.' Jasper's tubby face beamed. 'Something's afoot in Atourne. Stamen Magmason, Clay Odinson, your Shelter uncle Blesserson: that lot are clinging on to power by the scabied skin of their teeth.'

Usually Jasper's enthusiasm was contagious. Not today. 'Maybe. But I'm still public enemy number one. No one's going to let me benefit from any regime change.'

'Wrong logic, Astra.' He leaned back in his chair, laced his fingers and stretched his arms above his head, exposing pits like black forests and giving her a whiff of damp moss. 'Letting you access Hokma's memories of her last days, even if they prove she was killed by her own brother's fair hand, doesn't change your legal situation one iota. You did your deal with IMBOD, and that's that. Learning who murdered Hokma can only harm the killer. Or *killers*. There are plenty of folks in Atourne who would like to see Samrod Blesserson dislodged. Who knows, Odinson may be involved, too. It's more likely Blesserson was working with a senior IMBOD officer than Ahn Orson. There's a reason those memories are highly classified information.'

She'd believe it when it happened. 'What's the second piece of good news?'

'Hey. That was it.' He lowered his arms. 'And pretty fucking good news it was, too.'

'Oh.' Her forehead was itchy. She rubbed at a knot in the table grain with her finger instead. 'Nothing about Peat, then?'

Jasper's voice softened. 'I'm sorry, Astra. Peat, well, if there was word of him, that would have been Item One.' He placed a blank sheet of paper on top of the pile and took the pen from behind his ear. 'Item Six, then: you. How are you, Astra, really? Have you heard from Klor?'

She shrugged. 'Yeah. Everyone's okay. Nimma won another Craft award.' Her Shelter father Klor wrote once a year, formal letters that updated her on mundane developments in Or and the health of her family there. Jasper waited. She made circles on the tabletop with her fingertip. In the dream, she had been massaging Muzi's spine.

'How's your mama dog?' she asked. 'Did you get a Tablette collar for her yet?'

'She's good. Still totally bonkers and still proudly off-grid.'

'What about her puppy? The caramel one that joined the CONC police squad? Did they bring him back yet for a visit like they promised?'

Although not foolproof, the code was credible: Jasper did breed spaniels, and whatever he told Astra about them was true.

'Not yet,' he said. 'Everyone's just been crazy busy.'

So Muzi, as far as Jasper knew, hadn't returned to Asfar.

'The new litter is good, though. Really cute. Look.'

He leafed through the file folder and pulled out pictures of the puppies. His daughter was cuddling one in her lap and raising the mother dog's paw in a wave. This meant Muzi's family, the women and children for whom she had sacrificed her freedom, had emailed Jasper one of their brief updates from Asfar, where they were now living – without Muzi, who had left to join a guerrilla fighting unit over a year ago. For a moment, she felt sick with worry for Muzi – the war was over, why did he think he still needed to fight? Wasn't he getting along with his mother? How was his ear?

'Awww.' She feigned delight. 'What about that stray cat in your garden? Did she show up again yet?'

'Nah. She's still out prowling around.'

'She's been gone a long time.'

'Yeah. She could be in Zabaria for all I know. But she's a great mouser. She can look after herself.'

The cat was Lil. She had, over the years, sometimes written to Jasper using the name they'd agreed on, Emerald Dancer, but her emails had stopped six months ago. What she was doing in Zabaria was anyone's guess.

'I wish we could have animals in here.' She was playing a part – a little girl cooing over puppy photos – but for a moment the longing felt real.

'That's a whole other court case. For now, just be glad you don't have rats in your cell.' Jasper slipped the photos back into the folder and clicked the pen open. 'Did you see the dentist yet, Astra? Any abuse or infractions of CONC standards to report?'

She tongued the loose tooth. 'The dentist comes next week. So they say.' She paused, then made her useless report. 'Lichena disssticked me twice since you last came, once on 21.12.98 for not speaking when spoken to, and once on 3.02.99 for speaking when not spoken to. Charm Ambertondott witnessed both incidents. The groping continues. Even when the ion chamber starts, Lichena said they would still be frisking me. Vultura always gets shut down when it happens.'

He noted everything, then pushed his folder aside and assessed her. 'Twelve years next month. You're holding up very well. Still got colour in your cheeks, fire in your eyes. Hang in there, Astra, promise me that.'

She wouldn't be seeing Jasper properly again. Not like this, exuding the damp musk of his hairy armpits, staining the table with the sweat from his forearms. She could muster only half a smile and half a verse, one she had memorised a long time ago, from her father's anthology *Nights Beyond Measure*, which she was not allowed to

have in jail in case it harboured secret messages. It did, of course, but not the ones IMBOD feared. 'I'm okay, Jasper. Like Hafiz says:
    "Those whose lives are a shrouded sacrifice to Heaven
    drink the strongest wine, with me, the vagrant river."'

He grinned. 'Don't get too tipsy on those old poets, Astra. I'm telling you, Stonewayson's got a barnful of axes to grind, and with him on the bench of your INMA appeal we've got the best chance in a generation to help take out the whole rotten hub of the Wheel Meet. Then there's our case against IREMCO coming up, and the end of the Hudna to boot. It's All Change ahead. That Boundary's going to crack wide open, and I'll get you out of this shit-hole if it's the last thing I do.'

She shrugged. All in all, apart from the fact that her top law firm had refused to lodge a complaint with IMBOD over the violation of her right to human visitors, it had been an exchange of news that was no news.

'Next time I see you,' she said, 'you'll be a ghost in Amazigia.'

'Don't think about it like that. I'm telling you, the move will have advantages.' He grinned. 'You won't have to smell my fried-onion breath any more, for one thing.'

Next-best wasn't flesh-best. She didn't try to explain it. She had always thought it was important that her lawyer saw where she lived, met the guards, could impress his authority on them. But it wasn't just the illusion of protection she needed from his visits, she realised now. It was the miracle of seeing someone who had come from outside, someone who walked in through the door fresh from an adventure, energised by his epic journey over the steppes and the ashfields. Jasper brought the scent of freedom with him. That was the smell an ion chamber could never manufacture, a scent that had helped keep her going through the long hard years of captivity. For Jasper's visits, with their visceral reminder that physical freedom was a human joy and a birthright, did not make her wistful. Rather, that whiff of joy strength-ened her conviction that her sacrifice was worthwhile. If the Old Ones' vision could only be realised, everyone on Earth would experience marvellous freedoms, the profound liberties that mystics and idealists had always claimed possible for the human race – freedom from war and want, and the freedom to roam, not only over the planet, but deep into the shimmering web of consciousness that was the universe. If humanity at large rejected that vision, then she didn't want to spend the last months of her life in its company.

'Time's up.' The door opened and the sheer delight that was Lichena returned. The guard unlocked Astra's cuffs from the table and yanked her to her feet. Jasper thrust the file folder into her shackled hands and Astra twisted her head as she was dragged out, looking at him for as long as she could. Her lawyer's brown bear eyes were still gleaming with the promise he had made to her at their first meeting and repeated nearly every visit since – his vow to work for her until he secured her release. It was a promise she had doubted for years, had never required from him, but knew now that only Jasper's own death would extinguish.

Shadow Blue

The Windsands

'Hello. My name is Peat Orson. I am making this recording at six a.m. on the Vernal Equinox, RE 99. It is two days after the report of a Gaian breakthrough in spinal cord injury research. I send my love to my family and friends, and I thank everyone in the world who has not forgotten me.'

The Peat on the screen, standing in the desert beside a palomino stallion, gazed steadily at the Peat sitting cross-legged on the cushions in the tent, a dog in his lap. *Just look into my eyes*, the filmmaker, A'dula, had coached, and he had done so, into the videoglasses that had captured him from head to waist, bare-chested, clean-shaven, Starbrow's reins in his hand, the red desert rolling out behind them to the dawn horizon, a shimmering veil of rose pink, white gold and cornflower blue. Three hours later now, it was a bright day, even in the tent, the dirt showing on the camelhair cushions and carpets. Tent Peat fondled Smoke's floppy ears, let Screen Peat talk on as the hound licked his hand.

'I was taken into the keeping of the Non-Landers twelve years ago. At that time, I was a member of Is-Land's Security Generation. When I was eight years old, doctors in my country injected me with a serum that greatly enhanced my physique but inhibited the development of my capacity to make moral decisions. The serum also gave me ...' Screen Peat's face twitched. 'Non-human appetites that, to me, felt natural and right.'

In the dark behind Tent Peat, Dr Tapputu grunted softly. Tent Peat watched Screen Peat lean his head against Starbrow's neck, his gaze sliding off-camera, as if to a place no one else could ever see. He had wanted to stop, start over, but behind A'dula, Bartol had nodded: *Good, Peat. Continue.*

Smoke thumped his tail on the carpet and pushed his wet nose into Tent Peat's palm. Screen Peat continued, 'Today, thanks to years of medical treatment and psychological therapy, I am no longer a Sec Gen. I do not blame the Gaian doctors who made me what I was. They thought they were doing the right thing for our country. They also thought that human beings would be happier if we didn't have to make difficult decisions, if all we had to do was follow our instincts and obey a strong leader.'

From behind him came the restrained sound of Dr Tapputu sucking his teeth. Dr Tapputu did blame the Gaian doctors, Tent Peat knew. But this was Peat's message, not anyone else's. Again, Screen Peat paused. When he spoke again, his voice was tender and thick.

'Doctor Blesserson, you were very kind to me. But the sacrifice was too great. And the theory was wrong. I was not happy as a Sec Gen. People died, and I missed them. And worse things than that happened, too.'

The camera zoomed in. Now there was no horizon, just Screen Peat's face, the speckles of sweat on his cheeks, the sheen of his large, dark eyes. Steady as a march through the desert, his voice filled the tent. 'As a Sec Gen I did great harm, not to enemy warriors, but to innocent civilians. In RE 87 I entered Non-Land illegally with my team, travelling to Kadingir to kidnap a family, a hostage-taking mission IMBOD covered up with the false claim that the family had been trespassing in the Hem. During the mission, I unintentionally killed the elderwoman Uttu Dúrkiñar. In trying to restrain her, I accidentally broke her neck with my bare hands. That same night, acting with my team, I wholeheartedly participated in the annihilation of an alt-bodied woman from Zabaria.

I never knew her name, and after we had finished there was nothing left of her.'

Screen Peat's nostrils flared; his massive jaw flexed, but his eyes held the gaze of the world. 'Not long after my mission, I was taken captive myself. Then Uttu Dúrkiñar's two sons died in IMBOD custody. My Shelter sister, Astra Ordott, offered herself in exchange for the release of their wives and children and other Non-Land prisoners. I had no part in my sister's decision. For my safety and hers, I was denied contact with anyone but my carers. It took me several years, but eventually I acknowledged my crimes. I am a murderer, but the Non-Landers have not punished me. I have been housed in a beautiful place, well fed and cared for, allowed to live peacefully in Gaia's bounty with animals and understanding human companions. But I will not be at peace until I have taken responsibility for what I did. Of my own free will, I have asked to be transported to Asfar to be tried for double homicide, subject to whatever conditions the Mujaddid and the Non-Land government-in-exile may set. I hope that my former medical condition and my time spent here as a patient will be taken into consideration, but I understand if that cannot be the case. I have broken the fundamental law of any decent human society – to live and let live – and I must accept the legal consequences of what I have done.'

Starbrow tossed her head; Screen Peat stroked her nose, calmed her. The camera pulled back until man and horse were just small figures against the banks of the *wadi*, then panned slowly to reveal the tents, pens and huts that had been his home for the last ten years. There was no risk of discovery, Dr Tapputu had said: the animal sanctuary could be located anywhere in a vast region of desert. Screen Peat's voice returned, disembodied, floating over the dawn-stained image of borderless tranquillity.

'To accompany this video message, my doctors in Non-Land will be releasing the details of my restorative treatment. I, Peat Orson of Is-Land, urge IMBOD to cease their Security Generation programme immediately, and make this treatment freely available to everyone who has received the Security Serum shot. If IMBOD does not do this, I urge all Sec Gens to demand the treatment, and all Is-Land parents to refuse to allow their children to be injected in future. The end of the one-hundred-year Hudna is approaching and no country should be investing in war, let alone weaponising their children. The Sec Gens have not made Is-Land safe. Is-Land will be secure only when it respects the humanity of our neighbours, regardless of creed, diet, dress or their treatment of animals. We can only claim to be the guardians of our fellow creatures if we ourselves treat *all* living beings with respect.'

The camera returned to the place it had begun. Screen Peat was no longer there. He was riding Starbrow, bareback, towards a glowing gold horizon.

The screen blackened. Dr Tapputu set the remote down on the engraved brass table. 'Let some air in, will you, Bartol?'

Bartol stood and opened the tent flaps, then lowered his giant frame back onto his cushions. 'What do you say, brother?'

Peat stroked the fine hairs of Smoke's muzzle. 'It's good. Release it.'

Dr Tapputu clicked his tongue against his teeth. 'Are you sure, Peat? Why don't you think about it a little longer?'

He began to massage Smoke's back, the way the hound liked it, knuckles either side of the spine. 'I've thought about it for twelve years.'

The doctor sighed. 'Yes. But you still have time to change your mind. No one at CONC blames you for what happened. And we don't know how things will go in Asfar. Peat, I'll say it again: CONC would much prefer to take you into diplomatic custody and escort you back to your family.'

Smoke had a burr in his silky fur; Peat began to unpick it. 'No. Everything has to be done properly. The Non-Landers must witness me testifying. They have to know I really do repent. And they have to see for themselves that I'm not a Sec Gen any more.'

Tapputu fell silent. Peat freed the burr. Smoke yelped and he gathered the dog in his arms, burying his face in its soft coat. He had helped bring Smoke into this world, from its mother's belly. It would hurt saying goodbye to Smoke. That would be the worst part of his decision. But while there were no horses or dogs or rare foxes in Asfarian prisons, he had read that many prisoners kept hamsters and birds.

'I understand, Peat. I do,' Tapputu said at last. 'But crimes have been committed against you, too. Are you sure you don't want to pursue a case against Odinson and Blesserson?'

In response, Peat tickled Smoke's belly. The dog wriggled with pleasure, his tongue lolling out of his jaw.

'We talked about everything, a lot, Doctor,' Bartol said quietly in his rustic Asfarian. 'He means it.'

Peat let the hound tumble to the carpet and stood up. 'You gave me my free will back, Doctor. Now I'm going to use it. The video is fine. A'dula can send it to Shiimti for the Zardusht to see, and we can release it when she gives her approval.'

'All right, Peat.' Dr Tapputu stood, too, his small, stout, black-robed figure poised like a miniature chess piece between the two huge young men. He raised his palms. 'I won't argue with you any more. But remember, even after the video goes out, you can always change your mind.'

His mind had been changed enough, changed over and over, beyond recognition. Smoke at his heels, Peat left the tent and strode towards the horses. Starbrow looked up when he whistled. The horse was still in her pen, but Screen Peat was already halfway to Asfar.

SPRING RE 99

Acid Green
Desert Red
Burnt Orange
Desert Red
Acid Green

Misted Silver

Sour Gold
Bruise Purple
Shadow Blue
Bruise Purple
Sour Gold

Acid Green

Bracelet Valley
26.03.99

'What on *earth* did you think you were doing, Freki?' All the burning tension of the last five days burst out of Sif and sprayed like sparks over her small, stubborn daughter. 'We were frightened to *death*. The whole of Yggdrasila was out looking for you! And then you hurt Apa Vili. You haven't even said sorry!'

'Oma Sif.' Opposite her in the circle, Esfadur, garbed in the green, gauzy robe he had taken to wearing of late, addressed her sternly. 'Shouting won't help. And making demands is not the way of the Parents' Counsel.' Flanking the snowy-bearded elder, Esfadur's wife Brana shot Sif that haughty look of hers, while beside her Baldur glanced at the Common Room grandmother clock. On the basis of his grumbles when asked to attend the Counsel, the glass smith was no doubt impatient to be gone, back to his workshop.

Sif simmered quietly. It was just like Freki to make *her* look at fault in front of Yggdrasila's wisest elders. As if *she* were the miscreant, when it was the children who should be reprimanded. Perched on their two wooden toadstools in front of Sif, Fasta and Vili on the sofa, and the three Counsel Elders in their high-backed carved chairs, the twins dangled their legs and pouted. Ggeri was puffy-eyed from his bout of shamed tears. Freki, though, still harboured a mute glint of disobedience in her eye. She was the ringleader of this sorry escapade, Sif was sure of it. The sooner that girl had her Sec Gen shot, the better.

Yes, Sif knew that two children setting off to Lake Asgard with pilfered sandwiches and cake in their backpacks was hardly unheard of. But the children had been missing for three days! And when Vili's search party had found them curled up asleep in the woods, Freki had awoken with a screech to deafen the dead and fought like a hellcat to escape. Sif and Vili's Code daughter, the little Firewolf with the rebellious streak, had bitten and kicked and scratched her own father until Vili had finally held her upside down by her ankles, laughing his deep laugh as the girl finally went limp and burst into tears. The twins had barely said a word between them since. After two days of cajoling and threats from their three Shelter parents had produced no answers, Sif had demanded a Parents' Counsel meeting: she, Vili and Fasta needed help to get to the bottom of this.

Next to Sif on the old blue sofa, its cushions threadbare from years of hosting anxious parents' bottoms, Fasta leaned forwards. 'If you were upset about something, children, please tell us,' she wheedled, 'or else we can't make it better.'

Yet again, Sif wished she'd never accepted Fasta's offer to Birth Shelter mother her and Vili's Code children. A single straight woman and a heterosexual couple made the worst co-parenting schema, everyone knew that, but after six years with Vili, and four miscarriages, the doctors all said she was too frail to carry to term. She'd needed a Birth mother and felt sorry for her best friend Fasta, widowed in her early thirties; had somehow thought she'd be different – grateful, even! What a mistake *that* was. Increasingly, Fasta behaved as if carrying the children in her womb had made her their primary parent. She mollycoddled them, broke rules Sif had set, let them stay up late, eat what they liked, then astonishingly won community praise for her patience while the twins ran amok. Why couldn't Fasta just get herself another Gaia partner and Birth-Code Shelter some children of her own?

'I didn't hurt Apa Vili,' Freki muttered. '*He* hurt *me*.' She rubbed her arm and scowled at her father. The cheek of her!

'Now, Freki.' A warm, strong presence on Sif's right, Vili the pacifier intervened, addressing his daughter in his usual firm but soothing tones. 'You didn't hurt me very much, and I'm sorry if I hurt you. You aren't in trouble. We're all glad you've been found. Oma Sif is just upset because she was worried sick about you.' He squeezed Sif's hand and she sat straighter, daring any of the other adults to judge her. 'But we've called this meeting,' Vili went on, 'because we all want you to tell us why you ran away.'

'Has someone been teasing you, children?' Brana asked. 'Is that it?'

Tall and angular, like her barrel-chested husband in his long oak-green robe, the elderwoman was an imposing and, to Sif, somewhat unsettling presence. Brana too had recently taken to sheathing her still-fit physique, in her case in a loose gown of shimmering emerald gauze. The garments, the couple had explained to the community, were not insulation for old bones, but an expression of a deep inner commitment to Gaianism. *The true Gaianism*, Brana had said. Sif didn't understand how you could be truly Gaian other than by going skyclad, but no one dared argue with Brana. Now, under the elderwoman's expectant stare, the twins side-eyed each other, Ggeri silently pleading with Freki, his fierce sister forbidding him to speak. Personality-wise, the twins were chalk and alt-cheese, but in times of trouble they stuck together like a snail and its shell.

'N-n-noo.' Ggeri's voice wobbled.

'We wanted to have an *adventure*,' Freki blazed. 'A real adventure. Not some stupid *Sec Gen* game!'

So rude she was! Shouting at the elderwoman. And why was Brana's mouth twitching? She, of all people, a revered pillar of the community, shouldn't encourage this bad behaviour. Sif could not help her voice from rising. 'But you knew we would panic when you didn't come home! Look around you: everyone here dropped what they were doing to hunt for you. For days! Why didn't you think about *us*, Freki?'

'Sif,' Vili hushed. 'Children don't always—'

How many times had they discussed this? He wasn't to contradict her in front of them! 'She's got to be told, Vili!' she blazed. 'And she's not letting him talk. Ggeri.' She addressed her son. 'Did *you* want to have an adventure?'

'Sif, Vili,' Esfadur boomed. 'From now on parents must please let the elders do the asking.'

Sif clamped her mouth shut. An Yggdrasila co-founder, a Patriarch with five wives in his heyday, a grandfather fourteen times over and a great-grandfather to twenty-one children, Esfadur had headed the Parents' Counsel for years. Nearly everyone in the room had been subject to a decision by Esfadur at one point; somehow his authority permeated the very air.

'Freki,' he commanded, with a kindly twinkle. 'Go outside with Apa Baldur and have some cake in the dining hall. I want to talk to your brother by himself.'

The girl glittered at the elderman. Sif braced herself. Surely Freki wouldn't dare disobey Esfadur!

She didn't. Baldur stood and offered his hand. Shooting what could only be described as a warning glance at her twin, Freki got up and stalked past the glassworker to the door. Baldur grinned over her head back at Esfadur, who chuckled softly into his beard. Sif simmered. Brana was amused, too. Oh, it was easy for *elders* to enjoy naughty children – they didn't have to discipline the whelps.

'Now, Ggeri.' Esfadur resumed his kindly grilling. 'Your parents are right – we need to know why you left so that we can make sure you are happy here in the future. Tell us. Honestly. Why did you want to run away?'

'I didn't want to.' The tears began to tumble.

'Then why did you, my boy?' Brana asked.

'Freki said we had to. She *frightened* me. Oma Fasta, I'm f-f-frightened!'

'What are you scared of, Little Windwolf?' Fasta cooed at the boy.

Her son's stricken glance at Fasta was like a knife in Sif's guts. She waited for Esfadur to reprimand Fasta for speaking, but no stern injunction came. Into the silence, Ggeri lowered his damp lashes. 'You won't b-b-believe me.'

'We will.' His brown pate shining above his ridged brow, and his white beard cascading down his broad chest, Esfadur was as irrefutable as a mountain. 'If you tell us the truth, we promise to believe you.'

It took more promises, from everyone, but at last her son began to speak, waveringly at first, then in between bouts of sobbing. About a glade in the woods, and a man with a girl. Sticking her, with an electricity stick. A man hurting a girl, playing with himself, in ways Ggeri couldn't quite explain but were shatteringly clear to all listening. Though hands flew to mouths, and Sif could barely believe her ears, it was obvious Ggeri was telling the truth. 'She was only a girl,' he whimpered to a halt. 'That's *wrong*, isn't it?'

'Very wrong,' Esfadur rumbled.

'He was *kicking* her.' Ggeri blubbered again. 'Really hard. I was scared, Oma. I was so scared.'

'So why didn't you come to your parents right away?' Esfadur asked.

Ggeri wiped his eyes. His lip trembled.

'Tell us, son,' the elderman coaxed.

At last he forced it out. 'F-f-freki said the girl was a Sec Gen. That's why the man could stick her with the electricity stick and she didn't die. Freki said that's why Sec Gens are made so strong. So grown-ups can hurt them whenever they like.' His eyes welled up again and a tear splashed down onto his knee. 'Is Freki right?' he whimpered. 'Is that what the Sec Gens are for?'

'No, it is *not*,' Brana snapped, startling Sif. Severe as Brana was, she had never seen her quite like this before. The elderwoman's face was rigid with anger and her gaze could have cut glass.

'No, Ggeri,' Esfadur intoned from the deep core of all his majestic authority. 'I promise you that what you saw is not the purpose of Sec Gens.'

'Oh, Ggeri,' Fasta gasped. 'My poor baby.'

If Fasta could break the rules, Sif could, too. 'Don't be afraid, Ggeri,' she urged. 'You saw a bad man, that's all. A very bad man.

But he won't hurt you, ever. We'll never let him. Come here, darling, come.'

She held out her arms. Fasta may have lent the twins her womb,
but she, Sif, was their Code mother. Ggeri was made of her stuff,
hers and Vili's. It was to her he should turn first for comfort, and it
was she who should make the ultimate decisions in his interest.
Ggeri rose and stumbled, dazed and smeary-eyed, into her lap. She
clasped her son to her chest, Vili on one side, Fasta on the other,
three parents enfolding their hurt boy.

'The upper hill flank . . .' Brana murmured. 'That's not far from
the IMBOD zone.'

'Godstruth!' Vili swore, his voice roughened by the ancestors'
curse. 'What is happening to this country?'

'I do not know,' Esfadur boomed. 'But rest assured, parents, if it's
the last thing I do on Gaia's green Earth, I am going to find out.'

Desert Red

Asfar
03.04.99

Orson Video and Dayyani Victory: Two Giant Steps Closer to One-Land?
by Photon Augenblick

It may never be known if this week's shock international release of a statement by the former Sec Gen Peat Orson was deliberately timed to assist the cause of One-Land. In Orson's now viral video the supposed Gaian 'hostage' thanked his Non-Land medical team for reversing his condition and asked to be tried in Asfar for his crimes against Non-Landers. His courageous moral stance has clearly, if not influenced, at least chimed with global opinion. Today, Non-Landers from Amazigia to Pútigi are celebrating after the Council of New Continents agreed yesterday in a landslide vote to foot the entire bill for the loss and suffering caused by the founding of the Gaian state Is-Land.

Passed by 265 to 23, Commitment 1899A, Dayyani's long-fought amendment to Commitment 1899, *The Right of Reinstatement Act*, will see CONC alone paying thirty billion New Shells in compensation for the territorial, financial, emotional and physical loss and suffering inflicted by the Gaian dispossession of the people of the former state

of Somaria. C1899, passed in RE 92, required Is-Land and
CONC to fund the compensation equally, but for seven
years the Gaians have steadfastly refused to pay up. Now
that obstacle to reparations has been overcome, the moral
case against Is-Land gains ever more traction, strengthened
by Orson's defection.

Speaking yesterday from Amazigia, Una Dayyani, the
leader of the Non-Land Alliance, called the near-unanimous
vote, 'A decision that in its humility, generosity and perspi-
cacity is unparalleled in CONC history. Rarely have mere
numbers brought such sweet vindication.'

Fresh from her victory, Dayyani pressed further, urging
delegates of the Council of New Continents to keep pressure
on Is-Land to meet the other clauses of the original Commitment. First, the immediate liberation of occupied Zabaria;
and second, the opening of Is-Land's borders to a pilot group
of 1,000 Non-Landers to build agricultural settlements on
Is-Land's largely unpopulated steppes, an initiative that will
include CONC-administered cultural education in the Gaian
value system. Finally, Dayyani reiterated her support for the
long-term aim of *The Right of Reinstatement Act*, known
informally to many as *The One-Land Commitment*: to dismantle the Boundary and regenerate the toxic lands of the
Southern Belt, extending the borders of this new fully inte-
grated and expanded state to the desert town of Lálsil.

Is-Land, predictably, continues to refuse to negotiate. Stamen Magmason, Chief Convenor of Is-Land's ruling council
the Wheel Meet, having already banned the transmission of
the Peat Orson video within the country, today said from
Atourne – in a statement not expected to be relayed in full
to his people – 'I regret gravely that CONC representatives
may have been swayed by the fabrications of a vulnerable,
brainwashed youth, and I greet their decision with grave
disappointment. CONC payments to refugees should be

granted untainted by political agendas. The so-called *Right of Reinstatement Act*, with its demand to open our borders to an influx of hostile, meat-eating Abrahamic communities, poses an existential threat to our peaceable, skyclad, vegan lifestyle. If CONC and its allies in the region truly wish to create a sustainable solution to the conflict besieging my nation, they should invest this massive sum in creating another state for the so-called "Non-Landers", regenerating desert land in Asfar for them to live in. To approve this measure as part of a package to destroy the Gaian state is nothing short of a vicious, reckless act of fiscal warfare.'

But speaking for CONC, Colonel Akira Thames, the Non-Land Special Rapporteur, immediately shot down Magmason's call to settle Non-Landers in the Asfarian desert. 'Temperatures can reach 60 degrees Celsius here, so clearly re-greening is not a feasible option,' heesh responded. 'Convenor Magmason also ignores the emotional ties to one's homeland so perceptively recognised by Commitment 1899.' Heesh then reiterated the Non-Land Alliance commitment to adopting fear-free animal slaughter and extending its multicultural political infrastructure to the Gaian lifestyle.

Magmason's face may remain set against change, but recent events within Is-Land and beyond its borders hint that today's vote may yet lead to a 'crack in the Boundary'. Last month's reformation of the country's prison system has led to renewed calls for the release of political prisoners, including Astra Ordott, Peat Orson's Shelter sister, whom many Non-Landers believe to be an incarnation of the goddess Istar. With her Shelter brother now in the limelight, Ordott can expect her own international profile to rise.

Adding to the heat, Magmason faces internal resistance from the New Purists. Although it remains difficult to gather accurate information about the reclusive state, according to insiders the grass-roots social movement to 'rebalance the

Gaian relationship with nature and the body' has attracted
members from IMBOD, the Ministry of Penitence and the
Ministry of Spiritual Development. The rise of the New Purists, who take a more conservative approach to clothing,
dressing in green robes in public and going 'skyclad' only in
the privacy of their own homes, may offer N-LA hope of
bridging one of the greatest cultural divides between Is-
Landers and Non-Landers.

Meanwhile, Asfar's leader, the Mujaddid, has reaffirmed
his own commitment to justice for the Non-Landers, accepted
the responsibility of trying Peat Orson in an Asfarian court.
Whatever the results of that trial, Orson looks set to become
yet another icon of resistance to Gaian isolationism.

With pressure mounting both within and without the
Boundary, how much longer can Magmason maintain his
fifteen-year granite grip on the Wheel Meet? And how long
can Is-Land resist the will of the world?

Una Dayyani clapped and the wallscreen pixelated back from text
to a shifting mosaic of crimson, purple and gold tiles, sumptuous
tessellations of colour and light designed to harmonise with the
hand-loomed carpets, tapestries, sofas and footstools of her palatial
reception chamber. After the bland, echoing halls of CONC HQ,
it was good to be back in Asfar. She did not turn on the lamp; her
eyes were still tired after the Zeppelin flight, and the half-light was
conducive to reflection. 'All well and good, Tahazu,' she tsked. 'But
dare I complain that yet again *Is-Land Watch* has neglected to
acknowledge my role as chief bearer of the mantle of Istar, out here
in the world where words and actions can have some *effect*?'

His solid physique framed by two fluted pillars, her Chief of
Police, Tahazu Rabu, no waster of words, grunted. 'The headline,
though, is yours, as is the love of your people, stronger than ever.
Welcome back and congratulations again, Leader of Many Names
and One Vision.'

Don't complain, he was saying. It was not a response she would have accepted from her other ministers. Only Tahazu, childhood friend and most enduring ally, was permitted to offer less-than-effusive tributes to Una in her role as Istar, the long-prophesied saviour of her people; an accolade she herself, in public, modestly downplayed. She reached for her goblet of pomegranate juice on the gold-tiled table beside her high-backed velvet chair. 'To One-Land.'

'To One-Land.' He chinked his glass with hers.

'But I did not summon you here to laud me, Tahazu. I have returned early from the victory party to discuss matters of grave importance. The monster Peat Orson is gifting himself to us. Why?'

Rabu shrugged. 'The youth committed atrocities. Sometimes a young man does genuinely repent of his sins.'

Through a slit in the gauze curtains, a shaft of light was falling like a rapier across the floor at Una's feet. She toed it slowly with a bejewelled sandal, admiring the shining rubies, her matching nail polish. 'Badly enough to risk a life sentence in a desert monastery?'

'Countless others have freely chosen such a fate over the millennia.' Rabu stroked his beard – a worn boot-mat in comparison to her husband's silken curls, but it suited his lantern jaw. 'Look at the Ordott girl.' The crevice of his mouth split into Rabu's version of a smile. 'Perhaps an appetite for punishment runs in the family.'

She snorted. 'That one. Sitting on her half-Gaian bottom, eating three square meals a day, and keeping her name in the headlines by making preposterous demands and absurd ultimatums. Let's hope her brother's not going to start channelling the ravings of sandworms and cacti spines. We don't need two lunatics to contend with.'

Rabu drained his goblet and reset it beside hers. 'The Mujaddid heeds the Ordott messages. He is taking this new deadline very seriously. The Institute of Metaphysical Engineering has just doubled the prize money for the invention of a non-toxic global communications technology.'

She shot him a tart look. 'While the metaphysical implications of Ordott's messages may intrigue our host, she is a fringe figure in our community, irrelevant to our struggle to reclaim our ancestral land. Her call for sustainable technological development is a worthy one, of course, and her case against IREMCO a useful card in our hand; but her crackpot demand that the entire world abandon mining does not help the cause of Non-Land, nor does it inspire the loyalty of the vast majority of Non-Landers, who understand that it is only through mature negotiation at the international table that we will regain access to our beloved homeland.'

'Indeed.' Rabu acknowledged her riposte with a tilt of his craggy head. 'While Istar speaks through all Non-Landers, it is clear that the honour of shaping our future has fallen to Um Kadingir. But who knows, the Ordott prophecies may yet form a part of our victory. It costs us nothing to permit her minor contributions to the cause.'

'Of course not.' With a tilt of her chin, Una accepted the advice of her most stalwart supporter, sweetened as it was with the sound of her hard-earned title. 'These grumblings remain within these walls. Um Kadingir shares her glory with the weakest and most feeble-minded of her children.'

'And as Um Kadingir predicted,' Tahazu murmured, 'that glory is ever increasing.'

With a delicate flutter of her lashes, she graced him with a smile. Eleven long years ago, Tahazu had protected her government's caravan from bandits on its desolate journey from Kadingir to exile in Asfar. His loyalty since had helped transform that wretched humiliation into Una's current position as a moral force in international diplomacy. 'My people,' she had declared as she left the ruins of Kadingir, abandoning its flattened tents and bloodsoaked alleys to the vultures, 'do not despair. This is a battle that will be won over time, not over square metres. We will fight this battle on moral grounds, and we will win it.' Her enemies had laughed at her, attempting to gloss bitter defeat in such noble terms. But no one was laughing at Una Dayyani now.

'May the gods continue to water our dreams,' she replied modestly. 'With CONC and the Mujaddid on our side and funding to feed, clothe and educate our people, we have the Gaians on the backfoot and are ready to make the last push toward our return. And perhaps' – she cast him a shrewd glance – 'this wildly spinning Sec Gen may yet prove to be a wheel of our chariot.'

Tahazu's brow knitted. 'You know as well as I do, Una, the monster's fate is out of our hands. His crimes will be tried in the Mujaddid's courts and the families of his victims will help determine his sentence. A prisoner in the desert may in time receive the key to the kingdom of the invisible. But even with that key, he cannot open the gates to our homeland.'

Rabu had recently begun to leaven his ponderous discourse with the rhetorical flourishes of the Mujaddid's more obscure pronouncements. But two could play at that game.

'Indeed, Tahazu. We are guests of the Mujaddid, and his courts will judge all grievous and mortal crimes perpetrated or suffered by our people. That is the law we have agreed to abide by. But surely I do not need to remind you that in the Asfarian courts, as in our own, the views of the victims and their families are taken into due consideration before sentencing. So' – she lifted a manicured finger – 'given the diplomatic sensitivity of the Orson trial, do we not summon the victims and families and offer our counsel?'

'It would seem wise to at least know what they are planning to say.'

She tented her fingers, regarded him over the tips. 'And should they be faltering, do we not counsel mercy? For if we are merciful, if the Non-Land Alliance frees Peat Orson – indeed, if N-LA and YAC invite him to stay here in Asfar as our honoured guest, accompanied by the Non-Land friends he has made – surely we will add a priceless trophy to our war chest. Does the Mujaddid not say that the gratitude of a former enemy is a prize beyond rubies and pearls? And would not all the nations of the world be impressed by such magnanimity?'

Rabu considered her words. Though she could almost hear the granite cogs of the man's mind turning, she waited patiently. Over the years, running ideas through Rabu had ground their raw nubs and rough husks into the finest flour.

'Do we trust him to stay?' he said at last. 'If freed, he could return to Is-Land to a hero's welcome.'

'If he wanted to return to his vile home, he would have appealed to CONC for help to do so. He's ours for the taking, Rabu. And our friends in YAC are eagerly awaiting the return of his friend Bartol. To convert a Sec Gen into a YAC celebrity: think what a coup that would be!'

He nodded. 'Mercy, then, we shall call it.'

She smiled again. They still understood each other very well. She clapped twice, the tiny clash of her rings sending their spark of sound out into the air. The gold curtains over the arched stone doorway to her left parted and Marti entered the chamber, Tablette in hand.

'So, *habibti*.' Gesturing to a crimson stool, Una greeted her Karkish personal assistant like the daughter she had become. 'What news of this depraved creature's victims and their families? What news of Muzi Bargadala?'

Neat as ever in her pale blue diamanté-studded hijab, Marti swiped furiously at the device on her knee. 'We've found most of them, Una. Uttu Dúrkiñar's daughters-in-law, Habat Bargadala and Nanshe Emeeš, are still living together in the Old City, with or near their younger children. Muzi Bargadala, though . . .' She sucked her teeth. 'Hasn't registered for referendums in Asfar for over a year.'

Una stiffened. 'Muzi Bargadala is a highly significant individual. Tahazu! Surely we should be keeping track of his whereabouts?'

Rabu grunted.

Marti replied, 'We are. Well, we *were*. Last we knew, he was working at a camel racetrack in the outskirts. But around the beginning of last year, his citizen's account went quiet. He used to be a regular voter on municipal matters, especially anything related to the treatment of Non-Landers. We can only assume he's left the city.'

Una's cheeks began to glow. 'Marti. I've asked you to report on one of the most important developments in the Non-Land struggle for justice since the Mujaddid took up our cause, and you're telling me we've *lost* Muzi Bargadala?'

'He's a spent force, Una,' Rabu growled. 'Maimed by the Sec Gen, abandoned by the Ordott girl, he went kamikaze on the Hem in the battle for Kadingir but couldn't even manage to get himself killed. He's a shepherd, a country lad, outshone by his wife and ashamed of himself for escaping his family's fate in the jails. He came to Asfar with his tail between his legs, looked after his mother and aunt until their children grew up, and now he's gone back to the hills.'

Bargadala was a sleeper, that's what he was. An unexploded ordnance. Rabu should have had fly eyes, elephant ears and centipede legs on that boy. Did she have to do everything herself around here?

'Summon the family to a private audience with me, Marti. As soon as possible. We'll have to find out from *them* where he's gone. And this other most unfortunate woman . . .' She grimaced. Peat Orson's doctor had sent details of the Sec Gen's crimes, which even for a seasoned commander in this war had not made for easy reading. 'The alt-bodied woman from Zabaria. Do we have any idea who she was?'

Marti rubbed at the vertical line between her eyebrows with her forefinger, as if trying to swipe up a name from her brain. 'Artakhshathra is trying his best but we still can't find a way into the Zabarian server. In the meantime, though, the Singular Tiamet has come forward.' She jiggled her hands and wiggled her shoulders. 'You know, the YAC Attack percussionist and dancer, the one with the big Eid hit this year.'

'I know who Tiamet is. I haven't been living under a rock with the scarab beetles for the last twelve years!'

'Of course not, Una,' Marti murmured. 'I just thought you might not have been following her solo career.' Seemingly oblivious to Una's look of reproach, she returned to studying her Tablette. 'Tiamet saw the Sec Gen's confession on ShareWorld. She remembers the date of his crimes because two alt-bodied women she worked with in Pithar disappeared that night, along with her infant son. The women are called Neperdu and Anunit – she doesn't know their family names – and the boy is called Ebebu. She's desperate to discover if Peat Orson knows anything about them and has made an official statement to YAC.'

It was all just too much. Una clutched her throat and gestured wildly at the nearest window. 'Air, Marti! Air!'

Marti jumped up and flung open the latticed panes, then scurried over to her chair. 'Una? Are you all right? Do you want me to loosen your turban?'

'Oh!' Gasping for breath, she pushed the girl aside, then spat in Rabu's general direction. 'I might have guessed YAC would ruin everything!'

Marti retreated to the stool and looked at her, bewildered. 'YAC is our ally, Una. Ninti and Malku vote with us in Amazigia, and the Singulars all promote our cause in the cultural resistance. Tiamet's just trying to—'

'Pithar is a *brothel district* of Zabaria, Marti. She's trying to find two alt-bodied *sex workers*. Just what we need! Haven't we got enough on our plate with Astra Ordott's monstrous brother and jilted lover to cope with? No! Apparently not! We have to also contend with scandal, taboo sex, a whole poisonous snakes' nest of *sordid drama* . . .'

She sputtered to a halt.

'Alt-bodied sex workers have human rights like anyone else,' Marti said quietly.

'Of course they do! But it's matter of *timing*, Marti. We need to look dignified now in the world's eyes. Tiamet's not related to these women?'

Marti shook her head. 'Not as far as I know.'

'Then she's not invited to the private audience. She's got no right to petition the judge! No right to dictate our strategy.'

Marti looked to Tahazu.

'That's correct, Marti,' Rabu intoned. 'Direct Tiamet to my office. We'll take her statement again for our records.'

'Go, Marti. Go.' Una brushed her away. 'Do it *now*. And get Uttu Dúrkiñar's family here, yesterday!'

Marti stood. 'Are you sure you don't want a fan, Una? Or a glass of iced water?'

She stretched her leg and toed the carpet with a gem-encrusted slipper. 'Maybe another jug of pomegranate cordial. No, wait, lemon and mint.'

Murmuring, 'Right away, Una,' Marti floated out of the chamber. Una wiped her forehead with a silk handkerchief.

'Honestly, Tahazu. How could you let that boy escape?'

Rabu sighed, the sound of rocks crumbling into sand. 'He's no threat any longer, Una. No warrior, just another poor Non-Lander youth driven into battle by the forces of history, left a brittle shell of himself at the end.'

She stretched out her hand and inspected her emerald fingernail in the beam of light pouring in from the open window. 'Shells are hard and weatherproof and often hide poisonous creatures. I want to know what he's up to, and I want him to stand with his family in that court and speak with them in one voice for *mercy*.'

Tahazu rose, his massive form striped white by the light. 'Your word is my command, Um Kadingir.'

'Good.' She nodded. 'Now, are you and Iba coming round tonight? We have beer, a new batch just fermented. And a rather large windfall to celebrate!'

His grin was a chasm in his jaw. 'I won't tell the Mujaddid if you won't.'

Burnt Orange

Atourne & Bracelet Valley
04.04.99 – 05.04.99

Samrod's personal Tablette vibrated in his trouser pocket. He pulled out the device, glared at it, then picked up the call.

'Clay. At last! I've been leaving you messages for two solid days!'

'I'm sorry, darling. It's been a trifle busy up here.'

'Too busy to contact me about a fucking *disaster*?' He stood and began pacing. Three strides to the door, three back to his desk. His office, like his research portfolio, had shrunk badly in the wash of recent changes at the college.

'Samrod.' Clay tutted. 'Calm down. Everything's going to be just fine.'

At least he still had a view. Outside, the courtyard fountain was misting the air and students and faculty were lounging on benches, drinking coffee, laughing, reading; the brawny Sec Gens skyclad, a handful of the mature students and lecturers dressed in the green, gauzy robes of the Gaian New Purists, supposedly a symbol of being less concerned with having sex than 'returning to the original spirit of Is-Land'. Which was all about having sex – read the Pioneers' journals, for frack's sake, he wanted to shout at those sanctimonious geese – but never mind. Life was going on out there as normal, people preening and striving and kidding themselves, while Samrod's world was cracking and screeching and threatening to collapse around him like a climax forest on fire. But did Clay care?

'No. No, it is *not* going to be fine. They've turned him, Clay. And I don't know how!'

'I thought,' Clay drawled, 'the Non-Land doctors disabled Peat Orson's oxytocin hyperglands, which knocked out his loyalty gene, creating a vacuum of self-esteem which they treated with a combination of CBT, dream therapy and animal companionship. At least, that's what they told CONC they did.'

He marched back from the door, leaned his forehead against the window and lowered his voice. 'Those hyperglands were precisely engineered. If they ever stopped pumping, he should have dropped dead from a cardiac arrest!'

'It's the wonder of science, isn't it? Constantly evolving. Look, darling, in advance of the next Vision Council meeting, Stamen and I have been talking. We think it might be good to have some flexibility in the Sec Gen project. How long will it take you to figure out precisely how they did it?'

He spun back to his pacing. 'Tell Stamen Magmason to get his thoughts *off* my project and *on* to protecting me! This is a nightmare, Clay. International journalists have been ringing non-stop – I was tempted to flush my work Tablette down the toilet this morning. But funnily enough, when I seek to enquire who's been giving out a classified number to the world press corps, IMBOD's not returning my calls!'

'Oh, shush, Samrod. They're busy, that's all. And the Orson video is just a hiccup: it's highly classified in Is-Land, and who cares what the rest of the world thinks?'

'*I* care. And so should you!' He was flinging his arm about, his face prickling with sweat. It was just a matter of time before the Orson boy started talking about the firesands tower, but he couldn't say that on the phone, not even on his personal line. 'That video was released *two days* ago. You know how fast those damned Owleons fly. Every dissident cell in the country has got their grubby hands on the news by now. Where have you *been*, Clay?'

Clay gave a satisfied little yawn, as if stretching. 'I'm where I always am – picking fresh succulent blossoms on the path to paradise. Not to mention celebrating that CONC vote last night with Stamen and half the Wheel Meet. Such a great relief for us all not to have to worry any more about being forced to foot that absurd bill. The champers has been flowing, darling. You should be here with us.'

This again. Always trying to get him up to that foul place. 'I've told you a hundred times.' He stopped pacing by his awards shelf and straightened his collection of IMBOD Code Scientist of the Year trophies. Why did the cleaner always ruin the perfect chevron he'd arranged them in? 'I can't come to the Valley. I have classes to teach. Responsibilities.'

'You're overburdened. You need a break. Stamen has spoken to the Vice Chancellor. It's all been arranged, Samrod – a long weekend at Springhill, two days' sick leave due to stress. Go home and pack a bag. Wear your best trousers. A car will pick you up at five.'

The Vice Chancellor. Of course. He ran his hand over his damp scalp. He'd been waiting for her to call or email, too. Everyone in Is-Land security coded Orange had been granted access to the Orson boy's video statement. All right, Clay might have saved him a bollocking, or the ice-cold-shoulder treatment in the halls. But sick leave? What was the man thinking?

'Clay. A world-leading researcher in the field of post-traumatic stress syndrome taking time off for stress is hardly a *confidence booster*. Are you trying to get me fired?'

'Samrod.' Clay accomplished his classic feat of royally shafting you, then sounding mortally wounded when you pointed it out. 'Of course not. Your high profile means the world to me. For one thing, a bit of a situation has come up in the Valley. Something I need your help with.'

He swung back to the window. 'Oh, so it's not a nice little break for me? Not a long weekend in the lap of luxury? It's fucking crisis mismanagement on top of crisis mismanagement! How much longer do you expect me to—'

'*Darling*. Please. Don't argue. We need to talk, privately, don't we? So we'll talk. And the situation here's not serious. It just requires your reassuring presence.'

Samrod sputtered out of steam. He did have to see Clay, to talk freely with him about the mess they were in. But he didn't like decisions about his role at the college being made over his head. It was *infantilising*, that's what it was.

'It will be restful, you'll see,' Clay soothed. 'And Samrod – it's been too long.'

He sighed, gripped the back of his chair. 'Just for the weekend, Clay. I have to be back here on Monday.'

'A *long* weekend, darling. Your panting students can wait until Tuesday.' Clay rang off. Samrod tossed his Tablette onto the screendesk, sending it skittering against his porcelain vase of spring cherry branches. *Childish*, the delicate blossoms reproached him. Yes, well. He retrieved the Tablette, slipped it back into his trouser pocket. That was what a lifetime of dealing with Clay Odinson did to a man.

It was gone two p.m. He finished some form-filling, sent a couple of emails, watered the plants, then put on his college auto-reply and shut down the screendesk. At the door, he turned and said farewell to his cubicle. Disrespectfully small, yes; but well lit, with a pleasant view of the student body. When he got back, no doubt he'd be sharing it with a postdoc researcher.

It was just gone ten p.m. when the car cleared Springhill security and slid into the compound. Clay was waiting on the veranda of the main building, his silhouette straddling the path of light from the door. Stockpiling moisture and starlight, Samrod filled his lungs with valley air, then trudged up the steps.

'Samrod.' Clay opened his arms and enfolded him in the firm embrace of steel enrobed in bio-latex flesh. 'Welcome back.'

He air-kissed Clay, brushing his cheek against the twisted red rope that, apart from the slight dragging around the left eye, was the only visible sign of the dozens of operations Clay's face had undergone since his burn trauma.

'All right, I'm here,' Samrod murmured, aware of the receptionist's gaze flicking over them from the lobby. 'Just keep anyone under the age of sixteen completely out of my sight.'

'Of course, darling. We cater to all preferences here. Come.' Clay took his bag and Samrod followed him through the plush lobby to the elevator. Clay's repair was not seamless. But, fitted with four mechatronic limbs, his torso reupholstered with Sec Gen skin grafts and his groin refurbished with cock and balls the size of a carthorse's, the Director of Springhill Retreat liked to say that being dismantled in a Non-Land wavebomb ambush was the best thing that had ever happened to him. Swaggering down the plush corridor, he led Samrod to a suite overlooking the lake. The room was filled with buckets of mauve roses.

'Your favourites, darling.' Clay put Samrod's bag on the sideboard and purred over the velvet petals. 'I'm so grateful you've come.'

Samrod drew the curtains and stood on the opposite side of the bed. 'I'll see you at breakfast, Clay. Just you. I don't want to eat with any of these perverts, and that includes Stamen Magmason.'

Clay cocked his head, pouted. Samrod held his gaze.

'Don't worry, darling, everything will be as you like it.' Clay sat down on the bed, turned back the top sheet, plumped a pillow, inhaled. 'Lavender-scented. I asked the staff especially.'

'Thank you.' He suddenly felt ridiculous, standing stock still as if on IMBOD inspection. 'I'm tired, Clay.'

Clay rose, smoothed the sheet. 'Of course. Sleep well and rise refreshed. Birdsong is always so thrilling in the Valley.'

The dawn chorus came as a warning frisson, a collective alarm. Samrod wrapped a pillow round his head and lay in bed long enough for the bulk of Springhill's guests to eat and leave for the woods. Then he pulled on his new ivory linen trousers – no, he would not go skyclad here, thank you, Clay – and took his Tablette and binoculars down to the restaurant deck. The waiter had been instructed, led him through a cluster of Wheel Meet ministers, High Court judges and top-ranking IMBOD officers to a table for two, set away from the others in the corner over the herb garden. He clocked the crowd as he walked, nodding curtly at world-renowned faces. Like it or not, he, too, was famous here: Dr Samrod Blesserson, the love-struck fool who, in a moment of grief and shock and desperation, had agreed to bioengineer a travesty of human sexuality and, in so doing, placed his entire life's work in jeopardy. A table of silver foxes saluted him, raising two fingers each to distinguished brows; a buxom blonde, eating alone, smiled from beneath a white straw hat as she tore her croissant apart with fat, bejewelled fingers.

Each time he came to Springhill, more women had joined the club. This one was an unpleasantly familiar figure: Tulip Hiltondott, the Minister of Penitence. Director of the country's prison system, the woman liked to trap him in the lounge and give him updates on Astra Ordott, making jokes about getting rid of his Shelter niece in exchange for Samrod's services to Springhill, an offer that might have been tempting had Stamen Magmason not decreed that Ordott was an invaluable diplomatic asset, and any accident that should happen to befall her would be investigated with all the resources IMBOD could bring to bear. Samrod swerved around a table, lifted his chin in Hiltondott's general direction and sat down, his back to the breakfasters. Gradually the discreet murmur of butter knives and deal-making subsided as the other guests drifted away, off to the woods to indulge their repulsive predilections in Springhill's hidden cabins and nurseries. Burying himself in longevity research studies, Samrod waited with coffee and pastries for Clay to return from his own morning plunge in whatever underage orifice was entrancing him at present.

'Sleep well, darling?'

Clay's mouth pressed against his ear, then swiftly licked and nibbled the rim.

In front of whoever was left on the restaurant deck, he allowed Clay his pretence at coupledom. Clay sat down and reached for the coffee, his tongue protruding with pleasure from his lips as the mechatronic fingers patted the side of the jug.

'Ooh. Still piping hot.'

Life was a giant game to Clay. A game he was an undisputed master of. As he grasped the jug's handle and poured, time itself slowed to the careful measure of the movements of the prosthetic limb.

'That dreadful cow is here,' Samrod complained. 'She's such a chore, Clay. She'll stalk me all day, waiting to crush me against the bar with those absurd mammary glands of hers and moo on about bumping off Astra Ordott.'

'Sounds good to me.' Clay reached for a bread roll and prised it open. 'Why don't you take her up on it?'

'Don't joke, Clay. I've got enough problems without bringing Magmason down on me like a ton of hot lava. What actually worries me about that cud-chewing bore is the transparently obvious way she is' – he lowered his voice – 'fishing for *confidences*.'

'Oh, don't be such a worrywart, Samrod. She's only been in the post a year. She knows nothing about Hokma, I've told you that a hundred times.'

Clay grinned and twinkled and waved over Samrod's shoulder, presumably at Hiltondott, then began to butter his roll.

'Don't encourage her.' Samrod finished his own coffee. 'If I must be in the Valley, I'd much rather stay in the town, like last time.'

Clay put down his knife. 'Darling. We need to keep a low profile. The situation here is delicate.'

Samrod waited. In a few deft, airy, nonchalant sentences, Clay explained.

'He was enjoying himself with *what*?' The rage was rising, but before he vented it he needed to make sure he had plumbed the absolute depths of this disaster.

'A penitent prod. The discipline sticks they use in the jails. Well, an adapted one. Designed in a zigzag, like a lightning rod. Hilton-dott had them commissioned for us. The Sex Gens love them: you've made them so *impervious*, darling, they often benefit from a little extra stimulation.'

Hiltondott was in on this? Samrod tried to speak but choked on the words. He dropped his napkin on the table, got up and marched along the deck railings to the steps leading down to the lake. Heads turned. He did not care. Blindly, he descended the wooden steps. Away from this foul nest of arrogance, lechery and sheer stupidity. Pushing branches aside, he headed to the lakeshore, where he stood, breathing heavily, looking out over the calm, supple water. A bird flew up from one of the islets, a slim raised eyebrow on the face of the sky.

'Darling. You forgot your binoculars.'

Clay's face was gleaming, his smile forced. Steps and uneven ground were difficult for him, Samrod knew. He repressed a squirm of guilt, snatched the binoculars from Clay's hand. 'I told you this would happen,' he hissed. 'I *told* you, Clay. Springhill should have been located in the ashfields, or the white desert. That's what I said and you all ignored me!'

'Oh, shush.' Clay lightly balanced himself against a young oak tree. 'People are busy, they can't drive for days to get here. This is IMBOD-zoned land; it's been perfectly safe all this time. It's getting busier here, that's all. Harder to find a private spot.' Clay smirked and tapped the binoculars. 'Especially with the misuse of these.'

Samrod flushed, lifted the glasses to his eyes, sought the bird over the lake. 'Don't push me, Clay.'

'I'm just telling you what happened, darling. He was stupid to sneak off the grounds with the girl. Of course he was. He broke the rules and he's deeply ashamed. But the community affected is being very reasonable. They are willing to negotiate. One of their demands is to speak with you, in person. Darling, we just need you to reassure their Parents' Counsel that the Sec Gen project is all still right with the world.'

The bird dipped back into the wooded islet before he could focus. He slipped the binoculars in his pocket and confronted Clay directly, his face flaring. 'You want me to visit a *Parents' Counsel*? To associate myself with this . . .' He gestured back up at the dining deck.

'Just for an hour. And they don't know a thing about Springhill. Oh, they have questions of course.' Clay waved his hand airily. 'You just need to reassure them that what they saw was an isolated incident, one lost soul taking advantage of your handiwork. Honestly, Samrod, it's nothing more than a standard meet-and-greet and cover-up op. They're expecting you tomorrow at three.'

'*Expecting* me?'

'Oh, darling, of course I told them you'd come. They have questions about the Sec Gens only you can answer. But you won't be alone. The local officer will be with you, and of course you'll be fully briefed about the situation and what we can offer, depending on what exactly they know. Stamen's coming up again this evening to go over it all with you. And to discuss the Orson video: two birds with one stone, to use that cruel old non-Gaian idiom.'

Samrod contemplated that masterly disingenuous speech for a minute. 'Are you telling me that these people know about the Peat Orson video?'

'*No*. But if they do, don't worry, we're ready for them.'

He stared out over the lake again, tried to draw serenity from that long, silken gleam of water. He failed.

'Clay,' he fumed, 'that Orson boy has just joined his sister in the ranks of the greatest traitors this country has ever seen. Very soon, he is going to tell the whole world that you made him your underage sex slave in the firesands tower and I cleaned the sheets every morning. I know nineteen is practically *geriatric* for you now but believe it or not it is still illegal in this country for adults to have sex with anyone under twenty. The game is up, Clay. The plug is being pulled on this cesspit and I for one would like to avoid getting sucked down the drain with it.'

'Cesspit.' Clay pouted. 'That's not very nice, darling.'

The bird flew up again. Samrod fished out his binoculars, turned his back on Clay. 'Can't you be serious for *five minutes*?'

This time, he followed the black blur until it settled on a branch and exposed an iridescent blue throat. A growling riflebird. He'd seen the female before. His heart tightened in a little knot of satisfaction. Back in his room he could add the male on his Tablette, with a note of the date and weather conditions.

'We've Coded all the birds-of-paradise for the Valley's climate now,' Clay murmured. 'Except the Astrapias, of course. We do take traitors seriously, darling.'

Samrod lowered the binoculars again, shut his eyes and rubbed the bridge of his nose beneath his glasses.

'We're on the brink of ruin and all you can do is make jokes a Year Ten student would be ashamed of.' He looked Clay square in the face. 'You've been here too long, Clay. You need to come back to Atourne, catch up with the real world.'

Framed by the oak leaves, Clay struck a noble pose, knitting his formidable brow and speaking in a tone of grave tenderness. 'Samrod, I jest because no one here is worried. It's an unfortunate coincidence that these two situations have blown up at once, that's all. IMBOD shouldn't have given out your number to the press. That was a decision taken by someone dim and junior, not a malicious attack, darling. But we're on top of the Orson crisis. The boy was a weak link, you've said it yourself a thousand times. First his sister betrayed the entire nation, then his friend committed suicide in that *ghastly* fashion.' Clay shivered as if the thought of young flesh being devoured by carnivorous fish excited him beyond measure, then resumed his impersonation of an Old World classical statue. 'As authority figures, we did what we could to help Peat re-bond with us at the tower, but his loyalty gene was stretched to breaking point. Then the poor boy was kidnapped and subjected to medical torture and sophisticated brainwashing techniques! He's delusional, Samrod, crazed with revenge fantasies. No one's going to believe a word he says about us. There's absolutely no evidence. All the footage was wiped years ago. If you can just issue an official statement denouncing the Non-Landers' torture of a vulnerable hostage, we'll release it today. The journalists won't call any more, I promise. Leaving us free to sort out a little difficulty closer to hand.'

Clay was the delusional one. 'You think two children, their father and a community elder seeing a man beating and fucking a Sex Gen, and then telling their entire community about it is just a *little difficulty*?' Samrod sputtered. 'It just takes *one person* to email Blade Stonewayson and Springhill collapses like a house of cards. Then we're both heading straight to Atourne Max.' His voice rose. 'Did you know Stonewayson is in the frame for Ordott's INMA appeal?'

'It won't happen. Stamen is just placating these people with the illusion of respect. This "New Purism".' Clay waved his arm in a commanding arc against the frieze of trees, lake and sky. '*Pah*. It's a fad backlash, Samrod, having a moment, that's all.'

Samrod gazed along the shore to the sandstone ledge in the distance, a high outcrop beneath which the manatees gathered to sun themselves in the shallows. He wanted to walk there, recompose himself in the calm the lolling creatures exuded. But the beach was rocky, strewn with branches and stones Clay couldn't safely negotiate. Leaving him here would be an insolent act of able-bodied arrogance. And possibly an unpleasant adventure: Gaia only knew who else at Springhill was attracted to the inlets and coves of the lakeshore. He kicked at a pebble, waved an insect away from his ear.

'Some people,' he replied tightly, 'might argue that the New Purists have a point. Some people seem to think that since Is-Land clad the Boundary, you and I have turned our children into flesh-eating monsters, the Wheel Meet has become decadent and complacent and Stamen Magmason unfit to govern. And those people don't even know about this place. Yet.'

Clay placed his hand on Samrod's. The hand was light, warm,

pliable. Samrod did not squeeze it back. 'Please, Samrod. Don't say that about your own work. The berserker gene is a necessary adaptation for modern warfare, and we only tested the cannibal variation on a very small group.'

It had occurred over a decade ago, but that particular experiment still rankled. 'I've told you a hundred times,' he snapped, 'don't call it that. You said you wanted me to block the nausea reflex in case of accidental ingestion of human flesh. You didn't say you were going to deliberately order a group of Sec Gens to devour a living woman.'

'Samrod. I'm bound by complex confidentiality codes. I can't tell you everything. And no harm was done. Just as you engineered it, the loyalty gene enabled a full wipe of any distressing memories. All the Sec Gens are adapting very well to post-combat conditions.' Clay's hand squeezed Samrod's, a solid, rubbery grip. 'Samrod, come back up to the deck. Chat a bit with people. The commoners don't yet understand the gains we've made, but everyone here is eternally grateful to you. We're secure now, thanks in large part to your efforts. We just need the Hudna to end, and the New Gaian Vision to blossom globally, and all these detractors will simply melt away. Then we can be open about this place and all you've accomplished here. For now, we just have to tidy up a few loose ends.' Chuckling, Clay withdrew his hand. 'You have to meet the Patriarch of Yggdrasila. From what I hear he's positively Abrahamic! These people may very well call down the power of Stonewayson if we don't oblige them in what is after all a very touching demand. You're the expert, and they just want you to make everything right.'

Along the shore, up by the rocks, Samrod could see figures moving beneath the trees: an adult and two children holding hands. He turned his back on the lake.

'I'm going to spend my time here reading in my room. Stamen can visit me there and you can have my meals sent up on a tray. I'll be ready tomorrow when you call me for the meeting in Yggdrasila. With my bags. Afterwards I want to be driven back to Atourne.'

Clay regarded him quietly. 'You saved my life, Samrod, but you refuse to share its glories. That makes me sad sometimes.'

'My life is bound to yours, Clay.' He brushed past Clay's sweat-glistening chest, stole just one breath of its perfume. 'That will never change.'

Desert Red

Asfar
05.04.99

'He killed Uttu! Right in front of us! And . . .' Nanshe's mouth curled in revulsion. 'He *ate* Muzi's ear!'

'I know.' Habat twisted her wedding ring. 'But Peat Orson is Astra's brother. That makes him my *son*. And your nephew.'

'Ach!' Nanshe spat to a halt. They had been arguing all day, ever since Una Dayyani's summons had arrived on their Tablettes, and this point still rendered her speechless. But it was true. Muzi had married Astra, and that made the half-Gaian girl's family *their* family. In Habat's mind, at least. From the embroidered floor cushions on the other side of the tea rug, her two daughters and their husbands were all frowning at her. Only Suen looked contemplative, but that was his default expression. Her nephew, she suspected, used family meetings to puzzle out bioengineering problems in his head. Right now, he was stretched out over two cushions and fiddling with the tubing of his hydropac.

'Are you saying that you don't want to see the Sec Gen punished, Ama?' Hadis queried, in that neutral tone she had picked up so quickly at work. Hadis had a certificate in conflict resolution and was now working for the neighbourhood council as a family mediator. It was small surprise she was addressing her mother: they all knew Nanshe was mediation-proof.

'No, daughter. I just think—'

'Astra, Astra, Astra!' Nanshe recovered her momentum. 'I don't know why you keep writing to that creature, Habat. All she ever sends in reply are crazed ravings! Not even addressed to us!'

This was a very old argument. 'She saved our lives,' Habat replied implacably. 'She doesn't reply because she's not allowed to write to us. She sends her messages to the world.'

'It's because of *her* we were in that torture dungeon in the first place.' Her sister-in-law glowered. 'Turning herself in was the least she could do. It's *her* fault Kingu and Gibil are dead, Habat. It's *her* fault Suen is blind!'

Nanshe flung an arm out towards her son. Habat winced. But Suen was used to it. Still working away at the tubing, he said mildly, 'It's all right, Ama. I've told you lots of times, I'm happy the way I am.'

'Son.' Nanshe made a fist. 'You only think that because you're *blind*!'

Suen laughed, and so did his cousins. In the past, Habat had worried deeply for Suen, an only child subjected to all his mother's furious pity, but over the years, and especially as he began to excel at school, Nanshe's stubborn refusal to see his condition as anything but a tragedy had, fortunately, become a family joke.

Not to Nanshe, though. 'Yes, laugh at me,' she spat. 'Fatherless children, laughing at a widow. That is what that monster and his sister have reduced us to, Habat. And you want to show that thing *mercy*?'

'I'm sorry, Aunty,' Hadis, the peacemaker, responded. 'We didn't mean to upset you.'

Once again, a family meeting had been swamped by Nanshe's bitter anger. Perhaps, Habat thought, she ought to be angry, too. But while they were all in an IMBOD jail, her son had married Astra Ordott, and in the years before he left Asfar, Muzi had given her a different understanding of the half-Gaian girl's place in their lives.

'Istarastra also suffers at the hands of IMBOD,' Habat said quietly. 'She was courageous to give herself up to their jail, Nanshe. She did so because she speaks to the gods. Terrible misfortunes have befallen us, that is true, but in Their messages, the Old Ones tell us that our suffering is helping to bring about a great change in the world.'

'Oh, such helpful messages!' Nanshe erupted. 'Now she says we have a year to live! As if we need to hear that sort of nonsense!'

'It's a deadline, Ama,' Suen interjected calmly, 'for some important campaigns. Deadlines are useful. They focus the mind.'

'Oh yes, all these deadlines. I've had my fill of deadlines, my boy. The Gaians have already given us Kadingir back, haven't they, right on time! And now they are opening a gate in the Boundary. A gate so big I can see it from it *Asfar*!' She gestured at the glass doors to the rooftop patio, with its spectacular view of the city's minarets and domes. The doors faced south, but no one would have been so pedantic as to say so when Nanshe was in full spate.

'Aunty,' Geshti said softly, cradling her suckling babe's head, 'please don't shout.' Beside her, Esañ squeezed Mordi's bootie and waved at his son but did not speak. Her daughters' husbands were coming to the Listening tomorrow but had no right to a vote or a voice in the court. Esañ and Ahmad had not been members of the family when Peat Orson's crimes were committed. So far in this meeting, the two young men had wisely kept quiet.

'Campaigns,' Nanshe scoffed. 'She wants us to give up our Tablettes. How would Suen get around without his Tablette? She'd be better off sending a message about how to cure this plague of lost children. Does she say a word about that? No! It's as if she *wants* the human race to die out.'

Habat watched the baby's head move under the white lacy robe; saw Hadis, Ahmad's arm around her, glance down with sad eyes. Habat's heart went out to her elder daughter. After nursing Hadis through three miscarriages in two years, she had advised the young couple to stop trying for now, but not to panic. Geshti had carried her first pregnancy to term: having children was still possible. The problem was something to do with Old World pollution, she had read; CONC would surely sort it out soon.

'Istarastra's messages are morally correct and scientifically feasible, Ama.' As Suen spoke, he took a small knife from the hydropac and began splicing open one of the tubes.

'What are you *doing*, Suen?' his mother exploded. 'Do you want to lose a hand as well?'

Habat flinched. Like Nanshe, she always expected Suen to cut himself with knives. Unlike Nanshe, she forced herself not to say so any more. Still, though, that was a brand-new hydropac.

'It's for my project, Ama,' her nephew said calmly, still cutting the tube. 'Don't you want me to get into the Institute?'

For once, Nanshe had no answer. For all her savage woes about his blindness, she was proud of Suen. The whole family was proud of Suen, and equally mystified by what he did all day. After the family's release from the Gaian jail, N-LA had ensured the children attended the best schools in Asfar City. Suen had excelled in science and technology, completing four years of high school in two and entering university at the age of sixteen to study Eco-Physics. The apartment's rooftop patio had been turned over to his greenhouse, where he spent hours feeding plants with concoctions he and his fellow students devised in test-tubes at school. Now nineteen, he was applying for postgraduate study at the Asfarian Institute of Metaphysical Engineering under a world-famous professor. What was metaphysical engineering? Habat didn't really know, but it was obvious that Suen was destined to build a top-flight career in the field. Having aced the theory exam, her nephew now had to submit a practical project to get into AIME, and if a brand-new hydropac had to be sacrificed to that goal, he knew that Habat and Nanshe might grumble but they would not stop him.

'The Old Ones are right,' Suen went on. 'Rare-earths are toxic and have many military applications. Mining them is undermining global regeneration efforts and fuelling the possibility of war at the end of the Hudna. Humanity should now be moving to entirely clean energy and IT resources. Then we might see a reversal of the infertility crisis.'

'Yes, well, I don't see you giving up your Tablette, son!' Nanshe scoffed. 'Or getting married!'

'Yeah, bro,' Ahmad said with a laugh. 'When are you going to win the Mujaddid's prize and take us all on a holiday?'

'My project will provide an alternative to Tablettes, Ama. I just need to work out a few more ideas before I tell you all about it.' Where had Suen learned that confident manner? And how had he grown so *long*? You blinked and your nephew was no longer a boy, but a man, his grasshopper legs tripping everyone up. 'The Institute's research is the most advanced in the global field.' Done with the tubing, he slipped the knife back into the hydropac, thank the gods. 'I'll need to study hard for seven years in order to become a professor there. I don't have time to get married yet, Ama.'

'A wife would help you, Suen. And me. That's what wives are for.' Nanshe wanted a daughter-in-law – to boss about, Habat thought in her meaner moments – and a grandchild to raise her status to Habat's.

'Ama, we should be talking about the court case.' It was Hadis, using her professional voice, the one that always made Habat smile, remembering a little girl ordering her dolls to sit still. 'We don't have to agree. The judge will want everyone to say what they think. But the courts will want to know why Muzi isn't there. We have to decide what to tell N-LA about him.'

Habat was Muzi's mother. Everyone looked to her.

'We must not lie,' she said firmly. 'He went to the desert to find work.'

Hadis pursed her lips. Esañ and Ahmad exchanged glances.

'It's true,' Habat insisted. Let N-LA ransack her emails. Muzi knew how these people operated. He had never written anything that could get him, or any of them, into trouble.

'But what about all the things he was saying before he left?' Hadis probed. 'He talked to Ahmad one night all about how One-Land was impossible, that the Gaians didn't deserve to live with us, and we had to fight like men if we wanted the Boundary to fall. He sounded like he'd swallowed a NAARC Tablette whole, didn't he, Ahmad?'

Her husband nodded. 'I'd never heard him talk so much, about anything. He said Enki Arakkia was the only Non-Land leader left with vision.'

'So maybe he went to find Enki Arakkia.' Habat flushed. She hadn't expected this from Hadis. 'So what?'

'So what? Perhaps you haven't heard, but the Non-Land All Action Revolutionary Commandos, dear mother, are banned!'

'They're banned in Asfar, nowhere else.' Nanshe, for once, came to her defence. 'What harm have they done anyone? None. They just remind us that the Gaians aren't to be trusted, that's all.'

'Enki Arakkia is collecting weapons, Ama,' Hadis persisted. 'Everyone knows that. To attack Is-Land at the end of the Hudna.'

'Makes sense to me,' Nanshe interjected. 'When the Hudna is over, attacking those monsters won't be a crime!'

'Muzi doesn't want to attack anyone,' Habat said stubbornly. 'He's just never found his place after the war, that's all. His wife is in jail and the rest of us ended up in the city. It's all right for you young ones, you can adapt, but he was like his father, a born shepherd. Enki Arakkia's the same.'

'Arakkia was never a shepherd,' Hadis countered.

'But he's dyed-in-the-wool in his own way. A warrior to the bone. There's no place for men like Enki and Muzi in Asfar, so they vent their anger in the desert.'

'And if they dream about firing a rocket at the Boundary,' Nanshe finished off triumphantly, 'who can blame them?'

Hadis looked worriedly between her mother and her aunt. 'NAARC poses a serious threat to the political process—' she started to object. But it was six o'clock and Habat was saved by the *azan*. Through the glass doors came the wail of the neighbourhood Muezzin, the serpentine coils of her voice summoning them all to evening World Worship.

Ahmad stood. He was Asfarian and his family followed the

Mujaddid's version of the Old World Karkish religion. Hadis rose, too. Since the first miscarriage, she had begun to pray during Worship. Not to the Karkish god, she had told Habat, but to their own Sumerian pantheon: the sky-god and the earth-goddess, and the weaver-goddess in honour of her grandmother, Uttu. The couple went out onto the patio, where, facing southwest, Ahmad began his prostrations. Hadis knelt beside him, closed her eyes and folded her hands in her lap. The *azan* sounded louder through the open door. Suen followed and sat on the ledge beside the climbing plants he was growing, his face gilded by the lowering sun. For a reason Habat didn't understand – not just to do with the quiet, but the concentrated energy of a dense population – he said prayer time was conducive to innovative thought. Geshti and Esañ cuddled closer on their cushion, focused on the baby. Nanshe got up and went to the sink.

Chants and prayers were encouraged, and you were permitted to access spiritual texts on your Tablette, but no talk was allowed during World Worship, and except for essential services, emails would not send. Traffic halted, except for emergency vehicles, and wherever they were people generally stopped whatever they were doing. But there was no rule that you had to sit stone still during World Worship. Years ago, when they first arrived in the apartment, the sisters-in-law had signed and even mouthed messages through the silence. But though Nanshe still resented being cut off in mid-flow, stewing her resentments in the pots of prayer time, Habat had soon realised that Asfar's five daily doses of silence did everyone good. Why rush around all day crying and complaining, bleating and boasting, demanding or explaining things that could easily wait? Where was everyone going, after all, except to the grave? The Mujaddid was right: people should slow down and appreciate life, step as often as possible into its timeless wonder. As Nanshe clumped about in the kitchen, Habat sat and gazed through the open doors, grateful as ever for the sight of the quiet figures draped in the pink light of evening, and for the peace that the Mujaddid's city had brought her.

In the five daily silences, even small children settled, sometimes even stayed playing quietly afterwards for an hour or more. If you were out on the streets, all you could hear was the music of birds, the odd donkey-bray or dog-bark, the soughing of wind in the trees. For Habat, it was like being back on the scrublands, as if the huge stone buildings around them were just a mirage, curtains of light that might part any moment to reveal, not the sparkling waters of the Gulf or the majestic red dunes that surrounded the city, but a distant horizon of plain dun hills and, nestled among them, her own small lost home with its sheep pen and vegetable garden. Quite often, in the early days of exile, she had closed her eyes and visualised it, her home; now she mostly just listened to the conversations of nature: bird-calls, water splashing from a fountain, cats mewing from beneath a car. The meanings were a mystery, but the emotions expressed – joy, tenderness, fright – touched her own. Sometimes, listening to the voices of nature, she had begun to believe that her daughter-in-law Astra really was receiving messages from the Earth. There were languages other than human speech. Even humans had other ways of communicating than with words. After World Worship, strangers smiled at each other, were neighbourly, made offers to lend a hand with packages, help an old person cross the road. Between families or friends, interrupted arguments were not resumed, or were mended with apologies. Often, even Nanshe was calmer. This argument about Astra and Peat might not be easily resolved, but Nanshe would not pursue it again with such ferocity tonight.

At home, Habat sometimes read poetry during World Worship. Astra liked poetry, Muzi had said. Today, though, she closed her eyes and prayed, too. Prayed to the weaver-goddess that this unexpected news – a monster becoming a man, an invitation to show mercy – meant that soon everything would change. That Peat Orson's trial would bring her son galloping home from the desert, and with him her strange, powerful daughter-in-law, the girl who spoke to the gods.

Acid Green

Bracelet Valley
06.04.99

'I'm sorry. I don't know how to do that.'

Just for a moment, Fasta felt for Dr Blesserson. His voice strained, portly cheeks flushed, the IMBOD scientist was leaking hostile embarrassment all down the Meeting Room's head table. It was mid-afternoon and the table's polished oak surface was tinted with yellow, red and blue geometric shapes from Baldur's great arched windows; Dr Blesserson's humiliation was so strong she feared it might leave permanent stains.

Esfadur, a pillar of rectitude in his seat beside the scientist, responded sternly. 'Your international medical peers know how to reverse your handiwork. Why don't you?'

Beside Fasta, Sif wrung her hands in her lap, over and over, as if she had taken it upon herself to channel the anxiety everyone in the room must be feeling. *Esfadur! We can't let IMBOD know that we know about the Peat Orson video!* Sif had argued last night, to the point of tears. Fasta understood why she was upset. In the nine days since Ggeri's confession events had moved in an ever-more frightening direction.

First, Esfadur and Vili had hidden in the woods for three days running, returning on the third day with a Tablette recording that verified Ggeri and Freki's story. The footage was beyond repugnant, but the questions it raised had to be discussed with the community – or most of it. The children were of course not told, while Yggdrasila's grown Sec Gens were not invited to Esfadur and Brana's Earthship for a meeting that should, by rights, have been held in the Common Hall. This was for the Sec Gens' own protection, Brana stressed to everyone in her crowded living room: no one could predict how watching one of their number being so abused would affect the loyalty gene. But the decision had created a suffocating sense of secrecy that had only intensified since.

At their first meeting the community had voted to show the video to the local IMBOD officer, Major Brockbankson, with three demands: justice for the young Sec Gens, so appallingly abused; answers as to what on earth was going on at Springhill Retreat; and a guarantee of safe woods for their own children. However, Brockbankson had not responded to the video as the community delegates, Esfadur, Brana, Fasta, Sif and Vili, had expected. Rather than express outrage and immediately release a statement to the local media, warning people there was a predator in the forest, the Major had looked very stern. 'Leave this with me,' he had said. And then the next day he had made a personal visit to the five delegates, asking them to, 'under the circumstances', request the community's understanding of IMBOD's decision 'to handle this sensitive matter internally'.

Another meeting was called that evening. Strong voices were raised, some demanding that the video be sent to the national press. But Esfadur had counselled caution. 'IMBOD is hiding something. Don't we want to know what that is? We have power in this situation, and we should use it,' he had argued. 'Let us consider this situation fully: in addition to answers about the Sec Gen project, and their assurances that justice will be done, how might IMBOD be able to help us?'

It turned out that people had quite a few ideas about that. In the end, the community voted to demand a private audience between the Parents' Counsel and the IMBOD Code Scientist responsible for the abused girls' impossible ability to withstand electrocution.

We'll put them on the hot seat, Brana had declared. Major Brock-bankson had stalled, but finally promised to do his best to bring a senior member of the Sec Gen team to Yggdrasila. Then, two days later, Esfadur and Brana had summoned the community again, ostensibly to discuss the agenda for the proposed meeting, but in fact to make an unthinkable revelation.

Fasta still couldn't really believe it. Over the last year, it transpired, Yggdrasila's most respected elders had been *receiving messages from the outer world*. Not directly from an Owleon itself, thank Gaia – keeping unauthorised messenger birds was a charge high on the treason scale – but from one of the couple's New Purist friends, a woman who shared banned videos and news stories at a clandestine monthly meeting in the Valley of what Esfadur called 'concerned elders' from a range of local communities. Naturally, Brana announced, the couple knew that anyone aware of such gatherings had a duty to report them to IMBOD, but she and Esfadur were putting their trust in their fellow Yggdrasilans because what they had just discovered, that very afternoon at an emergency gathering of the group, had a direct and profound bearing on the community's negotiations with IMBOD. Then, to stunned silence, Esfadur had relayed the contents of Peat Orson's video statement.

There was much to gasp over and question, but everyone understood the relevance to their own situation: *the effects of the Security Serum could be reversed*. After the shock subsided, fierce debate had ensued. Several people had agreed with Sif – it was surely enough that they had incriminating footage of a man abusing a Sec Gen teenager in the woods. Revealing to IMBOD that they knew about Peat Orson's denunciation of the entire Sec Gen project could nullify this advantage and implicate the whole community in some serious crimes. But Brana and Esfadur had argued that the woodland video gave them protection. *With knowledge comes power*, Esfadur had concluded. *And it is time we reminded IMBOD that the true power of our people lies not in attempts to manipulate our DNA to serve perverse desires and political agendas, but in our living relationship with Gaia, upon whom we depend and to whom we must all in the end surrender. We must demand to speak to the lead scientist on the Sec Gen project: Dr Samrod Blesserson himself. We will tell IMBOD that our Parents' Counsel has questions only Blesserson can answer, and when he gets here we will lay our cards on the table.* It had been frightening but exhilarating to hear their elder speak in this way. Although Esfadur and Brana, in their gauzy green robes, were the only two self-declared Gaian New Purists on the Committee, when the vote came, they won the day by a large margin.

And now Esfadur was grilling Dr Blesserson, making him squirm like a schoolboy at the top of the table. 'There is an antidote that works if it is taken within three months,' the scientist snapped. 'Otherwise, I would have to study the CONC reports carefully. But I am not at all confident they will reveal a reliable reversal method. I suspect Peat Orson's doctors simply got lucky. And even if I *can* identify exactly what they did to make him renounce his old loyalties, or at least appear to do so, I can't guarantee their treatment would work on other Sec Gens. Psychologically, Peat Orson was severely weakened by the events surrounding his sister's expulsion from Is-Land.'

Opposite Fasta, Brana's lips tightened to a thin line. Fasta knew that look, but Brana remained silent, for now. On the other side of Dr Blesserson, Major Brockbankson nodded gravely. 'We are here to reassure you and your community, Esfadur, and to reward Yggdrasila's cooperation during this unfortunate situation. But we can only do so within the limits of known science, I am afraid.'

Brana tossed her long silver hair and glared towards the top of the table. 'I wish you could have been here fifteen years ago, Doctor Blesserson, to meet my little granddaughter,' she flashed. 'Halja was such a lovely girl. So playful and creative, and well adjusted. Even before her Security Serum shot she coped miraculously well with the loss of her mother. Didn't she?'

The others around the table nodded gravely. The death of Eya haunted the community still. Breast cancer was supposed to have been eradicated, a thing of the past, but the illness had raced through her: a spirited young woman who had become a dedicated mother, robbed of her future by an archaic disease all Is-Land's medicines were powerless to stop. Yet, everyone had agreed at the time, the tragedy confirmed the superiority of the Gaian parenting system: Halja, Eya's only Birth-Code Shelter child, had been well comforted by her other two parents. Parents who were now so distraught by their daughter's transformation that one had left for Atourne and the other had become a silent, brooding husk of himself.

'Halja developed into a happy, charming adolescent, like all the first Sec Gens, I'll give you that, Doctor Blesserson,' Brana went on. 'But since she came back from the Hem, all she wants to do is eat and drink alcohol and have sex with anyone who's up for it. Oh, she can work a full day training the younger Sec Gens in the gym, that's not a problem. But she hardly speaks to anyone. If we involve her in community activities, she just scowls on the sidelines, and if you hug her, she flinches. We took her for MPT, but she refused to go to the second session. If you try to make her do anything she doesn't want to, she barks and howls, howls like a *dog*, Doctor Blesserson. Her Code Shelter father is *destroyed* by the change in her.' The elderwoman's eyes blazed in her weathered face. 'You can throw me in your traitors' jail if you like, Doctor Blesserson, but it won't stop me wanting my granddaughter back. The way she was before IMBOD stuck your needles into her.'

Again, Fasta felt ashamed of her dumb tongue. Older people seemed to think they had nothing to lose. Brana's Birth-Code daughter Eya was dead, her only granddaughter Halja damaged, perhaps beyond repair. Perhaps not. Fasta wished she could be as brave, speak out on behalf of the wolf cubs, but just by being present, Esfadur had said, the parents would send IMBOD a message of unity. All around her, wan faces and tight lips signalled agreement: *We want our children back, too.* To her left, Rowan, the community's acupuncturist, sat composed and still. Only Sif's hands, still working away in her lap, rubbing her knuckles, picking at the skin around her perfect oval nails, registered protest, anxiety, refusal to pull with the community.

Beneath the table, Vili clamped Sif's worrying hands in his big paw. Vili, the soother, the joker, the oscillator. Fasta looked away from the couple. Which way would Vili lean? Although he had gone up to the clearing with Esfadur, had verified with his own eyes that, right on Yggdrasila's threshold, a young Sec Gen girl was being violently abused by a man of national status, her co-parent had not yet taken a position on anything other than the need for this outrage against innocence to be stopped.

'Don't worry, Brana,' Esfadur commanded. 'Doctor Blesserson doesn't have anything to do with jails. He's just a scientist, isn't that right, Doctor? And we are all here to speak our minds.'

The scientist's lips disappeared in a prim line. 'The Security Serum creates loyal and loving human beings, a close-knit generation gifted with superior warrior skills. Naturally, the Sec Gens will be affected by violent and upsetting circumstances, including the battle conditions in the Hem, but for the vast majority of these young people, a short course of Memory Pacification Treatment will return them to full mental health. Rare individuals prove resistant to MPT, and I am very sorry if this is the case with your granddaughter, madam. You mention the loss of her mother when she was young, and this is the type of trauma that can, unfortunately, deeply wound a young Sec Gen. We have all made sacrifices for Is-Land, and I salute you and your family for caring for this noble young woman. I cannot, however, as I have said, reverse her Sec Gen status. All IMBOD can offer is exemptions.'

'With thanks for Yggdrasila's discretion, of course,' Major Brockbankson concluded smoothly.

Blesserson had no need of her sympathy, Fasta saw now. He was arrogant, accustomed to telling people exactly what to think, a man who not only expected, as a matter of course, other people to mop up the mistakes that he made, but who would deny to the grave that he was at fault for any pain his work caused.

Brana, though, was uncowed. 'We *saw* that Orson boy's confession,' the elderwoman shot back. 'Never mind how we got hold of it, we watched it all. There was nothing left of that woman you set him on in Zabaria, he said. Nothing left! We know what you're doing, Blesserson – you too, Brockbankson. You turn our children into animals, don't you, bloodthirsty animals, and in the name of Gaia you send them out to commit inhuman acts. Then you try and wipe their minds clean of what they've done, but you can't, can you? Some of them are stained, *permanently* stained. They remember, maybe not like Peat Orson remembers now, but what they've done crawls in their veins, keeps them awake at night, drives them to seek out more violence wherever they go, extreme experiences to block the memories they can't quite recall. Yes, we can discuss keeping Springhill's dirty secrets. But if we take your offer and save our young children from the jab, their status would have to be kept hidden, too, all their lives. That didn't work with Astra Ordott, did it? It drove her mad!'

It was an extraordinary outburst. You could have heard a feather drop in the hall. Watching the elderwoman's eyes spit fire at the IMBOD officers, Fasta's stomach tensed. Attacking the Sec Gen project and accusing Dr Blesserson of crimes against humanity was one thing, but expressing sympathy for the Ordott traitor – calling the creature by *name* as if she were just any other woman – surely Brana had gone too far? Even Esfadur looked alarmed. And Blesserson was swelling up like a blood blister.

'I am sure, Brana,' Brockbankson intervened smoothly, 'that you do not mean to suggest that the actions of the traitor Ordott, who received expert care from medical professionals as soon as her condition was discovered, but wilfully rejected all help and demanded to be sent to live in the Southern Belt, are somehow the fault of IMBOD, let alone Doctor Blesserson?'

'I'm not *suggesting* anything, Major,' Brana marched on. 'I am stating the facts: that girl grew up hiding who she was, and despite all your best work to fix her, now she hasn't got a clue who she is. I've heard her messages, too. She grew up feeling like a pariah in her own community and now she's become a raving Gaia Messiah, lost to the world. I don't want that to be the fate of any child here.'

Fasta held her breath. Maybe Brana was right to force the issue wide open. This was the crux of the problem, exactly as Sif had argued last night after the meeting, before slamming her and Vili's door in Fasta's face: did they want their children to be social outcasts for the rest of their lives?

Dr Blesserson recovered himself: he now appeared to be smothering a sneer. 'Should you choose to exempt your children from the Security Serum shot,' he said, his tone implying this would be the gravest of errors, 'their status will not be a secret. Rather, IMBOD will consider it a pilot project. We would impose a media embargo for the time being, naturally, but all their teachers and peers would be made aware of their condition.'

It was a concession. Delivered like an insult, but clearly a compromise position. Around the table, the members of the Ethics Committee murmured to each other, emitting small noises of satisfaction. Fasta felt like hugging someone. But Sif would not want to be hugged, and she didn't know Rowan well enough to throw herself over her. So instead she smiled wildly across the table at Brana. The elderwoman's jaw was set in an expression of triumphant defiance, but she smiled weakly back at Fasta through watering eyes. Embarrassed, Fasta looked away, noticed Sif's hands, still worrying at her nails in her lap as Vili drew his partner closer to him. Fasta's heart tightened. Surely, whatever Sif wanted for Freki and Ggeri, she could not be so selfish now as to vote against giving other people a choice?

'A pilot project?' Esfadur enquired over the minor commotion. 'Are you saying the Sec Gen experiment is to be phased out?'

'Saving our country from invasion was not an experiment,' Blesserson retorted. 'It was a project of national necessity.'

'Yes, Esfadur, that is correct,' Major Brockbankson confirmed. 'Since the successful cladding of the Boundary, the security threat to Is-Land has been gradually downgraded each year. And IMBOD has always discussed eventually phasing out the Sec Gens and embarking on a new stage of transhumanist possibilities. You would be very welcome to trial these exciting new developments. I understand that Doctor Blesserson is currently working on a longevity gene that—'

'We don't want to offer up any more of our children as *guinea pigs* to IMBOD.' Brana was unstoppable. Fasta felt a pang of fear, but Esfadur radiated approval.

'The ancient prophets lived for one hundred and sixty years,' Blesserson said stiffly. 'In my current work, I am trying to understand—'

'Should you not first try to understand how Peat Orson came to hate himself and the things he has done?' It was Baldur, beside Brana, speaking for the first time. 'And why our Halja is so damaged, just as Brana has said? Or why my grandson, the descendent of generations of Craft workers, has no interest whatsoever in anything beautiful? I am a glassworker, Doctor Blesserson. I made these windows that shed their bright colours into our lives, and into this sordid meeting. If one of those panes should crack in the cold or cloud in the sun, I would want to know why, at the very least so that I did not repeat whatever mistake caused the fault. A human being is a window of sorts. Surely our children deserve at least as much concern as a piece of broken glass.'

'I have told you, I have requested the CONC reports.' The scientist reddened again. 'And I have given you all, as parents, the opportunity to avoid, in future, the very rare but sadly unavoidable failure of the Security Serum—'

'I'm sorry. I'm not comfortable with this opportunity.' It was Sif, interrupting in a high, thin voice. 'I don't care about exemptions, Doctor Blesserson. I care about my son and daughter. They saw things no child should ever have to witness. Now, I'm sorry, Brana, but I *want* them to have their Security Shot, to make them resilient, and help them recover quickly from this trauma. But I also want that evil man to be punished.'

Sif stared around the table, daring the other adults to disagree. Daring *her*, Fasta, to contradict her. She held her breath, waited for the community's response.

· 'Here in Yggdrasila, we speak with our own minds, Doctor Blesserson,' Esfadur murmured, 'each as different in colour and shape as
Baldur's glass panes.'

'My wife is right,' Vili spoke at last. 'We can't accept your offer if
it means letting whatever's going on in the IMBOD zone continue.
Are you not concerned about those poor girls, Major?' His face
darkened. Vili had wanted to run out and rescue the girl, right
there in the clearing, Fasta knew, but Esfadur had stayed him,
ensuring they took the necessary footage and returned home safe.
The Sec Gen girl, Esfadur had argued at the Ethics Committee
meeting, although fully capable of overpowering her attacker, was
not making any attempt to escape. For all they knew, she could have
been trained to turn on any would-be rescuers.

'That man should be *buried alive*,' Brana announced. 'As should
whoever programmed those girls to submit to him. Or are Sec Gens
no longer protected by the laws of the land?'

Around the table, another hubbub arose, everyone talking out of
turn, over each other. 'You don't have children, do you, Doctor Blesserson?' Helga, the Head of Kitchens, shouted down the table. 'You
just meddle with ours. Perhaps you don't care that young girls pumped
up with *your* loyalty hormones are being unspeakably abused.'

'*Of course* I care about the Sec Gens!' The scientist slammed his
palm on the table. 'I have spent my entire professional life caring
about the Sec Gens!'

'Good people of Yggdrasila,' Major Brockbankson said gravely
into the silence, 'I have daughters. Two beautiful Sec Gens, both
proudly returned from National Service and planning to start their
own families soon. I appreciate fully the horror of the situation. But
I can assure you, Vili, that nothing is going on in the IMBOD zone
except for authorised security training exercises. The man you saw
was suffering from chronic mental stress, the result of his own
grievous abuse by traitorous individuals. He is being treated accord-
ingly. The girl is being given counselling, far from harm's way.'

'The man we saw is *Ahn Orson*.' Brana jabbed her finger at the major. 'Don't think we never read the Atourne journals, my friend. We know exactly who he is, and we know he's not been arrested! *Nothing's* been on the news about it. Not a sparrow's peep!'

'That is correct.' There was still no menace in Major Brockbankson's tone, but Fasta found herself shivering. 'Ahn Orson is being dealt with by IMBOD. In the meantime, I know that none of us wants to cause irreparable damage to the reputation of an international icon. Why would we wish to bring yet more negative global media attention to the Sec Gens when there are other options – options that, as we are discussing, will benefit everyone here?'

In the quiet that fell again, Fasta found herself hurting; with a sharp pang suddenly wanting something more badly than anything she had ever wanted before.

'Our entire community of non-Sec Gen adults, including those not here in this room, will vote on the deal that you have offered,' Esfadur said. 'Our silence in exchange for a place on the exemptions pilot project for any child whose parents wish them to avoid the Security Shot.'

Around the table, parents pulled their Tablettes from their hip-belts. ACCEPT. REJECT. DON'T KNOW. Fasta's finger dived onto the screen. Beside her, Vili disentangled himself from Sif. Following the voting protocol, Fasta cupped her hand over her screen. In her peripheral vision she saw Sif, her Tablette tinted red in the light from the window, make her choice with a sharp swipe. Vili pondered a few moments longer, then pressed his screen with his thumb.

Esfadur rapped the table: all the votes were in. All heads turned to the elderman.

'Forty-one people agree to accept the offer. Six people in total don't know and four people have rejected the offer. We trust all members of our community will accept the decision of the clear majority.' As Esfadur announced the result, a wave of applause swept around the table, buoying Fasta up to the rafters of the hall. Brana shook two victory fists. Baldur nodded his heavy head. Beside Fasta, Sif exhaled sharply and Vili hugged her to him again.

'The exemption must be offered to all Yggdrasila families that want it,' Esfadur continued. 'But I also want regular reports from Doctor Blesserson on his investigation of the reversal method. As soon as he has perfected it, no matter when, we want our children to be first in line for the treatment. For now, Major, we accept your word that Ahn Orson is getting help for his problem, and that any children he has abused are in a safe place. We also agree to treat our discovery of his crime as a matter of the strictest confidence.'

He had not issued any warnings, but around the table, stony faces glinted threat. Major Brockbankson nodded. 'Thank you, Esfadur. Please, just let me know by next month which children you want to hold back from the next Security Serum shot. In order not to create community tensions, the pilot project offer will be extended to the parents of all children in the upper valley school district. Local authorities and media workers will be forbidden to discuss the project professionally until further notice.'

'So Ahn Orson gets off scot-free,' Sif muttered, loud enough to draw a reproving glance from Esfadur.

'The vote is binding, Sif,' the elderman warned.

Fasta's nerves tingled. Brana was pushing her chair back, getting up to return to the vegetable garden, Baldur rising to return to the glass workshop. From the top of the table, Dr Blesserson's eyes swept the hall. Fasta dropped her gaze. She could not worry about Dr Blesserson. Beside her, Sif's arms were folded under her breasts and Vili's arm was around his partner, his big knuckles grazing Fasta's shoulder.

'It's an option, Sif, only for families who want it,' he whispered.

Fasta put her hand lightly on Sif's wrist, leaned in to their coupledom. 'We can talk about it tomorrow,' she heard herself say before, without waiting for Sif's reply, she rose to go, the light of the window falling green across her body, sheathing her like a long, gauzy robe.

Misted Silver

The Ashfields
06.04.99

Catching up, settling scores, cracking jokes, placing bets, scraping the last smears of barely edible food from tin plates – the clatter and din of three hundred prisoners making the most of their lunch hour echoed from the basalt vaults of the dining-hall ceiling. Sometimes Astra found the racket life-affirming; sometimes oppressive; other times, like today, she wished it was louder. So loud that Cora couldn't be heard.

'Boycott absolutely. But it must be backed up by dirty protest.' Like a taut thread, Cora's voice drew half a dozen women's heads together around the far end of the Traitors' Table.

'Dirty protest?' Opposite Astra, Rosetta frowned. 'What's that?'

The elderwoman addressed them all, in a tone of command, not explanation: 'We refuse to wash or use our toilets. We piss on the floor and smear our excrement over the walls.'

'Whoah!' Rosetta wrinkled her pert nose. 'Why would we do that?'

'Because, sweetie' – Charm put her beefy arm around Rosetta's shoulders – 'our beloved prison authorities have just installed an ion chamber in this prison that will replace all of our visitors in the flesh. We don't like that idea, remember?'

'Because shit dries out more quickly spread on the walls than left in piles on the floor and therefore doesn't smell quite so bad,' Pallas,

Cora's tall, white-haired partner, replied evenly. 'Cora's lawyer did the research.'

'Ergh!' Rosetta shrugged off Charm's embrace and pushed away her plate. She only ever picked at her food as a rule. Other people were still eating: you soon developed a strong stomach in Ashfields Max. Astra finished her mouthful of green mush and inspected her brown slop. Often there were long, greasy hairs in the mush, and sometimes cockroaches found their way into the slop. Once, Rosetta had nearly eaten a tooth.

'In fact, it's the urine that really stinks to high heaven.' Cora wagged her knobbly finger. Her upper arm was purple and yellow from a recent confrontation with Bircha: the bruise was a warrior's band she was brandishing practically in Astra's face. 'So pee next to the door, everyone, and sluice it out into the hallway for the guards to mop up.'

Now Rosetta's face was a mask of horror. 'No, I mean why would we not wash in the first place? That's unhealthy. And smearing shit on the walls is totally disgusting!'

'Because the guards will hate it,' Cora retorted. 'And the public will realise the strength of our conviction.'

'No, they won't. They'll think we deserve to drown in our own faeces. Charm.' Rosetta swatted Charm's wrist. 'Astra. Tell Cora we're not doing that.'

Astra considered the question. Earth would approve of a dirty protest. But fighting the ion chamber ruling should not be the top priority right now. 'I—' she began.

'We can discuss other methods of protest as well,' Pallas said over her, just in case anyone was tempted, even for a moment, to think this was not a democracy.

'I dunno about the shit paint job, Cora, but boycott, yes!' Charm pounded her fist down on the table. Astra's plate trembled; Cora's bony, liver-spotted hand steadied a glass.

'Charm.' Rosetta's fawn eyes cast a nervous glance over the other tables. There was no privacy in the dining hall: the mics in their

Tablettes recorded everything they said and on the wall above the door Vultura's head swept from right to left, left to right, ever-alert for signs of infractions. But the prisoners had the right to organise, and to talk – until a guard said they didn't. Astra craned for a quick recce. Bircha was on the far side of the hall, leaning both fists on a table between the woman from the white desert who had killed two of her parents and the woman from the dry forest who had drowned her alt-bodied child.

'Relax, sweetpea.' Charm rolled her hulking shoulders and slung her arm across the back of Rosetta's chair. If it wasn't for the guards' diss-sticks, Charm could take on Lichena and Bircha simultan-eously. She had tried, four years ago, and still bore the scars, a constellation of white stars scattered over the exposed chest above her breastplate. 'The screw's nowhere near us. And yeah, boycott's only logical. We simply refuse to go in the thing. If they drag us in, we shut our eyes and don't talk.'

'Boycott can be an effective,—' Astra tried again.

'A dirty protest would make headlines, though,' Fern said at the same time. It was rare for Fern to speak nowadays. Astra hunched back over her plate and let the older woman continue.

'I think Cora's got a point,' she said, stroking her red, raw cheek. 'A controversial protest might galvanise our secret supporters. Loads of people don't want their children to become Sec Gens. They're just too afraid to say so. And other Gaians don't think mothers should be locked up for years for non-violent crimes. If our suffering becomes a national talking point, those people might at least defend our right to human visitors.'

Fern, with her burnt face, had suffered more than any of them at the hands of the guards, but her determination was stronger than ever. As she had before Lichena's 'accident' with the boiling kettle, when she spoke, she did so with conviction and authority. Sure enough, down the table, other women were exchanging queasy glances. Not everyone was speaking, but everyone was listening.

'Thank you, Fern!' Cora lit up. 'Dirty protest shows we mean business. You young lot should demand the removal of your hormonal implants. If you start bleeding again, you can write our demands in blood on your walls.'

'Ohhh.' Rosetta threw up her hands. 'That's revolting, Cora. And we can't not wash, Fern. What if we all get sick?'

Cora punched the air. 'Then we fill the infirmary. That's all to the good. To win quickly we have to cause chaos, overload the system, cost this place *money*.'

'Hang on, Cora.' Rosetta, for all her dainty ways, was not easily cowed. 'Can we stick to the boycott for a minute, please? If we reject the ion chambers, we won't get any visits at all. I've only *just* persuaded my mother to make the trip up from Atourne. Not seeing her? That's quite the sacrifice.'

Patience with those she deemed fools – meaning nearly everyone – was not Cora's strong point. 'A boycott, Rosetta,' she lectured, 'involves a short-term sacrifice for a long-term gain. Remind me again, how long is your sentence?'

'Long enough that I don't want to spend it never seeing anyone from outside!'

'Honeypot!' Charm tickled Rosetta's neck. 'The server's been down in this place for five days. What makes you think these ion chamber visits are going to be reliable? We've got an international right to have visitors. That's not much, but it gives us leverage. Can't you think strategically for once, lovebug?'

'Wow, Charm.' Rosetta shrugged off Charm's hand and folded her arms. 'You're my partner. Can't you think about me for once?'

'She is thinking about you, Rosetta,' Cora snapped. 'And about all of us. Thus she is demonstrating solidarity. And as history proves, over and over again, solidarity, my dear, is the only sure path to liberation for an oppressed population.'

Under the combined assault, Rosetta wilted. For a moment, Astra felt sorry for her. Rosetta was young and refreshingly self-absorbed. Even after two years in jail with Is-Land's most hardened political prisoners, she still always thought about herself first. After twelve years of thinking about herself last, if at all, Astra sometimes felt almost envious of Rosetta's ability to focus on her own needs. More often, though, she felt guiltily grateful to the woman for drawing Cora's fire.

'Charm. Cora. Shh.' Pallas, ever the mediator, intervened. 'We're never going to be allowed to see our children, Rosetta,' she said kindly. 'You mustn't hope for that.'

Like most of the other thirty-one women at the Traitors' Table, Rosetta had tried to preserve her first child from the Security Shot. She had done so clumsily, attempting to enlist the help of a teacher who had reported her, and was serving a ten-year sentence. Charm was in the ninth year of a twenty-five-year sentence for successfully protecting her twin boys, who were too old for the shot by the time she was discovered with them, living wild in the steppes. Pallas had saved four of her grandchildren from becoming Sec Gens before being discovered. And Fern, who had spared her two children and two of their friends by taking them to live off-grid for three years, was also a member of a dissident group that helped Non-Landers to live secretly in the country. Like Cora and Astra, unless there was a regime change in Is-Land, Fern would be in jail until she died.

'I know.' Rosetta thumbed the edge of the table. 'But maybe we'll get other visitors in the chambers. My Shelter aunt already said she would come.' She rolled her eyes. 'To tell me not to bite my nails, I expect.' She pouted, looked down at her torn, ragged nails, then hid her hands in her lap. 'I wouldn't bite them, but they get so dirty in here otherwise.'

'A little dirt under the nails is nothing.' Cora jabbed her finger at Rosetta. 'You need to not shower for a month and use your menstrual blood for blusher, then get your mother and that prissy aunt of yours to write to all the Atourne news channels about the unsavoury conditions their fallen flower is enduring for the sake of a simple human right.'

Beneath their pink powder, Rosetta's cheeks turned scarlet. Her near-religious dependence on make-up, which her mother sent in care-packages from Atourne, was a long-standing joke. Fern and the other women giggled. In the face of collective ridicule, Rosetta recovered her grit. 'And how's my aunt going to know how I am if we're boycotting all our visitors?'

'Our lawyers will get the message out.' Charm exhaled. 'C'mon, Rosie Posie. Don't you get it? These machines are soul-stealers. If your aunt does come, how are you even going to know it's her and not some hologram IMBOD's knocked up based on her Tablette Talk profile?'

'You haven't had a visitor request, Charm,' Rosetta informed the table. 'How are you going to boycott something you haven't been invited to use in the first place?'

The women fell quiet. Muscle-bound Charm and petite Rosetta had a red-hot-ice-cold relationship and, if you didn't want to get burnt or frozen out, you didn't intervene in their spats. Charm dug into her green mush so hard her spoon could have cut through the tin plate and Astra shovelled up a spoonful of her brown slop. The lumpy mound was cold now, but she needed whatever trace of protein it could offer.

'No, Astra!' Rosetta squealed.

She dropped the spoon back down on the plate. A small cockroach fell into the brown mush and lay there on its back, feebly waving its feet.

'It's alive.' Rosetta gasped and clasped her hands to her lips. Hushed again, the women craned to see.

'It's a sign we're doing Gaia's will.' Cora reached over, plucked the creature from Astra's plate and slipped it into a pocket on her girdle. 'I'll set it free in the yard after lunch.'

Trust Cora to steal *her* omen. But at least she had the table's attention at last. 'I agree with Rosetta,' she announced. 'The ion chamber campaign's a non-starter. Fern thinks we can galvanise public support through our suffering, and maybe we can. But the support we most need is in here.' She jerked her head, indicating the rest of the dining hall. 'Most of these women are keen to get new visitors. They won't support an ion chamber boycott, let alone a dirty protest. And we don't have legal backing, either – my lawyer thinks the ruling is a good thing, and so does yours, Cora. What we should be focusing on is amplifying Earth's recent message to the world.'

'Astra.' Cora tsked. 'Jasper and Calendula can be convinced. They work for us, remember. And the other prisoners just need to be educated—'

She'd had enough of being cut off and raised her voice, addressed the table. 'The living creature was on *my* plate. I do my best, but I'm just one voice: I need your help. I know there's not much we can do from prison to help humanity break the bond with Metal, but if we have ion chamber visitors, at least we can spread the word about the Old Ones' messages and get news about the campaign.'

Cora hrumphed, protesting Astra's rudeness. Astra couldn't help that. She respected Cora, Pallas and Charm, all of whom took brave stands against the prison guards every day. And she still didn't trust the ion chambers or accept the loss of in-person visits; part of her desperately wanted to fight the change. But around them at the other tables women were laughing, the mood in the windowless hall merrier than she could ever remember. Out there in Is-Land, from Bracelet Valley to the white desert, brothers, sisters, parents, school friends, ex-Gaia partners, people prisoners had only exchanged annual emails with for years, were, one by one, signing up for ion chamber visits. She'd thought about it carefully and come to the logical conclusion: there was little point in mounting a protest against a change most of the prison was embracing, and which even her own lawyer accepted. After all the effort and risk Jasper had taken to see her over the last twelve years, she couldn't demand that he take up the case. But more importantly, she and Jasper had other pressing priorities. With just a year to save humanity, they had to concentrate on her IREMCO and INMA cases, and, most import-antly, delivering the Old Ones' messages to the world.

The vital significance of which she still couldn't convey to a single soul in this jail. Down the table, women were finishing their food, wiping their mouths with coarse grey paper napkins, avoiding her gaze. Rosetta was inserting a wiggling finger into the gap between Charm's breastplate and girdle. As usual when she mentioned the Old Ones, it was as if she hadn't even spoken. All she'd done was remind everyone in earshot that she was a freak. As she sat in the silence, pushing the last spoonful of brown slop about on her plate, Astra felt a prickle up the back of her neck. That meant one of the prison's paedophiles was looking at her. She had learned to ignore those women, with their brittle laughter and darting eyes, their forearms razor-striped from self-harming binges and necks shiny and ridged like Fern's face from boiling sugar-water ambushes in the toilets. Perhaps the child rapists were human, too. Perhaps she should start a campaign to befriend them. But she couldn't. She just could not.

'Astra. Your messages are getting out into the world just fine as it is.' She braced herself. This was Cora's briskest tone. Sure enough, her cousin-who-acted-like-her-aunt launched into a lecture. 'We all want to support you, but frankly you're being naïve. We deserve a choice. We should be allowed to meet visitors in the flesh or in the ion chamber. The fact that we don't have this choice should make us highly suspicious. This is not just the Ministry of Penitence we're up against, but IMBOD itself. Hokma would have seen that instantly. Honestly, sometimes I think she over-Sheltered you.'

Astra's jaw tightened. 'I thought we agreed you weren't going to criticise Hokma any more.'

'I'm not *criticising* her. We all have our blind spots, especially mothers. Paloma thought it was fine to see me about four times a year. And she was convinced Samrod would grow out of his fascination with Clay Odinson. But at least she taught me never to trust IMBOD. Ever.'

'I. Don't. Trust. IMBOD.' She ground the words out.

'Then why are you so keen to dash into their fancy new surveillance chambers?'

'I'm *not*—'

'*Cora*,' Pallas snapped. 'Leave her be.'

She sat silently fuming. This was Cora all over. Any time Astra disagreed with her, she'd accuse Astra of betraying their entire illustrious family line of warrior women. Not just Hokma, but Cora's Code mother too, Hokma's long-dead older sister Paloma. Paloma, Astra had learned when she first entered the jail, was a leading campaigner in the late RE 50s for an amnesty for Non-Lander agricultural labourers who had secretly remained in Is-Land after the closure of the Boundary, and had been killed in a car 'accident' for her efforts. Her death had radicalised Hokma, who had joined her sister's network of dissidents, later recruiting Cora. Sometimes when Cora spoke about Hokma, it sounded as though Hokma had been two completely different people. She'd clearly never shared her spiritual side with Cora. Though who could?

'Hey, Astra.' Charm broke the silence. 'Don't the Old Ones want us to protest? Those chambers must frackin' suck up rare-earths metals!'

'Yes, Astra, surely the Old Ones object to the change?' Cora inquired with chilly courtesy.

Astra picked up her spoon again and returned to her brown mush. Brown mush had been known to harbour tooth-shattering stones. And sudden invocation of the Old Ones in an argument generally masked patronising attitudes and personal agendas. None of her fellow prisoners, especially Cora, really believed that the Old Ones existed. Charm had been with Astra once in the toilets when Earth paid an unexpected visit and knew that she was not simply making the messages up. And, through Calendula, Cora knew perfectly well that Astra had a small but devoted international following. But Cora and Pallas thought she was hallucinating as a result of taking lantern leaf in Shiimti; for them, Istarastra was just another playing piece in a complicated game of global geopolitics, and the Old Ones' messages interesting only insofar as they effectively challenged Is-Land's power – which to date, it had to be admitted, they had not.

Charm believed and had convinced Rosetta and the rest of the political prisoners that Astra was epileptic, a result of the neurohospice treatment she'd had before she was exiled from Is-Land. Everyone else in the jail thought she was psychotic, which was not a blessing. The guards and most of the non-political prisoners in Ashfields Max considered giving Code secrets away to Non-Landers, or trying to deprive the country of Sec Gens, crimes on a moral par with child sex abuse. Over the years, the political prisoners had won grudging respect by organising and sometimes winning campaigns for basic rights, but still, you never walked to the toilet on your own, and Astra had learned the hard way that a weakness like perceived mental illness only made you more of a target for persecution.

'I've told you before,' she muttered, 'the aim of the messages is to change the way humanity as a whole relates to the planet. It's not possible to enforce the Old Ones' demands inside the prison. We need Tablettes to communicate with our lawyers and the world. To get the message out.'

Rosetta's cheeks flushed again. Charm's hand was under the table, and whatever it was doing was giving her face a frisky glow. 'I don't know about the Old Ones,' she said, 'but Astra's right about one thing. If we are going to fight the system, there's better battles we could choose. Ones we can win. Proper dental care. Access to animals. The right to see the face of the planet again.' She tilted her face to Charm's and batted her eyelashes. 'Or how about the chance to masturbate every now and then?'

'Honeychild,' Charm admonished. 'We'll never get access to animals because half the lovely people Astra is so keen to keep happy' – she flicked a glance around the hall – 'are in here for torturing kittens and lambs. And us Traitor Ladies will never get even a glimpse of the ashfields because we betrayed Gaia Herself and don't deserve to look even at Her burnt face any more.'

Down the table, people winced.

'Aw shit, sorry, Fern. No offence.'

'None taken.'

'A bit of clit in the mornings would be nice, though, wouldn't it?' Rosetta cooed.

Fern grunted. 'She's right, Cora. We all could do with the occasional half-hour outside this anti-amorous armour.'

'Oh!' Cora slapped her forehead and jumped in her seat. 'Of course! That's the way forward – we should revive the conjugal visits campaign!'

Astra had tried. But once more she had failed to convince her fellow prisoners that the Old Ones' messages were addressed to them, too. Or maybe she should get the Old Ones to promise a little sex spice to co-operative humans. Around Astra, Pallas was murmuring approval, Fern and Sunflower were nodding and enthusiasm was dawning like a Summer Solstice in Charm's eyes.

'*Yeah*. Yeah, we *should. That* would get the rest of the prison on board. Astra,' she demanded, 'didn't you once say these ion chambers are like sex hotels?'

'Did you?' Cora cut in sharply. 'That could be highly relevant information, Astra.'

It was Cora's disappointed schoolmarm voice again, rebuking Astra, the uncooperative child. *Thanks, Charm.*

'No, I didn't say that. It's not like sex, exactly,' she reluctantly explained, wishing again that she had never spoken to Charm about her experiences with Lil. She'd done so in the early days, when she and Charm had been close, before sex stopped mattering to her, before Rosetta arrived. 'In the chamber, you can merge your body with the other person's ion form. It's like . . .' She tried to remember. 'Having a deep-tissue massage. Or a shower in particles of energy. It feels good. It has a calming effect.'

Pallas placed her cutlery neatly on her scraped-clean plate. 'So we could experience erotic intimacy in the chambers without removing our belts and breastplates. The prison authorities haven't told us that.'

'Of course they haven't!' Cora had reignited. 'They don't want us to start demanding our rights to conjugal visits again.'

Conjugal visits, forbidden in Max, could be viewed as a right of the prisoners' innocent Gaia partners. Or so the political prisoners had argued in a legal campaign that had failed ten years ago.

'"Innocence does not have the right to be tainted by guilt,"' Pallas dryly quoted.

'What?' Bafflement was a cute look on Rosetta.

'It's what the IMBOD judge said,' Cora told her. 'When we mounted our legal challenge to the prohibition on conjugal visits. I said at the time we should have followed up with a dirty protest or hunger strike, but only Pallas supported me.'

At the mention of a hunger strike, silence fell again over the table. Even Fern hadn't wanted to take that step. In Is-Land, hunger strikers invariably died.

'Come on, people,' Cora urged. 'Gaia's bounty is our birthright. What have we done to deserve a life of snatching kisses in the sewing-room toilets? And think of the victory – winning two campaigns at once.'

'But we lost last time,' Fern reminded her.

'If what Astra says is true, things are different now,' Pallas said evenly, backing up Cora as usual. 'The judge also ruled that removing our belts and breastplates would pose security issues, but the non-corporeal possibilities of the ion chambers put us in a much stronger position. I think a legal challenge could work this time.'

'Especially if backed up by boycott and dirty protest,' Cora finished gleefully.

Charm's arm was back around Rosetta, whose cloud of hair was brushing Charm's shoulder. 'So first you say we shouldn't have any visitors in these ion rooms, Cora,' she teased, 'and now you say we should be fucking in them? So that the guards can watch us like porn films?'

'What I am saying, Rosetta' – Cora poked that gnarled finger across the table again – 'is that we can't let IMBOD take away our agency. We have to participate in decisions here. We have to find a way to turn this rule change inside out: remind the prison authorities that we have rights in this place. We demand a choice of how we see our visitors. Building in a campaign for conjugal visits could generate enormous support for a protest against the rule change. And protection for us, too: if it's ever proven that IMBOD are recording the visits, or playing tricks with holograms, our guests would have substantial grounds for pressing charges as well.'

'You wouldn't like it if I had a sex visit,' Rosetta accused Charm.

'Light of what passes these days for my life.' Charm rubbed noses with Rosetta. 'This isn't some slave market. I don't own you.'

Astra cast a glance at the wallscreen. Vultura's eyes were amber, signalling not that the avatar had seen the kiss, but the near end of the meal. Good. The brown slop was disgusting; the green mush might finish off her loose molar; and she didn't give a shit about conjugal visits. Even if the prison would accept visitors from ion chambers outside Is-Land, Muzi and Lil would never be allowed to make contact with her. All of her former lovers in Is-Land were Sec Gens: Tedis or Sylvie would probably maul her to death as soon as look at her. And even if, by some remote chance, she attracted an innocuous erotic admirer who managed to wangle permission to visit her, apart from the rare wet dream she didn't have sexual feelings any more. Her mind was always elsewhere. She was detached from everyone; that was the problem. Just like now. Pallas, Fern, Sunflower, Charm and Cora were talking strategy, all five united like a fist, plotting the upcoming battle. Rosetta was nibbling a nail, a distant look in her eye.

'Look,' Cora hectored, 'this is the position we put to the other inmates. We all, the entire prison, boycott the visiting system until the right to flesh visits is reinstated and we are granted the right to ion chamber conjugal visits. We, the political prisoners, also volunteer to go on dirty protest until these two demands are met. Vote?'

Astra scraped the last spoonful of slopmush from her plate. Cora wouldn't have any visitors. Cora was badgering people into living in filth and isolation just so that she could get an ego-kick from running another campaign they would inevitably lose, along with who knew how many privileges. And all the time Earth's messages were going unheeded, unamplified.

'Shall we vote later, Cora?' Pallas murmured. Astra looked up. Bircha was bearing down the aisle, past the table of women from Silverberry, the isolated community in the steppes that had lost all its harvest money gambling in Atourne, then returned home and semi-starved their livestock all winter. Those women would be out in three years. In the meantime, they swanned around the prison with their noses in the air as if being convicted of cruelty to animals was some kind of prize.

'*Back to work!*' Bircha slammed the table with her diss-stick. 'Trays in trolleys. Single file at the door. *Now.*'

As the women stood, a chorus of muffled trills and bleats rippled through the hall. After five days down with a 'fault', the prison server had come back on. Astra's girdle vibrated against her belly: long long short, Jasper's Voice Talk code.

'Check your messages later!' Bircha barked. But everywhere women were flipping up their screens, taking a peek at their voice-message envelopes. She did the same. It was unusual for Jasper to call her. He was probably just saying he'd got back to Amazigia safe, but maybe he and Calendula had reconsidered their position on the ion chambers.

'Hey, Astra.' Rosetta nudged her hip. 'Can you hurry up? Charm and I need the toilet.'

But Astra was frozen to the basalt floor.

The message envelope subject line was 'Peat'.

Sour Gold

Occupied Zabaria
09.04.99

'Ama!' The boy wriggled like a gecko in her grip. 'I don't want to go into town. Everyone's playing *football*. I scored two goals yesterday. My team needs me!'

'Don't argue, Girin.' Anunit tugged his tracksuit zip up to his chin. 'You can play football tomorrow. Go and put your hat on.'

He pulled the zip back down, exposing the blue New Zonian football T-shirt she'd found for him in the latest CONC aid shipment. 'It's not cold outside!'

He spoke with authority, casual contempt, and a hint of anger: she hadn't left their two dank, windowless rooms all day. But she knew all about spring days in Zabaria. She pointed at the woolly hat in the basket by the door. 'It will be cold later.'

'Then you can carry it!' He stamped the floor, folded his arms. 'It's *dark* in here. These candles smell bad. Why don't we have light bulbs any more?'

She flung her arm up, as if to strike his face with the back of her hand. 'I am your mother. You don't ever speak to me like that! Or there'll be no football at all. And no more drumming lessons!' She gestured back towards the black, smoky cave of the living room. 'How much do you think that *doumbek* cost? If you talk back to me like that again, I'll *sell* it and use the money for light bulbs. How would you like that?'

He glowered at her, his eyes bitter embers in the gloom. When she began coughing, sinking into a chair as the fit seized her, he did not ask her if she wanted a glass of water. But neither did he storm out. As she put on her *niqab*, he stuffed the hat in the back pocket of his jeans. She blew out the candle on the kitchen dresser, then pushed him through the door and down the corridor to the market.

Girin's hand clasped tight in hers, she elbowed her way along the narrow aisle between the shops and the centre stalls, pulling him past stacks of onions, potatoes and cabbages, barrels of tea, nuts and spices, garlands of dried peppers and braids of garlic, bright shops filled with Tablette fascia and battery rechargers and dark alleys extruding jumbled heaps of solar generators, their black tangled wires climbing like vines up the walls of the market to the apartments stacked above its canopied roof. The scent of burnt sugar billowed into their path as they approached the confectionery stall and Girin dragged on her arm. She yanked hard and he complained but kept up. For now.

It was happening so quickly. He was learning this cheek from the older boys. The boys whose big brothers sold glue and morpheus in the alleyways, slept out all night at the cemetery, came home once a month nursing knife wounds, cleaned the kitchen out of fatoosh, stole the egg money, threatened their parents, thieved their mothers' jewellery to pawn. Soon he would learn power from the older boys, too. Male power. A year from now, Girin would not be scurrying resentfully after her through the market or dreaming of football glory. A year from now, he would be slamming the door in her face and running out to score drugs behind the waste heap.

They reached the end of the alley. Her chest hurt. She stopped for breath and Girin pulled his hand away.

'Look what Kaganu gave me!' He grinned, held up a red apple.

'He gave it to you?' Frowning, she peered back into the shadows of the market. From his stall, the elderly fruit seller raised a hand, waved.

'That was kind of him. You must thank him later.'

Juice running down his wrist, Girin held out the apple. 'Do you want some, Ama?'

This again. Suddenly still as touching and sweet as a seven year old. He was not lost. Not yet.

'No. You eat it all.'

'The doctor said you need vitamins,' he said knowledgeably, munching as they walked on, trotting of his own accord beside her now.

'I get my vitamins from the Gaian rice. Look. Let's play walking in the sun.'

He tossed the core in a puddle and pranced in front of her, a small tousle-haired boy weaving past carts loaded with schoolbags and pens, underwear and night clothes, bangles and *hijabun*; dodging scooters delivering kebabs and pizzas, shiny black cars with tinted windows parked up on the kerb; her boy, her confident guide to the thin crooked line of sun the tall buildings and overlapping canopies permitted into the narrow, rutted marketways. At the main street, wide and dusty and blaring with traffic, she took his hand again. He let her: they were out of his friends' orbit now.

'Are we going to the doctor?'

'No.'

'Are we going to visit Uncle?'

'No.'

'Where, then?'

This was the difficult bit. 'Don't buy the moon or the truth, my boy,' she intoned, 'for in the end they both come out on their own.'

'Whaaat!' He skipped around a fire hydrant.

'Apa used to say it, don't you remember?'

He screwed up his face. She was never sure what he remembered of her father and mother. 'Yes. But I don't want to buy anything. I just want to know where we're going.'

'It's not about buying things. It means "wait and see".'

'You never tell me anything,' he complained.

'I'll tell you when we get there. Why don't you play with your Sound Snatcher for a bit?'

He gasped, whipped out his Tablette, stuck in his earbuds. Sonic harvesting in the street was a normally forbidden treat: he got so absorbed in it he forgot to watch out for traffic. But keeping her hand on his neck, she let him trip along happily pointing the device at lamp posts, car bumpers, dogs, cats and shopping bags.

'Listen to this, Ama!' He held up an earbud and she took it, listened to the recording – car horns and tyre squeals, a stick clattering over metal, dog yelps and cat hisses, spliced up and rearranged in a pattern with electronic textures the programme generated: ruffling fur, swishing fabric, even simulated yawns were part of the composition Girin had been creating as he skipped down the street. She didn't understand music, but she knew Girin was good at it. His teacher said so, and because of his talent had been tutoring the boy for three years for nothing more than a place at the dinner table. Even when Lilutu had approached Todo with her false story about a back payment, Todo had not asked for any of it for himself. 'CONC is looking for you,' he'd said, over two weeks ago now, passing on to Anunit the number the woman had given him. 'You're owed some money. You could use it to send Girin to music school. I've taught him everything I know now.'

Disbelieving but desperate, she had called the number and made arrangements for a home visit from a social worker called Tira. The woman's voice had sounded familiar, but she couldn't quite place it. But when Tira arrived at the apartment and removed her *niqab*, however, she recognised her instantly: it was Lilutu, the half-Gaian from the Welcome Tent.

'I took him to keep him *safe*,' Anunit had hissed.

'I know. I just want to be able to tell Tiamet he's okay. But Anunit – there's no future for Ebebu here. With your help, I can try and get him out.'

'His name is *Girin*. You can't meet him, Lil. He can't know.'

She had broken down into coughing, a fit that lit a match to the papery bags of her lungs. Lil had opened her bag, brought out sage tea and honey, made a pot, waited.

'I won't tell him anything, I promise. But if something should happen to you, Anunit, and Girin knows I'm a friend of yours, I can help look after him, at least. Take this money for now – it's my savings. I can contribute more every month from now on.'

She had refused the money, sent Lilutu away. But then she had been ill again. For a nearly a week. And now, even though it might be a sprung trap, she was walking straight into her only option.

'Very good, son.' She gave the earbud back. 'We can play it to Todo tomorrow.'

Girin sniggered as a large woman walked by. 'Did you hear that lady's thighs rubbing together?'

She raised a hand. 'Do you want to hear a smack?'

Over the years, she had grabbed him, shaken him, shouted at him, pushed him along by the scruff of his neck, but she had never hit him. He grinned and pointed the device at a bottle top on the pavement.

'Sconul's Tablette can make bottle caps flip. You should see the cats jump when he aims it at them!'

'He'll put a cat's eye out and then he'll be sorry,' she replied sharply. Sconul would probably enjoy maiming a cat.

He wasn't listening. She walked on, past a garage and a white goods shop, a kitchen showroom featuring sinks larger than her and Girin's tin bath, picking up her pace as they crossed the archway entrance to a mall guarded by two security officers, ex-N-LA men, armed with sonic guns. This was the official centre of the city: the intersection at which the sprawling Non-Quarter, the hi-rise residential district where the traitor police and professionals lived, the spacious Gaian quarter and the entrance to the mine all met. Her heart pattering, she stopped and pulled Girin up against a round planter of giant aloe vera. This, the widest intersection in Zabaria, with its broad pavements and benches, used to give her a sense of freedom. But now, the white cement planters were all stencilled with the green, red and gold IMBOD Shield; at the end of the long avenue, the Boundary extension blocked the view of the windsands; and on the other side of the road, the Gaians had hijacked all the handsome old civic buildings.

'We're nearly here. Put the Tablette away. I want you to wear your hat now, please. With the brim down.'

He scowled. 'Why?'

She had swallowed some dust, had to wait until she stopped coughing. 'Because I don't want the Gaians to notice you.'

His eyes flashed. 'If you don't want the Gaians to see me, why did I have to come all this way?'

Beneath the veil, tears were streaming down her cheeks. She beat her chest with her fist and forced the words out between coughs. 'Because . . . I want you . . . to meet a friend of mine.'

He had learned enough from the big boys to mask his fear with anger. 'You're sick. Why can't she come and meet us?'

She leaned against the planter, glanced at the security guards. The men were sharing a joke, pretending they weren't looking at the naked Gaian women on the other side of the street. 'Because I want you to see where she works. There's a park opposite. Girin, listen to me. If anything ever happens to me, I want you to go to that park and wait for her to finish work. She has a nice place to live and she—'

He dug his hand into the soil and glared at her. 'Nothing is going to happen to you, Ama!'

'Don't *do* that.' She slapped his wrist away before the guards arrested him for damaging the aloe vera. She should have explained it all before, but he'd got home late from school, and then he'd argued with her, and she'd coughed, worse than she was coughing now. 'I said *if*, Girin.' She shook his wrist. 'I'm sick, yes. Suppose I have to go to hospital? Who'll cook your dinners while I'm getting better?'

'I'll go and live with Todo if you're in hospital. I don't want to live with a Gaian!'

Again, she was racked with coughing. She fumbled in her bag for her flask, slipped it up under her veil and drank until, 'Todo's got ten brothers and sisters,' she gasped at last. 'There's no room for you at his place. And Tira's not a Gaian. She's Somarian. She works for CONC.'

'If you're in hospital,' he said, 'you can just Tablette Talk with Tira. Then she can come to the market and pick me up.'

The water had helped. If she spoke softly, the cough remained at bay. 'I will if I can. But I might be too sick for the first day or two, mightn't I? So you need to meet Tira. She knows all about music: you might even like her.'

He pursed his lips, considered the conditions. 'You mean I can play in the park by myself?'

'Yes. There's a children's section there. You can play on the climbing frame. But you mustn't take any Tablette photos or do anything that a Gaian might not like.'

'What if a Gaian talks to me?'

'You just say you're waiting for your mother to come out of the CONC office.'

'But I can play with other kids, right?'

'Only other Non-Lander boys and girls, if there are any in the park.' She pulled his hat out of his pocket and tugged it over his head. 'Come on,' she whispered. 'We're going into enemy territory. You need to wear a disguise.' She glanced across the street. An IMBOD officer, tall, hairy-chested and naked except for his boots and belt, was waiting at the opposite light. She stood, took Girin's hand. 'Let's go. And don't stare at the Gaians.'

She had won him over, but beneath the *niqab* she was sweating rivers. In the centre of Zabaria, the black garment made her stand out more than if she'd dressed in feathers and sequins. But showing her face was not an option. The light changed to green and she stepped onto the crossing, keeping her gaze on the road and holding Girin close to her side as the IMBOD officer passed, his long, brown manhood swinging at the height of the boy's head.

Bruise Purple

The Great Depression
10.04.99

'So, brother.' Through the live coals burning in his throat and the VoiceBox medallion he wore around his neck, Enki croaked the question of the hour: 'Are you going to Asfar to do the will of the Non-Land All Action Revolutionary Commandos, or not?'

Though the VoiceBox transformed his eviscerated voice to a rich, rough baritone, and amplified his words to fill the tent, it couldn't dowse the fire in his throat. But, yet again in this abyss of a world the gods had abandoned, a heroic effort went unrewarded. Bargadala didn't even meet his gaze, just stayed silently hunched on the rug in the centre of the tent, looking as if he'd recently dug his way out of a desert grave. The man's hair was a rats' nest attacked with blunt shears; his robe, mottled with sweat, grease and what looked like bloodstains, was so stiff with dirt it could have been erected in the scrublands as a sheep hut; and as for that filthy canvas bag Bargadala was cradling in his lap, Enki wouldn't have been surprised to learn that it had been especially encrusted with camel dung to complete the man's signature look. For, as usual, he stank. Fresh, steaming camel shit, in fact, smelled far sweeter than this heap of human rubbish polluting the command tent. What was wrong with Bargadala? They were camped right by the River Shugurra: water, for once, was not in short supply.

'The date of the trial has been set, brother. The results could force us into battle. We have two months to prepare our response and we need to know your mind. Now.' Beside Enki on the cushions, Ñizal backed him up like the outstanding Commando he was.

In response, Bargadala side-eyed the tent opening. Warriors were walking past in the direction of the food tent, men and women chatting and whooping after the day's contests. For a long minute, Bargadala studied their shadows as if contemplating joining them. Then, that famous blue gaze flashing like sapphires in a sewer, he turned his attention back to his leaders.

'I tried to kill the Sec Gen. I failed. My word will count for nothing in the court.'

At the mention of the monster, Enki felt his chest tighten. They had never spoken of it, but he had been present the night Bargadala had launched himself at Peat Orson with a knife, a brave effort that had missed the monster's heart by a sliver of flesh and ended with the Sec Gen eating the man's ear. Enki had been too ill to witness the attack. Though those events had taken place years ago, there was always a whiff of insolence about Muzi Bargadala, a sly suggestion of lack of respect that might be traced back to having seen Enki semiconscious on a stretcher in the Zardusht's cave.

This meeting was making him too tense. Sulima would tell him to relax. He reached for his glass of sage honey tea.

Ñizal took the reins of the chariot. 'You did very well, brother. Attempting to kill a Sec Gen is no shame. And you have been tried and punished for that act in Shiimti. In Asfar you will speak as the Sec Gen's victim and the judge must take your views into account.'

'Your mother is going to ask for mercy,' Enki growled. 'You need to be there to speak for *justice*.'

Ñizal pursed his lips. Enki ignored the reprimand. Everyone knew Enki respected mothers – he had travelled to Pútigi on horseback to see his own on her deathbed two years ago – but against soft words of appeasement and the tug of home a warrior needed to stand up for the greater cause. Aware of the danger of such insidious pressures, NAARC had established strict communications protocols.

There was no internet in the Great Depression and no intranet in the camp. Owleons all arrived at the main perch, tattered and hungry after their long flights, and their messages were read by the comms team before the recipients were allowed to see them. Messages deemed sensitive to the cause of NAARC were passed on to the senior commanders, hence Muzi's summoning.

'My will is my own,' the dirtbag announced in his reedy monotone. 'I want to stay and fight. I want to help avenge Is-Land's Pain.'

Avenge Is-Land's Pain? Enki nearly shattered his tea glass in his fist. Shiimti or no, Bargadala was infuriating. He had turned up a year ago on a mangy camel, bearing no weapon but an old hunting knife, and since then had done next-to-nothing to earn the title of 'warrior'. He was a good forager, fair enough. NAARC was camped on the edge of the Great Depression, a vast, barren swathe of hard land surrounding the Salt Chott, and Muzi was soon supplementing their basic rations with herbs, roots, fruit, and small rodents and lizards from the scrublands to the south. Yes, he knew the land around here like Enki knew the pattern of his tent carpet, but when it came to firearms training, Muzi just melted away into the hills. And now he was refusing to co-operate on a matter of enormous strategic importance. For this soiled vagrant, this inert clump of toilet sludge, to defy Enki's express wishes in the name of avenging Enki's grandfather's sword quite simply beggared belief.

But shouting would do no good, yet. Enki held his tongue, let his brother-in-arms convey the will of NAARC to this useless lump of dirt.

'Of course you do.' Ñizal smoothed his beard. 'But the best way to help us is to go to Asfar. Astra Ordott is already attempting to pressure your family into showing mercy to her brother. She may even contrive to send another of her confused messages from the gods to try and influence the judge. Without you at the trial to speak for justice, Orson could be pardoned. Is that what you want, after everything that monster did to your family? After what he did to *you*?'

Bargadala screwed up his face and rubbed his neck with his short arm, a spot right beneath the ravaged remains of his ear – the warped scar tissue left from Orson's savage attack, over which, in the only act of personal grooming the man apparently permitted himself, he never allowed his hair to grow. 'Justice is not for men to decide,' he declared at last. 'We fight our battles, some to win, some to lose, but only the gods can rebalance the scales.'

This time Enki could not restrain himself. 'Did that monster eat your *dick* as well as your ear?' he barked. 'Justice for Non-Land is a matter of taking retribution and achieving liberation, Bargadala, simple as that – meting out punishment for Is-Land's crimes and wiping out the Gaians so those crimes can never be repeated. That's what we're fighting for and this is your chance to contribute. You're no warrior! If you want to fight for us, do it in the *court*.'

He had torched his throat. Eyes watering, Enki reached again for his tea. In front of him, Bargadala fondled a grey, bedraggled feather pinned to that disgusting bag. That was the other infuriating thing about Brother Muzi. You could taunt him all you liked, but he never responded in kind.

'I can cook and hunt and forage,' he said mildly at last, still stroking the feather. 'And I can keep the camp in gunpowder for as long as you need.'

That was overstating his usefulness. To give him credit, two months ago Bargadala had taken himself off to the Chott with his now healthy camel and returned with bags of brimstone. He had also taught the camp how to make saltpetre from horse urine. But everyone knew that recipe now.

'You have made a valuable contribution here, Brother Muzi.' Ñizal tried the familiar approach. 'But now we need you to speak for us in Asfar.'

Silence.

'The Revolutionary Commandos are a democracy,' Ñizal went on. 'We can't force you to go to the trial. But we're urging you to. For the morale of the camp. Think how many people here lost eyes and limbs, friends and family, to the Sec Gens. We need to see one of them suffer for his crimes.'

A sudden surge of bile rose in Enki's throat. 'Think how we lost *Bartol*,' he rasped, 'our best warrior, playing nursemaid to a *cannibal*. Are you going to sit back and watch the Sec Gen invite Bartol to get a medal from the *Wheel Meet* next?'

His face flushed and his heart juddered in his chest. He downed another gulp of tea, wiped his beard dry with his elbow. Uttering that name came at a cost, always accompanied by a hot spew of memories that threatened to shoot him into the fever zone. Bartol, Enki's best friend since childhood, his Karkish brother, the warrior he had fought with as one – a legless rhymer mounted on a giant's back, together leading the charge on the first night of the Battle of Kadingir, making headlines around the world – Bartol had betrayed their bond long before that weasel Tapputu had convinced him to stay in Shiimti and tend to the Sec Gen. Bartol, after killing fifty Sec Gens, had burst into tears at a Diplomeet, wept like a baby and refused to fight any longer. He had surrendered Is-Land's Pain, Enki's family heirloom, to lesser men he knew could not retain it; Bartol had let the weapon be wielded by weaker fighters, mere boys who had allowed the sword to be seized and ultimately destroyed by the Gaians. Enki still could not think of it without the blood rising behind his eyes: his grandfather's sword, hidden for years and gifted to him by his mother, only to be broken on an anvil in Atourne in front of a baying crowd of Is-Landers. And to top it all off, during the kidnapping of the Sec Gen Bartol had refused to allow Enki the honour of a hero's death on the River Mikku, condemning him to live on to see his dreams disintegrate, to witness Bartol form his degrading alliance with Tapputu, YAC merge with N-LA and retreat to Asfar, Enki's mighty vision of One-Land abandoned with the torn tents and rutted streets of Kadingir. All the pain and humiliation of those years pulsed like an infected wound whenever he spoke Bartol's name.

In answer, Bargadala picked at his big toenail, a curving brown horn that could have been transplanted from one of the wild goats the man doubtless fucked in the hills – what self-respecting woman would go anywhere near such a stink? Watching the man flick his toenail grunge out of the tent, Enki's stomach turned. For trying to kill the Sec Gen, for sacrificing his ear, for being the husband and desert guide of the supposed oracle Ordott, Bargadala was a hero to many. But he lived like a starved stray dog.

A dog who could suddenly turn and, not bite you, but bark like a sultan's hound. Bargadala lifted his head, his disconcerting eyes blazing blue fire. 'NAARC doesn't need Bartol. NAARC is stronger than YAC ever was.'

It was true. The Non-Land All Action Revolutionary Com-mandos lived up to their name: its core members were all hardened warriors, veterans of the Battle of Kadingir, Asfarians and other for-eign fighters; all committed to the destruction of Is-Land, they held no squeamish compunctions about stockpiling firearms in readiness for the end of the Hudna. But Bargadala was just using praise to divert attention from his own failure to obey. Enki glared at him until the mongrel dropped his gaze back to his cloven toenail.

'The time to show that strength is approaching,' Nizal stated. 'If the Sec Gen is punished as he should be, the Gaians will be furious. They will retaliate with crackdowns in Zabaria, imposing more and more repressive measures on the mine-workers. The world will call for action and CONC will do nothing. Then our senior patron will release the great weapon and we will strike for liberty.'

Muzi screwed up his face and drew a circle in the earth with his finger. 'If the Sec Gen is freed,' he countered mildly, 'Non-Landers throughout Asfar and the Southern Belt will riot. Perhaps our senior patron will also release the great weapon in that case.'

'If the Sec Gen walks free, brother,' Enki growled, 'Tahazu Rabu will arrest any rioters and throw them in jail for a year, and Una Dayyani will stuff the Gaian into her bosom and carry him off to Amazigia. There he will stand in front of all the nations of the world and beg Is-Land to let the Non-Landers squat like serfs on the steppes. Everyone will applaud and Dayyani will form a new committee. Our patron will tell us that diplomatic avenues have not been exhausted; our time has not yet come. Is that what you want? To see Una Dayyani stab the One-Land flag yet deeper into the corpse of justice!'

He was boiling again. The vision of One-Land was *his* vision, but it was dead in the water, long dead, killed by Bartol's betrayal, only to be resuscitated as a toothless ghost by Una Dayyani in her sick dream of building CONC-monitored villages of Non-Landers in Is-Land, living on sufferance, second-class citizens in their own homeland. Clearly Dayyani thought that hosting a Gaian turncoat would help her convince the world this humiliating scenario was a plausible solution to decades of oppression: she had already issued a public statement welcoming the Sec Gen to Asfar. NAARC's wealthiest patron, an Asfarian with both a reputation and a fortune to guard, would only risk releasing the great weapon, he had said, when Dayyani had conclusively failed and a military attack on Is-Land was the only option left on the table.

'Enki is right, brother,' Ñizal said. 'NAARC offers the only true resistance to the Gaians. Violence is the only language they understand, and with the help of all our patrons, we speak that language more fluently every day.'

Bargadala stood, shedding dried grass and mud flakes all over the carpet. 'It's an honour to serve you, Enki Arakkia,' he said, inclining his head toward his commanders. 'When the great weapon arrives and NAARC marches to free our people, I will lead the brimstone expeditions. I know where all the deposits are between here and Zabaria. Please excuse me now. It's time to curry the horses.'

A ghoul embarking on a barren quest, Bargadala shouldered that repulsive bag, floated to the entrance, slipped on his sandals and, ducking beneath the fringed canvas, disappeared. A wave of nausea overcoming him, Enki closed his eyes.

'You all right, Enki?'

His throat was killing him, but that was nothing new. The

queasiness was a reaction to Muzi. He ought to feel powerful compared to that skulking dog, but Muzi was a stray who had once witnessed a sultan at his lowest ebb. It was as if, Enki sometimes thought, their presence in Shiimti the night of Muzi's attack on the Gaian had forged an unspoken, uncomfortable bond between them. A bond of shame; as though they shared an intimate bruise. But somehow that camel-shit-licking bastard sensed that Enki's bruise was the more tender; Enki's shame the more deeply dyed. Enki's shame, which still visited him in dreams, and now was incapacitating him in front of his most loyal commander.

He shook the thoughts off, poured the last of the tea from the pot. The liquid had cooled to the perfect temperature and the honey had settled at the bottom: always the best glass.

'That pile of dirt's as stubborn as an arse-wart.'

'He's a Non-Lander.' Ñizal snorted. 'What do you expect? We're the warts on the arse of the world.' He stood, took the carpet brush from the shelf beside the entrance and began briskly eliminating the evidence of Bargadala's presence.

'He's a disgrace. We ought to expel him on grounds of hygiene alone.' It was a toothless grumble and he knew it. Apart from the obligation to work and train for eight hours a day, there were few rules in the camp. Bargadala slept and ate on his own, so there were no grounds to force him to wash.

Ñizal put the brush away and stuck his feet in his boots. 'Do you need anything, Enki?'

Outside, the light was pinkening. This was his favourite hour, the honeyed dregs of the day before dusk. He flexed his good arm. 'An hour alone with my wife would be welcome.'

Ñizal grinned, flashing his jumble of astonishingly white teeth. 'You go and summon Sulima if you like. I don't want to be the one to try and tear her away from target practice.'

He laughed. 'I can wait. I'm her night target. And her morning target, too.'

'Yes, brother, the whole camp knows that. When the great

weapon arrives, we're thinking of calling it after you. "Enki's Blaster", to be anointed with a barrel of goat's milk.'

He grunted into his own black cloud of a beard. 'It has to get here first.'

'Enki's Blaster' was good. But whatever they called the great weapon, right now the thing was infuriating: a monumental piece of heavy artillery, the key to NAARC's battle strategy, locked away in a desert warehouse until an overcautious billionaire finally decided he wanted to play his ace card.

'I suppose Bargadala could be right,' Ñizal mused. 'Whichever way the trial goes, Tibir might release the great weapon.'

'Maybe.' Enki drained his glass, the warm honey at last soothing his torn throat. 'But we want to liberate Zabaria *and* see the Sec Gen suffer.'

'People say the aunt will call for vengeance. And perhaps the blinded boy, too.'

Ñizal had his spies in Asfar City, and his own Owleons. Maybe Muzi's family would act with loyalty to Non-Land. But it was beyond galling that Bargadala didn't want to add his own voice to the call. The Sec Gen had killed his *grandmother*. Anger flared in him again. 'If Bargadala doesn't go to Asfar, we should question his loyalty to NAARC. Demand a vote of expulsion.'

Ñizal frowned. 'I don't know. Better he stays here where we can watch him. He's such a fool, if we let him loose with a grievance N-LA and CONC will find some propaganda use for him.'

'He's avoided Dayyani's clutches all these years. And he might stink, but I don't think he's a fool.'

'All the more reason to keep him close.'

That was Ñizal, the voice of caution. Sulima usually sided with Ñizal, and she was usually right. But neither of them could head the Revolutionary Commandos, and they knew it. Enki was the undisputed leader of the true Non-Land resistance. The Gaians, with their displacement of his people to a toxic wasteland, had taken his family's pride, had taken his legs before he was even born; the Sec

Gens had taken his arm and his voice, robbed him even of his best friend; his own supposed leaders, N-LA, had taken control of his organisation, hijacked and neutered his vision: but no one could ever take Enki Arakkia's thirst for justice, or his magnetic pull on his people. Every week brought more warriors to his camp, drawn by the lure of Enki's dream, and every last Gaian in Is-Land would soon rue the day IMBOD had broken his grandfather's sword.

To keep the love of his comrades, though, occasionally he had to lose a few small battles. He set his empty tea glass aside, slid off his cushion, waddled across the tent and mounted the ramp up into his new wheelchair. Electric, with a solar-powered battery that lasted a week, like the VoiceBox it was the best gear on the market: timid billionaires did have some uses.

'C'mon, we've wasted enough time on that bag of dirt. Let's go and watch my wife whip the new recruits into shape.'

Shadow Blue

Shiimti
10.04.99

'It is my professional duty to say it one more time.' Dr Tapputu's goat-gold eyes glinted at Peat over the rims of his glasses. 'It's not too late to change your mind.'

Peat and Bartol laughed. They were drinking mint tea in a café on the rock ledge at the foot of the Shiimti Complexity, waiting for a minibus to take them to Pútigi, the first stop on the long journey to Asfar. The Mujaddid had accepted Peat's request for a trial on the condition he demonstrate his sincerity by immediately surrendering himself into custody. Bartol would stay with old YAC comrades in Asfar City and visit Peat while he was on remand. Dr Tapputu had patients here in Shiimti: he would come down for the trial. But though Peat's bags were packed, his tickets bought and all the arrangements made, the doctor still hadn't stopped trying to convince him to go home to Is-Land, or on to Amazigia: anywhere but into the hands of the Mujaddid's justice system.

Beneath the table, Smoke licked Peat's ankle. He leaned down and ruffled the dog's neck. The Complexity's cliff-face edifice soared behind them like a marvellous castle, and ahead, in Shiimti's swathe of green gardens, bright-blue butterflies danced between twinkling flowers. But Peat's time in the healing beauty of this place was over. 'You told me to write my own script, Doctor,' he said simply. 'I've written it, and now I want to act it out.'

The doctor sighed. 'It is not a performance we're talking about. It's the rest of your life.'

Peat scooped Smoke up into his lap and let the dog lick his chin. After two years of planning this move he knew by now that nothing he could say would appease Tapputu. The doctor thought Peat wanted to sacrifice himself because he still had a death wish, or a deep-seated need to prove he was as noble as his Shelter sister had shown herself to be. Tapputu was also afraid that Peat would not be able to cope with a prison sentence, that subjected to conditions of hardship and isolation he would revert to the vulnerable, confused state of his early years of rehabilitation; might try again to take his own life. After reading Peat's first draft of the video script, the doctor had prescribed another year of soul-retrieval treatment, fasting and dream therapy at the animal sanctuary. Peat had completed the year, but he had not changed his mind, and nor did he share the doctor's fears. Astra's decision to swap herself for the Non-Land hostages might have got him thinking about his own options, but his Shelter sister could keep her saint's halo; he had no plans to start broadcasting divine messages from jail. As for his suicide attempts, they had frightened everyone but himself.

'I've told you, Doctor – my life was taken from me a long time ago. I can't ever get it back. All I can do is try and make amends to the people I've hurt.'

The doctor sighed. 'Your life is important to your family. They're desperate to see you. You could still go home to Or. If you did that, you could see Astra too, in an ion chamber visit.'

Smoke wriggled in his lap then tried to sniff out the honey pastries on his plate. Bartol clamped his hand over the dog's muzzle.

'Behave!' the big man said.

'She wants to see you, Peat,' the doctor persisted.

Astra's message had arrived three days ago. She wasn't allowed to send a video, but her lawyer had emailed the Zardusht to say that Astra admired Peat's courage, sent her love and hoped they could be reunited one day. In the meantime, the email said, Astra had promised to use her influence to press for mercy at the trial. The lawyer had also offered his services *pro bono* if Peat ever wanted to come back to Is-Land and mount a case against Blesserson and Odinson.

'She supports my plan.'

'She's going to try and help you get acquitted – that's not the same as wanting you to go in the first place. And she has a world-class lawyer. Look what he's offering, Peat: the best chance you'll ever get to go after the men who are *really* responsible for your actions.'

Peat buried his face in Smoke's fur. He had given up explaining. The doctor would never understand. For years, Tapputu had been coaxing him to launch a suit against Chief Superintendent Odinson, the senior IMBOD officer at the Non-Land barracks who had sexually abused him when he was still underage. But Odinson had been horrifically burned during the ambush that had taken Peat captive, losing all his limbs as a result: the man had been punished enough. Peat, though, had not been punished at all.

Tapputu hadn't snapped an old woman's neck. He hadn't savaged a limbless woman and devoured her flesh in a berserker pack frenzy. All of Peat's healers had told him that his deeds as a Sec Gen were not his fault: they were the crimes of those who had programmed him, like a computer, to do harm to innocent others. But *Peat's* hands had gripped that frail throat; *his* teeth had ripped into that doughy flesh; *his* mouth had watered for the hot cherry taste of human blood. The doctor didn't know what it was like to live with those memories, and neither did anyone in Peat's family. Like a sickness no one could cure, for years the memories had ground like cogs in his skull, churned in his stomach, at times so convulsively the only way to stop them was by slashing his wrists or banging his head against a rock. Now he was stronger, and the memories were weaker, but like an Old World leper, he had changed forever. He would never be Peat Orson of Or again. He was Peat Orson, former Sec Gen, now; and he belonged nowhere except to history.

'No one will ever put Odinson and Blesserson on trial for their crimes against the Non-Landers,' he said at last. 'Someone has to take a stand, Doctor. I'm the only person capable of doing so.'

'Peat's sacrifice is welcomed by Non-Landers everywhere.' Bartol, who normally stayed out of these discussions, contributed. 'And I'll be with him all through the trial, Doctor.'

Once again, Peat was grateful for his Non-Land brother's stalwart support. There was no internet at the animal sanctuary, but with Bartol as an escort, Peat had visited Shiimti to research the Non-Land legal system. He had discovered that Una Dayyani's government-in-exile in Asfar was restricted to assessing non-violent crimes: all cases of bodily harm, rape and murder involving Non-Landers had to be referred to the Asfarian legal system, which, he had learned with surprise, was considered one of the best in the world. Asfar was not like Shiimti, where culprits were given the choice of willingly submitting to healing or being cast out of the community; the country still had prisons, even life sentences, but sentencing was governed by mercy, and the prisons were large compounds in the desert, places of prayer in which to seek the forgiveness of the Asfarian god. Peat didn't believe in any god, but perhaps an Asfarian judge would know how long it might take for him to forgive himself.

The doctor shook his head and stirred his ginger tea. 'You don't need to sacrifice yourself, Peat. One martyr in a family is enough.'

The sun lit up the mint leaves suspended in his glass. A bird trilled in a palm tree. Smoke settled in Peat's lap. 'I'm not martyring myself,' he said quietly. 'It will be easier for me to live in Asfar, even in prison, than in Is-Land. In Is-Land, people will expect me to be someone I'm not.'

'It's always hard to go home, Peat,' the doctor said, just as quietly. 'But until we do, we can't chart our soul's growth.'

He didn't answer. People at the tables around them began to stand. The minibus had pulled up on the road below the ledge. This was it: the hard part. He pressed Smoke to his chest, buried his face in the silky fur between the dog's floppy ears.

'Goodbye, Smokey. Thank you. Thank you, my friend.'

He handed the dog to Tapputu. The soft bundle squirmed and scrabbled in the doctor's arms, trying to get back to Peat.

'He likes pumpkin cupcakes. And he needs brushing right after a walk.'

'I know. Don't worry. We'll take excellent care of him. He'll be waiting for you whenever you come back.'

Peat shouldered his backpack. Bartol picked up his bags.

'Good luck, Peat.' The doctor's gold eyes were shining. In the bright light, his grooved face suddenly looked as old as the cliff.

'Thank you.' Stooping, he held the man and the dog in a close embrace. 'Thank you, Doctor Tapputu, for never giving up on my soul.'

The minibus driver beeped his horn. Bartol turned to go. Peat didn't look back, but Smokey's whine followed him all the way down the steps.

Bruise Purple

The Great Depression
11.04.99

Chewing a grass blade, Muzi climbed the hill to the south of the camp. The sun toasted his neck, the scent of sage and wild thyme rose from the earth and the pain in his head, beating today like a drum, found its place in the sounds and sensations of the morning: just another rhythm to join the crackle of salvos from the training ground, the bursts of rifle fire, the shouts of the officers and the roar of battle cries. Out to the east, the River Shugurra glittered like a snake, muscular, diamond-scaled, writhing all the way to Asfar through the salt lands, the scrub hills and the windsands. He kept his eyes on the earth: the light on the water could kick the pain into skull-splitting.

At the crest of the hill, he turned to watch the cavalry drill. One of the woman warriors, Astarte perhaps, was at the head of the parade: a small figure swathed in sand-coloured robes, she drove her beast forward at a lolloping gallop and took aim at one of the metal targets set up on the hard, grey soil of the Great Depression. Whoever it was must have got a bullseye, or close: she pumped the air with her rifle as she wheeled her beast back in line. Shooting from camelback looked a good challenge, but Muzi didn't want to join the cavalry. NAARC was supposedly a democracy, but Enki ran a tight camp and the warriors spent all day following orders. Enki himself, a small figure from this distance but a mighty one, was directing the drill. Even the best Craft worker in Asfar could not design saddlery or tack that would enable a legless man with one withered arm to ride a mount into battle, but strapped into the seat of his specially adapted chariot, with his wife Sulima at the reins and his VoiceBox hooked up to loudspeakers mounted on the frame, Enki could lead a charge and deploy a mini-arsenal of sword, sonic gun and revolver. Ñizal was there too, on his race-winning steed with its red saddle and pom-poms. But no one in NAARC would dream of launching an attack on the Gaians without their spiritual leader at the helm.

For Enki was a visionary, sent by the gods, of that there was no doubt in Muzi's mind. From the start, back in Kadingir his prophetic wisdom had been obvious: *Pain is the path*, Enki had declared, his first great call to the people, and recognising that essential truth of their lives, all the alt-bodied youths of Non-Land had fallen in step behind the man with no legs. Even now, when the pain in Muzi's head got too much, and he had to lie in his tent all day in the dark pressing a wet cloth to his temples, he thought of all that Enki had suffered and lost, and knew that he, too, would endure, no matter what, to play *his* part in Enki's Dream. A dream that was slowly coming to life. From this height, even thronging with people and noise, the camp looked almost like a mirage in the heat. But it was a mirage that was stamping its mark on history.

All the commandos were in thrall to the story: how seven years ago, the wounded warrior, living in near-poverty in Asfar, in self-exile from his former comrades in YAC, had had a dream about the weapon he needed to destroy the Boundary and overthrow the Gaians. A dream so vivid and technically detailed Enki had convinced a billionaire Asfarian patron to fund research into its possibilities. On the basis of those scientific reports, Arakkia had issued his second great call to the people: *The summit is in sight: together we must topple the occupiers.*

At first, he had been laughed at. To topple a people, you had to get near them, and for years now the Gaians had been safe behind their

Boundary, its ramparts patrolled by Sec Gens, its walls clad in a hi-tech material that exuded a magnetic forcefield capable of repelling all metal projectiles – Muzi had seen the promotional IMBOD videos showing cannonballs bouncing right back at their gunners. How to outwit the Boundary engineers was a problem that exercised every red-blooded Non-Lander's brain. The forcefield extended fifty metres above the Boundary, a barrier which could have been easily surmounted with rockets. But rocket missiles were classified as 'weapons of war'. To manufacture, sell, purchase or use one invited even more severe punishments than the possession of unlicensed firearms – guns, due to their controlled use in hunting and policing, were classified merely as 'potential weapons of war'. For their misuse, jail terms began at five years; only when hundreds of firearms were being traded did serious sentencing begin. Billionaire Asfarians caught supplying rebel groups with a single rocket, however, could be stripped of their entire fortunes, or handed down life sentences in desert jails. At clandestine meetings in the Old Quarter of Asfar City, Enki had made it clear that his dream weapon was not such a missile – it was a unique, unclassifiable armament that would take years to acquire: years that would give him time to train an army.

For who was going to stop Enki Arakkia and his secret billionaire from buying truckloads of guns and setting up a guerrilla camp in the vast, roadless Great Depression? After the fall of Kadingir, CONC had withdrawn most of their troops from the Southern Belt, and the Gaians had agreed not to send the Sec Gens beyond the Boundary. You could never trust the Gaians, of course, but now their precious cladding was complete, the Is-Landers appeared disinclined to let their monsters out to roam, inviting bandit gangs of armed Non-Landers to shoot them. Thus, just as all had gone quiet in the Southern Belt, Enki had risen from the ashes of YAC. With no weapons. Just his dream. For talking and writing about that dream, for daring to publicly declare that the Gaians should be deposed, not appeased, Enki had been banned from Asfar. As he left, he had issued a summons through his underground channels:

all those Non-Landers who were tired of endless talking, who refused to share their homeland with monsters, who were determined to liberate Zabaria and take their country back should join the Non-Lander All Action Revolutionary Commandos, follow him into the windsands and learn how to fight.

Muzi had not come right away. He'd had family responsibilities. Now, though, his sisters were grown up and married, his cousin was going to college and his mother and aunt were living comfortably on their Heroes' Widows' allowance. A year ago, he had come to the camp, joining its atmosphere of electric anticipation and fevered industry. Right now, below him in the ammunition tent, used practice bullets were being melted down and recast and new armour was being hammered; in the gym tent, commanders were urging warriors through weights training and martial arts drills; in the garage tent, mechanics were checking every last bolt on NAARC's fleet of solar-powered vehicles; in the communications tent, media officers were tapping out messages to funders and journalists, storing them on memory sticks for Owleons to take to Asfar and beyond. And there, out on the edge of the Great Depression, Enki's chariot was wheeling in a cloud of grey dust, NAARC's leader preparing his army to reclaim their homeland.

Muzi stroked his short arm. Enki had scoffed at his fighting abilities yesterday. But he still had the CONC prosthesis at the bottom of his bag; and even without it, he could use his knife if he needed to. For now, though his contribution to the struggle might be quiet and solitary, it was still important. He turned his back on the camp and crested the hill, bending occasionally to snip a sprig of sage and slip it into his bag. But it wasn't the right time for foraging. The sun was soaring through the cloudless sky, honing the pain in his head to a jangly edge. Quickening his pace, he headed down the slope to his shepherd's lean-to. There were no sheep in the Great Depression, but early on in his time at the camp he'd brought sticks and tarp up over the hill and created a shelter, a private place to retreat to during the height of the day's heat. Sitting in the shade, facing the southern hills, he fished his Tablette out from his bag and read the Owleon messages again.

Asfar City
07.04.99

Son,
I trust that the gods are smiling on you. By the grace of the gods, we here are all well.

Before you left our home, I said to you that showing for-giveness is the pathway to peace in one's heart. I am writing today because our family now has a chance to show mercy to one who has hurt us.

Your wife's lawyer explains it better than me. He has writ-ten to us all, asking that we support Astra's brother in his time of great trial. Your wife also sent a message to you.

Please, son, return to Asfar as soon as you can, that we may discuss this matter and all appear united as a family together in the court of the Mujaddid, who has given us ref-uge in his land, and in the court of the gods.

Your loving mother
Habat
P.S. Here is the message from Astra and Mr Sonovason:

FWD: from sonovason@greenberg.ama
06.04.99

Dear Muzi Bargadala,
I trust this finds you well. I have asked your mother to for-ward this message to you as a matter of urgency. As you

might or might not know, Peat Orson has resurfaced. Thanks to the constant care of Non-Land healers in Shiimti, he has been pronounced cured of his Sec Gen traits and, in a public announcement that made international headlines, he has offered to stand trial in Asfar for his actions regarding your family; also for his part in the pack murder of an alt-bodied Non-Land woman in Zabaria. I have spoken to Astra about these developments and she is very concerned to ensure that her brother, who was not responsible for his actions at the time and genuinely repents of his deeds, not become a scapegoat for IMBOD. She is still forbidden from communicating with you directly, but I can confidentially relay that she has clearly indicated to me her wish that you and your family will attend the trial and, in your capacity as the bereaved family of Peat's victim Uttu Dúrkiñar, speak in favour of showing mercy to her Shelter brother. She also sends her love and best wishes for your own well-being.

It is my legal and personal opinion that a lenient judgement in Asfar would reflect very well on the One-Land cause. As the beneficiary of mercy, Peat Orson would become an ambassador for an eventual Truth, Reconciliation and Reparations process that could see Non-Landers reinstated with full human rights in their ancestral homeland. I would be grateful to hear of your decision, either way, as soon as possible, which I will discreetly relay back to Astra.

Best regards,
Jasper Sonovason
Greenberg & Greenberg
Amazigia

Astra, Astra, Astra.

He rolled up the Tablette and stuck it in his bag with the herbs. From its special pocket, he took out his knife and placed it in front of him. Curved, with an engraved blade and black handle, this knife had stabbed Peat Orson in the chest, missing the Sec Gen's heart by the faintest of shades. He should be proud of the weapon, but apart from declaring it when he'd entered the camp, he had showed it to no one, never used it.

The knife was only back in his possession thanks to Astra. As Peat's sister, she had been charged with the task of disposing of the weapon. Instead of destroying it, she had returned it to him, twelve years ago on their wedding night in the Shiimti camel stable. Whenever he looked at it, he thought of their kiss that night, that hot, twisted blade of a kiss, snatched in the dark before he had been forced out into the desert for his crime. The knife had cut him from everyone he knew and loved. The knife, he understood whenever he looked at it, was stronger than him: was waiting for him to learn how to use it.

Next, he unpinned from his bag the hudhud feather Astra had also given him that night. After travelling with him through sandstorms and dustbowls, camel racetracks and crowded beer tents, the feather, once a glorious tangerine with a sharp black-and-white tip, was grey and bedraggled now. But no matter how tired it looked, he would never discard it. It was not from a bird he had hunted, although he had stoned and eaten a hudhud just hours before he attacked Peat Orson. This feather was from an earring gifted to Astra by the Zardusht herself, the High Healer of Shiimti. Astra had pinned it to his shirt just before he married her with his grandmother's ring. Married like the cranes, he had said. Two cranes, flying in different directions. Astra had wanted to leave Shiimti with him, but he had refused to let her. He had killed his hudhud in violation of a pledge not to take life on his journey to Shiimti and was already suffering for it. His pilgrimage had failed; hers had just begun. She was Istar, the messenger of the gods, and he was just her shepherd guide. Her place was with her family and with YAC and the Zardusht; his place was out in the world, avenging the deaths of his father and uncle, and fighting to free his mother and aunt and their children. Crying, Astra had accepted his decision, had said the hudhud feather would be a messenger between them.

Ignoring the pain throbbing at his temple, he drew a circle with the knife in the dirt around the feather, thinking as he did so of Ildig, the woman who had finally helped him understand his relationship with Astra. For Astra's actions after they parted had been almost impossible to accept.

He had left Shiimti to fight on the Hem. But he needed to stop on the way in Lálsil, to pay his respects to the widow of Doron, the trader who had helped him buy the camel, and who, for his kindness, had been killed by IMBOD. Doron's shop, with the sign of the tree with ten fruits, had been locked up when he arrived, but he'd asked the neighbouring shopkeepers where the man had lived. The first two were suspicious, their faces as closed as the shutters, but the third took pity on him, showed him to Doron's house. Although Doron was Karkish, the neighbour said, his wife Ildig was Somarian and she mourned in the Somarian way: friends coming each day to bring food and praise her husband. Dragging the camel behind him, he had knocked on her door. When the woman opened it, he had fallen to his knees, pressed the reins into her hands, told her the beast had been a gift from Doron to him and now it was hers.

Ildig was older than his mother, her black hair streaked with grey, her long face grooved by the years. When she lifted him to his feet, he broke down, sobbing, 'It's my fault he's dead.' But she simply refused to hear the words. She led the camel into the backyard and tied it to a palm tree, then took him into the house and fed him chicken soup. After the meal, she dressed his mauled ear and gave him a bed mat for the night. In the morning, she brewed tea from Doron's famous samovar, and he explained as much as he could: about his grandmother's death, and his family's imprisonment; about taking Astra to safety and trying but failing to kill the Sec Gen who turned out to be his brother-in-law. About his marriage to Astra, and his dream of joining her again one day, when the war was over, moving to an oasis town and starting a camel racetrack. Astra loved animals and treated them like part of her own family. His friend Kishar's brother knew all about car racing; he and Kishar would help with the betting. In the meantime, he, Muzi, was going to Kadingir, to fight on the Hem and avenge his stolen family.

Ildig had listened. The next day, he hitched a lift with a man, Balag, who was going up to Kadingir, his cart full of food and medicines. It was chaos in Kadingir now, Balag said. The Sec Gens were swarming out of the Hem, rampaging through the camp, and the last die-hard YAC warriors were defending their ground, ambushing the Gaian monsters in the ruins of collapsed tents and the mazes of the Nagu scrapheaps. Under cover of night, aided by the element of surprise, it was just possible to trap and kill the beasts – two had been lured into the river and drowned. But still wave on wave of them kept coming, with their ferocious jaws and unquenchable bloodlust. No one was safe, not even CONC officials. Amazigia and Asfar had sent peacekeeping forces but plans for an international Diplomeet in the camp had been abandoned. Instead, Major Thames was trying to broker a deal. Una Dayyani was back from Asfar – her convoy of black limousines had shot past Balag's cart at high speed on his way down to Lálsil – but she had returned without the Mujaddid and was working out of the CONC fortress because, in her absence, the Sec Gens had trashed the Beehive, ripping out its wallscreens and destroying its collection of Non-Land pottery and weaving.

Muzi didn't say much; after what had happened to Doron he was afraid to tell anyone about his journey with Astra. Balag didn't seem to mind. He was a good travel companion and tried to take Muzi right to his home, but CONC had established sentries on the road who weren't letting anyone through. So Muzi joined the man and his warrior friends in a shelter in Nagu Four, squatting in a barricaded set of containers and feasting on the dried lizards, hummus and dates Balag had brought from Lálsil.

There was a phone signal in Kadingir, and after the meal he tried to find Kishar. When Kishar's brother finally called back, it was to say, in a dead voice, that Kishar had been killed two nights before.

'I'm leaving for Asfar tonight, Muzi, in the car, with my family. We've got room for one more. Kishar's seat. Come with us.'

But Muzi refused. Instead he tore his shirt, clawed mud over his chest, collected tent pegs, sharpened the metal ones, whittled the wooden ones into stakes and joined Balag and his warriors in their nightly prowl through Kadingir. His last memories of that night were of a Sec Gen lunging towards him, her mouth dripping with blood; then, as her skull hit his, a blinding white explosion. He'd awoken, bruised and bandaged, on a bed mat in the CONC fortress, wincing at the pain in his head that had been his constant companion ever since.

The improvised hospital was guarded day and night by peace-keepers. The Mujaddid's troops were also evacuating the wounded, in convoys to Asfar that left every two days. The ward was over-crowded, a jumble of bodies and languages, home; feeling strangely at peace, Muzi lay in a sunlit bay, listening to his people talk. He recharged his Tablette, read the headlines and, for the first time since leaving Shiimti, checked his email account. There was nothing from Astra. He thought about writing to her, but he wasn't used to email and didn't know what to say. If he'd killed a Sec Gen, he would have had news, but he couldn't remember doing anything on the battlefield worth telling. Then Tarez, a young woman with a mauled leg in the next bed, started talking and he forgot all about Tablettes and emails.

Muzi was lucky he'd left when he did, Tarez said. He'd missed having his heart ripped out of his chest by his own leadership. At the start of the war – fuck CONC, everyone knew this was a war – YAC had fought like demons. Before he decided to lay down his weapon, Bartol the Giant had killed fifty Sec Gens, decapitating thirteen of them with Enki Arakkia's family sword, *Is-Land's Pain*. The heads were priceless trophies, proof that the monsters were mortal; mounted on spinning plates under coloured lights, they were a thrilling sight. But – Tarez spat on the floor – YAC had sold its soul. Before the group could capitalise on this triumphant spectacle,

Una Dayyani had demanded they *give back* the heads to the Gaians. And, with barely a whimper, in exchange for a seat on the Ministerial Council and *community funding*, YAC had agreed. No wonder Enki Arakkia had pissed on the lot of them. N-LA hadn't even tried to trade the heads for hostages. Right now, thanks to the courage of the men and women lying savaged in this hospital, Dayyani had six more fallen Sec Gens in her possession, whole bodies. And she was planning to give those back, too!

Muzi had sat bolt upright, shivering with need. Where were the bodies? In a fridge in the fortress kitchens, Tarez thought. Muzi summoned a nurse and demanded to speak to Major Thames, Tahazu Rabu, Una Dayyani herself. He made so much commotion that at last a minor CONC official came to hear what he wanted, and he told her, not about Astra – the news was rife with speculation about Istar and he was wary of revealing her whereabouts – but about his family, kidnapped and held in the Gaians' firesands jail, hostages who mustn't be forgotten, who needed to be freed with negotiations. The official looked grave, took notes, promised to get him an audience with Major Thames. His head throbbing, he drifted off to sleep in a fever of hope.

But when he woke the next day, rumours of a diplomatic breakthrough, an end to the fighting, were spreading like a disease on the ward. Everyone was glued to their Tablettes but no one knew what was happening. The official did not come back. The following day, the news hit. Major Thames had brokered a deal: IMBOD had agreed to withdraw the Sec Gens into Is-Land, never again to set foot beyond the Boundary, and in exchange Dayyani had promised to leave Kadingir and form a government-in-exile in Asfar. Dayyani was wrapping fancy words around the agreement – 'the moral high ground', 'pariah state' – but it wasn't a deal. It was defeat. Thames hadn't even resolved the question of the Non-Land prisoners: their fate would be negotiated separately, once Kadingir had been evacuated. There was no chance, though, that they would be traded for the Sec Gen bodies. For, as if to seal this historic humiliation,

Dayyani had already handed the corpses over to IMBOD. 'By this humane gesture,' she had said, 'I show the world that Non-Landers honour our promises, and we honour the dead.'

No one spoke much. There were tears, random shouts, but mostly people lay on their bed mats, crushed under an invisible weight. Muzi was discharged that afternoon. There was no one to fight and nothing for him in Kadingir any more. He would join a convoy and leave it at Lálsil, he decided. He would work for Doron's wife, as if he were her own son, defend her from bandits and IMBOD spies. He would not cost her a penny. He would find a job in the market to pay for his food and stay with her for as long as she needed him.

Ildig took him back in, fed him bean stew, promised to let him mend her leaking roof. And that night, on his battered old Tablette, he read a news story that hit him like a blast of desert wind. Astra, too, had done a deal with the Gaians: to exchange herself for the Non-Land prisoners including his mother, aunt, sisters and cousin. She was in Kadingir right now, waiting for CONC lawyers to Zeppelin out from Amazigia and negotiate her re-entry to Is-Land.

He didn't know what to think or do. Joy, panic and confusion wrestled in his chest. His family were to be freed. He would embrace his mother and aunt, hug his little sisters and cousin. They would be together again, could mourn his father and uncle and rebuild their lives. He was blazing with happiness, wanted to cry with relief. But this happiness came with a sense of terrible falling, down a bottomless hole. Astra was being wrenched away from him. Astra, his wife, whom he had tried so hard to protect, was going to be driven into the bowels of Is-Land to be tortured. The thought of it made him frigid with fear.

But she had chosen to do it. Amidst the waves of emotion, a small uncomfortable feeling squirmed in his stomach. Astra *wanted* to be in jail? She preferred being in jail to being married to him?

He shouldn't think like that. It was ridiculous. He sat at Ildig's table like a stone.

'Did she write to you?' Ildig asked, so he checked his email account again – and there it was, Astra's announcement. Sent not to *ask* him if she should give herself up to save his family, but to *tell* him she was going to do so. 'Do not be afraid for me,' she had written in her schoolgirl Asfarian. 'The Old Ones will be with me. And our love will always keep me warm.'

He read the email twice before it dawned on him. Astra was in the CONC fortress. If she'd emailed before she left Shiimti, saying she was on her way to Kadingir, he would have got the message in hospital. He could have waited for her. They could have met. But more than that: he could have told her about the Sec Gen bodies. She knew Major Thames from when she worked at the fortress. And she was *Istar*, famous in Non-Land. Thames and Dayyani would have listened to *her*. They could have done it. They could have traded the Sec Gen bodies for his family, and Astra could have come to Asfar with them all.

But she hadn't consulted him. Acting as if he didn't exist, she had made herself the centre of the world's attention. He scanned the headlines again. Astra was all over the news like a rash. A Neuropean journalist had written a long story about other women dissidents in her Gaian family. A politician in Neuropa wanted to nominate her for a peace prize. Una Dayyani praised her for embodying the noble spirit of Istar. And a YAC splinter group was criticising the international media for focusing, not on the suffering of those left behind in Kadingir and the responsibilities of the international community, but on the ego-driven action of a half-Gaian with a messiah complex.

His face was wet. He felt dizzy. Ildig was looking at him in concern. 'I'm going for a walk,' he said.

Giddy and hot, he stumbled in a white daze out of the house. His head was pounding and his vision was blinded with tears. He was getting his family back, yes, but without his father and uncle. And who knew how hurt the others were. Everything he loved was dead or damaged. Everything had gone wrong for him after meeting Astra, *everything.* He staggered down Lálsil's longest avenue of palm trees, and at the end he was still listing all the misery she had inflicted on him. First Uttu had been killed and his family kidnapped. He had not blamed Astra for that; the opposite, in fact: he had tried to help her, taking her into the desert to find her father. There she had made him promise not to hunt on their voyage; a promise he never should have made. Not hunting was *her* religion, not his. But she had enchanted him, so he had agreed. She had bewitched him in the oasis, too, had shown him the magic of her beauty. That should mean that a man and a woman were getting married, but Astra had not wanted to do that. Rejecting his offer, she had forced him into a temporary marriage; again, not his tradition, but hers. Then, in the Black Desert, Astra's friend Lil had arrived in her dune buggy and told them that Doron had been killed. In Shiimti, the same day he had been rejected by Astra's father, he had learned of his own father's and uncle's deaths. When, in his grief, he had tried and failed to kill the monster who had snapped his grandmother's neck, he had also unknowingly nearly killed his wife's brother, tainting his heroic effort with indelible shame. He had accepted that shame, and his banishment, as the price of causing Doron's death and breaking his pilgrimage vow, but now, his head a storm of misery, he realised none of that was his fault. Running towards the Lálsil oasis, his heart pounding, he understood at last: Astra was a witch. A witch who had put a spell on him, had sucked out all his power to stoke her own.

But that was only part of the story. At the oasis, he slumped down on a tree stump and stared out at the moon path shimmering on the black water. Astra was a witch. Yet his people honoured her as Istar. She spoke to the Old Ones. And she was saving his family.

He stood, walked on, to the outskirts of town. Astra spoke to the whole world, but she didn't speak to him. What kind of a wife decides to send herself to prison without talking it over with her husband?

As his legs tired, the shame flooded him again. A wife who didn't respect her husband. And why should she respect him? She was Istar. And he was just a shepherd who didn't know how to write an email.

Only the gods could help him, he knew. Sitting on a rock, he watched the sun come up over the desert, and with it the morning star. Istar. Compared to the vast endless travels of these luminaries, what did his own ragged journey matter? Istar shining like a diamond above him, a beacon for his people, he realised that he had to be fair. Astra was not evil. She was a young woman the gods had chosen as a vessel, a well-intentioned but inexperienced magical being. In the process of coming into her power, though, she had clearly demonstrated that she didn't need him, or care about his opinions. He didn't need her, either. His role in her story was over. As strongly as he longed to hold his mother in his arms, he wanted to divorce Astra.

Ildig had helped him see things differently. 'She must love you a lot to give up her freedom for your family,' she said later that morning as she poured out the strong tea.

'She didn't do it for my family,' he replied. 'She did it for her gods. It's her gods she's married to, not me.'

Ildig was quiet for a while. Then she said, 'We can all speak to the gods.'

'I know. I ask the sky-god for advice. But he doesn't talk to me the way Astra's gods talk to her. He tells me if it will be a good day or a bad day. He might warn me not to do something stupid. But he doesn't tell me what to do with my whole life. He doesn't tell me why I'm here.'

She'd thought about that. 'Maybe you need to deepen your connection with the gods. Doron used to say that the sky-god needs the earth-goddess to manifest his power. He taught me a meditation, a way to communicate with both of them. If you like, I can show you. It might help you control the pain in your head.'

That night she taught him the secret of the tree with ten fruits. And when she was finished, Muzi remembered what he had understood in the stable in Shiimti: that his union with Astra was not a legal one, not anything like an ordinary marriage that was sealed with an exchange of sheep and pottery and a night of dancing in a rented tent and could be broken by a visit to the priest. Theirs was a union sealed with blood: the blood of Uttu and Doron, of his father and uncle, of Peat Orson the monster, and the blood of the hudhud, the bird whose feather he kept pinned to his bag. Though Astra was indeed a witch and had cast a binding, blinding spell over him, he could not unmarry her. He had been chosen to be her consort, and he must build his own power to meet hers. To do that, the gods told him over a painful week, during which he cried in Ildig's lap and walked for hours and hours, he must finish his journey to manhood. He must cleanse himself of his shame, not by avenging his father's death in a blood feud with Astra's family, but by making Kingu's spirit proud of him. He would look after his family, he promised the gods, as a man should do; and as a Non-Lander he would fight for freedom for his people.

After he had made this promise, he left Lálsil. Under the terms of Astra's deal, his family were being Zeppelined to Asfar, so he rejoined the overland exodus south through the windsands to the Mujaddid's city. His family had been housed in a large apartment with a patio roof in a pleasant part of the city. Safe there at last after her ordeal, his mother had wept over his ear, praised the gods he'd survived and thanked Astra over and over for her sacrifice.

His aunt had not thanked Astra. Uttu, Kingu and Gibil were all dead, Suen was blind and Nanshe had cursed the day Astra had ever set foot in their house. His mother, though, had wanted Muzi to write to Jasper Sonovason and ask him to convey her gratitude to Astra. He had refused. When he had fully earned his father's pride, come into his own power, that would be the time to write to Astra. So Habat wrote to the lawyer herself, but nothing much ever came back except those wild messages from Astra's gods, released to the world like burning flowers on the wind. His wife was Istar now, on her crane's journey, as he was on his. To start with, he had found work in Asfar, selling cold drinks down at the camel-racing track, earning extra money to help buy the children all they needed.

Sometimes, in the early days, journalists had come, wanting to talk to Astra Ordott's husband, Istar's husband, but he always sent them away, and soon they didn't bother any more. Then his sisters and cousin had grown up, and he had finally been able to fulfil his second promise to the gods. Determined to fight for his people's freedom, he had followed Enki into the desert.

Now he had been summoned. By everyone. Enki. His mother. The Mujaddid. Astra. Astra's lawyer. It seemed that Peat Orson's trial was going to be impossible to avoid. But what should he say if he went? His mother said peace only came through forgiveness. He knew that was not true: forgiving your enemies did not stop them from abusing you again and showing meekness often only invited more aggression. He didn't agree with Enki, though, that justice meant fighting for revenge. The gods had made it clear to him in Lálsil, and since, that warriors should fight with pure hearts. But Muzi understood Enki well enough to know that if he refused to go to Asfar, or if he went and asked the judge for leniency, he would no longer be welcome in NAARC. To obey Enki, however, would be to anger and disappoint Astra. But although he was not afraid of disappointing Astra, if necessary, refusing mercy would hurt his mother. It was a hard question. But thanks to Doron and Ildig, he had a way to find the answer. *It is a powerful method, but do not overuse it,* Ildig had said. *Ask only questions of extreme importance.*

He drew another circle in the dirt with the knife, directly above the feather. Beneath it to the right, he drew another, and opposite it another, and so on down towards his feet until he had mapped out the tree with ten fruits, the last one the circle with the feather, on its own, nearly touching his feet. To the right of this circle he drew a five-pointed star in the dirt, making the points all different sizes; one shorter, with a blunt tip, for his short arm. It was the YAC star, the symbol of One-Land, a place where Non-Landers and Is-Landers could live together in peace. Astra still believed in One-Land. To the left of the circle he drew the NAARC symbol: a jagged mountain summit haloed by a bright sun. It stood for aspiration and challenge and the goal of toppling the Gaians from the mountains they had stolen.

Finally, as Ildig had taught him, between the fruits he drew the lightning-bolt path of knowledge. Then he laid the knife down and stared at the tree, slowly travelling the zigzag path with his gaze. From the Spiritual Crown, he descended to the Third Eye and the Mind, soaking up their wise emanations before slipping down past Desire – a fruit that still stung – to swing for a long time between the Heart and the Sword. From there, he lingered on the Hand and the Foot, then descended from the Sap Fountain to the Root. He sat looking at the hudhud feather inside the Root circle for a long time, letting his gaze flicker between the YAC and the NAARC symbols. Then, climbing back up again on the electric ladder of the path, he focused on the invisible fruit, the one Ildig had taught him was the most important of all.

Around him rose the scent of the hot earth. He had stopped washing to be closer to the earth, so that the Tree of Life would trust him with its fruits. He was fully human now, a creature of both earth and sky. He lifted his eyes to the blue vault above the hills, then closed them. When he opened them he knew what to do.

With the edge of the blade, he erased the tree and the symbols. Then he picked up the hudhud feather. With a little difficulty – the task was a challenge with one hand – he pinned it on the inside of his robe, over his heart. With the knife, he turned and sawed through the clump of sage growing behind him. He put the plant in his bag. Enki drank gallons of sage tea. Then, blade in hand, he stood. It was time to finish the job.

Sour Gold

Occupied Zabaria
13.04.99

'Hey, Buttercup. What's wrong?' Bud tickled Lil's chin. 'Are you scared of the protests?'

She was lying on her back, staring at the cracks in the ceiling and chewing her lip. She rolled over to face him, shifting the sheet to expose her breasts. Bud responded well to breasts. 'No.' She sighed heavily. 'It's nothing you can help with, Bud, don't worry about it.'

'C'mon, Tira, you don't know that until you tell me what's wrong.' His milky-blue eyes soft with concern, he cosied up, tucking her under his meaty brown arm. It was, she thought yet again as she rested her head against his broad chest, almost a shame that Bud was a Gaian. The old bull might lack stamina, but he never ran out of cuddles.

'Honestly, Bud,' she protested, grazing her fingers through the thick silver curls between his sagging pecs, 'I shouldn't even be thinking about it. I'm sorry.'

'Don't be sorry. I got magic powers, remember. Green fingers and a golden nose for what's good for my little girl.' She giggled on cue and Bud hugged her tighter. 'Hey, skinnykins, you're not eating like I told you, are you? Every three hours, little but often, that's what I said.'

'I eat plenty, Bud. I'm not hungry, that's all.'

'You're not hungry because something's eating you. Tell me, gorgeous.'

It was the most peaceful time of the week in her room, late after-noon on a Sabbaday, as the Gaians called Bluday, no rush-hour traffic, just the occasional passing conversation and footsteps in the corridor, and a honeyed light flowing slowly through the shutters over her tangled pink bed throw, turning even the chipped orange paintwork and sticks of furniture golden with promise. The sense of hushed togetherness between the two bodies on her bed, though, Lil had worked for six months to attain. She trembled for real now. This was it. The moment when she needed her own magic to work.

She began in her most plaintive tone, addressing Bud's furry belly as he rubbed her neck. 'You know how I lived in Zabaria before?' On their third date, before they had even kissed, she had told Bud a potted version of her time in the mines and the sex tents, just enough to hopefully trigger a mixture of pity, protectiveness and salacious interest. The potent cocktail had done the trick: since that night, he'd pursued her with the doggedness of a St Bernard in a blizzard. She'd never seen a St Bernard, but her father had told her about them, another of the fantastic tales he'd spun when they were living wild in the dry forest in Is-Land. She hadn't breathed a word about her father to Bud, of course; as far he knew, she had been brought up in a Kadingir orphanage and learned her fluent Gaian from an idealistic CONC worker.

'I remember, Daisy Petal,' Bud crooned. 'But that time's over now. You're safe with me.'

He stroked her hair as lightly as he could. On their fifth date, he'd looked down at his big, clumsy mitts and sadly said he didn't think he had a lover's hands. She'd knelt in front of him and kissed his rough palms, rubbed them over her face, and even though his callouses chafed like sandpaper sometimes on her most delicate skin, apart from occasionally asking him to be gentler with her, she never complained. She took his hand and held it over her breast. 'I know. But I'm not sad about me. It's a friend I'm upset about. She was out of the city when you guys took over, and—'

He squeezed her breast gently. 'Hey, don't say "took over", Tira.

We restored order. Things were terrible here before, a real circus of corruption. Zabaria's running much better now. We cleaned up the sex tents, stamped down on the protection rackets. Everything's licensed and above board now. You've got a proper job and a room of your own, don't you? Not to mention a handsome brute of a man to take care of you.' He flexed his chest muscles, still strong under their pudgy man-boobs. Bud was a mid-ranking IMBOD communications officer farmed out to Zabaria to handle internal liaison with CONC; apart from tending his rooftop garden and humping Lil, he didn't get much physical exercise any more, but his beefy frame was surprisingly comfortable to lounge around on. He leaned over and snuffled her ear with his lips. 'And *he* says this room's a bit pokey for a wild girl like you, Tira. Why don't you pack all this stuff up in one of those itsy-bitsy handbags you like so much and bring it over to my place? You can keep your favourite lampshade, I promise.'

She'd told him a hundred times already: not only was she not ready to move in with anyone, but having a Gaian partner made life difficult for her at work – they had to be *discreet*. Having Bud over at her place was not ideal, but none of her neighbours were colleagues, and today especially she couldn't risk hidden sensors recording her at his state-of-the-art IMBOD dwelling. She exhaled dramatically and moved his hand to her waist. 'Anyway, like I was saying, during the period of *armed order restoration*, my friend was in Kadingir and her baby in Zabaria was being looked after by an aunty. During the chaos of all that *order-making*, the aunty disappeared, so my friend never found out where her baby was.'

She had never pretended to love Is-Land. When she'd done her shopping for a Gaian sex partner, along with a job handling CONC documents and a fundamental lack of interest in the political complexities of the war, the good-humoured ability to allow her to vent came top of her list of essential qualities. But she couldn't let this become one of their rare sparring matches. She snuggled closer to Bud, said quietly, 'That's partly why I applied for the job with CONC. So I could come here and look for him.'

'Oh, hey. That is sad.' He kissed the crown of her head. 'You're the best friend that girl ever had, I can tell you that, coming to this Gaia-forsaken place to help her. But you can't spend all your time worrying about this little boy, Buttercup. He's safe with the aunty, I bet. Look, if your friend wants to find him, maybe she could get a CONC job, too. I can help with that.'

She had cautiously sounded Bud out for weeks. For him, CONC was just another organisation in his supply chain, the Non-Land Alliance a distant group of sinister people he fortunately didn't have to deal with, and as for YAC, he had only dim recollections of the Battle of the Hem, which had taken place while he was on a long camping holiday in the steppes. She knew for a fact that Bud would have absolutely no clue that the YAC Singular Tiamet was famous for mourning her lost son in Zabaria. Still, although Non-Landers in Zabaria had restricted access to ShareWorld, CONC workers and Gaians could watch what they liked, and Bud's colleagues might be keeping up with YAC music videos, or 'propaganda' as IMBOD called them. She had no idea how much Bud talked about her, or to whom. On the topic of 'her friend', she had to tread carefully.

'I wish she could. But she doesn't speak Gaian or Inglish, and even her Asfarian is pretty bad. The thing is, Bud, last week I found him.'

'Hey!' He shook her shoulders. 'That's my girl. That's great. What are you so sad about, then?'

She sat up and flung her arms in the air. 'You don't understand! It's a terrible situation. The boy is healthy but his aunty is sick. She's got that coughing disease from the mine and doesn't know how long she'll live. All she wants to do is give the little boy back to his mother, but I can't even get a message to my friend.'

She was working herself up into a froth, and like always, he soothed. 'Sure you can. Just email her. You work for CONC, you can send messages outside.'

'No, I can't.' She pulled away, hugged her knees to her chest. 'IMBOD reads all the CONC mail, you know that. If they find out I'm trying to reunify a family, they'll accuse me of meddling in internal affairs and I'll lose my job. Then I'll have to leave Zabaria, forever.'

The threat was so bald it was nearly transparent. She couldn't believe he would fall for it. But like a rock from a cliff, he plummeted. 'Shh, don't say that.' He drew her closer again. 'Look, I know it seems like a harsh rule, but the closed borders are necessary. Otherwise Zabaria would be flooded by all sorts – spies and provocateurs, hostile agents pretending to visit their relatives. Then we'd be back to chaos, wouldn't we?'

Otherwise all the mine-workers and other Non-Landers would leave, she didn't say.

'He's just a little boy, Bud,' she sniffled. 'He's going to lose the woman he thinks is his mother. He doesn't remember his Birth mother. And she doesn't even know he's alive.'

She started to cry. It had to be his idea.

'Oh, Gaia. Shush, don't cry.' He patted her back. 'Where is the Birth mother now?'

She wiped her eyes. 'In Asfar. She's working as a maid. But don't worry about it, Bud.' She hit a note of accusation. 'I told you there's nothing you can do. There's nothing I can do. He's going to be an *orphan*.'

He was silent for a moment. Then he put his arms around her, pulled her close and said softly, 'I'm telling you, Tira, you should come and live with me. Then we can take him in. It would be fun, hey, bringing up a little boy?'

He was heading in the right direction. Now she just had to steer him correctly down the fork in the road. 'I can't do that. I can't *steal* him, Bud,' she wailed, pulling away from his embrace. 'He's *got* a mother. She wants him back. What's one little boy to IMBOD? Why can't they let him through? He could go out with a CONC van, they could drive him to Asfar.'

But reasonable, doting, obstinate Bud wasn't playing along. Yet. 'You can't hide him in a van, sweetie. He wouldn't get past the checkpoints. You know that.'

Of course she knew that. The CONC vehicles had to drive through a thermal reader: not even a Non-Land mouse could get through. Bud would need a hint. And some more bullying. 'If he had the right documents, he could,' she muttered. 'Like a medical certificate, to say he needed special treatment in Asfar.'

This silence was as long as the Mikku River.

'You know I can't do that, honey.'

'Why not, Bud? It's only one time. And he's not a terrorist! He's just a little *boy*.'

He squeezed her shoulders. 'Those medical certificates are like gold dust,' he explained, as though *she* were a child. 'The office issues them once in a blue moon. To highly skilled workers, not to little kids.'

'Sometimes people buy the certificates, though, don't they?' She was pleading now, beseeching him, gazing into those pale milky-blue eyes, running her hands through his old wolf's pelt. 'Through the network?'

It was true and everyone in CONC and IMBOD knew it. Rich Non-Landers in Asfar made contact through CONC with amenable IMBOD officers who, for a huge fee, issued the medical certificates to their relatives in Zabaria. Bud, she knew, was a fence-sitter when it came to the network. He had never broken the law himself, but neither had he squealed on colleagues who did. A troubled expression passed over his face.

'It's too risky, Tira. It's just a matter of time before the higher-ups decide to make an example of someone.'

She gripped his hand, held his gaze. 'But loads of officers are taking bribes all the time. There'd be way better people to make an example of than us. And with us, there wouldn't be any money exchanged. There'd be no proof, Bud!'

His jowls twitched and his droopy eyes regarded her with concern. '*If* he got papers, Tira, they'd just be a temporary exit visa. What happens when he doesn't come back?'

The sick person had to come back; to ensure that they did, the corrupt IMBOD officers never let single or childless people leave, or orphans, or more than one parent. If the person didn't return, then their loved ones would be punished and the whole network would freeze up for at least a year. Everyone knew that.

But Bud was wavering. She flung her arms around his neck, pressed her breasts to his chest, breathed in his ear.

'We get a death certificate from Asfar. We say he didn't make it. I can arrange that, honest. Please, Bud. Please do it for me. I'll be so grateful, you won't know what hit you.'

She squirmed against his warm bulk, nibbled his neck. He placed his hands on the small of her back, slid them down to her bottom, cupped her cheeks and squeezed hard.

'Daddy has to think about it, Tira.'

'I know.' It was time for her baby voice. 'And Tira has to be a very, very good little girl.' She reached down and found his erection with her hand. Fortunately, Bud never took long.

SUMMER RE 99

Misted Silver

Burnt Orange
Desert Red
Burnt Orange
Shadow Blue
Burnt Orange

Misted Silver

The Ashfields
15.06.99

Her blood had a will of its own. It obeyed gravity, but to its own capricious rhythms. Sometimes a scarlet clot escaped the tankini and crawled down her leg like a slug. Sometimes she seeped in her sleep, and woke to find her upper thighs damp and mottled with crimson womb-shadows. Sometimes black waves gushed from her and splattered on the floor of her cell. Other times she bent in cramped agony, gripping her stomach through the breastplate before catching her breath and soaking her hands in the pool of moon wine saturating her bed.

For the blood, flowing again after the removal of her hormone implant, was a libation, the pain in her gut as necessary and trifling a cost to pay as a smashed glass at a wedding. Far from the ordeal she had been dreading, Astra's first menstrual period in fifteen years was a vibrant reminder of her fertility of spirit, and she relished its rich shade in her earthy palette of protest. For two months she had smeared the basalt bricks of her cell with her own shit. Now she slathered her blood over the wallscreen, veiling Vultura's sour face not with the prisoners' demands, as Cora had ordered, but a palimpsest of her dreams. MOONLIGHT. COOL BREEZES. HOKMA FOREVER. ONE-LAND. A fresh red rush of blood-words, scarlet in the harsh light of the screen, the brightest colour she'd seen for years, a colour that set her tankini on fire and bathed her skin in an almost erotic glow. If the guards didn't immediately rush into her cell to clean the wallscreen, the bloodwords dried soil-brown, shedding the warm autumnal ambience of a forest hut. The bloodwords didn't stop the stink of piss and shit from burrowing into her nostrils, the itchy rash from spreading beneath her tankini, or the maggots from writhing in the corners of her cell. The blood-words made the guards beat her even harder, but they balanced these outrages, somehow, with another order of reality. Cross-legged on her bed, Astra could sit staring at them for hours.

Which was good because, except for when the guards dragged her down the hallway to the toilets to scrub her raw, she wasn't going anywhere. There were no dining-hall meals any longer, or workshifts, no mopping or sewing. Her life had shrunk to a small, hard cube of her own body's making, its floor wet with her own yellow waters, its walls rough with her own flaking excrement. Around those walls, like the wind she hadn't felt on her face for over twelve years, keened the cries of her comrades, howls of pain, outbursts of defiance, croons of comfort that came and went, sometimes so loud she thought she would float away on a sea of urine with that screaming wind in her sails. If only there were dry land beyond that sea – a person might be able to get used to the smell of her own unwashed body, but Astra now knew that you never got used to the stench of rotting shit and stale piss. Though she wore masks made of strips torn from her sheet, still every so often it would catch her off guard: her mouth would water, stomach turn, throat burn, and then the ripe scent of vomit would mingle with the perfume of the protest she hadn't wanted to join but now couldn't stop, not until its bitter end. Though the longer it went on, the more she thought there would be no end to the protest: that the end of the world would come first. That this was how Istar wanted her to depart from life, taking leave of her body from the dark heart of its powerful cycles of waste and decay, a death ordained by the Prophecy. *She will fly to the ashlands and bury herself in the earth.* She could accept that. It made sense. If dying this way, entombed in her own blood and shit, was a punishment, she deserved it for her failure to inspire the world to heed Earth's message. And if it was a reward for her service to the Old Ones, if she would arise in a placeless place, far beyond the walls of the material world, then, like a scarab beetle hatching its young in a dunghill, she would try and find beauty and purpose in her interment.

But then, two days after her period had finally trickled to a halt, Lichena and Bircha came barging into the putrid gloom again, not to punch and kick her, or to drag her to the shower room, but to haul her, blinking and gasping, into the yard. Where the bright light and blue sky of a summer's day, the cold air blasting from the vents in the walls and the urgent chatter of her comrades all shocked her back into life.

'Cora. Pallas,' Astra pleaded, her voice claggy with disuse, 'I'm telling you, I *must* have a proper visit with Jasper. There's stuff going on out there I need to know about! We're all here, can't we just vote on it quickly?'

'Please don't shout, Astra. It hurts my ears.' Rosetta winced and rubbed her arms. She looked peaky and green and was shivering in the arctic air blowing from the wall vents.

'C'mere, Honeypot.' Charm nudged Rosetta closer to the centre of the huddle. Astra faced Pallas, whose pale skin was a waxen mask, her lips chapped and blue.

'You can Voice Talk with Jasper,' Pallas said. 'That's how everyone else is communicating with their lawyers.'

'I *do* Voice Talk with him. But I told you already – it's not the *same*.'

'Astra. There is *no question* of a vote on this issue.' Cora's face was peppered with red welts and pus was running from her right eye. Her engine was still thrumming at top speed, though: she kept warm by wagging her finger furiously under Astra's nose. 'We have nearly fucking won this thing and we're not going to crack now. Everyone's got people they want to visit with. This is a collective protest. No special privileges. You know that.'

Astra snorted, sending a steamy cloud of breath into Cora's face. It was a fleeting pleasure, she knew, like the sight of the sky through the yard's grille roof and the reprieve from the foul stink of her cell. The air blowing from the vents smelled of metal piping, so despite their shitty hair, shitty tankinis and shitty skin, the women around her just *looked* awful. After so long in solitude, everyone was terribly thin: shoulder blades sawing the air above their breastplates, thighs bowed like dried wishbones, knees gnarled, and no wonder. It was becoming so disgusting to eat they were practically starting a hunger strike by default. Yet, although Rosetta was skeletal and ill, Charm bruised and scraped, Pallas scabbed and sallow, Fern ashen and grimy, Cora blotchy and run-down, everyone, except for Rosetta, was grinning, eyes shining, as if scenting victory. Standing in the electrical current of their determination, Astra had to admit to herself that Cora, for all her stubborn refusals, had been right: there was nothing like a protest to boost morale.

It was looking, in fact, as though Cora had been right about a lot of things. Not only had the Traitors' Wing won over the rest of the prison population with their demands for the reinstatement of flesh visits and the introduction of ion chamber conjugal visits, the chaos the dirty protest was causing at Ashfields Max was spreading throughout the whole prison system, stacking the pressure on the Ministry of Penitence and the entire Wheel Meet. Now that Astra was standing blinking in the light, it seemed an almost short campaign. Just two months ago, the Visiting Rights Committee of Ashfields Max had written to the prison Governor and the Minister of Penitence, Tulip Hiltondott, setting out their demands. Until they were met, all the prisoners in the jail had vowed to boycott the ion chambers, and the political prisoners had agreed to also conduct a dirty protest. That vote had been unanimous. Even Rosetta had been committed, if not exactly enthusiastic. After a deep conversation with Charm, who had assured her that true love was not jealous, Rosetta had decided that ion embraces with the Code father of her child were worth suffering for. With the whole

Traitors' Wing united and defiant, unless she wanted no one to ever trust her again, Astra had had little choice but to join in. Everyone had refused to wash their bodies except for teeth and genitals, to use their toilets or allow the guards to clean their cells. Any woman still fitted with a hormonal birth-control implant had demanded its removal. Everyone had agreed to squat by their doors to piss, aiming their urine out into the hall; everyone had sworn to smear their shit, snot, pus, blood and vomit on their cell walls. The women had each protested alone, catching only the occasional glimpse of each other in the hall, struggling bodies in the spotlight of the guards' hostility. For, just as Cora had predicted, Lichena, Bircha and the rest were furious about the repugnant extra tasks they were expected to perform. And now, at last, dragged out into the yard while the guards attacked their cells with hosepipes and mops, the women had snatched a campaign meeting from that fury.

'How much longer do you think it will take, Cora?' Fern asked.

Cora whistled through her teeth. 'Three weeks? A month? Especially if Atourne Max cranks up the pressure. Those men are hardcore and the demonstrations in support of them are getting bigger every day.'

'That's not long, Astra,' Charm said. 'Can't you just hang in there?'

'No. Three weeks is too long to wait. Peat could be serving a life sentence by then!'

'No talking!' a guard yelled from the gate. But her solitary diss-stick wasn't sufficient to enforce the command. The women moved closer together and Charm put her arm around Rosetta, who was picking at a scab on her wrist with a long nail – apparently shit-painting was a cure for nail-biting.

'Don't do that.' Charm pushed her hand away. 'It'll get infected.'

'C'mon, Astra,' Fern growled. 'The Visiting Rights Committee is meeting with the prison Governor tomorrow afternoon. We've forced that concession at last. We can't be seen to be weakening. Don't wreck everything now.'

'I'm not going to *wreck* anything. I just want to exercise my right to see my lawyer!'

Cora's grey eyes flashed, lightning at dusk. 'And what do you think the general population will think, knowing you've been having ion chamber visits? First whiff they get of that, they'll all want exceptions, too, and then bang goes the whole boycott.'

'They don't have to know. We don't have to tell them.'

'You think the guards will keep our little secret for us? What about the national media? What you don't seem to get yet, Astra, is that this isn't about *you*.'

She felt like crying. During the protest decision-making 'daisy chain', a painstaking process of whispers in toilets and hallways, she had argued long and hard for exceptions for lawyers' visits, but most of the women's lawyers did diddly-squat for them and she had lost that vote by a wide margin. She, on the other hand, was the only prisoner on the wing – the only prisoner in all of Is-Land as far as she knew – forbidden to communicate *about* another person, and that meant the others simply didn't know of, let alone understand, her dilemma. Peat's trial was scheduled for the end of the month and so far Muzi hadn't responded to Jasper's request to contact him. The prison censor listened in on all Voice Talk sessions, and she couldn't keep wittering on about Jasper's fucking puppies and the importance of training them to be gentle. She would blow the code, for one thing, but also she couldn't say anything significant to Muzi that way, nothing personal that would touch his heart and persuade him to show mercy on Peat. She needed to talk to Jasper over a secure CONC ion chamber connection. If IMBOD was somehow hacking it, she'd take the punishment, as long as she knew Jasper had received her message and could deliver it to Muzi.

But she couldn't explain any of that to the others. If her tankini mic caught even a hint that she was plotting to say something secret to her lawyer, the prison would have grounds to interrogate her in a neurohospice and scour her memories for contraband. If the neurohospice implant located her plan to contact Muzi, all her prison privileges would be revoked, forever. After the dirty protest ended, she would remain in solitary confinement in all but name, permitted only one group meal a week, not allowed to work any more with the sewing or cleaning teams, and denied access to all non-legal reading material. Now that she was back in the light of day and the thick of things, she knew, with a throb of panic in her gut, that she didn't want to abandon human society. If there was still a chance that human life would extend beyond the next Vernal Equinox, she didn't want to spend hers rotting in her cell. Not for nothing, at least – not for just *thinking* about Muzi.

Pallas put her hand on Astra's neck. 'We need to stay united, Astra,' she murmured. 'Of course you're concerned about your brother. But Jasper will tell you the results of the trial.'

'And you need to stop worrying about Peat,' Cora commanded. 'He made up his own mind to stand trial, and he must have accepted all the possible consequences. You have to let go, Astra. We can't control what other people do and think.'

That was rich, coming from someone who was trying to control her fundamental right to speak to her lawyer. Astra shrugged Pallas' hand off.

'This isn't about me and my family. It's about—' She raised a finger, the symbol for One-Land they'd adopted since what happened to Fern. 'If Peat gets sent to an Asfarian prison, all of Is-Land will want revenge. But if he's set free and speaks in defence of the Non-Landers, it could be the beginning of the end for Is-Land. I have to discuss *strategy* with Jasper.'

It was as close as she could get to the truth. She bit back a mention of Earth's deadline: no one would take that seriously at all.

'We agreed, babe.' Charm shrugged. 'Boycott and dirty protest. We can't start backsliding now.'

'I'm not *backsliding*,' she countered with as much dignity as she could muster, given that her teeth were chattering hard enough to bite off her tongue. 'I'm requesting an emergency exception. For political reasons.' She looked at Rosetta, who was slumped in Charm's arms, her face a rictus grimace. 'And Rosetta's ill. She should be allowed to come off the dirty protest.'

'No,' Rosetta moaned. 'I'm just tired. I'm so tired, Charm. But I can do it. I'm with you all, I am.'

'Astra.' Cora pinched a dewdrop from the tip of her nose. 'I know the news about Peat is unsettling, but there's nothing you can do to influence the outcome of the trial. You'll just have to wait and see what happens. It's what Hokma would have done.'

Astra's face flared. 'How the frack do you know what Hokma would have done?'

Cora raised an eyebrow. 'Hokma, Astra, was the most active campus campaigner in her year at Code College. After Paloma was killed, she practically ran the entire Atourne underground network for two years. If people got caught, though, you had to let go, forget you ever knew them, otherwise the whole network could be exposed. Everyone understood that. No silly risks, no power games or ego trips that could endanger everyone.'

'Hokma didn't do any campaigning when I knew her. She worked on her own. And she took a big risk for me. She even got Samrod to help her.'

Cora's grey eyes glittered. 'She worked with *me*, Astra. And look where trusting Samrod got her.'

Heat flushed through Astra's torso. It was all coming out now. Cora blaming Hokma for her own death. In fact, Cora was blaming Hokma's love of Astra.

'*Trusting Samrod* saved me from the shot. Are you saying you'd rather I was a Sec Gen?'

'Of course not. But she should never have asked Samrod for help. She should have brought you to me, in Atourne. I knew at least three people who could have falsified your records.'

Astra's stomach hurt. Wasn't it enough that Cora was controlling her future? Did she have to also claim jurisdiction over her past? 'Take me to Atourne? How would she explain that to Nimma and Klor?'

'By lying! She lied better than anyone I knew!'

Pallas touched Cora's wrist. 'All the mothers in here have taken risks for their children, Cora. And Samrod was Hokma's brother. But Astra, Cora's right about the protest. We can't start the whole daisy chain again for one non-essential question. We've just about got the whole prison on our side now and we can't risk fragmenting our position.'

Astra clasped her hands on the top of her head, craned her neck and stared up at the tiny black and blue squares of mesh and sky above them. She couldn't let Cora get to her like this.

'We all want justice for Hokma,' Cora kept on. 'Your INMA case stands an excellent chance of exposing Samrod Blesserson for the murderous rat that he is. We're all behind you. But you need to stand with us, too.'

'We all gotta lump it right now, Astra,' Charm said sympathetically, her chin on Rosetta's head. 'Rosetta stinks like a tropical latrine, but I put up with it coz it's for a good cause.'

'If we win,' Rosetta managed a wan smile, 'we all get some happy time. And if we lose, at least the whole jail is united against the guards again.'

'We're not going to lose, Rosetta.' Charm squeezed her lover's neck. 'And I'm just kidding. You smell like fresh-baked currant buns.'

Cora laughed, a bark of triumph, and her flint eyes struck sparks. 'This protest is exactly what this country needs. Solidarity, one step at a time. Be patient, Astra: we're priming the Gaians for what it will take to live in *One-Land*.'

She mouthed the last word and, around the huddle, the women's eyes shone. Very few had entered the jail believing in One-Land, but after years of abuse from IMBOD, most of them did now.

'*Time*,' the guard yelled. The women hugged, Charm and Rosetta clenched in a kiss, Fern and Sunflower enclosed in a tight embrace. Pallas clasped Cora to her chest, and then Cora turned and reached for Astra, gripping her shoulders with her bony fingers.

'Stay strong, Astra,' she commanded. 'We'll get that fucking uncle of ours, don't worry. We're going to bring the whole stinking Wheel Meet down.'

After two months of breathing piss and shit, it was strange how irritating she found the smell of industrial quantities of vinegar and citric acid. Astra lay on her bunk with her sheet over her mouth and nose, letting her anger course through her. On the wall, Vultura's bald head was sweeping rapidly back and forth, back and forth, until it made her sick to look at, and the clock was remorselessly marching on, not just the seconds and minutes, but the days and the weeks. It was 15.06.99. Nearly three months since Earth's ultimatum, and just over nine months until the Vernal Equinox, and what progress had been made? None whatsoever. Instead, the world was going backwards. Peat was going on trial, and if he was sent to jail it was highly likely that war would break out between Is-Land and Non-Land, a war that would surely involve Asfar. If that happened, other regional conflicts over the globe might ignite, dashing the dream of universal disarmament and provoking the Old Ones to devour humanity. As for the ion chamber campaign, the dirty protest could go on for weeks, even months, giving her no way to contact Muzi in time to help Peat; it could even continue until the end of the Hudna, in which case she was likely to die in here, buried alive in her own shit.

The clean floor and walls were an open invitation to befoul them all over again. She should get up, drink water from the tap, enough to make her piss gallons out into the hall. Instead, she pulled the sheet up over her eyes. Did it even matter if humanity went extinct? The Old Ones weren't important to anyone except her. She understood that now. To Cora, she was Eya and Hokma's daughter, a child playing at being a goddess. To Charm and the others, she was a torture victim, an epileptic survivor of the neurohospice, someone to care about, but basically deluded. Everyone, even her lawyer, was humouring her. She wasn't sure that Jasper was pushing Earth's message any more. When they did speak, he was focused on Peat and the protest: those were the important stories, he said, reminding the world about her and building a campaign to free her at last. But he didn't even seem to think it was crucial for her to communicate properly with Muzi and Peat. Whenever she said she was worried about his new puppies, he replied breezily that they were both fine.

And as for the Old Ones themselves, They had been silent since the start of the protest. Maybe this really was the end. In which case she would be joining Hokma soon. A lump rose in her throat. This wasn't the deal. She had chosen this suffering in order to give her life *meaning*.

Hokma? she soulspoke. *Are you out there? Please come back. I really need to talk to you.*

Nothing. Just the sting of vinegar, making her eyes water. A wave of self-pity flowed through her. Everyone else had somebody. Charm had Rosetta. Fern had Sunflower. Cora had Pallas. All the other women in the yard were at one in their desire to stick to the protest. Why did she have to be the outcast among outcasts?

You are alone, Small One.

The voice was light, a gentle breeze on her skin. Not Hokma. Air. Speaking the cool, undeniable truth.

And you're right as always, Air. She felt a little better already, her cells tingling with a delicate sense of anticipation. Air, detached, unemotional, clinical even, visited when the Old Ones had technical or legal instructions to impart. Air was here and would speak for an hour, imparting philosophy, facts, critical analysis; giving her data to memorise, logical arguments to follow, taking her mind off her wretched isolation.

Good, Air replied evenly. You must be even more alone for your next journey, one that only you can undertake. One you *must* undertake for humanity to survive.

Where had she heard *that* before? Although, coming from Air, it was a surprisingly illogical command. *How can I journey out of here? And how could I possibly be even more alone than I am now?*

Currently, Child, you are at war with yourself. So you are not truly alone: there are always at least two of you battling inside your head. If you can make peace with your-self, you can take your suffering and your solitude to a new level.

That sounds like fun.

It is the path you have chosen. And yet for some reason you now refuse to travel down it.

What does that mean?

A chill shivered over her skin. Learning what I mean, Istarastra, is the purpose of the journey. You must depart now, or you will miss your chance.

Depart now? I don't understand.

We cannot tell you everything. If you cannot deduce your next move for yourself, then your commitment to suffering has failed the test We have set, and humanity does not deserve Our largesse.

My next move? How can I move anywhere?

But Air had disappeared, and she was speaking only to the walls of the prison.

And then her body tingled again, and she knew exactly what she had to do. It was as if a razor blade of light had sliced through the cell, cleanly shaving her mind of its confusion and despair. Sitting on the edge of the bunk, she flipped up her Tablette from her tan-kini, swiped open Voice Talk and dialled.

'Astra?' Jasper sounded surprised but harried, his voice echoey, as if he were pacing down a high corridor in CONC HQ. For a moment, she could smell the coffee in his hand.

'Yes, it's me.'

'Fantastic. I was going to call you today. There's great news. *We got Stonewayson!*'

Blade Stonewayson, the Neo-Puritan Gaian judge with an axe to grind against the Wheel Meet, would be presiding over her final INMA appeal, deciding if she would be allowed to access Hokma's final memories. That *was* probably good news. But good news was irrelevant. She was stepping onto an elevator and moving into a new level of solitude and suffering.

'Jasper.' She cut him off. 'That's great. But listen. I want you to tell someone something for me. I want you to tell him that the sky-god has spoken to me. The sky-god says he must urge the judge in Asfar to show mercy. If he does that, tell him, then when I get out of here I'm coming to find him and we're going to start a camel-racing track togeth—'

'CAW CAW CAW. VIOLATION. VIOLATION. VIOLATION.'

Oh, Vultura was good at her job. The connection with Jasper went dead. The Tablette screen went blank. The wallscreen flashed blinding white and a driving storm of ice-cold water rained down on her from vents in the ceiling she didn't even know existed.

Burnt Orange

Bracelet Valley
20.06.99

Samrod had wanted never to return to Springhill ever again in his life. Except he had to talk to Clay about the Stonewayson situation, and Clay had refused to leave the vile place. 'Everyone wants to *thank* you, darling!' he had crooned. So here Samrod was, out on the restaurant deck eating pastries and summer fruits with that gross idiot Ahn Orson and that abysmal cow Tulip Hiltondott.

'Major Brockbankson told me how you held the line, Samrod. Valiantly, in the face of sustained and savage onslaught from the green-sheathed foe.' Ahn tore the tip off his croissant and dipped it in his glass of bergamot tea. 'I can never repay you.'

Yes, yes you can. You can conquer your odious predilection for beating and fucking young girls and go back home to live on your wilted laurels in Or, he didn't say.

'"The green-sheathed foe". Oh, Ahn.' Tittering like a schoolgirl, the cow batted her lashes at the once-renowned bio-architect turned Sex Gen molester. Didn't she know Ahn Orson was a washed-up wreck, creatively bankrupt, a has-been who no longer even bothered to pretend he was still designing buildings? Face drained, eyes puffy, he was a shadow of the man who'd won all those awards. And who dunked croissants in tea? Samrod repressed a shudder at the sight of the pastry flakes floating like soggy scabs to the bottom of the amber liquid.

'They really are destroying this country.' Ahn shuddered. Even his annoying hissy voice had faded to an insect whine. 'And this Stonewayson business is just awful. I can't believe the courts appointed him to the Ordott appeal. How on earth did that happen, Tulip?'

'It's an outrage,' Hiltondott mooed. 'Internal politics, of course. Pressure applied by the Ministry of Spiritual Development. I must have a word with Stamen about that.'

'Imagine giving Is-Land's biggest traitor a chance of winning access to classified material. I mean' – Ahn flicked his snakelike glance between Clay and Samrod – 'obviously there's nothing to worry about, but she shouldn't even be given the satisfaction of trying!'

Being probed by Ahn Orson was just the start of this new nightmare. Samrod took a peach from the fruit bowl, avoiding Clay's gaze. Fortunately, the cow was still lowing.

'Hokma Blesser should be *erased* from history, all the damage she's caused.' Hiltondott's eyes swelled with indignation. 'Imagine dragging your unsuspecting brother into a plot to betray the nation, and then expecting your lover to keep your filthy secret when he stumbles on it by accident!'

He tried to look humble, but it was difficult when peach juice was running from his knife all over his hands.

'Mind your trousers, darling,' Clay murmured, passing him a napkin. Hiltondott tilted her head as if unspeakably charmed by the gesture.

'How painful it must have been for Ahn and Samrod to make those statements to IMBOD, and what moral courage it took to do so.' She placed her fist between her udders and swung it out over the table. 'I saluted you both at the time, and I do again today. After all you've suffered, I can't bear to see Hokma's little protégée digging away like a thorn in your sides, stirring up utterly discredited rumours!'

Samrod abandoned the peach and, scowling, rubbed his hands with the napkin. Mildly gratifying as it was to hear his traumas with Hokma recognised with such vehemence, the cow was clearly fishing. At the time of Hokma's death, Hiltondott had been the Governor of White Desert Penitentiary; rumours about the circumstances had spread like wildfire throughout the prison system, and whatever Clay said, he was sure the now-Minister had her suspicions.

'Ordott can dig away as much as she likes.' He dabbed at his lips with the napkin. 'There's nothing in the files to worry anyone. They're classified as a matter of policy, not any nefarious necessity.'

In the wake of Hiltondott's sycophantic outburst, Ahn had adopted an air of wounded innocence. 'Astra Ordott belongs in a neurohospice,' he declared. 'She should have stayed in the one *I* had her committed to after her savage and completely gratuitous attack on me.'

Samrod's fingers were still sticky. He reached for his glass and, over the decking, poured some water into his hand.

'Oh for goodness sakes, Samrod!' Clay crowed. 'Just lick them clean! That's what I'd do if I still had my own fingers.'

'We're in company, Clay! I'm not going to slobber all over my hands to amuse you!'

He finished washing, shook his hands dry. Clay smirked. Ahn and Hiltondott exchanged glances. Then the cow trampled on. 'Ahn is absolutely right. Ordott should never have been deported – or allowed to pursue this case. Far be it from me to question IMBOD security policy, Clay, but sometimes I think it would be most expedient to let a certain political prisoner have an eensy-weensy lickle *accident* one day.'

She might be a cow, but she wouldn't be Minister of Penitence in Stamen Magmason's government if she wasn't a ruthless one, a bovine bully with sharp horns. People liked seeing a woman in charge of jails; never mind all this 'penitence' charade, a big mama guard with massive udders running the show made the public feel as though criminals were getting a good spanking.

'Hokma Blesser died of a stroke,' Clay boomed. 'Whatever nasty thoughts she might have been harbouring about her brother or her ex-partner before she popped her clogs are completely irrelevant. Stonewayson's been appointed as a sop to the New Purists, and if he lets Astra Ordott add some more deranged monologues to those already garbling in her head, we will doubtless thank him in the end. We're just waiting for the traitor to beg to be readmitted to a neurohospice, aren't we, Samrod?'

It wasn't that simple and Clay knew it. Why couldn't Ahn and Hiltondott leave so he and Clay could talk properly?

But he knew the drill, and he had to play along. 'Astra Ordott won't be a problem much longer,' he asserted. 'Once the New Gaian Vision rolls out, we won't be bound by these ridiculous CONC regulations any more. Then my niece will find her own memories harvested for INMA's shelves, filed right beside my sister's.'

They all laughed.

'To the New Gaian Vision.' The cow raised her glass of elder-flower pressé. The others solemnly clinked teacups and coffee mugs.

'And to Samrod,' Clay added. 'The brains behind it.'

'Yes, your work is truly extraordinary, Samrod,' Ahn purred. 'The Sec Gens and the Sex Gens. Youthful longevity. The Vision virus. So many breakthrough achievements. People say I'm a genius, but honestly, I don't know how you do it.'

I don't spend my life planning which pre-pubescent girl to electro-cute next, that's how.

'Now, if he'd just enjoy the fruits of his labour.' Chuckling, Clay reached for an apricot.

'Yes, Samrod.' The cow put her hand on his arm. 'Why don't you come and join us today? This new model is absolutely scrumptious. Somehow you've struck the most exquisite balance between resist-ance, compliance and sheer bloody *gratitude*.'

'I had no hand in the design of the current Springhill generation,' he corrected her over the laughter of the others. 'Delegating, Ahn. That's how it's done – in architecture, too, I am sure. And long hours. Thank you, Tulip, but I won't indulge. I have work to do.'

Ahn twirled a strawberry between his fingers. 'Well, don't

completely neglect us in favour of the geriatrics, Samrod. Even the freshest young things grow stale. We always stand in need of your innovations.'

Tulip stretched. 'Oh my. All this talk of fresh young things is rather *affecting*, wouldn't you say, Clay?'

'You go, dear.' Clay took a croissant from the basket. 'With Ahn. I'll join you later.'

Ahn ate the strawberry, dropped the crown on his plate and got up. 'Yes, must make the most of the weekend. It's so much more stimulating with more people here.'

'All work and no play, Samrod!' the cow mooed, pushing her chair back in so a pendulous breast grazed his shoulder. 'Tell him, Clay!'

Holding the pastry in one mechatronic hand, Clay filleted it expertly with his other thumb. 'Oh, I do, Tulip, I do!'

Samrod waited until they were out of earshot.

'Do you have to, Clay?'

'What?' Clay checked the marmalade pot.

'Collude in this offensive suggestion that I am somehow sexually repressed.'

'Oh, Samrod.' He dolloped a spoonful of marmalade on his croissant. 'I'm just waiting for you to dye those trousers green. Look, Ahn is right.'

Blood rose to Samrod's cheeks. 'Ahn Orson is not *right* about anything. Ahn Orson nearly destroyed us!'

Clay put his pastry down and regarded him gravely. 'It transpires that Ahn has been going through a very difficult time lately. You haven't been here. You don't know about his former partner.'

'Congruence?' He cast his mind back to the girl – she had just been a girl when Ahn met her, as he recalled. 'They've not been involved for years. She quickly became far too old for him, didn't she!'

'Actually, Samrod, they were very close.' Clay adopted a reproving tone. 'But over the last few years she fell ill. Some kind of chronic fatigue, depression, bouts of hysteria. Mysterious business, your sort of thing. But she wouldn't accept help. Ahn tried to get her to see you, he told us, but she pushed him away.'

Somehow Clay was making it sound as though *he* had refused to see the woman. 'So he turned his back on her and started coming here for eensy-weensy lickle underage *fuck* parties. Charming!'

'No, Samrod. This spring she committed suicide. That's tragic enough. But to make things worse, she left behind a deathbed confession in her suicide note, telling her Shelter parents that she had set a fire in her teens, a fire that killed two of her peers.' It was the kind of gossip that Clay normally told with gusto, but his tone remained solemn, with a note of reproach. 'There was a love triangle, the usual sort of thing that bedevilled people before the Sec Gen era, and her rival was canoodling with her young man under a table in a common room. In the note, Congruence claimed she didn't mean to hurt them, just smoke them out, but the fire took hold of the tablecloths and that was that. She said she'd wanted to confess at the time, but she went rigid with fear and locked all the feelings up inside her.' Clay paused, and for a moment he sounded almost baffled, an unusual state for him. 'She said that she felt she deserved to die young.'

Samrod vaguely remembered the fire. More vivid was the memory that flashed up of Clay in the burns unit. He winced. 'It's tragic, as you say, Clay. But what on earth does it have to do with Ahn's complete lack of self-control?'

'Come on, Samrod. Show some sympathy. The man's rattled: he's learned that he never knew his own partner, who has now violently abandoned him. And on top of his shock, grief and anger, he feels persecuted. The woman's confession upset everyone in Or, and some of them blame him. They think perhaps he knew about the fire and took advantage of her distress to get involved with her before she was of age.'

Samrod's exasperation was building again. 'Well, they're clearly thinking straight, unlike some people around here. Frankly, we should have learned from Ahn's relationship with Congruence, which I have no doubt began when she was underage and was conducted under her parents' noses. We should have realised the man has no respect for authority and is addicted to risk and banned him from ever setting foot in this place.'

Clay's eyes sparked. This was the kind of debate he thrived on. 'Ahn's a healthy Alpha male, Samrod. He seizes what he wants out of life, empties the cherry bowl, then comes back for more. He took those girls out of bounds because that is precisely the essence of desire: the need to transgress. We here at Springhill must cater to that need by constantly transgressing our own boundaries. We can't have our guests feeling bored, Samrod.'

That took the croissant, it really did. 'Are you suggesting it's somehow *my* fuddy-duddy fault that Ahn broke practically the only rule this place has, a rule fundamental to the security of everyone here?'

'No, no, no, no, *no*. I am saying that I understand why he broke it, and as the Director of Springhill, I see it as my duty to ensure no one is ever tempted to do so again. Ahn is right, Samrod, when he says we must *innovate*.'

Clay raised an eyebrow. Samrod snorted. 'I'm working on two other major projects, Clay. And anyway, how much further can I push the Sex Gens? There are blind ones and limbless ones and babies pumped with growth hormones to reach the size of three year olds while still looking like infants. There are children engineered to die before puberty and stunted amnesiacs who will live in a state of confusion for decades. There are multi-orifice models, for officers returning from Zabaria. There are even pregnant children eagerly offering up their newborns into service. The Sex Gens already cater for every perversity under the sun!'

Clay was silent for a moment. 'You think you can't hurt me, Samrod. But you can.'

'Oh, for Gaia's sake, Clay. I'm not some naïve young officer with goo-goo eyes for you. Don't try and play me!'

Clay tossed his napkin on his table. 'I mean it, Samrod. You created the Sex Gens for me, to help me recover my zest for life. And now that I'm well, you spit all over the project, call me a pervert for enjoying activities human beings have indulged in since time immemorial. With one crucial difference.' Noble and wounded, he gazed out over the lake. 'The Sex Gens enjoy what we do to them. You don't understand that because you never take part in our games. I feel misjudged, Samrod. Ridiculed and misjudged and held in contempt by a man I love. And the worst thing about it,' Clay turned back to Samrod, his brow furrowed, eyes gleaming, 'is that you're so *unhappy*. When you should be proud and fulfilled, enjoying the prime of your life!'

Consummate Clay. Samrod's anger drained away. Clay's love wasn't like other people's love. It didn't manifest as cosy concern, or anxiety, or an obsessive desire to please. It was bedrock love: hard and enduring. He gazed out over the trees to the lake.

'Physical violence doesn't turn me on, Clay,' he said at last. 'It's crude. So obvious. Psychosexually, I prefer mental anguish. That's why I've stayed by your side all these years.'

'I know that, darling.' Clay reached across the table and placed his heavy hand over Samrod's. 'But you're taking your masochism too far. Don't hate me. Come with me to the woods and watch today. There'll be no hitting, I promise. No blood. It's the innocence I love about them, that's what keeps me young, Samrod, their innocence.' Clay lowered his voice, squeezed Samrod's fingers. 'Sweetheart. This new group of toddlers call me their *teddy bear*. When I take off my limbs and they clamber all over my stumps, they call me teddy. It makes me cry, every time.'

A large bird floated over the bushes. Its giant wingspan made him think of the albatross, though of course it wasn't a seabird but one of the storks the Bracelet Valley Council had introduced last year. He itched to take his binoculars out. Instead, he slid his hand up Clay's arm, to the seamed flesh above the elbow, gripped it hard, feeling the scars from the skin grafts ridged under his palm, the muscle solid beneath.

'Thank you for telling me that, Clay. I'm glad you've found healing here. That's the goal of all my work, psychological healing. But I can imagine your games with the Sex Gens. I don't have to watch.'

'*Do* imagine them, darling.' Clay's voice was thick with desire, the fresh-baked-bread scent of his breath as potent as the first time Samrod had ever leaned in for a kiss. 'Think about them, all day and all night. And if you get aroused, text me, any time, and I'll come, wherever I am.'

Samrod pulled away. 'Thank you, Clay. As I said, I have work to do, but I'll bear it in mind.'

It was the closest he had ever come to seeing Clay crestfallen. Just a flicker of disappointment, quickly smoothed over by a dignified, long-suffering mien. 'Have it your way, darling.' Clay popped the last piece of croissant in his mouth, washed it down with his coffee, brushed the flakes from the table into his palm and flung them over the balcony into the bushes.

Pastries and marmalade. Crumbs for the birds. A day of pleasure ahead. For a moment, Samrod felt a pang of regret. Why couldn't he sleep with Clay again?

Because he simply couldn't, that was why. It wasn't Clay's changed body. They had tested his new penis together a decade ago, to mutual satisfaction, and at that time Clay's stumps had aroused a wellspring of compassion in Samrod's heart that had made their sex the tenderest it had ever been. The problem was his sense that Clay, by immersing himself completely in Springhill, had travelled so far away from him that, sexually, he now would only ever be a visitor, from a land Samrod couldn't bear to be soiled by, not by so much as a drop of peach juice on his trousers.

'I'm sorry, Clay,' he said. 'I didn't mean to sound callous. I'm just tense. This Stonewayson decision. It's unsettled me. And it should concern you, too.'

Clay got up. 'I know, darling. You are uber-conscientious. That's one of the things I love about you.' He leaned over, took Samrod's head in his hands and planted a kiss on his forehead. 'But please don't disparage your work on the Sex Gens any more. You've done a great thing here. History will thank you, not just me.'

After Clay left, he sat for a long time with his binoculars, watching the storks glide through the sky, devoted parents carrying nest-sticks in their long, rude beaks over the glittering lake.

Desert Red

Asfar

22.06.99

'In short,' the professor concluded, his scratchy voice echoing from the dome of the lecture hall, 'the Old Ones' messages require humanity to thoroughly re-envision our relationship with our natural environment. The "pact with Metal" refers not simply to our love of jewellery or our over-reliance on toxic industrial processes. The pact is an ontological one, the very ground of our historical conception of technology. Since the dawn of civilisation, human beings have manipulated nature for materialist ends, privileging this utilitarian attitude toward the planet and its creatures above other vital modes of appreciation, most particularly empathy, humility and wonder. Truly breaking the pact with Metal, as the Old Ones demand, will require us to bring our rational capabilities and physical requirements back into balance with our emotional and spiritual needs.'

The professor paused, giving Suen's earbuds time to tell him that, 'On the left side of the slide is an image of Ibn Sina, a man with a beard.'

'To accomplish this,' the professor continued, 'the Institute of Metaphysical Engineering fosters a return to the value our ancestors placed on the figure of the polymath. Intellectual versatility is the first pillar of our pedagogy. As well as physics, philosophy and information technology, students are expected to study across a wide range of subjects including poetry, pottery, music, dance, horticulture, psychology and theology. All these disciplines will be taught in a manner intended to help each student acquire deeper self-knowledge and healthier self-disregard.'

As some students laughed, the earbuds informed Suen that: 'An image of the Grand Mosque in Asfar City has appeared in the middle of the slide.' He summoned the mosque to his mind, its deep pile carpets and crystal-clear acoustics, an airy open space in which words sounded like delicate bells.

'Allied to this vision, and the central pillar of the Institute's mission, is the Mujaddid's radical commitment to inclusivity. Within the land of Asfar, the Mujaddid has decreed, submission to god means the acceptance and worship of the Oneness-of-the-Many. Believers in all faiths and none are welcome in our land and in the Institute – as long as they, too, reject the false idols of money, beauty, youth, political power and fame, and uphold our respect for the Other and for the Beyond-Human world. Finally . . .'

The professor paused again for the audio description: 'On the right-hand side of the screen has appeared an image of a woman in a hijab and modest swimming costume, standing on a diving platform.'

'. . . the Institute's third pillar is creativity. Knowledge is not enough. To truly excel at the arts and sciences, one must be prepared to dive into the unknown, to experiment, to take risks, to occasionally fail. We will encourage such explorations, and nowhere more so than in our enthusiastic response to the challenge laid down by the Mujaddid's Post-Metal Communications Prize. On this auspicious day, when we welcome a new cohort of students, it is my great pleasure to announce that the Institute will hereby be dedicating itself to solving the problem that the Old Ones have set us, and meeting the deadline They have set. Every day we will hold an open forum on the question, sharing ideas and establishing teams of researchers to develop and test non-metal-based information technology. Should the Mujaddid's prize be won by members of the Institute, the award money will be used to fund travel scholarships for the key researchers, enabling them both to develop their expertise abroad and to take the new technology to all corners of the globe. Students! Let us begin. Tell me your answers to the Old Ones' question. How would you develop a metal-free communications device that does not force human beings to relinquish the convenience of instant messaging or ordering a kebab while riding side-saddle on the back of a motorcycle?'

The other students tittered again. Suen's fingers flew over his Braille keyboard, taking note of the three pillars, and the challenge the professor had set. The sun from the skylights warmed his hands; the scent of jasmine rose from his Mapvest. No ideas sprang to his mind; he felt awed still, wished he could sit forever on the polished wooden bench of this hallowed hall, photosynthesising like a plant the wisdom of his elders.

'Yes – you in the front row,' the professor demanded, and a young woman's voice rose in the hall.

'Before Tablettes, before telephones, before letters and writing even, people communicated through their dreams. We need to learn how to harness our inherent powers of telepathy. In Shiimti they've been working on this skill for many years: we should invite the Zardusht here to speak.'

'The Zardusht does not travel or use Flock-Talk. But extending an invitation to one of her colleagues is certainly possible . . . Mona, is that right? Developer of a lunar-powered self-correcting moon-dial, as I recall.'

'Yes. That's me.'

'Good. Anyone else? Problems with Mona's suggestion? Other ideas? You – yes, you in the back.'

'All the evidence for telepathy suggests it's a skill, like singing.' Behind Suen, a young man challenged Mona. 'It's undemocratic tech. Not everyone can do it. Even if psychic phones were possible, we'd be creating a new elite.'

The discussion went on, some people defending Mona, others raising more objections. Suen's face flared. Why wasn't he speaking? How could he go home and tell his family he'd remained silent during the very first lecture? An idea came to him, a vague one. He lifted his hand halfway. If the professor didn't see it, then at least he could tell them he'd tried.

'The young man in the centre, wearing the plant jacket. Suen, correct? Inventor of the haptic, phototropic, hydroponic Mapvest, which uses living, colour-sensitised plant fabric to guide visually impaired wearers through physical environments. If there were a prize for entry projects, I think we can all agree Suen would have been a strong contender.'

He blushed so violently he was afraid he'd trigger a seizure in the plants. But he found his tongue and heard himself say, 'I agree with Mona. Plants communicate through their roots. The roots of human beings are our ancestors. Our ancestors, like all indigenous cultures, communicated through dreams, so perhaps telepathy isn't a rare skill, but a neglected human capacity.' He was warming up now and the ideas flowed. 'Metal tech is like sight – very convenient – but the problem is, people become over-reliant on it. Look back at the Old World: as soon as writing emerged, people stopped relying on their memories and the culture of the druids and bards disappeared. When Tablettes were invented, people outsourced their minds altogether! We've relied on mechanical and electronic devices for so long, we've forgotten how to access different levels of our conscious-ness. But human neurochemistry hasn't changed. Perhaps, if we try, like Istarastra has done, and like Yosef did in the Mujaddid's Holy Book, we can all re-learn how to communicate through our dreams.'

'Thank you, Suen. A most bio-theological contribution. Well, it looks like we're agreed, then. The next guest speaker at the Institute will be a dream voyager from Shiimti. The sceptics among you will have a chance to hone your arguments against a specialist in the field. Thank you all for your attention and enjoy your classes. I'll see you next week.'

He had spoken. On his first day at the Institute. He had made a bio-theological contribution to a cohort discussion, and afterwards

Mona and her friend Cyrus invited him for tea in the lunar garden. Over mint infusions, Mona described her moondial, with its mobile gnomon and lunar batteries, in elegant detail and Cyrus passed around his Calmcap, a temperature-variant massage skullcap that helped alter the wearer's brainwaves, which Suen tried on but Mona didn't, because, she said, her hijab kept her calm. Then both his new friends admired the Mapvest. Mona slightly inclined to smell the jasmine he'd threaded through the reeds, so that he caught a whiff of the rosewater scent she was wearing, and Cyrus asked if he could touch the water-tubing, the youth's hands tugging at Suen's waist sending an unexpected jolt through his stomach.

'How does it work?' Mona asked. In a tumbling rush, he explained, elated by the knowledge that, unlike his family, his new friends would *understand*: how he'd crossbred reeds with algae to increase their colour sensitivity then planted them in hydroponic tubing, putting phototropic hormones in the water to enhance that sensitivity so the reeds reacted instantly to anything with a colour that came within a metre of their blades. After much experimentation, he'd arrived at a modified alarm reflex, triggered in the roots but activated in the tips, so the longer reeds, woven up his front, over his shoulders and down his back, could detect obstacles in front of him, but direct him from behind. It couldn't help him walk through a glass sculpture garden or avoid anything barrelling fast, but the Mapvest made negotiating an ordinary street or building like . . . moving through a dream, he told Mona and Cyrus: after a while, your body just reacted automatically, leaving your mind free to wander elsewhere.

'Wow, cool,' Cyrus said. 'It must be like being hugged all the time.'

Then it was time to go home and he walked to the bus stop with Cyrus in a haze of street dust and happiness, the Mapvest steering him like a hand on his back with its gentle pressure and heat, the tendrils on his chest warning him when to stop.

'It's such an innovation, on so many levels,' Cyrus enthused. 'I bet there are psychological applications. Let's talk. On a Tablette for now.' Then he gave Suen his number and hopped on his bus.

It was an interesting idea. Waiting in the dusty shelter and sitting on his own rumbling bus, Suen considered it. Yes, perhaps the hormones in the water could be altered so that the plants could detect pheromones. They *could* hug you when you felt lonely . . . warn you about strangers approaching with hostile intent . . . or let you know if someone was attracted to you . . .

'I'm home!' he yelled as he barged into the kitchen, fishing in his pocket for his Tablette. He stopped short of the patio doors. The hint of a strong smell was hanging in the room, musty and stale and masculine. 'Muzi?'

'Turns out it was Muzi, yes, under all that dirt,' his mother commented archly.

'He's been travelling for days,' his aunt retorted. 'Are you sure you don't want a nap, son?'

'Peace, Suen.' His cousin's voice was sticky, as if from years of disuse. 'They told me you were at school. Why don't you show me your plants?'

They went out onto the rooftop patio together. Suen washed his hands and feet for World Worship and left the tap running.

'I'm okay, cousin. I just had a shower. And Ama gave me some of your clothes.'

Suen turned off the tap and took his cousin to his little greenhouse. Muzi admired his plants and the Mapvest, and then the *azan* sounded. They sat in silence in the sun, their backs against the balcony wall. Now he was close to Muzi he could smell Habat's olive oil soap. But he didn't think Muzi had washed his hair.

Beneath them, the city revved to life again. 'In the desert it's always World Worship,' Muzi said.

There was a long pause. 'Do you hate the Sec Gen?' Suen asked.

'No.'

He felt like cheering. Everything was going to be okay. 'Can you

talk to my mother?' he asked. 'She wants to demand a harsh punishment. But the rest of us are going to ask for mercy. Like Astra asked
us to.'

He waited. So long that, if he hadn't been with Muzi, he would
have thought the other person had stolen away for a joke. He was
getting used to his cousin's scent of baked earth and soap, soured by
the fragrance of a billy goat in a pen.

'Did you get Astra's messages?' Suen asked at last. 'The lawyer
said she was being punished for sending the second one.'

That was all he knew. Only Habat had read the lawyer's two
emails for Muzi. Though Nanshe had complained about the expense
and the risk, his aunt had put them on memory sticks and taken
them to the Owleon station in the outskirts of the city.

'I got the first Owleon. Then I left the camp. Ama showed me the
second message today. You don't have to worry about Astra, Suen.
She can't be punished.' Muzi spoke slowly, as if his words were echoes
of thoughts he'd had somewhere else, ages ago, in a different dimen-
sion. 'It doesn't matter what happens to her: the Old Ones are inside
her and They give her strength. Like the gods give us all strength, but
more so. You should understand. They gave you extra strength, too.'

It was more than Suen had ever heard Muzi say in one go. And
he didn't understand it. 'But I'm free. She's in an IMBOD jail,' he
said. 'She can't go anywhere. She's not even allowed to smell a
flower. And the Gaians hate her. The Old Ones are just in her head.
They can't be protecting her from the guards.'

'She's Istar. The guards mean nothing to her. None of us mean
anything real to her. She's not here for us.' Muzi spoke flatly now, as
if stating an obvious truth. 'She's here for the Old Ones. And even
she doesn't understand what that means.'

He didn't understand Muzi, he realised. All he really knew about
his cousin was that his mother said Muzi had completely changed
since the war, from a spring afternoon into a winter's night. Was he
really saying now that he wouldn't help save Peat Orson?

'But her message is clear, isn't it? She's asking us to help humanity survive. If we send her brother to jail, Is-Land will rise against us and war might break out. Then the Old Ones will punish us. But it doesn't have to be that way. I want to help solve the Tab-lette problem, so we can meet all of the Old Ones' demands by the spring equinox. Don't you want that too?

There was another very long pause. 'The Old Ones didn't ask us to help free the Sec Gen,' Muzi said at last, again in that ancient, distant tone. 'Astra did. In her second message she said that she spoke to the sky-god, but really she misunderstood Him and just used His words to say what she wanted. When I was in the desert, I spoke to all the gods and they told me there are different ways to show mercy. I will do their will in the court and Astra will thank me one day.'

Suen still didn't get it. 'You mean you're not going to ask the judge to set Peat Orson free?'

'I mean I'm going to do what the gods tell me to do, not what Astra says I should.'

Muzi, as far as Suen knew, had never taken another partner. He'd always assumed that deep down, Muzi still loved Astra. 'She's still your wife,' he said, puzzled. 'Don't you want to make her happy?'

Thinking about that seemed to cost Muzi some effort. His sour scent deepened. 'People believe that you marry someone to make them happy,' he said at last. 'But you don't. You get married to help each other grow.'

Suen didn't know how to reply to that. He had memories of his parents fighting, his father drinking and his mother nagging; of Muzi's parents, in contrast, laughing and stealing kisses when they thought no one was watching. But his father and uncle were gone with his sight, and he didn't know what a marriage was for. You'd think his mother would be happy now his father was dead, and his aunt would be grief-stricken forever, but it was the other way around. Maybe nothing could make his mother happy; maybe it was true that she'd driven his father to drink. Maybe Habat's mar-riage had been strong because she was naturally a happy person.

'But Peat Orson's her brother. Aren't you even going to explain your decision to her?'

Muzi gripped his arm. 'I'm going to do the right thing, cousin. And the world won't end. You have to win a prize and finish your studies.'

'Dinner, boys,' Nanshe called over the patio.

Muzi released him, grunted softly. 'Tell them I'm not hungry. I'm going to sleep out here.'

Suen got up, uncertain. His Tablette, still on silent from the lecture, vibrated in his pocket. Letting it ring, he walked back to the kitchen, leaving his cousin to steep in his great half-washed mystery.

Burnt Orange

Atourne
26.06.99

Super-Helpless Sex Gen: Pre-order Now! This new model will take tactility and submission to the next level. Lacking sight, hearing, taste and smell, the entirety of the child's sensual experience will be focused on its skin and genitalia. Engineered with varying levels of intelligence and mobility, fully house trained and maintained for you at Springhill when needed, this model will be capable of learning haptic language skills sufficient to communicate with their primary adult and can be kept at home with little more care than an old cat. Natural mortality will vary according to consumer demand. Please place orders now, stating all preferred characteristics.

Samrod deleted the email and shut the screen down. Outside in the college courtyard, the fountain splashed, and skyclad and green-robed figures sat reading in the morning light. Inside his office, a veil of darkness had descended. What was Clay thinking? The utterly repulsive nature of the new model aside, letting people keep a Sex Gen at home was suicidal insanity. His chest hurt.

There was a knock at the door. He jumped. A figure in green robes, a man, stood outside the wall window.

Go away.

But the man could see him, too. He couldn't pretend he wasn't in. He got up and opened the door to a middle-aged man, a nonentity with sapless features and thinning blond hair, wearing those ghastly green robes. A New Purist, someone without an idea of his own in his head, a mature student or postgraduate researcher; someone who should have emailed first, made an appointment.

'Yes,' he snapped.

'Doctor Blesserson.' The man flashed his Tablette. 'I'm Harald Silverstreamson, National Prosecutor, from Justice Blade Stonewayson's office. Campus reception told me you were in. Can we go somewhere quiet for a chat?'

Samrod stared at the Tablette and back at the man's bland face. His stomach churned.

'Yes. All right. Yes.'

They walked off campus a couple of blocks, to the wildflower meadow in Atourne Park, where they sat on a bench beneath a pear tree, out of earshot of everyone except whoever was listening in Stonewayson's office. Silverstreamson had strongly suggested that Samrod, for his own protection, leave his Tablette behind, but doubtless his own device was recording everything they said.

'This is rather an unorthodox visit, is it not?' Samrod enquired, with an effort at dignity. 'Surely you should be communicating with me through my lawyer?'

It was a meaningless preamble and Silverstreamson brushed it aside.

'We'll involve your lawyer at a later stage. I'm here to offer you a deal, Doctor. I wouldn't refuse it if I were you.'

'A deal? How kind,' he murmured. 'But I don't need any green trousers, thank you. I'm quite happy with white.'

'I'm speaking of a legal offer. Direct from Blade Stonewayson.'

'Indeed?' He mastered another stomach cramp. 'Look, Silverstreamson, pleasant as it is to take the air with you, I'm a busy man. Perhaps you might get to the point?'

'Of course.' The man paused, gazing out over the park. His skin was impossibly smooth, with a glowing tone: he looked like a butterscotch.

Get on with it, Samrod's stomach panged.

'Last week, our office received a call from a woman using a public call box in Bracelet Valley,' the man said at last. 'She didn't want to give her name, but she made some significant claims regarding serious crimes occurring at Springhill Retreat, including an eyewitness account of a meeting she had attended with you. The woman was very distressed. She hastened to say that she was breaking confidentiality by calling us, which she was doing without the knowledge of the rest of her community, but she felt she had to let us know about a horrific incident involving a minor – an act of physical and sexual abuse that took place recently on public land near her home.'

In the distance, picnickers were melting in a heat haze. A dog ran barking through the meadow. Samrod was immobilised. But now it was actually occurring, that which he had feared for years, the trap opening up underfoot, all his weight bearing down into it . . . he learned that a man suspended above a pit of alligators could, by sheer dint of will, walk on air. 'How curious,' he remarked lightly, 'that you would take as Gaia's gospel the word of an anonymous caller.'

'As it happens,' Silverstreamson went on in his smooth toffee way, 'the woman's statement, shocking as it was, did not come as a surprise to our office. Rather, her call confirmed suspicions Blade has had for some time about the true nature of the activities at Springhill. Doctor Blesserson, our office has nearly all the evidence we need, not only to send you, Clay Odinson and Ahn Orson to prison for a very long time, but also to topple Magmason and his entire regime. I think you'll find that the public's appetite for industrial-scale child sex abuse is pretty small. I'll be seeking life terms for all of you. Unless, of course, Doctor, you would like to co-operate with the investigation. In which case, Blade would be pleased to offer you immunity from prosecution.'

The picnickers had practically disappeared in the warped air.

The dog barked and barked. *Nearly all the evidence we need.* Silver-streamson was fishing. And Samrod was no salmon farm. This woman, someone at that horrendous meeting, breaking confidentiality at the risk of sabotaging her community's relationship with IMBOD; she could be dealt with. He drew himself up. 'Please forgive me – Harald, is it? – if I am rendered momentarily speechless. Springhill is a private retreat for this country's hardest working politicians and legal professionals. I am there rarely, and when I am, I do not mingle with local communities. I think *you'll* find that spurious and self-serving attempts to trump up charges against Stamen Magmason in aid of a political coup will be met with stiff resistance by the Wheel Meet and the general population. This country is at war, you know. A little loyalty would go a long way.'

'I'm fully aware of Is-Land's current geopolitical situation, Doctor. I also know that your work on longevity is considered essential to Is-Land's survival. But Is-Land will be healthier when it has rid itself of a government whose true interests lie in committing acts of sexual brutality against children. We are aware that you spend very little time in Springhill these days; quite curious considering that you used to be up there nearly every weekend. That's partly why we're giving you this choice. You can wait for us to gather decisive evidence against you and your cronies, or you can testify against them, end their unspeakable practices and continue with the work you really want to do.'

A figure in the park stood up and whistled. Samrod watched the dog bound back to the picnickers. As the animal disappeared, the grass near the path began to wave. A child was running towards them, a small girl in a flapcap, brandishing a toy. He began to feel profoundly irritated.

'I don't have to visit Springhill often to know that nothing sexual is going on there apart from some innocent Gaia play in the woods, between consenting adults. This is a ludicrous effort at blackmail based on pure fabrication. A nameless woman claiming she's met me? You think any court in the land will fall for that?'

'I understand, Samrod.' The man smoothed his robe over his knee. 'You did a deal with the community, you thought you were safe and now you need time to put pressure on them to flush out the whistleblower. But even if you succeed at that task, Doctor, you will need our help to survive the Astra Ordott case. Blade has reviewed the Hokma Blesser files. He was surprised to discover enough evidence to charge you with conspiracy to murder and obstruction of justice, which would send you away for, oh, probably ten years. I expect, considering your influential friends, you could get that reduced, and early parole, but still, the trial and any jail time would not be a pleasant experience.'

There was a roaring in his ears. His body was filmed with sweat. He was running and running, against a headwind, getting nowhere, just slipping down, down, as reptile jaws snapped beneath him. But instinct was a marvellous thing. Although his heart was hammering so hard he thought it would explode, he ran on, kicking out at that smug, tanned face, those sickly green robes. 'I'm terribly sorry,' he announced. 'I've had enough of this game. You really will have to speak to my lawyer. Much as I would like to defend myself against yet another set of crass accusations, you know perfectly well that I cannot discuss my sister's tragic, unexpected stroke with you. Hokma's twisted fantasies about me, her groundless suspicions, are, like all traitors' memories, classified information. Publishing them would undermine national security. The Wheel Meet was fully in agreement on that point. And it is my hope that Stonewayson will uphold that contract with the public trust.'

He should have got up and stalked off. But he was glued to the bench. He couldn't leave without knowing exactly what cards Silverstreamson held up his green sleeve. And Silverstreamson knew that. The man smiled calmly.

'The public deserves to know that traitors have been dealt with to the full extent of the law. Our office maintains that Hokma Blesser should have gone to trial. IMBOD had good evidence against her and we needed to know more about her network. Instead, she ended up dead in her cell, conveniently unable, as her memory probe reveals, to tell the courts that you helped Astra Ordott avoid the Security Shot. A terrible thing, to kill your own sister, but I do understand that her evidence about your complicity in her treason would have been rather a blot on your professional record.'

'Kill my sister?' he spluttered. 'I never laid a *finger* on my sister. I never even visited her in jail.'

'No, you were too much of a coward to do the job yourself. Instead, you sent Clay Odinson into her cell. And Clay just can't help himself, can he? Really, we were surprised at how telling the conversation was. We understand that Clay couldn't remove the memory probe, but we thought you, Doctor, would at least have made sure he edited the files before the probe was archived.'

Fury was stronger than fear. He knew that now. *Clay.* He'd given Clay probe-edit software, told him to remain in the cell after the suffocation and erase all evidence of his presence. Clay wouldn't even have needed to remove the probe from Hokma's head: he could have jacked in wirelessly. Ten minutes, that's all it would have taken; the guard would have allowed it, the guard and the coroner had both been paid enough to agree to anything Clay demanded. But Clay hadn't done it. Hadn't taken the simplest precaution. The probe didn't matter, he'd said: traitors' memories were classified for seventy-five years; they'd both be dead long before anyone could prove that they had taken justice into their own hands and dispatched Is-Land's Public Enemy Number One. Clay, Samrod had accused, had *wanted* history to know of his deed. Clay had laughed off the suggestion, saying that with the amount of Memory Pacification Treatment Hokma had received, no one would believe any of her memories anyway. That had perhaps been true thirteen years ago, and Samrod had stopped arguing with Clay about it. Probe analysers today, though, could assess the difference between a dream, a hallucination and an experience with nearly ninety-eight per cent accuracy.

He stared out at the meadow, where the child was running in a circle, her hair haloed in the sun. His face burnt and his body ran cold. What the hell had Clay said to Hokma about him?

Silverstreamson waited.

Waited, Samrod slowly realised, for him to confess. There was no ace up the prosecutor's sleeve or he'd have sent an arresting officer. The man was fishing, that was all. *Fishing.*

'I recall that Clay visited Hokma the day she died,' he retorted. 'I can't be held responsible for anything he may have said about me while he was with her. Clay was one of her interrogators. *Interrogators*, as I understand it, use various techniques to extract information from their subjects. Some of which might involve *lies* and *bullying*.'

Silverstreamson half-smiled, acknowledging the barb. 'Lie-detector tests would certainly help determine the extent of your involvement, and of course there's Clay's testimony to consider. He may well wish to lessen his own charges by implicating you. A jury would have to decide in the end. But it doesn't have to come to that, Doctor. In exchange for your help in the Springhill investigation, Blade is willing to maintain the embargo on any incriminating files and grant Ordott's access to non-sensitive material only. I must make it clear, though, that your decision to co-operate would protect Clay from the murder count, but not from the Springhill charge. He has to go down for that, Samrod. For a very long time.'

The child's screams of glee punctured the long silence that followed. Samrod wiped his glasses on his trousers. His hands trembled as he replaced them on his nose. 'You will be aware that I have a close relationship of long standing with Clay Odinson.'

'We are aware of that, yes.'

'And yet you think, after supporting him through his accident and protracted recovery, that I would be prepared to sacrifice him on the altar of Blade Stonewayson's political ambitions?'

'We think, Doctor Blesserson, that you are a highly intelligent man with an entirely natural desire for self-preservation. We also know that CONC is pursuing a case against IREMCO, in which

you, as a member of the IREMCO Board of Directors, are implicated in charges related to the serious sexual misconduct of Gaian
officers in Zabaria. We feel for you, Samrod. We know you have just
been following orders, the orders of a madman. We also have a need
on our team for a Code Scientist willing and able to learn from the
Peat Orson case and reverse the Sec Gen condition for the many
families that are requesting the procedure. Should such a scientist
be experiencing legal difficulties, we would be willing to do everything in our power to help him. We have contacts in CONC who
would appreciate any insider information you might be able be provide about IREMCO. Minimum-security prisons in Amazigia are
surprisingly comfortable, I am told. And serving a short sentence
out of the country would be a safe place to await a regime change in
Is-Land.'

Samrod's armpits were soaking wet. He must stink. Stink of
fear. He stood up.

'It seems that whatever I do, I am to be found guilty by association simply for pursuing my IMBOD responsibilities. Tell Blade
Stonewayson I have committed no crime, and therefore I can make
no deal with his office.'

Silverstreamson looked up at him, shading his eyes. 'The offer
stands until the day before the trial. Call me any time. Day or
night.'

Refusing to reply, Samrod strode away, back into the meadow. As
he crossed over to the path his foot landed on something soft and
his ankle buckled. The thing was a teddy bear, its orange glass eyes
staring up at him. He kicked it viciously into the grass and marched
on back to his office.

Shadow Blue

Asfar
28.06.99

Black-robed, hunched and frowning, Dr Tapputu dominated the front row of spectators like a bird of doom. But from Peat's vantage in the witness box, he could see, as clearly as he saw Bartol's tall figure seated considerately in the back row, that doubt and fear had no power in this place. Lofty and light, this was a place where justice was done.

The Merciful High Court of Asfar was so beautiful, in fact, it was hard to keep his mind on his testimony. The court's whitewashed arches and vaults were embellished with intricate tessellations of small blue, red and gold tiles, their delicate patterns twisting like vines up to the dome in the centre of the ceiling. There, sunlight filtered down through a brick and glass lacework of stars to the marble floor, its gentle beams caressing the judge and the lawyers in their blue and white robes, the witnesses and spectators on the benches, Peat's hands on the polished wooden edge of the witness stand. Whose soul could not be rinsed clean of dirt here? Who needed even to go through the motions of a trial to be made pure?

He did, of course. He bowed his head and focused again on the question.

'You have admitted killing the grandmother Uttu Dúrkiñar,' his lawyer said in Asfarian. 'You claim this was unintentional, is that correct?'

'Yes,' he replied in Gaian. He understood Asfarian now, could make himself understood in return, but the judge had decreed that all who spoke in the court should give testimony in their mother tongue. At the back of the room, he could see the court interpreters in their curtained booth, translating his words for the earpieces of everyone present. 'She was struggling,' he went on, 'and I was trying to control her. I wasn't supposed to hurt or kill anyone on the hostage mission, but I didn't realise my own strength. I accept responsibility for her death, and I am deeply sorry for the pain my action has caused her family. I am willing to accept any punishment they wish to give me.'

For the first time, he looked directly at the family, seated on their own bench in the front row. The women, two older, two younger, stared back at him, their expressions unreadable. The blind youth, in what looked like a vest made of plants, cocked his head as if listening for everything that Peat did not know how to say. Muzi – for it could be no other, Astra's husband, who had attacked Peat in Shiimti – did not meet his eyes. Dressed in rags and seated at the end of the bench, separated from his kin, the man was leaning against the back of the bench, craning up at the dome.

'And in the case of the woman Neperdu?'

'I was part of a pack that tore her apart and devoured her. We ate her flesh and bones like wild dogs.'

There was a split-second delay for the interpretation, then a collective gasp rushed like a wind through the court. Behind the family, a tall alt-bodied woman with multiple arms, one of the Singulars he had been told about, emitted a sharp cry. Beside Tapputu, a large woman in a turban folded her arms in front of her impressive bosom. That was Una Dayyani, his lawyer had told him, the leader of the Non-Land government-in-exile.

He raised his voice. 'Neperdu spoke to me before she died. She told me I was a dog, and I was. I was a crazed animal, not worthy of the name human being. I am filled with shame at my actions. For many years, I begged my doctor in Shiimti to erase my memories of that night. But that was not possible, and nor, I understand now, is it

desirable. Forgetting our crimes does not heal our souls. I beg forgiveness, and I accept whatever punishment this court deems necessary.'

Tapputu was shaking his head. But Peat's confession rang out in
the clear dome of justice, entered the Non-Landers' ears, if not yet
their souls. His own soul felt as light as a feather on a swaying
golden scale.

His lawyer pressed on. 'So you do not ask for mercy? Even
though you yourself were being controlled at that time by your
military superiors?'

'I committed those crimes. With my hands and my teeth. I
caused those deaths and I carry the memories. I must pay the price
for them or I will never be free. My superiors must pay their own
price for what they did to me.'

Una Dayyani whispered something to the lantern-jawed man
beside her. Muzi examined his fingernails.

'Thank you,' his lawyer said. 'No more questions, your honour.'

As expected, the prosecutor declined to cross-examine him. Peat
left the stand, nodding at Bartol and glancing at Tapputu as he
returned to his seat beside his lawyer. The doctor gazed back at him,
his face sagging with the weight of his worry, his eyes glazed with
tears. *It wasn't your fault, Peat,* Tapputu had kept repeating during
his visit to the cell. *None of it was your fault. Call me as a witness.
Let me take the stand and explain to the court how the Security Serum
affected you. Let me help you go home to your family.* Peat had
remained mum, enduring the pleas. Now he sat down with his back
to the doctor as the judge made his announcement: there would be
a break, and then the victims would give their statements.

No one from Zabaria had been allowed to come to Asfar, so the
judge would use his discretion in sentencing Peat for Neperdu's
death. His decision about Uttu's death would be influenced, however, by the statements of her family. One of the older women,
Habat Bargadala, took the stand first.

'I speak for myself,' she said softly.

The family had chosen to make separate statements. This was not a good sign, his lawyer had said. It suggested they were divided in opinion, and he'd just have to hope that a majority, or at least half of the six, were in favour of mercy.

He didn't hope for mercy. He hoped for whatever punishment was deemed to fit his crimes.

Habat looked at him with her quiet, dark eyes. Thanks to him, this woman had lost her mother-in-law, her freedom and her husband. Her calm gaze was like a poultice on an open sore. At first contact, it burned through to his core.

'This boy has wounded my family,' she said in her language, Somarian, interpreted into Gaian in his ear, 'but he is also part of my family. His sister, Astra Ordott, is married to my son, and therefore he is my son, just as Astra is my daughter. Astra willingly gave up her freedom for mine, and in return I wish the court to grant freedom to her brother. My daughter-in-law Astra is also a messenger of the gods. I am a follower of Istarastra, and I believe her vision of One-Land will only come to pass if we forgive this boy. If we Non-Landers take him into our hearts, if we create peace within ourselves, then we and the Gaians can begin to create a shared future in our land.'

Another murmur rustled through the spectators behind him. Habat looked at Peat again and smiled.

'My mother-in-law wanted to visit her home town with Astra. I hope one day, Peat, we can all go there together.'

He could not smile back. Habat returned to her seat and the next woman, Nanshe Emeeš, took the stand.

This woman's eyes were bullets. She had lost her husband and her mother-in-law, she railed at the court. She had been imprisoned and tortured by the Gaians and her son had been tortured with fire ants, blinded by the Gaians for *sport*. He was a genius, her son, everyone said so, but think what he could have accomplished with eyes! This creature before them was a monster, created by the Gaians to destroy them. He was a Gaian, and you could never trust

Gaians. He should be sent into the desert and baked in the sand, blinded by the sun, just as her son had been blinded by the fire ants. She would never forgive him. As for Astra, Astra might want them to show mercy, but the Old Ones had remained silent. This was not a political decision; it had nothing to do with One-Land. It was a matter of personal *justice*.

On and on she went. He took her fire, each word ripping a hole in him, a hole that would let in more light. As she stood and returned to her seat, someone at the back applauded. The judge reprimanded the court.

Peat sat, glowing with light, as one by one Hadis and Geshti Bargadala took the stand. The girls spoke with their mother, for mercy, one shyly, addressing him as brother, one with confidence and legal sophistication. Then Suen Emeeš, the blind son, walked to the stand, as smoothly as if the blossoms on his vest were eyes.

'The Gaians blinded me,' he said. 'That is true. But Peat Orson didn't give that command and he wasn't there when that happened. Also, being blind has some advantages for me. For one thing, I have had to be clever to invent ways to get around more easily; but also, I think that if I had sight, I would be too easily distracted from my work. Every day I think hard about Istarastra's messages, and I study at the Institute of Metaphysical Engineering to develop non-metallic information technology. The work I've done with seeing-eye plants is helping me solve this problem that humanity faces. So, for myself, I cannot blame Peat Orson for hurting me. He killed my grandmother, that is true. I loved my grandmother, and I miss her very much. But Peat has asked for forgiveness, and when I listen to his voice, I believe that his remorse is genuine. I have also read a lot about the Security Serum, and I think that he was drugged by the Gaians, and therefore can't be held fully responsible for his actions. I know that my cousin by marriage, Astra Ordott, wants us to show mercy to her brother. I forgive him, and I ask for clemency from the court for his crimes.'

As the boy returned to his seat, the call to prayer sounded, as it did five times a day in Asfar. The judge adjourned the court and a guard took Peat to an antechamber to wash his hands and feet before the fifteen minutes of silence. He didn't have to, the lawyer had said, but it would be polite. He went willingly. He wanted to abide by the customs of Asfar. He wanted to be clean for this place.

After World Worship, the judge called on Muzi. The man shambled to the stand in his patched robes. Beneath the faded material he was thin and raggedy, a scarecrow from one of the fields back in Or. His short, tangled hair exposed a gnarled wart of flesh where his ear ought to be. Peat's stomach knotted. He had eaten that ear.

Muzi did not look at him. Again, he gazed up at the lacework ceiling, then out across the room. 'I saw the Sec Gen kill my grandmother. I watched it with my own eyes.' His voice was so ravaged and soft Peat had to lean to hear him. The court fell as silent as a tomb. 'But I do not want to speak for myself. I avenged my grandmother, my father and my uncle in Shiimti and in return the Sec Gen ate my ear. Those deeds were tried in Shiimti, and I have been punished for my part in them. Nor do I speak for my wife. I speak' – he spread his arms wide – 'for the gods.'

Was it Peat's imagination, or did the court brighten? Did the sun send a pulse of light through the lacework dome, gilding Muzi's tangled hair? Peat didn't know, he just watched, mesmerised, as this battered man rasped on.

'The Mujaddid has his god, and I have mine. The Somarian sky-god and the earth-goddess have told me that the Sec Gen has asked to be tried in Asfar because he wishes to be sent to the desert. The Sec Gen is my brother, and I understand this wish. In the desert, there is no crime, no right and wrong, no war and no peace. In the desert, there is just the soul. The endless empty soul of the world and the endless earth and the endless sky and the gods who send stars in the night, and cool darkness, and rain that causes plants full of water to grow in the sand. I look at my brother here, and I say that his soul is stained, like mine was by his deeds, stained like light pouring through an ocean of blood. In the desert, my soul has been cleansed, and in the desert my brother Peat's soul will be cleansed too. I say the court must show mercy by sending Peat Orson to the desert for the rest of his natural life.'

Muzi looked at Peat. Astra's husband had blue eyes, dazzling blue eyes in an earthen-brown face and a gaze that seared Peat like lightning. The shock ran through him and his body went limp. 'Thank you, brother,' he whispered. 'Thank you.'

Burnt Orange

The Ashfields
07.07.99

First it appeared on the horizon, a glint in the lava field that became a bright dot travelling down a grey road beneath the grey sky; then it was a toy vehicle, a miniature white van roaming over a lumpy black carpet; and finally it was pulling up in front of him in the lay-by, a large, square paddy wagon, its hood stamped with the IMBOD Shield. Samrod got out of his car, nodded at the driver and waited, scowling, as the guards dragged Astra Ordott out in front of him.

As requested, she was blindfolded, shackled and straitjacketed. A guard at each arm, she stood barefoot on the gravel, sniffing the mild, damp air. He beckoned to the guards and they followed him up the path to the stone bench on the volcano slope, dragging her between them.

'Fix her here. Then leave us,' he ordered.

She went rigid as a hound on the scent. 'Blesserson?'

She struggled but was no match for the guards. They secured her shackles to the bench then trudged back to the van. He sat beside her, watched her shake and strain against her chains. Let someone else feel afraid. Let her fill to the brim with fear.

'Just do it,' she hissed.

'Do what?' he enquired archly.

'If you're going to kill me, do it now.'

'No one's going to kill you, Astra. If we wanted you dead, you would have been dead a long time ago.' He reached behind her head and removed her blindfold. 'I've come to talk to you, that's all.'

She blinked. Gasped. Stared, not at him, but at the valley stretched out below them, its long, rumpled slopes of dried lava creased with swathes of mauve lupins and mottled with mossy green rocks, all the way to the distant peaks of the Firetongue Range.

'The ashfields have their own bleak beauty, do they not?' he remarked.

Her head swivelled like a wooden doll's, in every direction but his: up to the soft grey clouds, out to the steep volcano flank, down to the earth beneath her feet.

'I understand you haven't seen the face of Gaia for twelve years,' he commented, 'and I know you are now living under an even harsher prison regime, brought on by your own insubordination.'

Seemingly transfixed by a clump of small yellow stonecrops quivering in the faintest of breezes, she ignored him. She was, he presumed, soaking up what she thought would be her last sight on Earth. But she was listening. She had no choice but to listen.

'Under the terms of your incarceration, this near-solitary confinement could last indefinitely. But much as I admire your tenacity, Astra, as your Shelter uncle, I hate to think of you suffering. As you might imagine, I have some influence with the prison authorities. I can, for example, order the reinstatement of your privileges. I could even arrange for you to benefit from extra entitlements. Did you know there are mineral hot springs at the foot of Mount Hephaestus? I can arrange for you to take the waters there once a month, in the out of doors. I can also arrange for food hampers to be delivered to your cell. All your favourite delicacies, once a week. None of the other prisoners would know about it.'

He remembered her vividly as a child. She was still small, snub-nosed. Nondescript. Her scalp was shaved now, though, her tangle of curls a thing of the past, and when she spoke, her voice was as rough as the lava field. 'No one at Ashfields Max gets to spend time with Gaia. It's not allowed.'

'I brought you here, didn't I?'

She looked at him for the first time. She was no child. Prison had etched a cobweb of lines in her face and her eyes were shrewd as a hawk's. She squinted, as if in distaste, then turned again to look out over the slopes.

'What do you want from me, Samrod?'

He wrapped the blindfold around his fist, gripped the cloth. 'I want you to drop your INMA appeal. Nothing you can find in Hokma's memories will bring her back, and nor will a victory in that case set you free. I also want you to instruct your lawyers to exclude the Board of Directors from personal culpability in the IREMCO case. Cease this pointless vendetta against me and let me help you enjoy your life as best you can under the circumstances you have freely chosen.'

A muscle worked in her jaw. 'You killed her, didn't you? You killed Hokma.'

'I did not kill my sister!' he flared. 'She died of a *stroke*. High blood pressure runs in our family, my father had it, and so did his mother. Those INMA files are classified for good reason – for reason of national security. Stonewayson's using you, Astra, as a pawn in his own game against the government. He won't look after you. I *can*. I can get you books, films, fresh fruit, weekly walks in the lava fields. I'll talk to Klor and Nimma, urge them to visit you. Your campaign worked, didn't it? People can visit the prison any way they like now – you could see your family at last, in the flesh. Who knows, maybe we could even get your sentence commuted to house arrest in Or. Just let go of the past, Astra, and let me help you build a better future for yourself.'

She swivelled her head back towards him. Hunched and furious, she looked for all the world exactly like a helmet-headed hawk. Her gaze searched his face; found it wanting.

'There is no better future for anyone,' she croaked. 'You brought me here in a metal box. You've chained me to stone with metal chains. You send your commands to the prison authorities with a metal tongue and gag me with a metal gag. You are a slave to metal, like the rest of humanity, and you are bringing the fury of the Old Ones down on our heads.'

'Astra.' He shook his head. 'You need help. Psychiatric help. New medication. I can arrange that for you, too.'

'*I don't need your drugs.* You see these clouds?' She jerked her chin to the sky. 'They are going to blacken and *burst* and drown us in scalding-hot rain. You see that mountain?' Her gaze jolted across the valley, then returned to scour his face, hers twisted with hatred. 'It is going to erupt. Soon. Then, within a month, two months, the entire planet is going to erupt and bury us all alive in molten lava.'

On and on she went, her apocalyptic visions creaking like an old gate, blood rising in her face. Her condition was worse than he'd thought. She clearly believed all the messages she'd been pumping out of her cell all these years. 'Astra,' he said sharply. 'The planet is fine. You should be thinking about your own welfare—'

'We have eight months left to live, and all I want is to see you *ruined* before we all *die.*' She lunged at him, the shackles surely scraping her wrists and ankles raw. 'You killed Hokma, Samrod, or you wouldn't be here trying to shut me up. You killed Hokma and I am going to *destroy* you if it's the last thing I do.'

She couldn't touch him, but, instinctively, he flinched. She was straining at him like a mad dog on a leash, practically foaming at the mouth. Sweat prickled his forehead and his gorge rose. What was he doing, trying to negotiate with this deranged creature, this constant thorn in his side? She was so small. She was bound, immobilised, helpless. He could strangle her with the blindfold. Or smother her. He could shake out the piece of cloth and bundle it over her face. Clay had told him how easy it was. How suddenly the struggles ceased and your chest ballooned with an enormous airiness. An almost mathematical delight, Clay had called it. The algebraic delight of problem-solving for x.

Down by the vehicles, the guards were watching. Not her. Watching him.

He stood. 'I am sorry to see, Astra, that you have been so badly affected by your prison experience. If I were your doctor, I would recommend a long spell in a neurohospice, but sadly you have yet again rejected medical treatment for your mental ill health.' He replaced the blindfold over her eyes and, with fumbling hands, knotted and yanked it tight.

'I'll see you put in *jail*, Samrod,' she screamed after him as he strode back to his car. 'Right before Is-Land is consumed by the Earth's molten core.'

AUTUMN RE 99

Desert Red
Sour Gold
Bruise Purple
Misted Silver
Burnt Orange
Acid Green
Shadow Blue

Desert Red

Asfar
07.09.99

'Do you think the Old Ones disagreed with the judge's decision?'
Mona's question wove a soft path through the background chatter of
other students and the wild rhythms of rain on glass. They were sitting on cushions in a greenhouse seminar room at the Institute, two
months after Peat Orson's sentencing. Suen pondered the question.

'Various political arguments have been raised in favour of mercy,'
the judge had said that day in his cool marble tone, 'but this court
does not tailor its decisions to suit political agendas. We work here
to provide justice for the souls of victim and criminal alike. I have
considered all the statements carefully. I am impressed by the
defendant's willingness to take responsibility for his crimes. I also
take into consideration his fragile mental health and troubled history, which make it unlikely that he will find peace back in his
belligerent home country. The former Sec Gen, Peat Orson, has
come on a pilgrimage to Asfar, seeking Asfarian justice: redemption,
not retribution. He is on a healing journey that began in the desert
of Shiimti, and for him the desert has clearly been a wise teacher.
Taking the Mercy and Compassion of the Oneness-of-the-Many as
my ultimate guide, for the crimes of manslaughter, cannibalism and
fatal affray, I therefore sentence Peat Orson to, respectively, ten
years, twenty-five years and thirty years in the Asfarian desert, to
run consecutively with no chance of parole.'

As he banged his gavel, there was a rumble and crash, and as the drumming of rain began on the skylights, Nanshe had cried '*Yes*' and clasped Suen to her chest, and the court had exploded into a barrage of cheers and applause. It had been raining on and off ever since, a wet summer, unheard of in Asfar, that had now become a monsoon of epic duration, turning the streets into rivers of mud. Sighted people complained about getting wet and having to travel on a packed Underground, but Suen liked the rain. It made the smells of things richer and their locations crystal clear. Right now, by tuning in to the steel-pan patter at the edge of his hearing, he could sense the dimensions of the long, low greenhouse sheltering the Psychosphere Team from the orchestral onslaught of rain.

'No,' he replied slowly. 'Astra didn't mention the Old Ones in her messages to us and I don't think Peat Orson's sentence mattered to Them. If this rain is a warning, it's probably because the deadline is only six months away and humanity is no closer than ever to giving up metal.'

'Yes we are.' Cyrus' knee pressed against his thigh. 'We're here, aren't we?'

The knee sent a warm message through his muscles. He didn't move away. Cyrus often touched his arm, or his shoulder, signals of affection Suen still couldn't fully decipher. Although he found himself waiting for them, sometimes left strangely flushed by their vigour, the brief nudges and clasps were probably nothing more than gestures of brotherhood. He and Cyrus had quickly become like brothers, after all. They Tablette Talked often about college work, ate lunch every day with Mona, and now they were working together: after the professor's opening lecture nine students had volunteered to pursue a psychic-tech solution to the Old Ones' challenge, a 'dream team' of which Mona was the unofficial leader, and voice of caution.

'Yes,' she said now to Cyrus, 'but don't start planning your prize voyage just yet. We won't know what direction we've stepped in until after we've eaten the leaf.'

A bubble of excitement rose in Suen's torso. So far the team had mainly done a lot of reading and brainstorming, but they had also received funding to invite a psychic practitioner to tutor them in experiential research, and today Ñeštug, a dream voyager, was going to initiate them into the secrets of Shiimti.

'Friends!' From his place at the end of the greenhouse, Ñeštug addressed the seminar. 'We are ready to begin. Please form a seated circle and unroll your mats. Make sure your sick buckets are within reach. Then sit quietly with your eyes closed, and together we will set our intention. Remember, all we are hoping to do today is meet in the psychosphere, so please do not focus strongly on any other desire.'

Cyrus' knee disappeared. Suen shuffled into place with his yoga mat and bucket, guiltily aware of the impurity of his intentions. In his lecture yesterday, Ñeštug had said everyone who ingested the leaf would first throw up and then see visions and hear voices. Normally one would ask the plant for advice before embarking, and even on a first voyage the plant usually delivered powerful messages to the seeker. Given the goal of establishing a shared psychic space, however, individual aspirations had to harmonise with the collective experience, and therefore the team would chant a shared intention. Even so, Shiimtian shamans had discovered that initially, in a group voyage, the plant spirits would deliver any personal messages they saw fit, might even 'weed out' members of the team who were not deemed suitable. After three or four voyages, the lantern leaf would begin to facilitate a powerful collective experience. Suen wanted that to happen. But he also knew that he had a private intention.

Ñeštug had said that manifestation in the psychosphere usually varied within a group. Generally, everyone experienced an exchange of voices, or the sense of words. But to some voyagers other group members also appeared as visual images; and to others, for example people who had been blind since birth, as felt presences. Suen had found himself dwelling on this information. Normally he didn't care what people looked like. His memories of his family's faces, and his own, were like photos in an old album: treasured, but rarely looked at. He and his family would look different now, and besides, people's voices, and what they said with them, created a vivid and, he thought, much truer impression of who they were. But then, creeping alongside the anticipation, it had come: a secret desire to see Cyrus' face. Just once, he told himself. Just a glimpse to file away in his family album.

It wasn't a bad intention, surely. It didn't contradict the group's goal. Still, he shouldn't focus on his own selfish needs. Trying as hard as he could to push the thought of Cyrus from his mind, he followed Ñeštug's commands and together with the team chanted the collective intention:

'We, the Asfar City Dream Team, humbled and inspired by the Old Ones, and grateful as always to the Oneness-of-the-Many, thank the lantern leaf spirits for their guidance. We ask them to lead us to a meeting place in the psychosphere where we may begin to understand how to break humanity's toxic bond with metal and enter into a new relationship with the Earth and all its creatures.'

Ñeštug's assistant came around and pressed a plant into his hand. He held it to his nose: the leaf was thick and tough, and smelled of sage and something bitter. As instructed, he chewed it carefully, trying not to gag, then lay down and waited.

Afterwards, the other team members could talk for hours about their experience, as if recounting every detail of a long journey. Suen couldn't. For him, everything had happened very quickly, and all at once. First, he had vomited violently into his bucket. Then the Lantern Leaf Grandmother appeared, a spirit everyone had seen, a flickering figure with long, grey vines for hair, beckoning him down green tunnels that opened around him everywhere, into a shifting, mesmerising pattern of colours, music, voices, each twist of the kaleidoscope more ravishing than the last. He marvelled with no sense of sorrow at the intense visuality of the experience, rather with thankfulness, as he felt sometimes after sleep dreams. Then his father was there, and his uncle, shadows and voices, both booming with pride over his accomplishments, and then his grandmother Uttu, laughing and tweaking his big toe, saying, *Don't get too big for your boots, my boy, listen to your mother, listen to your mother.* He felt a little annoyed, wanted to argue – he was trying to help humanity survive, and if his mother had her way he'd be married and trying to create children with no future . . . But then he heard Cyrus shout, 'In water!' and Mona whisper, 'Under the moon,' and suddenly he was awake, back in the greenhouse, rain still pelting the roof.

He was stunned to learn that six hours had passed. Gradually each team member awoke and, to ensure objectivity, wrote down an account of their journey. When they read these back to each other, it transpired that while no one had entered a shared meeting place, the lantern leaf spirits had given others on the team the name of a plant and special instructions on how to tend it. As the excitement in the group mounted, and the greenhouse panes rattled and shook in the rain, Suen waited his turn with a deepening sense of gloom.

He was being weeded out. The spirits wanted him to leave the Institute, to return to his family. If he stayed, he would hold everyone up and humanity would suffer the fatal consequences. Tears prickled his eyes and all around him great crashing sheets of rain threatened to wash away all his dreams.

Then it was his turn, last before his two friends. Miserably, he told his story, all two minutes of it.

'That's incredible, Suen.' Mona gasped as Cyrus grabbed his arm. 'You were in my dream: that's exactly how the grandmother spirit told me to sow my mountain sage.'

'You joined my journey too, brother.' Cyrus was shaking him. 'That's how I'm supposed to plant my tiger root!'

'No.' He shook his head. 'I was lying between you both. You must have spoken out loud while you were dreaming and I heard your voices, that's all. I'm sorry, everyone. I'm holding us up. I'll step down from the group.'

'Suen.' Ñeštug's voice rumbled like a timpani drum in the symphony of the rain. 'I was awake the whole time. No one spoke aloud. Mona and Cyrus are correct – you joined their voyages. Congratulations, everyone. The lantern leaf spirits have accepted you all on a journey that will become more collective each time you chew the plant. You need to recover now and follow any instructions you were given. We will meet again here at the same time next week, and every week henceforth, to continue your journey. The gods willing, it will lead us to the answer that we seek.'

Then everyone was cheering and talking, and Cyrus was hugging him, the soft cloud of his beard and the rosemary scent of his musk more distinctive and compelling than any snatched photo could ever be. 'When this rain stops,' Cyrus pulled away to announce, 'we can do the planting at my uncle and aunt's house. They have a field with a stream, and greenhouses. You can all come and stay the night. My family have plenty of tents, and a cook-fire, and a big yurt. We can plant under the moon, and at dawn, just as the spirits demanded.'

Listen to your mother, Uttu had said. Not *tell your mother everything*.

Sour Gold

Occupied Zabaria
16.09.99

'I got honey!' Girin yelled, slamming the door behind him, slinging his bag on the kitchen table, kicking off his shoes and jamming his feet into his slippers.

Anunit was coughing in the living room, still in her nightdress, her *niqab* folded on the table and her hair haloed in the lamplight. Tira was with her, sitting on his bed mat.

'Hey, Girin,' Tira said.

'Hi, Tira.' He hovered at the doorway. Tira was nice. She was pretty, and she liked music. When they'd met at her office in the Gaian quarter, she had played him a tune on her Tablette. It was a song from Asfar, she said, by a Non-Lander musician, a Singular called Tiamet. His mother hadn't wanted him to listen, but Tira said, 'He should hear it, Anunit. She's a good drummer,' and his mother had caved in and let him take Tira's earbuds. The words were a chant about One-Land, which was cool, and the track had lots of drumming. Tiamet had eight arms and drummed with six of them, which was wicked. He'd wanted a copy, but Tira said it was pirated and he shouldn't keep it on his Tablette in case a Gaian ever stopped him for a propaganda check. She'd deleted it from her Tablette right after he'd listened to it. 'But I can get others.' She'd put her finger to her lips and widened her eyes. 'By Owleon, shh.' Since then, she had come to the apartment a few times over the summer, bringing money to help out his mother. They had electricity again now, and they ate better – alt-meat twice a week and fresh fruit and vegetables every day. When Tira came, she always listened to Girin's drumming, and clapped, and played him more songs, new tracks by Tiamet, solo and with YAC Attack, the Non-Lander band in Asfar all the One-Landers listened to on pirate radio. Some of the lyrics were messages from the Old Ones, all about the end of the world, but Ama and Tira said not to worry about that. The world ended every time you went to sleep and began again when you woke up, his mother said.

Yeah, he liked Tira. But recently she'd been coming more often. Because Ama had been coughing more, and harder, and getting up less often. The neighbour had banged on the door the other night and refused to go away until Ama had let her come in with a pot of parsley soup for them both. His mother wasn't well. And if she went to the hospital, then he was supposed to go and stay with Tira, in the Gaian quarter, far away from his school and his friends. He didn't want that to happen, so he lingered at the threshold, where he could still pretend that Tira looked happy, and his mother was just resting after a day doing housework and visiting with the neighbour.

'Don't stand there like a broomstick, Girin. Come and keep me warm.' His mother waved him over. He crossed the room, sat down in her arms and fished out his Tablette.

'Hey, Tira, want to hear my new Sonic Soundscape? The mine-workers were demonstrating on the main street, there were loads of shouts and chants and then someone set a dumpster on fire and everyone started banging it with sticks. I recorded them and made a new tune. It's called "The Wall Must Fall". It just needs a drum track.'

If his mother had been well, she would have told him off for hanging out at a demonstration. But she just held him close as he played the track.

'That's great, Girin,' Tira said. 'I really like that zipping sound you added.' She dug in her bag. 'Hey, I've got a new Tiamet video to show you. It's a live clip, from a concert in New Zonia.'

He scrambled forwards, his mother's arm still around his waist, to take the Tablette from Tira. 'Do you want to listen, Ama?'

His mother hugged him harder. 'No, son.'

'It's one of her early solo hits,' Tira said as he stuffed the earbuds in. 'A bit different from the ones you've heard. It's called "Tears for My Son".'

It sounded soppy, but he'd never seen Tiamet live, and Ama was the most comfortable cushion in the world. Leaning back against his mother, he watched the footage, nodding his head and tapping his feet. The stage was flaming with a million orange and gold lights, the band were on platforms at angles so steep he thought they'd slide off, but then they disappeared into the darkness and Tiamet, her hair wild as an Old World lion's mane, stood in a spotlight in a sparkly dress, drumming with just finger cymbals and a *bendir* and a *naghara* as she wailed the words of her song, which was all about a Non-Lander mother crying over her lost baby. 'You were torn from me in Zabaria,' she howled. 'I'll seek you as long as I live.'

'Cool lighting.' He took an earbud out. 'But she's better with the band. Do you have a clip of the next song?'

His mother placed her hand on his and pushed the Tablette down to the bed mat. 'Girin. Shhh.'

What? He'd been doing everything right. 'I brought honey,' he repeated. 'Like you asked. And Old Man Endu gave me dill for the fish soup.'

'That's good. You're a good boy, Girin.' Then his mother started to cry, and Tira was leaning over with a tissue saying, 'I know it's hard, Anunit, but it has to come from you.'

And then it started, the walls of the apartment, of his whole life, falling, falling, into a heap of rubble, his mother-who-wasn't-his-mother saying that she loved him very much but his mother was really Tiamet, who was a friend of Ama and Tira's from the old days before the Occupation, but Tira and Tiamet had been in Kadingir the night of the Occupation, and his mother-who-was-really-his-aunty – she wasn't Tiamet's sister but everyone knew that Anunit was Ebebu's aunty, and no, his name wasn't really Girin, it was Ebebu – had been looking after him and had taken him when the Gaians came, to keep him safe, and there was no way to get a message to Tiamet, and all she wanted was for him to be happy, but soon she wasn't going to be here any more, because she was sick, very sick, and Tira wanted to look after him, and if he wanted, Tira would try to take him to Asfar, to be with Tiamet and go to a proper music school. It wouldn't be easy, and the plan would have to be kept secret, but Tira had a friend at CONC who would help her get the right papers, and if Girin lived in Asfar he could get an education and have a future and travel wherever he wanted to go in the world. And then everyone was crying, and Ama who *was* his Ama, would always be his Ama, was coughing and coughing and coughing, until blood came up on her handkerchief again, and again the neighbour knocked, but again his mother refused to let them get the doctor, just lay choking with the effort of not coughing, and as the neighbour laid cool cloths on her forehead, Tira put her hand on his shoulder and he stood up and helped her make fish soup in his kitchen that no longer had any roof or door or walls.

'I don't want to leave Zabaria,' he said after Tira left. 'I don't ever want to leave you.'

His mother smoothed her blanket. 'When I'm gone, Girin—'

His face went hot. 'You're *not going anywhere.*'

She waited for him to calm down and went on, 'I'm very sick, Girin. I can't look after you properly. When I'm too sick to care for you any more, you can do what you want. You can live with Todo – I asked him, and he said yes. Or you can live with Tira. But Tira won't stay in Zabaria forever. You should only stay with her if you want to try and get to Asfar and be with Tiamet.'

He sat still on his bed mat, aware of a cold feeling in his stomach. 'Will I grow more arms?' he asked.

Ama smiled a rare smile, her crooked yellow teeth gleaming in the lamplight. 'No. You didn't inherit your mother's alt-bodied genes. But you got the drumming from her, didn't you? She could teach you a lot about drumming, I'm sure.'

He wasn't sure if he was relieved or disappointed. Having more arms would be a great advantage as a drummer. Across the room, the ceramic base of his *doumbek* gleamed in the lamplight. Tiamet had tons of stage lights, all different colours.

'Ama?'

'Yes, son?'

'Was my father really Karkish? Did he die, like you said?'

Her face crumpled, and he felt bad for accusing her of lying. 'I don't know, Girin. I don't know who he was. Tiamet would have to tell you about him.'

Sometimes he wanted Todo to be his father. But Todo was more like an older brother, and his small apartment was already crammed with children.

'Why did you say he was Karkish, then?'

'So that I could wear the *niqab* and keep us safe.'

'Why wasn't it safe to be seen?'

She paused. 'Because the night that I took you away, men came to the tent where we worked. Gaians. They didn't like Tiamet or Tira, or YAC, and if they ever recognised me, and discovered that you were Tiamet's son, they might have hurt you. Girin, you mustn't tell anyone about Tiamet, not even Todo. Do you understand?'

He was the son of a famous YAC Singular. His mother was even more famous than Astra Ordott. He nodded slowly. 'What do you want me to do?' he whispered.

There was another long pause. Again, Ama's face twisted in pain. 'She misses you.' She pulled him to her soft chest, spoke into his hair. 'I wanted to give her a message, but I couldn't. Tell her I'm sorry, Girin. Tell her I just wanted you to be safe.'

Bruise Purple

The Great Depression
02.10.99

'Well, Brother Muzi.' As agreed, Ñizal spoke first. 'You took your time getting back to camp.'

Bargadala shrugged. 'My mother wanted me to stay in Asfar City for a while.'

Impatience swelled up in Enki's chest. 'We know what you said in the court,' he informed that heap of dirt in his tent. 'You didn't exactly howl for the monster to be hacked into pieces and fed to the crows.'

'The Sec Gen is in the desert,' Bargadala replied. 'And it's just like you said it would be: Is-Land is killing the mine-workers in Zabaria now. I came back to help collect gunpowder.'

Enki glowered. Gunpowder was always useful for firearm practice, but what good were his stockpiles without the great weapon – long-promised, but not yet released. The namby-pamby stipulations of Asfarian billionaires were not something, though, that he needed to discuss with Bargadala.

'We understand. But first we have to debrief—' Ñizal began.

'Why did you call the Sec Gen your brother?' Enki barked.

Bargadala stroked the grubby feather dangling from his bag. 'He's my wife's brother, so he's my brother, too.'

Enki narrowed his eyes.

'The gods told me what to say,' Muzi offered suddenly. 'They said if I didn't use those words the judge wouldn't listen.'

Enki stroked his beard. The Asfarian courts were proud of their reputation for mercy; that was true. But the judge also knew that letting the Sec Gen off could have turned Asfar City into a riot zone. To be able to frame a life sentence as a merciful decision was quite the coup. The point of this meeting, though, was not to contemplate the nature of the gods, or of Asfarian judges, but to ascertain whether he could trust Muzi Bargadala. Reports of the Orson trial, followed by Muzi's long absence, had given rise to speculation that the man was a secret One-Lander, even a YAC spy. No one had expected to see him again, but here he was, footsore and foul as ever, seeking readmission to NAARC. Did he really think it would be that easy, after claiming kinship with a Sec Gen?

'Some people think you're soft on Gaians,' Ñizal pressed. 'They say you're still a One-Lander, like your wife.'

Bargadala squinted. 'The land is one. The people are too many.'

Enough gnomic utterances. 'Who knows you're here?' Enki demanded.

'My mother.'

'What about N-LA? YAC? The Ordott lawyer?' Sonovason had sent observers to the trial; Bargadala could be plotting with them, too.

'No. I told the newspaper I lived in the desert. By myself.'

'Were you followed here?'

For the first time ever in Enki's memory, Muzi looked offended. 'I took the hard paths and the creeks. I travelled at night. I doubled back, left no tracks,' he replied, his tone as stiff as his filthy robe.

Enki sighed. Muzi was here; in his own inscrutable way, he'd done what they'd demanded in Asfar; and he was a good forager.

'Let him back in,' Enki growled. 'But no Owleon privileges. We find out you're sending messages and we'll have the other ear.'

Bargadala wrinkled his nose, as though it were Enki and Ñizal who hadn't washed in weeks, and got to his feet. 'I'll pick some wild roses for cordial. The warriors will enjoy that.'

Trailing flakes of dandruff and scabs of dried mud, Non-Land's most aggravating man drifted out of the command tent.

'He did get the job done,' Ñizal murmured. 'And in the continued absence of the great weapon, we need something to celebrate. Why don't you toast him tonight?'

'Toast *Bargadala*?'

'At least use his return to remind the camp of our goals.'

'Oh, all right,' Enki grumbled into his beard.

Ñizal stood to go, too. 'Any chance of a rhyme?' he asked from the tent door. 'I miss your rhymes.'

'Better go back to Asfar and join YAC, then,' Enki shot back. 'NAARC is for warriors only.'

Misted Silver

The Ashfields
10.10.99

'Keep *still*, Nutdott.' Lichena slapped her cheek. Hard.

'*No*,' Astra bellowed, straining against the straitjacket and jerking her head back and forth. 'I don't *want* to see them.'

'You *fought* for the right to see 'em, you *won* the right to see 'em, and if you *don't* see 'em, CONC's going to land like a ton of bricks on *my* skinny arse.' Lichena forced the headset over her skull and yanked the chinstrap tight. 'So just relax, will you, and let the iris tracker take the strain.'

'I demand to speak to my *lawyer*!'

'You can call your fat boyfriend when you've watched the fracking files, Ornut. So sit still and watch! And keep your mouth shut this time or we'll gag you again. Your screaming upsets Vultura.'

So it resumed, the slow unspooling of INMA_Hokma_Blesser_ 01-52_ZIP. Two hundred and forty-eight hours of Hokma's final memories. Two hours ago, Astra had begun watching them. One hour and twelve minutes ago, she had screwed her eyes shut and begun shouting for the guards to take the headset off. Lichena had done so and left the cell, only to return with an eye-clamp, a device attached by a thin tube to a bag of fluid that moistened Astra's eyeballs every thirty seconds. She could not shut her eyes or close her ears. She could not avoid reliving Hokma's last week of life, had no choice but to experience all the files Justice Blade Stonewayson had granted her permission to view, once only, on a marathon schedule of ten hours a day for twenty-five days. Ten hours a day of grainy images, garbled words. The first two hours were horrific, a torture. Hokma's impressions of a cell like hers, but worse: no Vultura, but filthy, damp and freezing cold, with rats running over the bed. Hokma's stray thoughts of her, Astra. Hokma's screams. Hokma's whimpers. A pointless immersion in grief. A torture that would result in no justice, no justice ever. Because Stonewayson's order had excluded three hours of memories on Day Six and the very last hour of Hokma's life.

There was no evidence here, no evidence of anything at all except for the fact that Hokma had not been strong. Hokma had been afraid. Hokma had been confused, broken, tearful, terrified, and Astra couldn't help her. Astra had lost Hokma and would never get her back except as a shadowy, nauseating confusion of images and phrases, the memories of a woman broken by solitary confinement, her memories blasted and harvested by neurohospice drugs and probes, a woman shattered into irretrievable pieces.

Hokma. Hokma. Hokma. Please come. I need you. Please come and help me. Please come.

Afterwards, when Lichena had taken the headset away, and Bircha had released her from the straitjacket and removed the chair from the cell, she lay naked on the hard bed, shivering though the cell was warm, knees hugged to chest, rocking back and forth. She shouldn't be doing this, she knew that. She should be stretching, meditating, exercising, recovering from the ordeal, reviewing in her mind exactly how the guards had violated her rights so she could recite every instance of abuse to Jasper when finally permitted to speak to him; she should be reading her case files, calming herself before it began all over again tomorrow; she shouldn't be descending into this abject pleading, she knew she shouldn't, but she couldn't help it. She needed *Hokma.*

Astra. Shhh. I'm here.

She drew a long, hoarse, juddering breath. Her shaking subsided. *Really?*

Yes. Really me.

The soulvoice was faint, but unmistakable. Tears flowed. *I'm sorry. So sorry. They hurt you. All because of me.*

Shhh. None of it was your fault, Astra.

Yes, it was. You wanted to protect me. Without you, I would have become like Peat. I would have killed people. I might have eaten *people. I might have died on the Hem. You knew. You knew what IMBOD was trying to do, and you wanted to protect me. They tortured you because of me.*

No. Protecting you was just part of my resistance, Astra. I sent Code to the Non-Landers, helping them create the Rookowleon. My downfall was my own foolish pride: sending the Code via an old Owleon. I should have known Helium couldn't keep flying those long journeys, but I was convinced I'd created a bird with superavian strength. Poor Helium died of overwork, far from home. I was a negligent birdkeeper. I deserved what happened to me.

Hokma's presence in her body was tender and calm, but Astra couldn't stop shaking. *They hurt you so much. I can't stand it, Hokma. I can't stand it.*

They didn't hurt me. They scrambled some of my memories, that's all, just for a short time. What you're watching isn't me, Astra. It's a fever, a bad dream. You mustn't confuse it with me.

But they're making me watch it. All of it.

It's not all bad. There are peaceful moments, too.

Please stay with me, help me. Watch it with me. Tell me it's okay when you scream. Tell me the peaceful part is coming right up.

No. You must watch it alone. If you can do that, you'll be stronger than ever, Astra.

That was Hokma's stern tone, the tone that brooked no dissent. Astra fell quiet. Hokma was here. She wasn't promising anything, but after so long an absence, she had returned. That was a miracle, fortifying. From being a storm-lashed puddle on the bed, she could feel the resolve stiffen again in her bones. *Then tell me now. Tell me what happens at the end, when the footage is cut. Did Samrod kill you? Is that why he tried to bribe me to drop the case?*

It doesn't matter how I died, Astra.

Yes, it does. I have to get justice for you.

Once, I would have agreed with you. But things look different from the tunnels. If I tell you what happened, you'll fixate on it. You don't have time for hatred now. You need to focus your energy on Earth's message, on convincing humanity to break its pact with Metal. Your success will be your contribution to the creation of One-Land. It would be better, Astra, if you could forgive Samrod.

Forgive Samrod? What had IMBOD done to Hokma? *I can't do that. He killed you. I know he did. You're practically admitting it. I can never forgive him.*

Then you will never be free of him, even if you walk out of this prison, all the way to Asfar.

I don't care. I don't need to forgive him. As long as I have you, it doesn't matter if I hate Samrod.

But you won't have me any more, not like this, Astra. I've come to say goodbye.

Hokma's tone was softer now, the softness in the air before a storm.

No, she pleaded. *Why?*

Because I am travelling deep into the tunnels now, leaving this world behind me, to emerge on the other side of eternity.

But you can't do that, Hokma. You can't leave me here by myself.

You are not alone, Hokma soothed. And it is my time to go. Only ill souls, suffering from the disease of attachment, linger on in the astral tunnels. Souls that have used their time well on Earth, to learn compassion and detachment, must merge with the universe, surrendering their precious sense of self to the ecstasy of oneness: oneness with all that is and was and will be. Death is not absence, Astra, but the ground of presence. Death is the wellspring of life.

No, no. Hokma, stay.

Goodbye, my dear child. The best thing I ever did was love you.

No. Come back!

But though Hokma's words, like all soulspeech, were seared into her mind, echoing there as if down infinite tunnels, there was no reply. Astra opened her eyes, stared wildly around the cell as though Hokma might be standing there still, watching her. But only Vultura's eye pierced the gloom.

I can't do this. I can't. She sobbed and sobbed, her heart crumpling in her chest.

Yes, you can, Young One.

Soft, supple, a cool liquid swelling in her cells, Water's voice had never been so welcome. But it could not absorb the rising flood of her fear and grief.

I can't. I need Hokma.

Hokma died, Young One. And now she is gone from your realm. Be happy for her. Her flesh has decayed into humus and what you call her soul must now decompose into the field of universal consciousness. She told you herself she was ready to completely disintegrate, did she not?

Water's voice slowly sponged up the worst of her distress. *Yes, she said that,* Astra acknowledged. *But I'm not ready for Hokma's soul to decompose. Bring her back, please, Water. Follow her. Bring her back.*

Who and what you knew as Hokma no longer exists, Istarastra. That is the nature of living creatures. They die. And in dying, their bodies enrich the dark soil of the Earth, and their souls enrich the dark matter of the universe. As above, so below. As without, so within. Hokma has decomposed, Young One. As will all human beings soon if you do not convince them to mend their ways. She told you to concentrate on conveying Earth's message, didn't she?

Astra was floating now, floating on Water's gentle currents. *Yes.* She sniffed. *And it's getting through. The IREMCO trial is in the new year. And on the Vernal Equinox CONC will vote on making the Hudna permanent. But we still don't have a non-metal communi-cations technology. Can't you give us a little longer, Water? Ten years?*

The Old Ones didn't set the deadline, Istarastra. Humanity set it, with the Hudna. You need to make good on that promise of peace, now, or there is no hope that you ever will. The Mujaddid has offered his prize. You have a chance.

But what can I do from in here? I can keep sending messages out, but people think I'm crazy. Or an artist. They turned Your last mes-sage into a song. People bought it and played it on their Tablettes. Suddenly she was overwhelmed by a wave of exhaustion. *I've done my part, Water. I'm tired. I've suffered enough. If Hokma can't come back, I want to follow her. It's time for me to go, too. I can stop eating, and leave this body, join you all in the tunnels. The Mujaddid's engin-eers can find a solution without me.*

There was a ripple of coolness over her eyelids, and a light blue shimmering, and then an image appeared inside her head. A man. She was above him, in a room, a bare room with just a desk and a bed. The man was sitting at the desk, his head haloed in Tablette light, typing with long fingers, his shoulders hunched. His shock of white hair, thinning at the temples, and wire-rimmed glasses looked famil-iar. She floated down and around him. Of course. It was Photon. Her heart hurt. Photon. So close she could touch him. But she had no hands, no voice, just a craving for contact. What was he writing? She looked over his shoulder, peered at the words on the screen. He was in a search engine, typing a phrase that made no sense to her: 'mycelia circuit board technology'. Then suddenly his shoulders caved in and he was crying, crying over his Tablette, soundless, heaving sobs that made the walls wobble, the image blur, until her head was swimming again in blue.

That was Photon. What's wrong?

His partner left him, taking their baby with her.

She was staggered. *Why did she do that?*

He's been working two jobs for years: copy-editing for a regen-eration charity in the day and writing for *Is-Land Watch* in the evening. When she got pregnant, she insisted he had to choose between his family and his writing for *Is-Land Watch*. He reminded her that he'd said when they met that he couldn't abandon you. He loves his child, and he tried to be a good father, but he just didn't have the time or energy to also be a good partner. She returned to her family in New Zonia, and she's just emailed to tell him that she's met another man. He's been trying to distract himself by working on an article about Earth's message, but he can't stop thinking about her. He knows now that he'll never get her back.

Water sounded sad. Unlike Earth, Air or Fire, Water had time for people, cared about them, felt for their sorrows. *But that's terrible. He shouldn't be sacrificing his life for me.*

He does it because he loves you, and because he cares passionately about achieving justice for Non-Land and peace on the planet. Do you think if you go on hunger strike and die he will take heart from the end to your suffering?

She felt the shame rush to her cheeks. Her slow suicide would kill him inside. *No.*

And if you watch all Hokma's memories, and give Jasper an account of your ordeal?

Photon would write about it, she responded slowly. *He always writes about me.*

When he blogs about you and Is-Land, he feels powerful. He feels he is influencing others, contributing to a great work. He celebrates whenever CONC restates its commitment to One-Land. And although he worries about you, he is cheerful when you send a new message to the world, because he believes that your continued faith in the Old Ones must mean that your spirit is strong.

My spirit is *strong.*

Is it?

Yes.

Strong enough to absorb Hokma's memories?

Yes. But now I'm worried about Photon. He looks so lonely.

He is lonely. He is trapped in Tablette land. Sometimes he stays in his room for days on end, writing, researching, emailing others in his network. The sooner you humans develop better methods of long-distance communication, the better. Then you will be able to speak with Photon as intimately as we are doing now.

Really?

But Water had slipped away. Astra opened her eyes and got out of bed. Ignoring Vultura, she crossed her cell to her bookcase and withdrew the first of the three thick *Is-Land Watch* files. Photon had been writing about her and Non-Land for ten years. She had a lot to reread before Lichena came back in the morning.

Burnt Orange

Atourne
11.10.99

'You must come this weekend, darling! It's a triumph. An absolute triumph! Magmason is *thrilled*. He wants to celebrate – you have to be here.'

Samrod was standing at the window, his forearm resting against the glass, his forehead resting on his arm. His back was sore. He felt as if he had stood this way forever, propping up the Code College, propping up Clay, propping up the whole fucking Wheel Meet. 'We haven't done anything noteworthy, Clay,' he said wearily. 'I told you after the trial: we've both just had a very lucky break, that's all. And a temporary reprieve. Stonewayson must be waiting for some sort of critical mass before helping the New Purists attempt the coup they clearly have in mind.'

'Oh, Stonewayson knows what side his bread's buttered on. He was never going to grant Ordott access to all those files, Samrod. What, and risk allying himself with Is-Land Enemy Number One in the public imagination? That's not the way to win a popular revolution! But you – you've triumphed! Tulip told me all about it, how you tried to persuade that creature to drop her petty case and she refused, not for all the lichen in the Ashfields.' Clay chuckled. 'And now that the traitor is finally watching her precious files, she's begging the guards to stop the show.'

Outside, the fountain glittered in the autumn sun, students

paraded. The proportion of green-robed mature students to skyclad Sec Gens had increased in recent weeks. Though not all New Purists dressed in green. That IMBOD officer there sitting on a bench reading his Tablette, as he had been for the last hour, dressed in standard black boots, cap and armband – the college's head security officer, responsible for all the campus Sec Gen security guards: who would have guessed that *he* was an adherent of the new philosophy? And yet the man was not ashamed to admit it; thanks to the Vice Chancellor's notorious liberality, such ideas were debated freely at the college, and the security officer had stood up just last week to wonder aloud – 'with all due respect to Doctor Blesserson here' – if Is-Land had enough Sec Gens now to be getting on with, a view for which no one had fired or demoted him. Samrod wiped at a small stain on the window with his thumb.

'She's lost her mind, Clay. She's hardly a serious foe.'

'Oh, Samrod. You're always such a sourpuss.' Clay sounded cross now. Cross, or mock-cross. 'Why aren't you overjoyed?' he cajoled. 'Magmason is – he wants to fête us. He's due any minute, for the launch of the new model.'

Samrod's body felt as though it were made of stone: a crumbling stone buttress for the iron tower block that was Clay Odinson. 'I'm tired, Clay. It's been exhausting, worrying so much.'

'So don't worry. Come to the Valley. Do some birdwatching, wild swimming, take a dolphin cruise on the lake. I'll send a car.'

'No.'

'I don't understand you. If you're so worried about your place in the world, you could do without alienating the Chief Convenor of the Wheel Meet.'

Outside, the IMBOD officer stood up, put his Tablette in his hipbelt, glanced up at the window. Samrod stepped back into his office.

'No, I mean don't send a car. I'll drive myself. I could do with some time on my own.'

'Good, Samrod, I'm glad you're seeing sense.'

'And Clay...'

'Yes, darling?'

His lips were dry as dust. 'I've been thinking about what you said. About joining you in the Woodlands. Maybe you're right. Maybe it has been a bit all work and no play for dull Samrod lately.'

'Oh.' Clay's surprise seamlessly morphed into a deep rumble of satisfaction. 'Samrod. *Never* a dull moment.'

'I'll arrive tonight, at nine. Don't wait for me. I want to join proceedings as the promised punishment. Uncle Samrod, arriving as threatened.' His face flushed and his stomach turned. 'I'll text en route.'

'Darling! Delicious! Stamen will be absolutely *tickled*!'

He rang off. The window was on the shady side of the building now, but the sweat was pouring off his back. He picked up his bag and took one last look around his office. His gaze lingered on his IMBOD Code Scientist of the Year trophies: five cloudy-white marble sculptures, smooth twisting ovoids, somewhere between a cell and a helix, arranged on their pedestals in an out-of-kilter V. Three for the Security Serum and its new editions over the years; two honouring the breakthroughs in the post-traumatic stress disorder treatment he'd devised. Beside them was a smaller trophy, a smooth ball of pink granite. He picked it up, felt its solid heft in the palm of his hand, stuffed it in his briefcase and flicked the lights off.

It was dark when he arrived at Springhill. The little lamps along the compound wall twinkled like fireflies and a pool of warm light fell on the road from the guard's booth. The Sec Gen inside was expecting him, didn't come out, just raised her hand and pointed at the entry post. Keeping one eye on her unconcerned silhouette, he rolled down his window. The night was loud with crickets, the air smelled of dried grass and a distant bonfire, and the sky was a black metal dome.

It was useless to pretend he still had a choice. He placed his forefinger against the scanner. The gates slid open.

He rolled up the window and sent one last text.

I'm here. x

Then he drove through the gates and braked in between them.

For a split second, nothing happened. He crouched in his seat, in the crash position. But although he had been expecting a thunderstorm on the roof of the car, nothing hit or rattled him; there was no sound except the thud of feet striking the ground in front of the car. He peered over the dashboard. They were landing just inside the beams cast by his headlights. One, then another, then another, then another. Sec Gens, the first model. His finest creation, some said. And they were beautiful to watch in full flow. Young men and women, tall, in perfect physical condition, leaping like big cats over the car and landing in the compound, huge thighs pumping like pistons, disappearing into the dark, bare soles flashing like binary Code, on-off, on-off, heading straight to the lodge or veering right towards the Woodlands.

SKKKRRAWHAACK. With the grating shriek of metal on metal, a massive force struck the car, jolting him sideways and cricking his neck out of alignment with his head. He ducked again; then, when no one tried to get into the car, he cautiously looked around. The gates had slammed shut against the back doors of the car. He turned the headlights off. In front of him, lights were blazing on in the lodge, shadows spilling out to wrestle on the lawn. He could hear faint calls of alarm and then the hunting horn: Springhill's own elite force of Sec Gens being activated to defend their masters and mistresses with their lives.

But thanks to his own detailed report on Springhill security, submitted an agonising month after his return from the ashfields, and a month before the INMA trial, Springhill's Sec Gens were vastly outnumbered by those now vaulting Samrod's car: a furious legion of Sec Gens, warriors who had been fed a diet of sickening videos over the last four weeks, whom he himself, their most venerated elder, had addressed and counselled and commanded; youths who knew exactly what was happening to their kinfolk in the

Woodlands; a revenge-and-rescue murmuration of outraged Sec Gens doing what Sec Gens did best – swarming and completely overpowering the enemy. He glanced in the rear-view mirror. Two massive shadowy figures were bundling the gate guard into a van, one of at least four blocking the road.

'Oh, and don't bother to try and run,' Silverstreamson had warned. 'They'll catch you in a fingersnap, and then we'll arrest you and try you with the rest of them. Stay in the car and wait for me. We'll tell Odinson we arrested you at the gate and are interrogating you separately.'

People were being dragged from the Woodlands now. Some were fighting back. Others, children, were being carried away, struggling and kicking and howling. As the last of Stonewayson's secret regiment leapt over his car, flicking up dirt, Samrod laid his head on the steering wheel and, for the first time in decades, wept like a newborn baby.

Acid Green

Bracelet Valley
12.10.99

'The potential ramifications of last night's raid on IMBOD's exclusive Springhill Retreat in Bracelet Valley are still unfolding, but what is shockingly clear at the moment is that overnight, Is-Land has become a rudderless ship of state.' The news van had sped up the road just this morning, roaring past Fasta on her way back from shopping in Lakeville, and now the journalist was beaming his report to the country.

'Turn it up please, Esfadur,' Brana urged. Her husband did so, and Yggdrasila's non-Sec Gen adults fell silent again, hanging on the journalist's every dreadful word.

'In a move that IMBOD spokespeople strenuously deny was an attempt at a coup, a Sec Gen regiment loyal to Minister of Spiritual Development Crystal Wyrdott was dispatched to Springhill Retreat to break up what is being described as an alleged paedophile ring composed of Is-Land's elite. Among those arrested and charged with crimes too abominable to relay over public broadcasting were Minister of the Eco-Economy Flint Cascadeson, Minister of Childhood Watt Grandcliffson, Minister of Penitence Tulip Hiltondott and Wheel Meet Chief Convenor himself, Stamen Magmason, leaving the Wheel Meet Deputy Convenor Riverine Farshordott to declare a state of national emergency. Local IMBOD officer Major Brockbankson has also been named as one of those rounded up in the raid, while celebrity figures now behind bars include renowned bio-architect Ahn Orson, former Top Ten singer Petal Blacksteppedott and Clay Odinson, the wounded hero of Kadingir reborn as Springhill's Director. While details of their alleged crimes must remain opaque on this channel, having done some digging in the sordid soil of Bracelet Valley, this reporter can reliably inform you that the action was taken after a tip-off from an anonymous local resident to the offices of prosecuting Justice Blade Stonewayson appeared to confirm longstanding suspicions about activities behind the compound walls. Justice Stonewayson's office has yet to make a comment, and with key seats on the Vision Council now empty, whether Deputy Convenor Riverine Farshordott succumbs to demands from other prominent New Purists to call an election remains to be seen. Stay tuned for live updates on the hour.'

Esfadur turned off the wallscreen, Brana drew open the curtains and together the two Elders faced the nearly fifty non-Sec Gen adults gathered in the Common Hall. A blade of red light from Baldur's long window fell over Fasta's hands in her lap. Although she had been watching the news all day, and nothing she'd just heard was a surprise any more, she felt a deep chill.

'An anonymous tip-off, he said,' Esfadur boomed. 'A phone call that could only have come from someone in this room, violating our communal word of honour, and undoing our collective decision to ensure our children's safety. We have no trump card now, my friends. Brockbankson and Orson are exposed for the vermin they are, and any effort to insist that Blesserson honour the terms of our agreement may well result in charges of treason against Brana and myself. If this *tipster* is seated here among us, would he or she please have the courage and decency to confess?'

No one spoke.

'Sif?' Esfadur looked straight in their direction.

'What!' Beside Fasta, Sif reacted, but her outrage met a cold circle of faces. Fasta's stomach flinched for her. 'You don't think . . . ? That's not *fair.*'

'Esfadur, what is this?' Vili demanded. 'Some kind of witch-hunt?'

'Vili. Sif was unhappy with the result of the vote, we all know that. She stated openly that she wanted Ahn Orson punished for his crimes. And now someone has called a prosecuting judge to alert his office to obscene goings-on at Springhill Retreat. I have to ask, Sif.'

Sif's face reddened. 'I accepted the democratic result, Esfadur. Vili and Fasta and I are still discussing what to do about the twins.' She stood, walked up to the two Elders and offered her Tablette to Brana. 'Check my calls. Read my emails. I had nothing to do with it.'

Brana raised her palm, rejecting the Tablette. 'It wasn't Sif, Esfadur.'

Esfadur regarded his Gaia partner. 'And how do you know that, Brana?'

'Because it was me.'

Fasta didn't want to stare, but she couldn't keep from glancing at Esfadur. At first, the elderman looked as stunned as everyone around her; then, briefly, his face was so stricken with hurt that Fasta felt the knife-stab in her own gut. Beside him, Brana drew herself up.

'I should have discussed it with you, Esfadur, I know. You are my life partner, the father of my only Birth-Code daughter, and the grandfather of our *two* Code granddaughters.'

'Two granddaughters? Halja may be a different person today from the girl she was, but she's still just one human being. Brana – are you well?' Esfadur's weathered face now expressed deep puzzlement, his voice finding its way through confusion to concern.

But Brana held up her hand. 'I am sorry. I have something to tell you, to tell the whole community. Meeting with that scorpion Blesserson, that *despicable* liar, has stung me into telling the truth.'

'The truth?' Esfadur flashed. 'And what truth would that be?'

It was excruciating to watch them but impossible to move. Fasta felt as though she'd been turned into stone. 'A difficult truth' Brana announced into the silence. 'Before Eya died, she told me a secret.

She made me promise not to tell you, Esfadur, because she didn't want you ever to be disappointed in her. But that promise was made in a different age. Our country is in crisis and the time has come to reveal to you, Esfadur, my friends, that Halja was not Eya's first child. My daughter had another daughter, while she was at Code College in Atourne. She was afraid to tell us, Esfadur my love, because she said we wouldn't like the father. She never told me anything about him other than that he made her laugh.'

'Brana, why are you telling everyone this?' Esfadur stared at the woman he loved as if snakes were pouring out of her mouth. 'And what has it got to do with Springhill?'

'Hear me out. One of Eya's friends at college was a young woman by the name of Cora Pollen.'

There was a second's delay, processing time. Someone gasped. Esfadur recoiled. Brana marched briskly on into the breach.

'Cora suggested that Eya take a work holiday at Cora's aunt's community. That was the year Eya went to the dry forest. She gave birth there, named her daughter Astra and left her infant in the care of Cora's aunt, Hokma Blesser.'

Again, the news took a moment to sink in. When it did, Fasta thought the roof would fly off the Hall.

'*We are Astra Ordott's community, Yggdrasila,*' Brana declaimed over the cries and gasps and snorts of revulsion.

'Shhh. Shhh,' Esfadur commanded. 'Finish what you've started, Brana. Finish.'

'Thank you, my love. Astra might be a traitor and has surely lost her mind just as poor Halja has lost hers, but what we know now is that her actions are not her fault.'

That generated another round of objections, but Brana overrode them all.

'She was given MPT as a teenager for what? Do you recall?' People exchanged glances. Fasta thought back with a struggle. To be honest, she didn't quite remember the extent of the Ordott creature's crimes.

'For attacking Ahn Orson.' It was Baldur. His statement hung in the air, a sword of light cleaving understanding from uproar.

'Correct.' Brana was blazing now. 'And so perhaps we now know why a young woman might attack that odious man. Astra has spun out of control. But she has been pushed into madness by a corrupt, debauched regime, hostile to the founding principles of Is-Land, which we must stand together to bring down. Esfadur' – she turned to her partner – 'what is the point of attending all those Concerned Elders meetings if we never act, except to protect our own little corner of the world? We know that Blade Stonewayson is a New Purist. We know that Crystal Wyrdott wishes to bring this country back to a state of spiritual harmony with Gaia. Knowledge is power, you said, Esfadur my love. And after that meeting with Blesserson, after seeing him and a senior IMBOD officer cover up what was clearly depraved, systematic child abuse, I knew that we must use our knowledge to root out the evil riddling the heart of this country's elite. We had to tell what we knew to people who could do something decisive about it.'

'But Brana.' Esfadur found his voice again. 'We're a community. We act collectively, and we respect collective decisions, as Sif has done. Sif, please accept my apologies for suspecting you of Brana's deed.'

'I didn't tell you I wanted to make contact with Stonewayson,' Brana replied, 'because I knew you would all need time to adjust to the truth of our relationship with Astra Ordott, and I feared some of you would never accept it. I didn't know that Stamen Magmason would be found up at Springhill, but frankly it did not surprise me.'

'You took a grave risk, Brana.' Esfadur shook his head. 'Riverine Farshordott could still put the whole country under martial law, with Sec Gens on every corner.'

'She does not have the will of the people.'

Brana, so implacable, so righteous. Anger boiled up in Fasta, could not be contained. 'Esfadur's right, Brana,' she flared. 'You didn't have the authority to take that risk for us. We did a deal with

Brockbankson and Blesserson. Now Brockbankson's in jail, and that means our children are right back in line for the Security Shot. You, you with Halja to worry about, how can you sleep knowing that our children might end up the same way now?'

'We don't know what will happen yet, Fasta,' Brana said. 'There's been no news of Blesserson: that poisonous toad was clearly working for Springhill when we met him, but from the results of Astra's INMA trial, I suspect he must have done some deal with Stonewayson. He will probably be put in charge of reforming the whole Sec Gen project.'

'You trust Blesserson?' Baldur snorted.

'Just to look after himself.' Brana stood. 'Again, I am sorry, my community. In acting as I did, I violated a central tenet of how we live here. I will make amends. I am willing to risk jail to help anyone preserve their child from the Security Shot. But for now, please excuse me. I need to make a Tablette call to Atourne. I am going to make an appointment to hold an ion chamber visit with my granddaughter in the Ashfields. Esfadur, you are welcome to join me.'

And with that, Brana turned on her heel and, in her translucent green gown, floated between them, out of the Common Hall.

Shadow Blue

The Asfarian Desert
14.11.99

People said the desert was golden, or red, or white, even black, but those people had never really *looked* at the desert. The desert was a ghostly flock of birds-of-paradise, forever ruffling its rose, violet, apricot, flame and tawny-gold feathers. The desert was a restless lover in bed, its contours shifting with the wind, continuously revealing new curves and dimples. Sometimes the winds whipped up a cyclone of sand, a distant spiral that spun across the horizon, which the Asfarian guards called a *mergallá*, a demon spirit it was best to avert one's eyes from in case it took offence and came hunting for you. Sometimes the rains blew in, driving hard for days, and the desert became a soup of sand and the guards whistled through their teeth, saying this was new, this was bad, this was a warning from the Old Ones, no, this was a gift from the Oneness-of-the-Many, for afterwards there would be streaks of greenery in places, he was told, where plants had never spouted before. But for all these ceaseless changes, the essence of the desert never changed. Its horizons never disappointed; its immensity always humbled him. Even with his eyes closed, Peat was happy: he could sit and inhale the desert all day, feeling its mineral smell feed his bones. He had no idea why the Asfarians called this place a prison.

They had installed him in a cave, in a craggy orange cliff gouged by other caves, dwelled in by other men. 'You'll garden with the group every morning,' the guard had said. 'You're new and they won't trust you at first, so they'll ignore you. Then they'll ignore you because they're happier that way.'

One man did try to talk to him, a small, wiry man with darting black eyes, who leaned over a row of carrots to whisper about escaping, some garbled plan to join forces and overcome a guard with their hoes, but before he could respond, a massive man, not as tall but nearly as broad as Peat, stepped over and told the would-be conspirator to be quiet or he'd bash his head against that rock, tear his flesh from his bones and feed it to the vultures. The small man blinked with furious spite, then returned to jabbing the ground with his hoe.

'He hasn't been here long,' the older man said to Peat. 'He doesn't know. Here you are with yourself again, and with god, and from that reunion there is no escape.'

After that, there was silence. And if not happiness, simple relief. The relief of using his muscles in the garden to grow his own food; his hands in the lean-to, to weave baskets from reeds the guards brought in from the coast; his mind in the morning or early evening, reading the Asfarian Holy Book – made of stiff paper, and the only book he was provided with unless he wanted to request a Holy Book from another tradition; his legs on the cliffs and the sands, walking at night, as far as he wanted, then back to the cliff. He could have walked on to evaporate in the heat of the day, there was nothing stopping him; men did, and then later the guards released vultures, muzzled vultures with electronic tags on their legs so the guards could find them, pacing the desert, their wings spread in frustration, the man's eyes bloodied but not plucked out, his flesh bruised but not torn by the birds' blunted beaks, his body a spent force, ready to be buried in the cemetery a day's drive to the north, in the village where the families came for their annual visits.

No family would visit him. Tapputu and Bartol had said they would come, but he didn't need visitors. There were animals, traces of rodents and lizards in the rocks, and birds. But happiest of all, he slept without dreaming.

So it went. Until the letter came.

The guard handed it to him at the garden entrance, on his way back to his cell to make soup. A single sheet of blue paper, folded and sealed. He slipped it in his robe pocket to read after lunch. But after lunch, he sat and watched the wind undress a dune, one thin billowing sheet of sand at a time. Then he slept on his mat of rushes through the oven hours of the day and rose to work in the lean-to. After work, he went for a walk. With every stride, he was aware of the letter in his robe: not heavy, but present, insistent, with its faint slither against his thigh. When he returned, it was too dark to read. He took the letter out of his robe and placed it under a rock, so the wind would not take it in the night.

In the morning, after he'd boiled water for his tea, he opened it. It was an email in Gaian, one that had been read and printed out by the prison.

From: sonovason@greenberg.ama

Dear Peat Orson,

I trust this finds you well treated in your new environment and well served by your legal team. I write to you in my capacity as the lawyer for your Shelter sister, Astra Ordott. As you may know, Astra took an active concern in your trial, sending messages to Muzi Bargadala and his family, asking them to show mercy to you. You may not know that, in sending these messages, Astra violated the terms of her incarceration and as a result is now enduring extremely harsh conditions in her prison, Ashfields Maximum. All her privileges have been revoked, and she is currently unable to read or socialise normally with other prisoners. Although allowed daily exercise, and to eat one meal a week with other people, she is virtually in solitary confinement, and her case is high on CONC's human rights watch.

I understand that Astra and you have had a difficult

relationship over the years, and that both of you have changed so greatly since you last saw each other that you may not feel you know her any more. But I wish to assure you that in all the time I have known her, your welfare has always been uppermost in Astra's mind. Hoping that her love and concern for you will mean something to you, and might indeed be reciprocated, I write to you, not at her behest, but because I believe you are her best, if not her only, chance at improving the desperate situation she now finds herself in.

The letter finished on the back of the sheet. He raised his head and gazed out at the desert. The horizon was rimmed with gold. He watched for a long time as the dunes began to glow more deeply. Then he refolded the letter, placed it back under the rock and got up and went to the garden.

WINTER RE 99–100

Desert Red
Misted Silver

Acid Green
Burnt Orange
Acid Green

Misted Silver
Desert Red
Acid Green
Misted Silver

Bruise Purple
Sour Gold
Bruise Purple
Sour Gold
Bruise Purple
Sour Gold
Bruise Purple

Desert Red

Asfar
01.12.99

'Your fingernails are dirty.' Suen's mother swatted the back of his hand, making him lose his place in the Braille.

'I've been gardening, Ama.' He searched, found the equation, sped on through the text.

'You'd never know that from the greenhouse. Who's been looking after all your plants?'

'Thank you, Ama.'

'You're not listening to me, are you, son?'

'I'm reading, Ama. The book is on special loan from the Institute library. I have to finish it tonight.'

'That's all you do here these days. Read and eat. And then you're off again, back to sleep in the cold and the dirt at that drug haven. What kind of an education do you call that?'

Sighing, he put the book down. *Listen to your mother.* If he broke that promise, perhaps the plant spirits would not reward him with insight. But doing so was awfully difficult when *she* refused to listen to *him*.

'It's not a drug haven,' he said patiently. 'I've told you before, Ama – it's a Psychosphere Garden. We're working with the Spirit Molecule, DMT, to develop plants that will expand our ability to communicate with each other in the realm of shared consciousness. Shamans have taken psychotropics for millennia, but we're trying to refine the process. It's fascinating work. Look, Ama.' He reached for the vase of flowers he had brought her from the garden, took a long-stemmed daisy and offered it to her. 'Every plant has a spiritual vibration. So, for example, everyone knows that the daisy represents humility and innocence, and the rose embodies passion.'

Nanshe took the flower and put it behind his ear. 'You should be growing roses for your sweetheart, Suen. Not giving daisies to your mother.'

The rose greenhouse at the garden was already nicknamed the Love Plot. One day he would find a way to tell her. But not today. 'I'm explaining things to you. All those associations aren't just symbolic or based on the way the plant looks. When we ingest a plant or inhale its perfume, aspects of its DNA trigger reactions in our bodies. Our physical bodies are vehicles for our subtle bodies, therefore the plants affect us spiritually, too. So combining lantern leaf with other plants invests each collective psychotropic experience with a complex spiritual lesson. You can do that by consuming more than one plant at the same time, but in the long run cross-breeding takes less land and water and is more cost-effective. To fuse plants effectively, though, you need to understand their spiritual DNA. This book was written by a Gaian mystic in New Zonia and lists the chemical equations for the vibratory energies of hundreds of plants.'

'Written by a Gaian!'

He clutched the book to his chest, afraid she would rip it out of his hands. 'The Gaians had some good ideas before they got obsessed with Is-Land, Ama. This book enables me to ascertain which plants would bond most easily with each other.'

His mother clumped away and turned the tap on full blast, a cataract in the kitchen sink, as if trying to drown out his ideas. He put the book back on the table and continued reading, one hand pondering interesting plants, the other skimming ahead for possible matches. Chemistry was so satisfying; he loved the way molecules bonded, like hooked fingers or . . . He flushed as his mind drifted. It had been hard to leave Cyrus, even for one night.

'It's drugs, that's what it is.' Nanshe started in again from the sink. 'The only good thing about leaving Kadingir, son, was getting you away from those morpheus users, and here you are, making drugs in *school*.'

He set down the book again. 'They're not drugs – not recreational ones, anyway. They're medicine. Soul medicine. Morpheus is a private experience and highly addictive. Psilocybin-based plant voyaging is very different. Ingesting DMT helps people stop taking drugs or drinking too much. Our technology will not only provide a practical replacement for metal-based communications devices, it will help people break their addiction to Tablettes.'

His mother hrumphed and clattered. She was stacking the dishwasher now, with such vehemence he expected a bowl to smash. 'So we're going to be able to talk on the plant-phone to people, and send plant-emails, and look up the weather on the plant-internet, and read plant-newspapers and share plant-videos and download plant-books and plant street-maps right into our DNA?'

'Yes. Well, sort of. I'm not sure yet exactly how the psychosphere will depart from the internet. We're still working on all the details.'

'We we we.' She slammed the dishwasher door shut. 'You've given up all your own work. You could be marketing that vest of yours. How many poor blind people could benefit from your inventions?'

He laughed. 'You mean, how much money could I earn from the vest, Ama?'

'What's wrong with earning money? You'll need it to start a family one day.'

She was back to her default position. But despite his annoyance, he felt a twist of guilt. His mother had lost nearly everything in their dislocation from Kadingir – her husband, her home, her sheep – and all she wanted now was a grandchild to give her old age some purpose. He hadn't talked about it yet with Cyrus, of course, but Cyrus liked kids. His little cousins were always underfoot at the garden, trailing Suen around the polytunnels, climbing on him and asking interesting questions. And now Cyrus wanted to meet *his* family. The plan was to invite his mother to the upcoming open day, when the team would show off their work to their families and other students. If she could just see how happy he was out there, and how impressive and well-loved Cyrus was, then – if everything that was happening between him and Cyrus wasn't simply a beautiful dream bubble, as he sometimes woke up terrified that it was – then maybe one day he could risk telling her of his real desires for the future.

The daisy was tickling his cheek. He took it out from behind his ear and slipped it back in the vase. 'We've got just over three months left to meet the Old Ones' deadline, Ama, or no one will be starting any families. If we make it, and win the prize, I can get back to my own work after that. Everything I'm learning right now will help me make better plant-based assistive technology.'

'You can take one day off. I want you to volunteer tomorrow at the neighbourhood council house.'

'What?'

'Hadis told me about it. They're having a Living Book Day. People, special people who have overcome hardship and challenges, sit in the Common Room and talk to anyone who wants to ask them questions. There's a girl who used to be a boy. And a man who swam the whole length of the Mikku from Kadingir to the Gulf. Hadis thought you could go, too.'

He was aghast. 'I'm not a "special person", Ama. I'm a totally average person, seeking to reach his full potential, if you would just let me alone for a minute!'

'You *are* a special person, son.'

His chest hurt. What did his mother think he was, a freak show exhibit? 'Special to you, maybe, but not to anyone else. I'm a team member. I have to go back to the garden tomorrow.'

'It's just for one day. You could tell people about your invention,' she persisted. 'Maybe someone would like to invest in it.'

'Ama, please stop nagging me.' He bookmarked the page and got up. 'I'm going outside for some fresh air.'

'Put a sweater on!'

Ignoring her, he marched onto the patio, sliding the door shut behind him with a thud. Outside, in another alarming bout of strange weather, it was cold – not the normal light winter's chill in the evening air, but bitterly cold. Goosebumps rising on his arms, he fumbled for his Tablette and earbuds, calling Cyrus as he ducked into the greenhouse.

'Hey, Suen.' Cyrus chuckled. 'How's your mother?'

He switched on the solar heater and reached for a robe on the back of the door. 'She's driving me crazy already!' In a burst of anguish, he explained: the distractions, the interruptions, the humiliation, how she never took him seriously. She had complained about the vest when he was working on it, but now that he'd finished with it, it was all she could talk about. And now she wanted him to go and try and make people feel sorry for him and beg them for money. Cyrus listened to it all in silence.

'Actually, I think it's a good idea.'

He couldn't believe his ears. '*Cyrus*. It's a terrible idea.'

'No, it's a *great* idea. You could talk about the psychosphere! Canvas opinion. Prepare people for the plant-tech revolution!'

Cyrus was ignited, flaming with the enthusiasm that normally thrilled Suen to the bone. But not right now. Today, Suen was dumbfounded. 'They're coming to talk to some poor blind boy about how he manages to stumble around the city. They won't know a thing about psychotropics. They'll be just like my mother and think we're no better than morpheus-heads!'

'So enlighten them! If we want Plant IT to take off, we must have public support.'

'If we want Plant IT to take off, we have to win the prize. I can't afford to be away from the project for a whole day.' He felt a pang between his ribs. Was there another reason Cyrus didn't want him to come to the garden tomorrow?

'We have to be ambassadors for the psychosphere, Suen. And you're not some poor blind boy. You're an inventor, who was imprisoned by IMBOD, and Astra Ordott is your cousin-in-law.

You've got tons of important things to tell people. Look, if you want, I'll come with you. I could chat with the other Living Books.' Cyrus paused. 'I could meet your mother.'

Suen's ribs eased a little. Shivering, he reached for a blanket. The space heater wasn't strong enough to deal with this cold snap. 'I don't know if we should do that yet. I thought we should wait for the open day.'

'That's not for two weeks.' Cyrus hummed. 'There'll be a trans woman at the event, too, right? And your mother wants you to appear at it with her?'

He knew where this was going. It was all right for Cyrus – he was out to his family. 'Cyrus, my mother thinks trans people are like . . . some kind of regenerated exotic *animal*. Like a liger or tigon. Some kind of wonder of science, but nothing to do with her or her son.'

'Okay, but she doesn't think they're a sin, or disgusting. That's a good sign, Suen. And if she knows I helped persuade you to come, she might like me a bit better.'

He was being assailed on all sides. He didn't want people to look at him with pity or marvel at his abilities, to go home and tell their families, 'Imagine who I met today – a blind boy who studies science, fancy that?' He didn't want to be a Living Book. He wanted to go back to the garden.

'But we were planning to have the bonfire tomorrow.'

'This is more important. If you don't want to take advice from me, then heed the lantern leaf. It told you to listen to your mother, didn't it?'

He wanted to pull the blanket over his head, never come out. 'Suen?'

Listen to your mother. It was as if the plant were still in his veins. 'All right.' He accepted it. 'I'll go. But only if you come too.'

'Speaking of coming . . . where are you?' Cyrus asked, in *that* tone of voice.

'*Cyrus.*' Cyrus deserved to wait. 'I'm in a glasshouse and my family will be coming back for supper soon. Plus it's cold in here.'

'Here, too. All the more reason to get the blood flowing.'

His blood was already tingling, but he stood up. 'I've got to finish my library book. As in my real library book. If my mother lets me, that is.'

'Tell your mother I'm coming tomorrow, and that I said you get all your genius from her.'

'Ha ha.' He rang off and stepped back out onto the patio. As the cold air brushed his nerves, something damp landed on his forehead and cheeks. Puzzled, he patted his face and head. They were wet, but there was no sound of rain. Everything was quieter, the symphony of the city dampened, too. He held out his hand, felt it fill with gentle blossoms of wetness. Gingerly, he licked at his palm, felt cold, fluffy crystals melt on his tongue. Could it be . . . ?

In his pocket, his Tablette burbled. Cyrus' ringtone.

'Suen, get outside. It's *snowing.*'

'Yeah, I know.' He lifted his face, let the flakes kiss his eyelashes and mouth. Inside him, a field of winter roses bloomed.

Misted Silver

The Ashfields
15.12.99

'Big day for lickle Ordotty,' Lichena sneered. 'All ready to meet Omma, are you?'

Goosepimpled and shivering, Astra shifted from foot to foot and, as best she could with cuffed hands, clasped her blanket around her. It was freezing in the cell, an unprecedented natural atmospheric cold. Yesterday she'd exercised for an hour in the snow. The tiny flakes melted as soon as they hit the concrete yard, but still, snow was unheard of in Is-Land. At the one weekly meal Astra was still allowed to take with the other prisoners, Cora had told her that the long cold snap was creating havoc in the country. Farming, transportation, elder mortality, all were being badly affected, and the hospitals were full. Astra wasn't surprised. Her nose and throat were raw and her left nostril was leaking steadily, her sheet damp from wiping the snot. Even Vultura was cold: a row of icicle icons framed the wallscreen and the avatar shivered melodramatically every five minutes.

'Am I supposed to go wrapped in a blanket?' she complained. 'I requested winter clothing five days ago.'

Lichena, clad in a fleece jacket, earmuffs and wool trousers, scowled. 'Warm clothes are on sale in the shop. Now c'mon, drop the blanket, let's go.'

She held her ground. 'You want me to walk around half-naked in this temperature?'

'Aw, poor baby. I'm not having your blanket removed from the cell. Security risk, isn't it?' Lichena slapped her palm with the diss-stick. 'Now get going. Or do you want me to give you a bit of heat?'

So far, the cold had made Lichena slightly less aggressive: she didn't like leaving her lukewarm office to loiter in the cold cells, not even to torture the prisoners. But her unexpressed sadism could be building up steam, and there was no point risking further 'security' measures. Astra let the blanket fall to the floor and followed Lichena out down the hall.

'You know my Privilege Account is frozen,' she grumbled as they waited for the elevator. 'I can't buy anything in the shop. And the normal winter blanket ration isn't enough for this cold. I've got a human right to be warm.'

'Yeah, well, Hiltondott left some pretty big holes in the budget.' The guard thrust her fleeced arm under Astra's nose. 'You think this gear is so cosy? It's crap, that's what it is. Might as well be made out of cobwebs. But when we asked for another layer, did we get one? Hell we did. The guards aren't getting any special winter treatment, Lady Ordott, so why should traitors be any different?'

It was a rare concession of news from a guard; though, thanks to Cora and Jasper, Astra already knew all about the political scandal. Although two months had passed since the Springhill raid, the arrests of Ahn Orson and Clay Odinson still charged her with joy; she could happily endure any hardship the prison threw at her, knowing that two of her arch-enemies had fallen on their own spears, brought down by their own relentless depravity. The broader ramifications of Springhill were still unfolding. In the latest twist to the crisis, it transpired that Tulip Hiltondott had been diverting large sums of public monies to a fictitious 'Internal Security' company and, allegedly with Stamen Magmason's knowledge and approval, investing heavily in Sex Gen development. After the slew of Wheel Meet arrests, a new Minister of Penitence had been appointed, but so far, the prisoners had failed to see any benefit from the change. It was nice to know, she thought, watching

Lichena stab the elevator button again, that the guards were suffering, too.

'Fracking *at last.*' Lichena pushed her into the elevator. 'C'mon, Princess Nutdott, grandmama's waiting.'

Astra descended in silence, refusing to rise to Lichena's bait. This 'Lady' and 'Princess' goading was new and persistent, but only mildly irritating. Nor did she feel excited about the visit. Hearing, a couple of weeks after the Springhill raid, from Eya's Birth-Code mother, a woman named Brana Yggdrasiladott, had come as a shock, but had not raised any great hopes of an ally: it was clear that her relative thought she was mad. 'I am concerned about your mental health and the negative impact that growing up in Or had on you,' the brief letter had said, going on to explain what Astra already knew – that her Birth mother was dead – and concluding with a request for an ion chamber visit to 'meet you properly and hear your story in your own words'. She'd filed the letter in a new folder on her shelf and spent a few days deciding how to reply.

Cora had long ago told her that Eya's family were typical Bracelet Valley snobs: wealthy, ultra-conservative Gaians who would have been horrified to learn that their daughter had conceived a child with a Non-Lander. When she'd told the other women in the dining hall about the letter, Cora had tried to persuade her not to see Brana. Her grandmother would be a Gaian Hymn Book thumper, Cora said, visiting to try and convert her, and to blame Hokma for all her problems. If Astra had any sense, she would refuse the request.

'If she really cared about you, Astra, she'd come and visit in person. If she can't see how much you've suffered to win back that right, she won't understand a *thing* about you.'

'Aw!' Rosetta had objected. 'It's her grandmother, Cora. Maybe she's too old to travel. Astra's got to meet her at least.'

After considering all the options, Astra had decided in the end to accept. Who cared if this woman was an evangelical New Purist or emotional blackmailer? Nothing could be worse than watching

Hokma's memories. More importantly, it was warm in the ion chamber. She'd let her name be put on the list.

The prison's sole ion chamber had been installed as an extension on the ground floor. Lichena led her in and handcuffed her to the solitary chair, then left her under Vultura's watchful gaze, the avatar filling the back wallscreen of the windowless cube. For a minute or two, as the guard communicated with the chamber in Atourne, Astra luxuriated in the heat. Then a ghostly silver-grey form appeared in front of her: the translucent figure of an elderwoman in flowing robes, her long garment masking the chair she was sitting on in her own ion chamber, hundreds of kilometres away.

VISIT BEGINS. A red announcement flashed over Vultura's head and the wallscreen clock switched to stopwatch, starting its countdown. In front of it, the ion woman gasped, her hand flying to her mouth.

'Granddaughter. Oh, goodness. What on Gaia's green earth are they making you wear?'

It was a no-frills chamber. You couldn't choose different wallpaper. There were only two ion shades on offer – silver or bronze, which Jasper preferred – and either the audio connection or the wallscreen speakers weren't great; there was static on her grandmother's voice and her lips weren't quite synced. But the visual transmission was pretty good: Astra could see the fine creases in the woman's face moving in an almost comical expression of shock and concern.

'It's a chastity tankini. All prisoners in Is-Land wear them.'

'Yes, I knew that.' The woman recomposed herself. 'But I'd never seen one before. Does it hurt?'

'It's okay, Brana. I'm used to it.'

They stared at each other for a long moment. It was nothing like looking in a time-lapse mirror; where Astra was short and compact, with a short, dark pelt of hair and a small round face, Brana Yggdrasiladott was tall and angular, her long wavy locks framing a handsome, square-jawed face. Her attire was an understated blend of elegance and comfort, the long robe augmented with a sateen hip-purse on a thin shoulder strap, finely crafted sandals, small droplet earrings and a wedding ring on her left hand. But there was something similar about the shapes of their eyes. Astra felt a sudden pulse in her chest: this was it, the Code-recognition moment. She'd experienced it before, around Non-Landers and then with her Code father. She'd forgotten what it was like. As if life were a giant puzzle and part of you was being clicked into place, whether you liked it or not.

Astra broke the silence. 'Are you in Bracelet Valley?'

'No. There isn't a prison in the Valley. I took the sky train to Atourne, and then a taxi out to the prison. I must apologise that it's taken me so long to arrange the visit. I had to acquire many relevant permissions.'

She spoke High Gaian with an accent Astra had only ever heard on Tablette dramas when she was young. Nimma would have called it 'refined' or 'cultured'; Astra and her friends would have said 'hoity-toity' or 'la-di-da'.

'Is this your first time in a prison?' she asked.

'Well, I'm not exactly in prison, dear. The ion chambers are in a separate block.' Her earrings trembled when she laughed; she looked nervous now.

Who was this woman? 'Are you a New Purist, Brana?'

Brana smoothed her robe over her knee. 'Well, yes, I suppose I am. Though I certainly don't think that's all that I am. I'm a painter – a watercolourist – and a herbalist, and an Yggdrasila elder.' She smiled again, a generous smile her handsome face wore well. 'You can call me Omma, if you like.'

She shrugged. 'I call my Birth mother Eya.'

The smile shrank and the ion eyes shone with tears. 'I wish she could have seen you. You're so pretty. A different pretty from hers, though. Here, this is Eya. Just a year after you were born.' She leaned forwards and pressed a button Astra couldn't see. 'They said I could show you.'

Ion chambers transmitted the diaphanous echo-shapes of human beings and selected objects; they couldn't reproduce two-dimensional images. Even so, visitors weren't allowed to bring their Tablettes with them. But with 'relevant permissions', photos could be shared on the wallscreen. Behind Brana's form, Vultura shrank into a corner box and a young woman's face filled the chamber. Eya, trapped in time, younger than Astra was now.

She looked like Brana. Fine-boned and square-jawed, with tumbling blonde hair and tanned skin. Astra stared at her, aware of an inner shield, stronger than the tankini, a shield against Eya's beauty. This was her Birth-Code mother. She should love her. But Eya had abandoned her. Had gone back home to Bracelet Valley after giving birth, never tried to re-establish contact, never written. She had become a fairy tale, a princess Astra had dreamed of meeting one day, a childish dream wrapped up in a Belonging Box she'd left behind years ago.

'I take after my Code father,' she said.

'Yes. I imagine you must.' Brana's expression formalised itself. 'And how is he?'

'He returned to Gaia. Nearly four years ago.'

'Oh. I didn't know.' Brana's lips disappeared for a moment. 'I'm sorry.'

She waited, but Brana asked no questions about Zizi. Probably to Brana it was just as well that her inconvenient Non-Land father was out of the picture. There was, however, something Astra urgently wanted to know.

'Did Eya tell you about me, or did you just find out recently?'

'No, no. Eya told me. Before she returned to Gaia.' Brana blinked rapidly, and again her lips twisted into a nearly invisible line. 'Before she died, she gave birth again. You have a half-Code sister, Astra. Halja.'

Brana offered the information like a bright gift through her tears; a gift Astra didn't need. 'I know about Halja. Eya's friend Cora Pollen heard about her and told Hokma, and Hokma told me. That's my Shelter mother. She returned to Gaia, too.'

'I know who Hokma is. I have been following your case ever since you were deported.'

She should, she knew, be warmer to Brana. The woman must be taking a huge risk to see her. But she felt, suddenly, furious.

'Why didn't you visit me before, then? You could have come and found me in Or after Eya died, when I was little.'

Brana smoothed her dress. 'Astra, in our community, families are supposed to be formed with the approval of all sets of parents. Your father and grandfather would have been very upset to know Eya had a secret relationship and bore a child during her college years, and she made me promise never to tell them. I could hardly cross the country to find you without breaking that promise. But I thought about you every day, I can assure you. When you were declared a traitor and deported, it was quite a shock for me to learn from the news that your Code father was a Non-Lander. I was very angry with Eya for some time after that discovery.'

She understood why Cora had advised her not to see Brana. She wanted to shout at this prim, cowardly, self-righteous woman with her quivering earrings, who had never met a Non-Lander in her life.

'You don't know anything about my father. Don't you *dare* judge him.'

'Astra.' Brana drew herself up and lifted her chin. 'I am not judging your father. But the fact remains that he was a Non-Lander, living illegally in Is-Land. By entering into a relationship with my daughter, he was seriously endangering her and her family. I can understand you wishing to reunite with him, but your own actions in rejecting Is-Land and becoming a symbol of the destruction of our country have been challenging for many people to accept.'

With difficulty, Astra mastered her anger enough to demand, 'So why are you here, then?'

Brana contemplated her wedding ring. 'Recent events have given me a different perspective on your actions. Astra, do you know about Ahn Orson's arrest?'

Her lip curled at the sound of his name. 'I know all about Spring-hill. Well, what's been on the news, at least.'

Brana looked straight at her again. 'Do you recall from the reports that there was an informant in Bracelet Valley?'

She thought back. 'Someone called Stonewayson's office, didn't they?'

'Yes. That person was me.'

'You?' Incredulous, she stared at the ion form. Brana might be wearing New Purist robes, but this high and mighty Gaian lady secretly reporting on IMBOD sounded about as likely as her piss-ing all over a Wheel Meet flower bed.

'Yes. Two children in Yggdrasila saw Ahn Orson abusing a young Sec Gen in the woods. Your grandfather returned to the spot and took photographs: it was unmistakably him. It made me think . . . about the way you attacked him when you were a teen-ager.' Brana's mouth twisted. 'Oh, Astra. If he hurt you. If he . . . touched you when you were little . . . and made you . . . the way that you are . . . so help me, Gaia, I'll kill him.'

Brana was crying. Astra was invaded by confusion, her contempt for Brana's ignorance suddenly punctured by a guilty desire to com-fort the woman.

'No. No, he didn't touch me. He hurt Hokma. He had an affair, with . . .' She paused, not wanting to name Congruence. 'With an underage girl. An older teen, not a child. They went public when she came of age and the community accepted it. But before that, he and Hokma fell out, over me, mainly, when he discovered I hadn't received the Security Shot. When Hokma died in jail, I thought Ahn and Hokma's brother had arranged for her to be killed, to stop her telling the court that they both knew about me. That's why I attacked him.'

Brana was dabbing her eyes with a hanky. 'Are you sure? Some-times children repress the memory. And then later on, they act out all of their feelings of rage.'

It had never occurred to her that she might have been abused by

Ahn. She searched back, but all through her childhood Ahn had been remote, untouchable, gliding by with his head in the clouds of his genius. 'No. Honestly, no. I had enough to act out, just by not being a Sec Gen.'

Brana sniffled. 'Well, I'm glad of that.' She put her hanky back in her purse. 'I met Samrod Blesserson. He's a nasty piece of work, up to his neck in Springhill's foul business. By rights he should have been arrested, too, but he seems to have slipped the noose. My theory is that he did some kind of deal with Stonewayson and will be testifying against all those vile people.'

Again, Brana had dumbfounded her.

'Blesserson was involved with the Sex Gens?' Her pulse quickened. 'Are you *positive*?'

'Well, he didn't say as much, but after we reported the photographs we took of Ahn to the local IMBOD officer, Springhill sent Blesserson to barter with us for our silence. I'm ashamed to say we struck a deal at first. He said we could be a pilot project, to start phasing out the Sec Gens, and our children wouldn't have to receive the Security Shot if we didn't want them to. We voted on it, and though I desperately wanted to protect our children, I voted 'Don't Know'. Why should *anyone's* child be forced to be a Sec Gen, I thought? If Gaia wanted us to evolve into superhuman warriors, She would alter us in Her own good time. And it was so patently obvious that Ahn Orson wouldn't be punished. Would *keep on* abusing children! And of course I couldn't get you out of my mind. So in the end, I called Stonewayson. I knew from the New Purist network that he and Crystal Wyrdott were starting to question the need for the Sec Gen programme, and I thought if he knew about Springhill and could expose their despicable practices, public opinion might swing our way. I suppose it was a big risk, but there's still a chance we might win.'

Astra sat back, taking it all in. 'When did you meet with him?'

'I didn't meet him. I called him.' Brana smiled proudly. 'On an untraceable Tablette I got through the New Purist network.'

'No. I mean Blesserson.'

The woman's brow furrowed. 'Sometime in the late spring. I called Stonewayson just after the solstice, as I recall.'

'That explains it!' She strained against her shackles. 'Why he wasn't arrested. Brana, Blesserson came *here* in the summer. Two or three weeks after the solstice. He tried to get me to drop my petition to access Hokma's memories. I refused. I assumed he was afraid Stonewayson would grant me access to the files, and that must mean they contained incriminating evidence – that he killed her. But Stonewayson didn't let me view all the files in the end. *That's* why Blesserson hasn't been arrested. You're right, he did do a deal with Stonewayson: to betray all his cronies at Springhill in exchange for getting off *scot-free* for Hokma's *murder.*'

She was sweating, she was so angry, and her raw nose was splashing snot onto her bound arms. It was Brana's turn to stare.

'Won't they even let you wipe your nose?'

'No. Not while I'm talking to you.'

Her grandmother glanced around the cell. 'Do you think there are microphones in here?'

'Supposedly not, but yes, of course,' Astra said crossly, shaking her head to clear her nose. 'But I don't think it really matters what you say. Just coming to see me will have put you on IMBOD's radar. You're the first visitor I've ever had, except for my lawyer.'

Brana's eyes widened. 'Really?'

Astra shrugged. 'Yeah, really. I'm a traitor, remember? I want the people who used to live in this land to be able to come back and share it with us. To be able to farm it like they used to, and fish in the rivers, and go for hikes in the dry forest mountains.'

Brana flinched. 'I'm sorry, Astra. This is a lot for me to take in. I'm sure most of the Non-Landers are perfectly ordinary people. But they can't come and live here. They don't share our values.'

'No. They don't. They don't turn human beings into killing machines. That's what's wrong with Halja, isn't it? She's like my *brother.* They *destroyed her mind* on the Hem.'

'Please don't shout at me, Astra.'

She simmered down. 'I'm sorry. But I'm not a traitor. There's plenty of space in Is-land, especially if we knock down the Boundary and regenerate the Southern Belt. I don't see why we can't all learn to live together. You wear robes now, don't you? Well, the Non-Landers can learn to respect skyclad people and not eat meat. They've said that they'll try. My father lived in a permaculture community, Brana. The Non-Landers know plenty about living in harmony with the land.'

Brana's face twitched. 'You have the right to think that,' she said at last. 'You have the right to think what you like. It's for the people of Is-Land to decide if they want to try and share their home with neighbours who've bombed us and killed us, and who eat meat and don't respect our way of life and can't be relied upon to control their sexual urges when surrounded by skyclad men and women. So far it seems that the people of Is-Land don't want to risk that experiment. And for good reason. If we let the Non-Landers live here, Astra, before you know it, there will be more of them than us, and they'll change the laws, and Gaia and Her creatures won't be protected in Is-Land any more. Is that really what you want to see happen?'

Oh, for Gaia's sake. What a pathetic argument. 'Veganism and animal-welfare rights are enshrined in the Constitution,' Astra shot back. 'No one can change those laws. If the Non-Landers want to eat meat, they'd have to do that in the Southern Belt. Dayyani's just holding out on that point to get some negotiating leverage on numbers.'

Brana's jaw set and her eyes glinted. Suddenly, her grandmother looked exactly like Astra. 'I didn't come here to entertain such misguided ideas, Astra. I came to see if you were all right. You appear to be sending out distress signals. I've seen your messages and I'm worried about your state of mind. I know humanity isn't living yet in fullest possible harmony with Gaia but absorbing yourself in alarmist prophecies and unrealistic political demands won't help bring about world peace.'

Again, Astra was utterly confounded, unsure whether to feel patronised or astonished. 'You've seen my messages?'

'Yes. With my New Purist elders group. We get monthly reports from the world outside, sent via Owleon by contacts beyond the Boundary. I can assure you, Astra, that the world is not ending after the Hudna. The climate is still unpredictable after the Dark Times, that's all.'

She took a deep breath. *It's not worth it.*

'You need to stay strong mentally,' Brana ordered. 'I know that's hard under your current conditions. I tried to send some money so that you could buy some warm clothes, but I was told you have no shopping or reading privileges right now. I want to help you repeal that decision. In the meantime, I will send you some robes. Nice brown woollen ones. I checked the rules and they can't stop you receiving gifts from your family.'

This woman was one surprise after another. 'Thank you,' Astra muttered.

'And you need to get some perspective on Hokma's death.'

The stab of resentment returned. 'Please don't criticise Hokma.'

'I'm not criticising Hokma. Yes, she did a wrong, *very wrong* thing in sending Is-Land secrets abroad, but she looked after you, and Eya, and I owe her a debt of gratitude. I can understand how angry it must make you to know Doctor Blesserson will escape justice for any role he may have played in her death. He should be punished also for his role in creating these terrible sex slaves. He hasn't even lost his job! He's still being treated like some kind of expert! The gall of him, going on the news to say he knew nothing about what was really going on at Springhill, and proposing to give all the victims that ghastly memory treatment. Gaia knows if those poor creatures can ever live normal lives, the way they've been programmed. The whole thing makes my blood boil. But you are young, and you must *not* let yourself be eaten up by your anger.'

Much as it chafed to be lectured, it was clear that her grandmother was cross with Blesserson. And she was far more politicised than she looked. Cora had been wrong: Brana, Astra was beginning to realise, might somehow become an ally. 'I'm not eaten up, Brana. I'm very strong. And I've got one more chance to get Blesserson. Did your contacts in Amazigia tell you about the IREMCO trial? It's finally started.'

'Yes, I know. Though I have to say, dear, that trial does look rather unfair. The birth defects in the Southern Belt are the result of the Dark Times, not Gaian mining practices.'

It wasn't Brana's fault, she tried to remember. The woman had virtually no other source of information but the Is-Land internet; of course she would view even illicit Owleon files through that lens. 'It's not just birth defects,' she tried to explain. 'The Non-Landers in Zabaria suffer from terrible diseases and premature deaths. I think there's a link . . .' She stopped. Brana was never going to believe IMBOD had anything to do with the infertility epidemic. 'Look, Blesserson was on the Board of Directors at the time. He's deeply implicated in malpractice at the mine, sexual abuse, too, and if CONC finds that IREMCO was negligent, or worse, and imposes massive sanctions on Is-Land, he could be held accountable for the damage. Maybe he'd finally lose his job then, or even be sent to jail here in Is-Land.'

Brana looked doubtful. 'I suspect, dear, that the College and the Wheel Meet would keep on standing behind him. They want us to believe Springhill was just a bunch of bad apples, not that the whole Sec Gen programme was rotten from the start.'

Astra knew that, but she didn't want to hear it. 'It depends, doesn't it? On who's in charge. Farshordott might be angry with him for squealing on Magmason. And if Wyrdott's the next Chief Convenor, maybe she'd like an excuse to get rid of him.'

VISIT OVER IN FIVE MINUTES.

Eya's face disappeared, consumed by Vultura's beady eyes and yawning beak. In the corner of the screen, the hands of the stop-watch swept around.

Brana sighed. 'Astra. You should really focus on remaining calm, getting through each day and winning your privilege appeal. I'm going to send you some nice food, too. You look a little peaky. Now, is there anything else you want while I'm shopping?'

She felt deflated. But what could Brana do about Blesserson and the IREMCO trial? Nothing.

The clock hands sped around, sweeping away the last of the after-image of Eya's face. And suddenly, there was something she wanted that only Brana could give her.

'Eya left me a present,' she said slowly. 'A Bracelet Valley bracelet, with blue stones for the five lakes. But I wasn't allowed to bring anything with me from Non-Land. It's safe – my lawyer has it still in Amazigia, but if you sent another, maybe the prison will let me have it one day. I can't wear jewellery right now, but if I get my privileges back, I'd be allowed to.'

Brana nodded slowly. 'I remember that bracelet. I gave it to her. It's a traditional design. I'm staying in Atourne for a few days, but I'll buy you one from the same Craft stall when I get home.' She paused. 'I'd like to hug you, Astra, but there's a glass partition in this chamber.'

In an ion chamber hug, the two visitors occupied the same co-ordinates, their forms melding, flesh saturated with healing ions. No contraband could possibly be exchanged, but erotic intimacy was possible, and hugging was forbidden to prisoners unless they had permission for a conjugal visit – a right which had been won by the dirty protest, but only for previously recognised Gaia partners. Friends and relatives had to remain partitioned. Brana stood up and stepped forwards. She placed one hand on her heart and the other flat on the invisible wall bisecting the chamber. Astra bent her wrists in their shackles, raising her palms. Brana blinked again, bathing her in that warm, generous smile. From somewhere lost and forgotten inside her, Astra found a small, brief smile in reply, and then her Omma faded from view.

Acid Green

Bracelet Valley
15.12.99

Snow. In Bracelet Valley. Unheard of, impossible. And yet the skies were leaden grey all day, the temperature not flirting with the normal damp chill of the season, but steadily plunging into an iron cold that numbed the skin and ate into the bone. No one had sufficient warm clothing to stay outdoors for long; even the Purists' thickest robes were inadequate protection against this unheralded blast of real winter. All of Yggdrasila stayed indoors, watching through their windows as the skies darkened and a tempest of snowflakes whirled up from nowhere, a freak blizzard that blotted out the whole community.

For a while it was cosy. After work in the polytunnels, Fasta dashed back to her Tiny House for extra blankets, then joined Sif and Vili and the twins in the Earthship. As Vili made a pot of stew on the woodburning stove and the children ran about playing arctic explorers, she and Sif rooted through cupboards and storage boxes for more warm clothes – work trousers and Vili's boiler suit, worn for protection during tree pruning and house building; scarves and fleecy blankets kept on hand for when people caught colds.

'What will happen if it snows all week?' Freki asked as they ate.

'Don't worry, Freki,' Vili reassured her. 'We have plenty of warmth in the Earthship walls, and wood for the fire.'

'Most of our food is grown in the polytunnels this time of year, so there's plenty to eat,' Fasta added.

'It will stop snowing tomorrow,' Sif declared. 'It's a freak storm, that's all.'

Then, as Sif and Fasta were loading the dishwasher, Vili's Tablette rang. He stood in front of the stove, listening. Then he put his Tablette in his hipbelt, turned and frowned.

'It's Esfadur. He's just had an email from the Regional Council. He says we have to wrap the fruit trees. With cardboard if there aren't enough blankets.'

'Go out?' Sif objected. 'In this weather?'

Vili was already at the backdoor porch, pulling on his boiler suit. 'We have to, or else the bark will crack. You two stay with the children. I'll go.'

Fasta stood. The cherry and apricot trees were essential to the life of the community, their fruit sold at market to fund the purchase of grains and other necessities. 'I'll come, too.'

'You can't go out in that snow, Fasta!' Sif fretted. 'What will you wear?'

She picked up Vili's work trousers, shook them out. 'These. My boots. And I've got some robes at home. On the shelf in the cupboard. Vili, can you pick them up for me? And my rain cloak.'

'Robes?' Sif frowned.

Fasta focused on buttoning up the trousers. They were miles too big but the sturdy denim should help keep her dry. 'Yes. I bought them in town last week.'

'Oh. So you're a New Purist now, are you? When were you going to tell us?'

She bent down to roll up the trouser cuffs.

'Sif,' Vili said sharply from the door. 'This can wait. Okay, Fasta. I'll be right back.'

'Can we come?' Freki piped up.

'Yeah,' Ggeri chimed in. 'I want to help save the fruit trees.'

'No,' their father told them. 'You'll catch colds. You're to stay here with Oma Sif.'

'But—'

'Quiet!'

The children obeyed until he was gone then, thankfully, resumed their pleading and clamour. Fasta let Sif deal with them, ducking into the porch to hunt about for a rope to use as a belt, and a pair of gardening gloves. She found an old blanket, too, which she quickly made into a poncho, cutting a hole for her head. Then Vili was back with her robes. Long-sleeved, olive-green hemp with dark green embroidery, they weren't winter gear, but added another layer against the cold. With the poncho and rain cloak on top, and the wool scarf wrapped round her head, she was as snow-proof as possible.

'Here.' Vili had brought her rain hat, too. Leaving Sif to simmer, they trudged out into the snow. She walked gingerly behind him over the wet stepping stones to the recycling barn. Esfadur's word had spread like frost-fire. Dressed in every stitch of clothing they owned, topped with impromptu ponchos and tea-towel turbans, over half the community was there. People had ransacked their attics, cellars, porches and sheds, filled two wheelbarrows with flattened boxes and packaging, old blankets, rope and string. But the recycling trucks had just come and the two loads were nothing like enough to cover the whole orchard.

'Friends,' Esfadur greeted them. He looked worn out. Not just cold: something vital had drained from him since Brana's announcement about Eya. And now Brana was gone, off in Atourne for a few days on a prison visit with Astra Ordott. No one knew quite what to say about it all. But this was a practical emergency, over which Esfadur still retained his authority. 'The Council are going to deliver cardboard to as many communities as possible,' he announced, 'but the dirt roads are turning muddy and their vehicles may not be able to get this far up the slopes. We have to do our best with what we've got. And please, don't make yourselves ill. If you're feeling at all unwell, you must donate your clothing to a fitter person and go home.'

Fasta's throat felt a little raw. But she had energy. And the trees needed her. Silently, Vili and Baldur pushing the wheelbarrows, the community headed out into the snow, walking in a huddle up through the whirling white darkness to the orchards. Her fingers and toes were burning with cold by the time they got to the gate and her body was shivering, but the rain cloak was a good one and she was still dry beneath it. In teams of two and three, working as fast as they could, people wrapped the cardboard, blankets and towels around the satiny trunks of the cherry trees and the fissured bark of the apricot trees, tying them in place with the ropes. It didn't take long: there was enough protection for only a third of the orchard. Beside Fasta, Baldur took off his poncho and wrapped it round a cherry tree, securing it with his own belt. Across the orchard, others began to follow suit.

'No!' Esfadur's voice rang out. 'We can't afford to all get ill.' He conferred with Baldur, then the two men moved between the teams, giving orders to go home and undress in the warmth, then nominate one person to return to the orchard with the ponchos and any other blankets that could be spared. Fasta went back to her Tiny House with Vili and handed him her poncho.

'Go to the Earthship,' he urged. 'It's warm in there with the stove. Sif can make you a hot lemon and whiskey.'

She had a space heater and the Tiny House didn't take long to warm up. 'No. It's okay. I'll see you both in the morning.'

In the morning, though, she woke late, with a painful throat. But she couldn't stay in bed. Outside, the sky was pale grey, and her robes had dried in front of the heater. She had to help assess the damage to the trees, do what she could to repair it. She made a flask of lemon and ginger tea, wrapped a couple of sheets over her robes and headed out to the orchard.

It was a ghastly sight. The night's thin white blanket of snow had melted, exposing trampled grass and muddy soil, and the few remaining leaves on the branches dangled limp and shrivelled as if in shock. She walked through the gate in a trance. Half the trees stood in mute indignity, sheathed in a pathetic armour of cereal

boxes, cardboard packaging and worn blankets; the other half had
been left exposed, and of those, she saw as she trod between, nearly
all had split and peeling bark. Almost worst of all was the sight of
the birds. Scattered around the orchard were the corpses of dozens
of birds-of-paradise, their scarlet and turquoise plumage blotching
the soil like the lesions of a contagious disease. If she hadn't felt so
wretched, ill and numb, Fasta would have wept. But there was no
time for tears. Their faces drawn and grim, people were busy tending to the trees or gathering the birds and heaping them in a
wheelbarrow. Fasta picked up a bird, clasped it to her chest, and
walked over to Baldur to add the stiff body to the funeral pile.

'They must have been trying to migrate.' Baldur squinted up at
the blank sky. 'Then they either froze in mid-flight or had heart
attacks.'

'It's unbearable.' She stared down at the heap of crushed feathers,
grasping claws, glassy black eyes. 'An extinction.'

'We'll be lucky to have any Yangtze dolphins or manatees left.'
The Craftsman's voice was as cracked as the tree bark. 'Over a hundred bodies have been beached.'

'Do the Lakekeepers need help?' she asked. 'I could drive down.'

'We have to cure the trees first.' He lifted the wheelbarrow. 'And
return these birds to Gaia with all due ceremony.'

As he trundled the barrow back down the path, she approached
Esfadur. The elderman was working on a cherry tree trunk with his
knife, whittling the edge of a long crack in the bark.

'What can I do?' she asked.

He grimaced. 'We need to clean the wounds to prevent infection. Go home and fetch a knife and some water and white
spirits – vodka or gin – to sterilise the blade between cuts. Get Sif
and Vili to come, too, if they're well.'

She looked around. 'Aren't they here?'

He rested his knife against the tree. 'No one's seen them. Vili
worked until nearly three a.m. I assumed you'd all slept late.'

But her co-parents would have had to get the children to school.

Perhaps they were all sick. Worried, she headed quickly back to the Earthship. It wasn't locked – no one ever locked their doors in Yggdrasila – but the home was empty and the children's school bags weren't on their hooks. She went to the community centre, thinking Sif and Vili must be having a late morning tea, but only Gretel and Halja were in the dining hall, the old woman wiping down the tables, Brana's granddaughter drinking coffee and playing a Tablette game.

'Sif and Vili?' Gretel rubbed at a porridge stain. 'I saw them getting on the school bus with the kids.'

'Go to town together, on a day when everyone's needed here?' she puzzled aloud. 'Why would they do that?'

'I don't know.' Gretel flapped out her cloth and moved on to the next table. 'Maybe to buy some warm clothes?'

Without texting her? She found her Tablette, called Vili and got voicemail. She rang off, tried Sif. Same thing. She felt hot. Something was wrong.

'I know where they went.'

She started. Quiet as a cat, Halja had sidled up beside her.

'Do you, Halja?' She tried to sound calm. At the best of times, she found Halja disconcerting. The young woman had Brana's bony features, fine blonde hair and imperious demeanour, but where her grandmother was controlled and articulate, Halja was wild and shifty, given to gnomic utterances, epic sulks and unpredictable temper tantrums. With her Sec Gen strength, she should be out helping in the orchard, but mostly people just left her to do as she pleased.

'Yes.' Halja's breath carried the sour smell of tobacco, giving credence to the rumour that she was sleeping with the hermit in the woods, an older man who'd been evicted from his community for not-so-secretly smoking a pipe. Fasta tried not to let her distaste show.

'Can you tell me? I'm a little worried about them.'

'I heard them arguing in the polytunnel last week. They were talking in big whispers. But I was lying outside in the grass and they didn't know I was there. Sif wanted to do something with the twins today in town and Vili said no. But now they've gone off all together, I guess he said yes.'

Her skin was buzzing, as if a thousand little alarm bells were sounding in her cells. 'Thank you, Halja. Do you know what exactly Sif wanted to do with the twins?'

'Well, Fasta . . . how about I tell you in exchange for a favour?'

She didn't have time for Halja's sly glances and crude game playing. She couldn't keep the impatience from her tongue. 'What favour would that be?'

'*You* tell *me* the secret everyone is keeping from me. The thing people stop talking about whenever I come near. The reason everyone looks at me different now.'

Her stomach twinged. All the Sec Gens had been excluded from the emergency meetings this year, but surely they knew the gatherings were occurring.

She couldn't break the silence, though. Brana had made everyone promise not to tell Halja about her half-sister, the traitor Astra Ordott. Who knew what effect that discovery would have on the damaged Sec Gen's loyalty gene?

'You're imagining things, Halja,' she said.

'No, I'm not. Sif and Vili talked about community meetings. How come I wasn't invited to any?'

Suddenly, Fasta stiffened. There could only be one reason Sif would want to secretly take the twins to town.

'Halja,' she said sharply. 'Is IMBOD at the school today? Are they doing a drop-in Security Shot clinic? Is that it?'

Anger and confusion briefly flickered over Halja's face. 'Maybe.'

The girl was cunning. Liked to hide, to spy on the adults. But she was a Sec Gen and Sec Gens couldn't conceal their emotions for long. Anger had ignited in the girl's eyes, anger at losing her trump card. Adrenalin surged through Fasta's body. There was no time to lose.

'Thank you. Thank you for telling me, Halja.'

'I didn't tell you. I didn't tell you anything, and *you* didn't tell *me* anything yet.' Halja, standing between the tables, was blocking her way to the door. The young woman's fists were clenched and outrage was rising in her voice. She was large, taller than Fasta, and broad. For a moment, Fasta felt queasy with fear.

'Are you two okay there?' Gretel called from the window.

'Yes. We're fine.' Fasta reached out and touched Halja's wrist. 'Look. You're right. People *are* keeping a secret from you. It's because your grandmother doesn't want to upset you. But I think you should know what it is. When Brana gets back from Atourne, I'll tell her that we should inform you.'

Halja's face twisted into a triumphant sneer. 'I *knew* there was a secret. I want to know what it is. Tell me *now*.'

Her breath was turning Fasta's stomach. 'I can't, Halja. It's a long story, and right now I have to get to Lakeville. You understand that, don't you? I need to make sure Freki and Ggeri have a choice about what's going to happen to them. Just let me go now and I'll talk to Brana when she gets back.'

She didn't know if Halja had any concern whatsoever for the twins. The young woman's eyes burnt with unreadable fury. 'Promise?'

'I promise.'

The damaged Sec Gen's face recomposed into its usual sullen expression. 'Okay.' She stood aside. 'But I want to know my secret as soon as Brana gets back.'

Lifting her green robes clear of the mud, Fasta ran to the community garage, signed out a car and roared off down the dirt road. The surface was rutted and she feared getting stuck, but at last she was on the tarmac road to Lakeville, berating herself the whole way. She was so *stupid*. She should have known Sif would try and do this: get the children injected with the Serum before the whole Sec Gen project was abandoned. She, Fasta, had been lulled into a false sense of security by the Springhill arrests, that was the problem.

For after the raid on the retreat and subsequent revelations, a furious, completely unexpected debate about the whole Sec Gen project had kicked off in Is-Land. On the day that Stamen Magmason, Clay Odinson, Ahn Orson and the rest of the so-called 'Sex Gen' ring had been charged with multiple counts of the sexual abuse of minors, the Minister of Spiritual Development, Crystal Wyrdott, had issued a statement questioning the need to continue the Security Generation programme: *We are safe behind the cladding now,* she had argued. *Why do we need to breed warriors any longer?* It was a heretical statement. The whole country had held its breath. And yet Wyrdott hadn't been arrested. Instead, it was as if a dam had burst. Other ministers and Wheel Meet Spokes had waded into the debate, some suggesting that the Sec Gen programme be phased out, with the Serum administered to just one child in each family from now on; some had called for the shot to be made available on a volunteer basis only. It was surely only a matter of time before the issue became the centre of a national election campaign. But for now, Riverine Farshordott had responded defensively, claiming that her opponents were endangering the security of the nation and offering in-school opportunities for children to get their dose of Serum early, ahead of the official schedule.

Anxious about the developments, Fasta had gone to see Esfadur and Brana. 'Don't worry about Freki and Ggeri,' Esfadur had said. 'Farshordott's running scared. It's just a matter of time before Wyrdott and Stonewayson gain control of the Wheel Meet and the whole Sec Gen programme is a thing of the past.'

'You see, Fasta,' Brana had said. 'There is hope for this country after all.' The elderwoman's dignity had impressed Fasta. Back at her Tiny House she had entered 'New Purism' into her Tablette search engine. A month later she found herself in Lakeville, looking for green robes.

Sif, though, had wanted to get the twins injected right away. 'If there's going to be a civil war in Is-land, Fasta,' she'd hissed one night in the Earthship, tears shining like diamonds in her eyes, 'then we need our children to be on the winning side!'

'There's not going to be a *civil war*, Sif,' Vili had boomed. But his eyes were full of doubt, and Fasta couldn't tell what he did or didn't believe in any more. For the time being, caught between the two mothers, he had postponed making his own decision, saying they didn't need to decide until the spring, when the children's shot was scheduled.

'But what if the programme is abandoned?' Sif had objected.

'It won't be abandoned,' Vili had soothed. 'It might be phased out, that's all.'

Clearly, Sif had convinced Vili to change his mind. Half an hour after leaving Yggdrasila, Fasta was pulling up at the school. There it was, in the yard, a mobile IMBOD clinic. And as she got out of the car, she saw them: Sif and Vili and the twins, heading across the yard from the gymnasium to the caravan. Ggeri was tripping along happily, out in front. Freki was a small stiff symbol of resistance, the girl being hauled by the elbows by both Code parents, her feet dragging over the yard.

'Stop, stop,' Fasta yelled, running as hard as she could across the yard. '*Stop!*'

Vili had the decency to look ashamed. He dropped Freki's arm and the girl pulled loose from Sif's grip and hurtled into Fasta's waist.

'You can't do this,' Fasta raged at her co-parents. 'You need my permission.'

'No, we don't,' Sif flared, defiant. 'Two parents are enough.'

She glared at Vili. 'If you want to keep this family together, you need my permission. They're not old enough. And Freki doesn't want to get her shot. How can you do this to her, Vili? Without even telling me!'

They were making a commotion. Faces appeared at the school windows. The door to the mobile clinic opened and an IMBOD officer looked out, a young man with a Tablette in his hand.

'Freki Yggdrasiladott and Ggeri Yggdrasilason?'

'Just a moment, Officer,' Vili told him. 'We're having a family conference.'

The officer pursed his lips but disappeared back into the clinic. Sif stepped forwards. 'You've joined a cult, Fasta,' she accused, her eyes blazing pinpoints of light. 'Without telling *us*. A cult that's trying to divide this country, to pit us against each other and make us easy prey for our enemies. How can we trust you now?'

Fasta was trembling. She hugged Freki tighter, who was burying herself into her robes. 'I haven't joined a cult. New Purism is a social and political movement. I'm seeking change, that's all. Lots of us are. I just want this country to get back to its roots, Sif. To become a haven again for biodiversity – including *human* diversity. And for us to live in peace with the rest of the world.'

'I'm cold!' Ggeri was hopping from one foot to another. 'Apa. Omas. Hurry up! I want to get my shot and go back to the gym.'

'Good boy.' Sif held out her hand. 'Let's go into the clinic, then.'

'Ggeri. No.' Fasta held out her hand, too. 'Freki's frightened of the shot. Don't do it now. Wait until you're older.'

'Don't do it, Ggeri,' Freki wailed from Fasta's waist. 'Don't let them *do it* to you.'

Ggeri, suddenly confused, looked between his mothers. His lower lip trembled. Like an eagle, Vili swooped down and scooped up his son.

'Sif,' he said, rubbing Ggeri's back, 'Fasta's right. We should have informed her. I know Ggeri wants to become a Sec Gen, but we have to do this as a family. We can *all* wait.'

Relief flooded Fasta's body. 'Thank you, Vili. Thank you.'

'Vili?' Sif screeched. 'It's all agreed. You signed the form!'

'*Sif.*' Her husband raised his voice. 'We'll discuss it later. Right now, we're going to tell the school we've changed our minds, then take the children to the quiet room to calm down.'

The school receptionist was also wearing a green robe. The woman smiled brightly as she altered the twins' records on her screendesk, then offered the children a carob cashew ball from a tin. 'I know it's a disappointment, but there's plenty of time to get your shot, Ggeri,' she twinkled at the boy.

The adults drove home in silence. Vili sat up front and Fasta avoided Sif's gaze. But when she glanced in the rear-view mirror, Sif's expression was as dark and turbulent as the blizzard that had ruined the orchard.

Burnt Orange

Amazigia
17.12.99

The studio apartment was small and clean, with white walls, a polished parquet floor and a separate kitchen, thank Gaia. The living space was appointed with minimal but acceptable furnishings: a hand-loomed rug with a bright geometric design; a not-uncomfortable futon in a frame that opened like an Old World book; patterned cushions to match the rug; an armchair, a desk and a coffee table, bare save for a vase of pale yellow desert flowers, two ceramic coasters and a remote control for the wallscreen and its 218 channels. Samrod didn't want to watch the news. There was no such thing as news. Human history was just the same old story, told over and over again. An entirely predictable story of desire, vain effort and disappointment, scrawled by desperate individuals in the sand, only to be erased by the inevitable flood of events beyond any single person's control. He sat in the armchair, contemplating his briefcase. A new one he'd purchased in the summer, it had been packed for weeks, waiting in his closet at home for Silverstreamson's call. It hadn't taken long to unpack last night – an extra pair of trousers on the shelf in the cupboard; toilet items in the bathroom – but the task was not quite done.

He got up, retrieved his work Tablette and tossed it onto the futon beside his personal device. Then he unzipped the inner pocket of the case, took out the pink granite ball and placed it on the windowsill, adjusting the trophy so that the brass plaque caught a slanting ray of sunlight. Beyond the glass lay a white beach and a dark blue sea, sounding its ceaseless roar as the waves broke against the sand. Now that was something worth watching. He stood, contemplating it for a time.

The guards are for your own protection, Silverstreamson had said. *One will accompany you on the flight, and then another will keep an eye on the apartment building. You're not a prisoner. If you want to go for a walk, just ask her to accompany you.*

It was seven a.m. The car was coming at half past eight. He would walk along the beach shortly. First, he needed to get a few things in order on his work Tablette and iron his white trousers. These people all wore clothes. Surely there would be an iron somewhere in the kitchen.

The Zeppelin had arrived near midnight, so the morning drive provided him with his first proper view of Amazigia. He'd been housed in a satellite town, a bedroom suburb for international workers that had accreted around an ancient village. The salty air of the harbour and the bland concentric rings of apartment blocks were soon behind him, erased by the dunes of Western NuAfrica, a vastness of white sand edged by the glittering sea. The car sped quietly north, the occasional tatty cluster of palm trees, mud huts and weathered fishing boats spoiling the tremendous monotony. Then, just as the steady rhythm of the drive was lulling him into the false belief that it would never end, CONC HQ loomed into view. There it was: the huge, iconic, conch-shell-shaped temple to global harmony, symbol of humanity's regeneration, its elegant ridges and curves not the pristine white of the publicity photos but yellowed by the region's sandstorms and rains. A distant thin whistle greeted him as he got out of the car: the wind keening through the apertures in the roof. Samrod thought of Ahn Orson, and his oft-repeated professional opinion of this particular design feature: *Buildings shouldn't sing*, Is-Land's most famous bio-architect liked to snipe. *Imagine trying to work with that going on around you, like a bad case of architectural tinnitus.*

Ahn, who was infamous now; in prison in Atourne, facing, like Clay and Stamen and the rest, a life sentence.

A lawyer met him on the steps and the guard accompanied them inside. The building's high atrium, soaring through seven or eight stories of offices, courtrooms, lecture halls and meeting rooms, was lined with curved white balconies. Around him, people, all shades, garbed in robes and suits and traditional dress, an international fashion show, moved in purposeful currents towards whatever important work preoccupied them today. Samrod let security check his briefcase, then followed the lawyer through the turnstiles and, the guard on his heels, joined the flow. He was taken on an elevator to the third tier. People sat on cushioned benches along the balcony, sipping coffee, reading, making whispered Tablette calls. He was ushered to a seat, offered a drink. He took some water. As he'd suspected, there had been no real need to arrive first thing. The judge was late and the lawyer did what lawyers do, leaving him with the guard to 'check something with a colleague', returning to assure him 'it won't be long now'. Then he was being led into International Courtroom Three, a small panelled room, its twelve or so spectator seats half-empty. The judge, a dark-skinned man with greying temples seated behind a wooden stand, was presiding over four lawyers, one of whom stood and turned to face him.

'CONC calls Doctor Samrod Blesserson to the stand,' she announced.

In the spectator seats, a couple of heads swivelled, then bowed back down over Tablettes: journalists doing what journalists did. He took the witness seat and, avoiding the eyes of the IREMCO lawyers, vowed on the name of Gaia to tell the truth, the whole truth and nothing but the truth. Had he met that older IREMCO lawyer once, long ago at a cocktail party in Atourne?

'Thank you for joining us, Doctor Blesserson.' As the CONC lawyer – *his* lawyer – spoke, her colleague, a round furry man, looked up from his Tablette and smiled at Samrod. Bile rose in his throat. That was Sonovason, Ordott's lawyer. He picked a spot on the back wall to stare at.

'We understand,' the woman went on, 'that you wish to make a statement regarding malpractice at the IREMCO mine in Zabaria, incidences of which took place during your tenure as a member of the IREMCO Board of Directors.'

'Doctor Blesserson. Is this the precise duration of your seat on the Board?' Sonovason stood and, triumph practically bubbling from his voice, gave the dates of Samrod's Board membership for the court stenographer to note. At least his colleague was attempting to maintain a professional demeanour: Ordott's lackey wasn't even bothering to try to hide his glee at their coup.

But one must rise above temporary indignities. 'Yes, that's all correct.' Samrod smoothed his trousers over his knees, cleared his throat. 'As a Board member, I was fully aware of inadequate safety protocols in place at the mine. Everyone on the Board knew that, in contrast to similar mines within Is-Land where illness was rare, mine-workers in Zabaria were routinely contracting coughing sickness and skin diseases, many female workers gave birth to children with high rates of disability, and other women and men were rendered sterile by exposure to the rare-earths they quarried. All of these conditions could have been prevented with better decontamination procedures at the mine, more investment in medical care and longer periods of holiday time and sick leave, but these measures would all have cost money and were not implemented.' He reached into his briefcase. 'I have proof here, in the minutes of the Board meetings and in signed electronic documents, that IREMCO deliberately ignored international health and safety standards and allowed mine-workers to suffer. I hereby submit my work Tablette as evidence for this claim.'

He held out the Tablette. A lawyer on the Gaian team jumped up as, out in the spectator seats, the two journalists' heads jerked to attention: a comical piece of puppet choreography that, under other circumstances, might have provoked him to laughter.

'Objection!' the IREMCO lawyer barked. 'We need full access to these documents.'

'Copies will be made available to both teams.' The judge nodded at the court recorder, who stood to take Samrod's Tablette. His lawyer continued her scripted probing, all the questions he had been prepared to expect.

'You are a medical doctor, are you not?'

He recomposed himself. 'I am.'

'So why did you not speak out at the time?'

'The Board took the view that the people of Zabaria freely chose to work at the mine, the pay being better than the financial support CONC aid provided. We were also highly aware that Non-Landers, as a whole, were hostile to Is-Land – were, indeed, at war with us. The Board did not feel an urgent need to protect them and to speak on their behalf would have been considered a highly suspicious intervention. Certainly, I would have been ejected from the Board had I done so. I might also have lost my teaching post and any chance of funding for my other projects.'

The journalists' fingers were galloping over their Tablettes, the Gaian lawyers exchanging a furious whisper. 'I see,' the CONC lawyer responded. 'And so why have you decided to testify against the mine now?'

He blinked. 'I am a Gaian, a medical doctor, as you say, and a Code Scientist. I have spent my life trying to ensure the security of my country and the health and well-being of its inhabitants. For my efforts, I have been honoured in Is-Land, not only with public acclaim and awards, but also with a seat on a key governmental body, the Vision Council. Until recent arrests were made in Is-Land, the Vision Council was headed by Wheel Meet Chief Convenor Stamen Magmason and included several senior Wheel Meet Spokes, as well as experts in various fields of importance. I took a seat as a senior consultant to the Security Generation programme but was privy to other decisions of strategic importance. Many of these decisions were public knowledge. Some, however, were made behind closed doors, ostensibly in the interests of national security. Over the years these secret directives became, in my view, more and more self-serving, decadent and, frankly, dangerous. I began to deeply regret my involvement in the Vision Council and remained a member only in hopes of moderating their more extreme positions. Recent events in Is-Land have demonstrated to me that this is not possible. The Vision Council's current plans endanger not only the health and well-being of the people of my country, but the future of the human species.'

He was aware of a buzz of interest and confusion in the chamber, of the eyes of the Gaian lawyers trained on him like guns. But he was shielded from their hostility, clad in the shining armour of the truth. The truth being a story that a person had polished until he could see the whole world reflected in it.

'That is a strong accusation,' the lawyer commented.

'Indeed. But my work Tablette contains email chains and minutes of Vision Council meetings that will substantiate my testimony.'

'Objection.' The Gaian lawyer jumped up again. '*Irrelevant*. This has got nothing to do with practices at the IREMCO mine.'

Samrod turned to the judge. 'I can assure you, Your Honour, that I am giving testimony deeply pertinent to this trial.'

The judge raised a palm. 'Objection overruled. Witness may continue.'

'Thank you, Your Honour. Research I conducted while on the Board of IREMCO resulted in the discovery of a particular radioactive isotope that causes infertility in men and women but not cancer, or at least, not for decades. This was simple enough research, but later, in the hands of the Vision Council it became weaponised. Over my verbal objections, the isotope was embedded in a sexually transmitted virus carried by flies that were designed to only lay their eggs in raw meat. The virus was engineered to survive cooking temperatures. When the meat is eaten, the human host becomes sterile, as does anyone they exchange bodily fluids with. The virus causes no other symptoms. It has been easy enough over the last three years for Gaian agents to release these flies in international eating establishments of dubious hygiene and let human nature do the rest. Currently only meat-eaters and their partners are affected, a test sample, one might say. Come the end of the Hudna, anticipating either a full-scale military attack on our nation, or the imposition of crippling economic sanctions, the Vision Council plans to release the virus in mosquito carriers and cause a worldwide epidemic of infertility, ultimately the near-extinction of our species.'

A great scoffing arose from the IREMCO legal team. 'Objection! Irrelevant! If not to say absurd!'

The judge frowned. 'The witness is testifying to the long-term ramifications of the alleged malpractice at the mine. Objection overruled.'

Samrod asked for a glass of water, took a sip, continued. 'I say nearly extinct because Gaians would remain safe, quarantined behind the Boundary, the cladding of which emanates a magnetic forcefield the insects cannot penetrate. And in any case, even should the epidemic permeate our national epidermis, so to speak, we have the antidote to the virus. The Vision Council was fully confident of the success of this full-scale assault on the rest of humanity. Even the arrest of Stamen Magmason has not eliminated the threat. Currently, Riverine Farshordott is the acting Head of the Vision Council and if she remains in power, then I fear that Is-Land will release the virus in a matter of months.'

'If what you say is true,' his lawyer reflected, 'then this plan was a highly classified piece of information.'

'Yes. Including the Vision Council and the IMBOD agents in the field, I'd say fewer than twenty people knew about it.'

'So what risk are you taking by breaking the code of silence?'

Behind the spectators, the courtroom doors were opening and closing and opening, people coming in, filling the seats, then standing at the back, more journalists, no doubt, summoned by their colleagues. He waited for the door to close and raised his voice slightly.

'Even if the Vision Council is disbanded tomorrow, for revealing national defence strategy to the outside world, I will be called a traitor by many if not most of my compatriots. But I have no choice other than to betray this secret. I may have been complicit in IREMCO's negligence at the mine and guilty of disregard for the health and safety of Non-Landers, but to perpetuate the mass murder of a billion innocent people has never been my life's ambition. I have never wished to harm any living creature. Currently I am researching ways to prolong human life, and of all the work I have done over my career, I am most proud of designing the Code for a pest-resistant, multivitamin-enhanced, all-season Pink Lady apple that has preserved countless children across the globe from rickets and other diseases. As proof of my complete rejection of Gaian aggression, I have brought with me, on my Tablette, the equation for the antidote to the infertility virus. Your Honour,' he turned again to the judge, 'I hereby defect from Is-Land and seek the protection of this court.'

The Gaian lawyers were hissing. The journalists were buzzing. There would be a break in proceedings, as there always was after a bomb dropped from a clear blue sky. After that, he would be cross-examined, every grain of his character impugned, his relationship with Clay, his involvement with the Sex Gens raked over like a muddy plot. But the IREMCO lawyers were just actors in a long scripted play. The deal was done. This evening, Silverstreamson's guard would take Samrod back to his studio room, back to the white beach and blue sea and his polished pink granite apple, waiting on the windowsill to be repacked up in his case and taken away, far away from Amazigia, from CONC HQ and the courts and the journalists, back to the airport for his scheduled Zeppelin to New Zonia. Central New Zonia. Where there were apple farms, and colleges with large offices and intelligent, respectful young men and women keen to learn the deep intricacies of agricultural Code Science from an world-renowned expert; where off-grid rural communities sheltered international refugees and a man could live in a spacious A-frame house with an orchard, spending his mornings on the veranda with a pair of binoculars, watching quaint little birds with red caps and yellow beaks squabble in the dust, and the late afternoons scanning the sky for golden eagles – monogamous pairs of giant raptors circling their prey in the grasslands, beautiful predators at one with each other and the world, unlike their human counterparts.

Acid Green

Atourne
18.12.99

'Brana. It's not safe in Atourne. I can see it on the news. You must come home now.'

'Oh, Esfadur. You know what the *news* is like.'

Voices carried; you couldn't be too careful. Pushing aside her breakfast tray, with its divine offering of fresh peaches, skyr and a croissant with raspberry and champagne preserve, Brana got up from her four-poster bed and, feet sinking deliciously into the hotel's plush white wool carpet, crossed the room to the window and shut it tight. Outside, over the road, an IMBOD officer was posted on the street corner, directing passers-by around a large black charred stain on the flagstones.

It was cold outside. Of course people would light a fire if they wanted to stand on the street all night. Apart from a little bit of shouting and shoving around the Wheel Meet, the demonstrations had all been peaceful. In fact, when Brana, emboldened by the sight of other green-robed figures congregating in the park across the road, had ventured beyond the hotel last night, she'd had a lovely time. Warm in the light of the bonfire, she'd discussed matters of great mutual interest with local New Purists, eating roasted chestnuts and drinking mulled wine from a flask someone kindly passed around. There had been some opposing voices in the park, a few taunts about their robes, but under the watchful eyes of the five

IMBOD officers assigned to the park, mainly people had been most civil. Not that she would tell Esfadur any of that; he had left a voice message and sent two texts last night, forbidding her to leave the hotel room.

'The streets of Atourne are perfectly safe,' she informed her husband, 'and I am not coming home. *You* must come here. Today. With as many members of the Council of Concerned Elders as possible, and an Owleon.' She checked her watch. 'If you leave within the hour, you'll be here by two o'clock.'

'Transporting Owleons is against the law, Brana.'

The lake-chain bracelet, draped elegantly around her watch, glinted in the morning sun. She lifted her wrist, admired again the five ovoid sapphires in their delicate silver settings. The classic Bracelet Valley design, given a filigree twist by the designer, a woman from a community just south of Lakeville, the Atourne market-stall owner had told her. Brana had bought three of the bracelets yesterday, one each for Astra, Halja and herself. But her granddaughters would have to wait for their adornments.

'The laws of this land are about to shatter!' She closed the curtains for good measure, and to keep the heat in. 'Today's demonstration is the largest planned in Is-Land for nearly two decades. New Purists are coming from all over the country. We *have* to be there to support them, Esfadur.'

'What about supporting your own community?' he grumbled. 'I can't leave Yggdrasila, and if you had any concern for this place you'd be back here already instead of taking a holiday in Atourne. Half the trees in the orchard are cracked from crown to root, and half the community is ill in bed.'

'You've got the situation under control. I'm taking a little break, and a good thing too, or you wouldn't have an eyewitness in Atourne to the potential downfall of Riverine Farshordott.'

Her husband sighed. 'We can watch that all on the news, Brana. There are problems here with the young parents too. Sif has thrown Vili out of their Earthship and he's staying with Baldur, while

Fasta's taken it upon herself to tell Halja that we're keeping a big secret from her. We need you, Brana. Your granddaughter is demanding you return.'

'Fasta's a good woman. I'm glad to hear Vili appears to be listening to *her* for a change instead of his paranoid nitwit of a wife.'

'Sif's frightened,' Esfadur boomed. 'And so are many people, with good reason. Samrod Blesserson has just given CONC and Asfar all the excuse they need to send a rocket blasting through the Boundary, cladding and all. Then we'll see how paranoid Sif is!'

'*Oh.*' How could her husband, a man renowned for his wisdom, spout such blatant propaganda! 'CONC doesn't want to violate the Hudna in its final months. They want *us* to overthrow our corrupt regime and renew our country's founding principles of radical democracy. Now is our *chance*, darling, to clear out the final dregs of rot in the Wheel Meet.'

She peeked out between the drawn curtains. A couple of green-robed figures were entering the park, carrying screenplacards. One of the Atournians she had met last night, a teacher, had offered to bring her a placard holder today so she could use her Tablette to display a message to the country. Perhaps even a message to the world. All of her new friends, a doctor, agricultural researchers, had inspired her with their sense of hope. But her bright urging was met with silence. When Esfadur spoke again, his tone was heavy.

'We've yearned for something like this scenario, I know. But Riverine Farshordott isn't going to step down willingly, Brana. She commands a huge swathe of public opinion and an army of Sec Gens.'

'Not everyone—'

'Yes, I know. Crystal Wyrdott also has many followers, and a loyal Sec Gen regiment. That's what concerns me. Things could become very violent, very quickly.'

'Not if there are enough concerned citizens on the streets, calling for a national election and a full impartial investigation into

Blesserson's claims. Farshordott would never dare turn the Sec Gens on their fellow Is-Landers – for one thing, the Sec Gens wouldn't know how to attack their own people. We're on the brink of real change at last. I need to be here.'

'*Our* Sec Gens couldn't harm a fellow Gaian, but who knows how Farshordott's been training her guard? Brana. Why are you so hungry for action? Isn't it enough that your phone call to Stoneway-son was likely the root cause of Blesserson's defection?' He sighed again. Bless him, her dear husband: he was less angry than baffled. 'Come back, I beg you, before the demonstration starts, while the streets are still clear. You can tell me about . . . your ion chamber visit. You can talk to Halja about . . . *her.*'

He still couldn't bring himself to say Astra's name. 'Our grand-daughter Astra has been falsely accused and unjustly imprisoned for over a decade,' she said briskly. 'She needs this country to change. Tell Halja I'll be home as soon as I can. And if you want to witness history for yourself, Esfadur, come to Atourne and join me on the march. I'll keep my Tablette on.'

She hung up over his sputtering objections and, returning to bed, thumbed through her Tablette address book. Now, who on the Council of Concerned Elders had some *spine*?

'Thank you, Sapphire. Yes, I understand. Esfadur told me. It sounds just awful damage. And of course it would be safer to leave Swoop at home. But it would be wonderful if you could make it. I'll keep my Tablette on.'

She rang off, stretched and got out of bed again to re-open the curtains, enjoying the spill of sharp winter light over the hotel's creamy settee. Time for another cup of coffee. She made a strong cafetière, took a pear from the fruit bowl and returned to her four-poster office. It was a peculiar situation, true, to be lounging in the lap of luxury while the country plunged into crisis and her own community suffered a dreadful storm. But Gaia had led her here, to Atourne, into the heart of the drama engulfing Is-Land: Yggdrasila would just have to wait. She returned to her Tablette and thumbed through the latest updates.

Apart from her hour by the bonfire, she had been glued to her screen since last evening when the six o'clock news had broken the story of the century: on the basis of the testimony of Dr Samrod Blesserson, CONC had called an emergency meeting yesterday and, after a six-hour debate, had voted 252-13, with three abstentions, to declare Is-Land a Rogue State and subject it to an immediate blanket economic blockade. As of today, with the exception of emergency medical supplies, all trade with the outer world was banned. Until Is-Land proved itself a responsible member of the international community, it could import no more steel or iron ore, vehicles, heavy machinery, Tablette tech, gems or luxury foods and alcohol, and Gaians would no longer be able to sell their Code or Craft or innovative eco-tech work abroad. It was rare to get news of CONC decisions on Gaian media, but this catastrophic insult, fall from grace, act of war, whatever you wanted to call it, was too huge to be hidden from the people. Within the hour, a furious crowd had gathered at the Wheel Meet. About half – as far as Brana could make out from the rolling coverage – were calling for Is-Land to establish itself as a self-sufficient eco-state, while the rest – many, but by no means all, in green robes – were demanding a national election. At eight p.m., Riverine Farshordott had appeared on the steps and made a taut statement. Brana had watched the video twice. Now she searched for the text and pored over it, word by word:

In the Face of Betrayal and Persecution, Riverine Farshordott Calls for Unity

The Full Text of Deputy Convenor's Statement to the Nation

Today our small nation stands accused of a crime beyond imagining, the wholesale genocide of the entire human race beyond our borders. And who accuses us of this fantastical crime? *Down with CONC* some of your placards read. And yes, the Council of New Continents, to whom Is-Land has always been grateful and generous, with whom Is-Land has always co-operated, has gravely betrayed us with this outrageous designation of Rogue State. But let us not forget that the finger that has pointed CONC in the direction of this malign and disastrous untruth belongs to one of our own citizens: Dr Samrod Blesserson.

Who is this man, the man we know as the key architect of the Security Generation programme, a celebrated figure to whom we all entrusted the lives of our children? How could such a man tell brazen lies in a court of international law, some of you ask. Such a good man, perhaps he is telling the truth – let us investigate!

Yes, indeed, we all want answers. But let us recall that even before his duplicitous flight to Amazigia, Dr Blesserson's reputation stood on the verge of ruin. Who, ask yourselves, was the only Code Scientist in this country capable of the kind of vile mental and physical doctoring of our youth brought to light in the Springhill scandal? Rest assured, IMBOD has its own files on Dr Blesserson. Believe me when I tell you that this venerable doctor, the long-term Gaia partner of Springhill Director Clay Odinson, was a prime instigator of the so-called Sex Gen project and a frequent visitor to that den of repulsive iniquity. Was it sheer luck that the good doctor was not present on the night that our leader, Stamen Magmason, making a surprise inspection of the premises, was unjustly implicated in the depraved practices of Odinson and his cronies? Or was Blesserson's absence that fateful night in fact a case of cunning design?

Dr Samrod Blesserson, let us not forget, comes from a family of known dissidents, a veritable nest of traitors. He is the Code Shelter brother of the traitor Hokma Blesser and the Shelter uncle of the arch-treasonist Astra Ordott, and he never quite shook the suspicion of being complicit in the Ordott girl's evasion of her Security Shot. Just bad luck, you say? But those of you with long memories will recall that Samrod Blesserson's oldest sister, the late Paloma Blesser, was also a dangerous rebel, a woman who campaigned for the right of Non-Lander agricultural labourers to take up permanent residence in this country, an unthinkable policy that would have destroyed our way of life. Paloma Blesser, in her reckless rush to sabotage her own country, died in a car accident. Hokma Blesser made mistakes and got caught. But cautious, cunning Samrod Blesserson has been playing the long game. My government urges patience: all will be revealed at the trial of Stamen Magmason, when Samrod Blesserson will be exposed for the devious and deviant traitor and liar that he is, and CONC will be forced to retract its offensive and erroneous slur upon our nation. Until then, my people, my noble Gaians facing a hostile world, stay strong and stay united! You are welcome to keep vigil here until the truth is established and our reputation is restored.

Beneath the article was a photo of Samrod Blesserson. Brana squinted at it in distaste. That poisonous scorpion. Imagine the craven hubris of the man: scuttling away to safety and fame while his lover and cronies and, more importantly, poor Astra languished in jail. Clearly Blesserson had done some kind of major dirty deal with Stonewayson.

But as she'd discussed with her new friends at the bonfire, just because the man was a greasy, self-serving little rat, didn't mean he was lying about the Vision Council. And she was not the only person to suspect as much. The crowds at the Wheel Meet had quieted after Farshordott's speech last night but had not dispersed. More people had arrived, bringing tents and blankets, the numbers of those in green robes steadily rising. The Wheel Meet was only a half-hour taxi ride away and Brana had considered going but, with her new friends, had decided in the end that it was better to save her energy for tomorrow. For at ten p.m., Crystal Wyrdott had appeared outside her gated residence in the Atourne hills and, flanked by a dozen Sec Gens garbed in green hipbelts, made a statement of her own. Finishing her coffee, Brana reread it, too.

Following Riverine Farshordott Statement, Crystal Wyrdott, Minister of Spiritual Development, Calls for National Demonstration

Full Text of Crystal Wyrdott's Address

Fellow Gaians, I speak to you with a sorrowful heart. Today our country has been accused of an unthinkable crime. But difficult as it is when we feel slandered and under attack, if we are to rise above this outrage against our very souls, we must accept that the decision made today in Amazigia is not the result of international discrimination against our Gaian land. Rather, it is rooted in the decades of spiritual corruption that have blighted the very heart of this country's ruling body. Do we believe the Deputy Convenor when she blames the messenger, when she lays at Samrod Blesserson's door the crimes for which a whole cohort of our leadership stands accused? Do we really think a perverse lovers' pact is responsible for the obscene gatherings that took place at Springhill Retreat? Do we want to wait for the trial of our disgraced Chief Convenor before we decide that Stamen Magmason, a man found at midnight supposedly 'investigating' a bioengineered orgy of child sex abuse, is unfit for office? Surely, rocked as we are by the Springhill revelations, we must demand the deep truth about this government and *all* of its secrets.

Come to Atourne, my fellow Is-Landers. Come to your capital from every bioregion. Leave now, travel all night.

Come to the Wheel Meet to demand a national election and a
full impartial investigation into the claims of Samrod Blesserson and the doings of the so-called Vision Council! Come
while it is still legal to gather peacefully in this country.
Tomorrow we will meet at two p.m. in every park in Atourne
and converge at four p.m. at the Wheel Meet, to peacefully
demand the return of democracy to Is-Land. For just as compassion is the measure of the spiritual growth of a person,
informed democratic elections and transparent and fully
accountable government are the measures of the spiritual
development of a nation. In the spirit of the Pioneers, come
and join me tomorrow at the Wheel Meet and demand a return
to the founding principles of this great nation: Political Freedom, Spiritual Growth and a Deep Commitment to All Life
on our Beautiful Planet!

Reading the words roused her again. No, Esfadur, she could not go
back to Yggdrasila. She had to be there today: she had a message for
the Wheel Meet. She opened up Notepad and, using her best calligraphy skills, began to write with her stylus.

It took some time to complete to her satisfaction but, eventually
happy with the result, she took herself down to the hotel restaurant
for a substantial hot lunch. Afterwards, dressed warmly in the new
felt-lined boots and green woollen cloak she had bought in the market on her first day in Atourne, she packed her Tablette, some fruit
and a flask in her bag, and went outside.

Even from the hotel steps she could see people were assembling in
large numbers near the fountain, a small group in green cloaks standing in a cluster, holding screenplacards, while a much larger group of
people in blanket ponchos stood behind a line of IMBOD officers,
shouting and shaking their fists. There were far more IMBOD officers on the street today, and outside the hotel an IMBOD wagon was
parked on the street, a large black vehicle with small barred windows.

For a moment, fear froze her belly. But there was her new friend,

Gladioli, waving at her, an extra placard holder in her hand, as promised.

Brana crossed the road, quickening her step, and threaded her way through a heaving mill of people and a forest of screen-placards.

BRING BLESSERSON BACK TO FACE THE WOLVES

Gaia Loves **ALL** Life.

Is-Landers are NOT Mass Murderers.

STAND WITH STAMEN: EVICT ALL TRAITORS

WHO NEEDS CARS? The Cart and Horse were good enough for the Pioneers!

Sec Gens Are Loyal to OUR MOTHER

Demand a National Election NOW

'Lovely to see you, Brana.' Gladioli kissed her cheek. 'Don't you look well dressed for the occasion.' Resting her own sign – GLOBAL GENOCIDE: NOT **MY** VISION – against the fountain, she helped Brana unfold her Tablette to the largest screensize and click it into the placard holder.

'And I can video everything while I'm marching, you said?'

'Yes. And you can watch the live footage here.' Gladioli's husband Cloud took over, his hands red in the cold, showing her the controls and the small flip-out viewscreen.

'But what if my husband phones?' she fretted.

'The handle will vibrate. And there's an inbuilt mic. Just keep your earbuds handy.'

Ah, so that was how it all worked. Very neat. Reassured, Brana opened the poster file she had written in the hotel room:

To Become a Sec Gen
Should Be a Choice:
FREE ALL
POLITICAL
PRISONERS

'Oh, that's excellent!' Gladioli clapped her gloved hands.

'My my, you're bold folk up there in Bracelet Valley!' Cloud teased.

Brana had been afraid they would think it was too dangerous a message. Perhaps one day she would tell Gladioli and Cloud about Astra. But for now, there was no time to bask in the pride. The demonstration was on the move.

Chanting and chatting, they left the park, stewarded by the IMBOD officers to merge with the crowd on the main road. Brana and her new friends fell in step with a group marching behind a large green silk banner, its carefully sewn white letters declaring NEW PURISTS CALL FOR A NATIONAL ELECTION. As they walked, their own placards held high, the crowd swelled and extended like a gorging python, protestors joining it from the city's parks and side streets, an endless flow of Is-Landers marching towards their Wheel Meet. It was astonishing. Brana had never seen so many people in her life. She saw banners from the dry forest, the white desert, even the ashfields: it must be true that people had driven all night from every bioregion. And though large swathes of the crowd were composed of people in brown robes, woven warm against the cold in skin tones to assert their affinity with the sky-clad, although these people brandished signs reading 'FALSE CONCsciouness', 'ARREST ARCH-TRAITOR SAMROD LIARSON' and 'FREE STAMEN MAGMASON', although some of them shouted and bared their teeth when they saw Brana's placard, there were also countless people marching in green robes, walking together for protection and good cheer, holding signs reading 'Rogue States Don't Vote', 'Our Children are Not Your Sacrificial Lambs', 'Crystal Wyrdott for Chief Convenor' and even – her heart leapt – 'Bring Peat Orson Home'. Between the brown- and the green-robed groups marched people garbed in blue and red and yellow and purple, all the colours of the rainbow. People who might frown at Brana's sign and quickly look away, but whose own signs read: 'Is-Land is a Land of LIFE';

'NOT IN MY NAME'; 'NO SECRETS'; 'LET THE PEOPLE DECIDE'.

And then they were there: at the entrance to the Wheel Meet. On her placard handle viewscreen she could see the top of the steps leading up to the famous round building, its redstone walls curving ahead in the near distance. The park was thronging already with marchers: her group would never get near the front doors, but screens had been set up, and portaloos and food shacks. This was no festival, though. The atmosphere was tense, the crowd's shouts met by stern commands from the IMBOD officers and troops of Sec Gens were everywhere: some in black, and some in green – Crystal Wyrdott's force. Brana needed the loo, but the momentum of the march drove her on, officers herding the protestors in green and brown to opposite sides of the park, allowing those in rainbow robes to mingle between them. As she shuffled along, Brana checked her watch. Three-thirty p.m. Esfadur had not rung.

But as the banner ahead came to a halt and people jostled for a view of the screen, her placard handle vibrated in her hand.

She fumbled with the controls, fished for her earbuds. 'Hello?'

'Brana.' It was Sapphire. 'We're here. Where are you?'

She smothered her disappointment. Sapphire was here. That was marvellous.

'Behind the green and white banner! The big one by the cherry trees.'

She didn't ask about Swoop. On the phone in the morning, Sapphire had wholeheartedly agreed that it was essential to get images of the demonstration out to the wider world. Riverine Farshordott might try to disguise the numbers of dissenters to her regime, but if people beyond the Boundary could see images of the march and footage of all the New Purist signs, then they would know that Is-Land was not its leaders. Is-Land wanted change. Swoop was the answer: the Owleon that had brought Peat Orson's video to the Council of Concerned Elders on a memory stick clipped to its ankle. The Owleon flew to and from a camel-breeding farm just outside Lálsil, an oasis town in the Southern Belt. The farmers were part of Cora Pollen's long-established network: within a day, images of the march could be emailed to CONC officials, concerned ex-pat Gaians and media outlets all over the world.

But Sapphire had also agreed with Esfadur, insisting it was beyond stupid to take an Owleon anywhere near a national demonstration in Atourne. She'd told Brana to bring her video footage back to Bracelet Valley, where it could be dispatched on a memory stick tomorrow. Brana had never been involved in sending messages before but it was clearly time to start: she had agreed at once to the plan.

'Yes?' Gladioli asked. 'Is your husband coming?'

Brana peered down at the sea of heads filling her viewscreen. 'No. Another friend from the Valley.'

But it wasn't true. The crowd parted behind them, and he was there, bumbling into their little group beside Sapphire, her husband, his large white beard flowing down over his sombre green robes.

'Oh, Esfadur.' She opened her arms. 'You came.'

'Brana.' He hugged her, then glanced up at her placard and shook his head. 'Look at you. I knew I had to come. I can't have you getting in trouble here on your own.'

But his eyes were twinkling, and then she was proudly introducing him to her new friends and showing him the placard camera controls, and Sapphire was opening her large wicker basket, bringing out solar-battery-powered hand-warmers, a flask of hot apple juice and a batch of home-baked cookies to share with the young green-clad Sec Gens, and soon it was the best day of Brana's life, a day of cold fingers and toes, bright cheeks, laughter and hope, inspiring speeches from Crystal Wyrdott and Blade Stonewayson, of conversations with strangers, a day that became a candlelight vigil, an evening in which her voice joined with thousands of her countryfolk, chanting over and over again: 'What do we want? A National Election. When do we want it? NOW!' A chant that rose again and again, louder and stronger, over the calls from the other side of the park, angry calls for Blesserson's arrest and Magmason's release, until, at last, at ten minutes to midnight, Riverine Farshordott appeared on the steps of the Wheel Meet.

'The people are the Wheel Spokes of a nation,' the Acting Chief Convenor declared, 'and Is-Land's people have spoken: I hereby call a national election, to be held in six weeks. To all my supporters, thank you. I hereby also announce my candidacy for Chief Convenor. I call for Unity, and I ask for the chance to deliver justice for Stamen Magmason, and justice for Is-Land!'

The crowd erupted. Somewhere outside the park, fireworks went off. Brana cried then, and Gladioli and she hugged each other, Esfadur, Sapphire and Cloud, too. She pulled away, swiped at her placard. When she raised it again, it read:

FREE ASTRA ORDOTT

'Brana!' Esfadur looked around. Was that IMBOD officer staring at them? Who cared? There was going to be an election, and people had to seize the opportunity to speak their minds.

'Astra Ordott is a political prisoner.' Her voice trembled, but she held Esfadur's troubled gaze. 'IMBOD hates her because she successfully managed to avoid her Security Shot.'

Beside Esfadur, Cloud frowned and nodded. 'I am sure there's a lot about that story we haven't been told.'

Sapphire was hoisting her wicker basket on her back. 'Job done here, folks. And I'm cold. I say we find a bar and have a stiff hot chocolate before I drive back to Bracelet Valley. Who's coming?'

She had to give the memory stick to Sapphire tonight. 'Ooh. Good idea.'

'Brana, darling, give the placard holder back to Gladioli,' Esfadur commanded.

'I'll give it back to her at the bar, darling.' The IMBOD officer was still looking at her, talking into his Tablette, and her heart was thumping, but she raised the placard high. 'This demonstration isn't over yet.'

Misted Silver

The Ashfields
28.12.99

'How's Omma today, then?' Charm drained her mug of tea and addressed Astra over the dining-room table. 'Did she send the Tooth Fairy to ickle baby's cell?'

'Ha ha.' Astra grimaced, baring the brand-new gap in her gum-line. A lower incisor had fallen out last week, making three teeth in total she'd lost in jail. With the amount of jaw grinding she'd been doing since Blesserson's defection, she'd lose the rest before the year was out. At least she was warm at last. Brana, true to her word, had sent her a care-package from Atourne: leg-warmers, a fleecy sweater and trousers, thick hiking socks, fingerless gloves, woolly slippers, fennel toothpaste and floss.

'Don't tease her.' Rosetta slapped Charm's hand. 'I think it's nice Astra has a loving grandmother. We all need a little looking after in here.' She reached across the table and stroked Astra's wrist. The lake-chain bracelet slipped out of Astra's sleeve.

'Oo. What's that? It's lovely!' Rosetta squealed.

She flushed, tried to pull her arm away, but Rosetta had hooked her pinkie around the bracelet and she was afraid that it might break. 'It's a traditional bracelet from the valley. I had one before that my Birth mother gave me. Brana sent me this one with the care-package.'

'I thought you weren't allowed to wear jewellery.'

She let Rosetta admire the sapphires and silver hoops. 'Brana hired a lawyer who told her it was a religious symbol, a tribute to Gaia. She threatened the prison with a lawsuit if they didn't let me wear it.'

'Clever!' Pallas whistled.

'I must say, it's a strange thing for a doomsaying crusader against metal to be wearing,' Cora commented dryly.

'No one's listening to my prophecies,' she muttered, tucking the bracelet back up her sleeve. 'If you don't mind, I'd like to indulge in a connection to my Birth mother before we all get swallowed up by an earthquake.'

'C'mon, Cora. Don't be mean,' Rosetta scolded. 'It's a present from her grandmother. That's so special! Is Brana going to send you anything else, Astra?'

Brana wrote to Astra nearly every day. The letters, penned in exquisite calligraphy, arrived in batches, heavily redacted. Reading between the blacked-out lines, it was clear Brana was bursting with hope. Hope, though, was a feeling Astra didn't experience any longer. 'I don't know.' She pushed her porridge bowl aside. 'IMBOD obliterates most of what she writes. I can tell she's excited about the election, though.'

There were, she knew, reasons to be excited about the election. Although prisoners weren't allowed to vote, most of the women on Traitors' Wing stood to gain a great deal if the New Purists won. Crystal Wyrdott was running for Chief Convenor on a platform of reforming the Wheel Meet and renewing the country's democratic traditions, thereby re-establishing Is-Land's status of esteem in the eyes of the world. Her major campaign promises were to order a full investigation into the so-called Vision Council; to suspend the entire Sec Gen program pending a thorough review of the current security situation; and to unconditionally pardon all parents jailed for trying to save their children from the shot. If Wyrdott won, Rosetta, Charm, Sunflower and most of the other prisoners on Traitors' Wing could be freed within weeks. Astra knew from

Jasper's ion chamber visits that Brana had started a campaign to free her, too, which explained the redactions. But she failed to share the general excitement. Like Cora and Fern, she wasn't an ordinary traitor. If Farshordott stayed in power, Brana was likely to join them in Ashfields Max. She almost wished her grandmother would drop her campaign: Brana was far more useful to Astra outside the prison walls.

'Brana Yggdrasiladott is an excellent example of the intersectional potential of single-issue campaigns.' Cora wagged her finger at Charm for once. 'No normal Bracelet Valley matron would dream of getting involved in a prisoners' rights campaign. But the Springhill scandal has cut across lines of class and political allegiance. What Astra needs to remember, though, is that Brana and the entire New Purist movement are still, at core, deeply nationalistic. Crystal Wyrdott is focused entirely on rehabilitating Is-Land's economic and international social status – her campaign offers no hope at all for One-Land.'

'There's hope for us, though.' Rosetta clapped. 'We could be out of here in a month.'

'Rosetta,' Charm chided. 'Don't gloat in front of Astra and Cora.'

'Oh.' Rosetta scrunched up her face. 'Sorry, Astra. I forgot.'

'That's okay, Rosetta,' she said. 'I hope Wyrdott wins and you guys are freed. And don't worry, Cora, I'm well aware of Brana's limitations.'

They had hashed all this over a dozen times already. For anyone interested in justice for Non-Land, the election was no cause for excitement whatsoever. Wyrdott was already espousing a hard line on negotiations with N-LA, stating Gaians could never compromise on the founding principles of Gaianism, including veganism and the right to go skyclad, or on national security or economic needs. And despite Blesserson's revelations in Amazigia, Wyrdott was only calling for reform at IREMCO, promising that under her rule, Zabaria would remain annexed and the mine would be run according to the highest possible standards of human and environmental health. Astra had tried writing to Brana about all this, had tried telling her more about the suffering of the Non-Landers, their dignity and their care for the Earth, but doubtless those letters had also arrived scored through with black blocks.

'You have to be *careful*.' Cora turned her guns full square on Astra. 'Brana's got a deep emotional investment in remaking you in her image of an abused granddaughter, psychologically damaged and not responsible for any of your actions. She'll try to make you palatable to all her Bracelet Valley friends, diluting your revolutionary potential.'

Heat spread through her blood. Since when did Cora believe Astra had revolutionary potential? 'Cora. She's my fracking grandmother. Let her spoil me a bit.'

'*Phhwweet*.' Lichena whistled from the door. Astra's weekly social hour was up. And not a minute too soon. She stood. 'Have a good afternoon, everyone. See you next week.'

Back in her cell, she resumed her daily furious pacing, from the door to the window, the window to the door, working up such heat she didn't need Brana's fleece. Her irritation with Cora evaporated in minutes; it was Samrod Blesserson who made her blood boil all day, whose face she stamped on and ground into dust, over and over, as she wore a groove in the floor. She still couldn't believe he had got away with it: not just evading arrest for Hokma's murder, the Sex Gen scandal, IREMCO's crimes and the genocidal schemes of the Vision Council, but reinventing himself as a courageous moral crusader, practically the saviour of the human race! According to Jasper, CONC wasn't interested in Blesserson's culpability in the infertility plot. A deal was a deal: they'd taken the antidote recipe then Zeppelined Samrod away from Amazigia the day after the trial and relocated him in a witness-protection programme, likely in some cushy villa in Neuropa or New Zonia. Sure, his testimony had saved a billion lives and might yet bring the Wheel Meet down. But there were only three months left before the Vernal

Equinox, and Samrod was going to spend his last days on Earth in some peaceful paradise, fêted by the world press, while she fell apart, tooth by tooth, alone in jail. All she could hope for now was that his death would be slow and painful: the result of famine or disease unleashed by climate chaos, while hers would be quick: struck on the head by a falling brick as the prison collapsed in an earthquake and Lichena and Bircha, she vividly imagined as she paced, were trapped alive and broken beneath the wreckage, to suffocate and starve in claustrophobic tombs.

You are burning badly, Child.

The voice flickered through her, a hot tingle, verging on a rash.

I'm burning my way, Fire.

Being eaten alive by your own anger is not what Hokma wanted for you. She asked you to forgive.

Stomp. Stomp. Stomp. She paced faster, harder, six strides from window to door, her toes nearly kicking the walls at each end. *Hokma was in the tunnels. Things looked different for her. From where I am, Samrod still deserves to suffer.*

The voice licked at her skin, tickling, annoying.

Forgiveness isn't about what the other person deserves. It's about what *you* deserve.

Oh, don't weep all over me like Water. I thought you understood anger.

I understand anger, Child, yes. Channelled correctly, anger is a great cleanser. Misused, though, it will burn your heart to ashes.

Yeah, well. What's the fracking point of having a heart anyway? I've tried to love people. I've tried my best to save us all, but is anyone listening to me? I did what Earth told me to do, I gave humanity the deadline to break the bond with Metal, but is anyone taking me seriously? No, I just get called crazy, that's all. I did what Air told me to do, made the biggest sacrifice I could, gave up all my privileges to get a message to Muzi, but did Muzi listen to me? No, he sent Peat to jail and gave Farshordott and Magmason their biggest propaganda boost in a decade. I did what Jasper told me and attacked Blesserson on all fronts. Did I catch him? No, he's a fracking international hero, laughing at me from some garden palace in New Zonia. I did what Hokma and Water told me to do: I watched every hour of her torture. Did that make my life any better? No. I just died with her, that's all. Died with her before I die, along with everyone else!

Istarastra! Enough! Fire roared. You must find your stillness. Now!

Her skin heated to the edge of violent crackling pain. She stopped pacing and, shaking, leaned her forehead and palms against the cold windowpane, resting as the Old One admonished her.

Yes, you died with Hokma. You died and were reborn. Sharing Hokma's death has made you stronger. Nothing will ever be as difficult as that. Experiencing her memories, you learned that who a person is under torture is not who they are in spirit. That the spirit is an inextinguishable flame.

She *had* felt different since watching the INMA tapes. She had felt angrier than ever before. But also more determined to fight on. She pressed her cheek to the cold glass, let it cool her, cool her and calm her, as Fire's voice flickered on under her skin.

Speaking with Hokma before she entered the tunnels, you learned that death burns away the inessential emotions that so burden you humans in life. Now you need to learn how to experience anger without hate, how to let anger flare and subside, and burn alongside joy and gratitude and a desire for justice so great that in its presence disappointment is but a fleeting sprinkle of rain on a blazing bonfire. You are a leader, Istarastra, and you must learn how to inspire people with your passion, or they will never listen to you.

Her skin was glowing now, but not sweating; glowing with an inner radiance. In her mind an image rose, a childhood memory of the dry forest, the swathe of burnt woodland on the hillslopes beneath Or.

Fire, can you tell me something? Are there trees in the firegrounds these days?

There are. Tall trees, shining with a radiant green blaze of light and leaves.

She imagined it, the wasteland of her childhood, transformed. For a moment, a fierce, sad, wistful yearning leapt in the hollow where her heart used to be.

You have been razed to ashes. Now soak up the sun, let the rain fall as it may, let the shoots and saplings grow. In time, their cool shade may lead you to forgiveness. For now, Istarastra, you must speak to the people of growth!

Fire's voice faded. Astra remained at the window for a long time, eyes closed, breathing steady, her mind swimming in green light, the delicious winter chill stealing like frost through her limbs.

Desert Red

Asfar
31.12.99

'Are you *sure* you want to do this, Una?' If Marti's hands were dish-rags, they would have been wrung to shreds.

'No, Marti.' Una touched up her lipstick in the jewel-framed compact. 'It's New Year's Eve, the last day of the first century of the Regeneration Era, and I don't want to drink a foul-tasting concoc-tion that will make me vomit and hallucinate for hours. But I don't have much choice, do I?'

'You could say you have heart problems. Or digestive issues.'

'And have the media claim that Istar has lost the heart and stom-ach for her people's fight for freedom?' Tahazu boomed from his velvet chair. 'No, Marti. Una is our leader, and leaders must always think of the people first, their own comfort second.'

She popped the lipstick and mirror back in her purse and snapped it shut. 'Marti, have you been asleep all week? Today, the Institute of Metaphysical Engineering is presenting the first viable Ordott Prize entry to the Mujaddid and a Non-Lander boy, a childhood victim of the worst of the Gaian jails, is on the team. If his team's disgusting potion wins, all the world's attention will be on Non-Land and our exemplary response to the injustices meted out to us by history. We cannot miss the opportunity to stand in that limelight.'

Marti stiffened. 'It's an unapproved drug, Una. I'm just repeat-ing what the doctor said. What about your asthma attacks?'

'I have asthma attacks when I'm under stress! When I'm having to explain things that don't need to be explained! The boy is blind, Marti, *blind*! What greater gift to our cause could there be?'

'All right, Una.' Marti stood. 'Don't follow medical advice. Shall I pack towels? What about an extra robe?'

'I believe they have minimised the vomiting,' Tahazu said. 'It won't be a viable technology if not.'

'Oh, for goodness sake.' Una's hand hovered over her trinket tray. 'It can't be worse than that pickled sheep's brain I had to eat at the Northern Neuropean delegates' party in Amazigia. I managed that without a change of clothing, as I recall.'

Marti's Tablette bleeped. 'The car's ready, Una.'

She chose a garnet brooch and asked Tahazu to hold the mirror as she pinned it to her turban. There, now she looked every inch the spiritual leader of her people.

The Institute of Metaphysical Engineering was a compound of bulbous buildings surrounded by long, gleaming glasshouses a short drive from N-LA headquarters. It took some time to arrive, however, as the streets were lined with people: her people demonstrating on the pavements, spilling out onto the road, celebrating their young brother's success, but also still outraged by the Blesserson defection and its shocking revelations, and agitated by the upcoming election in Is-Land. 'We Want RESTITUTION for our LOST CHILDREN', one placard read. 'Free Zabaria NOW' another demanded. 'COMMAND CONC to CLOSE the MINE'. 'ONE WORLD ONE HUMAN FAMILY ONE-LAND'.

'You see, Marti?' She adjusted her turban. 'Already a media opportunity.'

In fact, a party. They heard the music half a block from the Institute, a wailing tune she vaguely recognised.

'YAC's here,' Marti commented.

'So I gathered!' she snapped. Yes, that was it, one of those tedious Ordott messages the YAC Singulars had somehow transformed into a

minor-hit song. The car pulled up and there they were on the steps,
turning her red carpet into a stage for a pop-up performance of Non-
Land's biggest celebrities: the eight-armed Tiamet with her drums and
cymbals and the two-faced Simiya ululating away in her eerie double
voices. The duo was flanked on one side by Asar, the tall deafblind seer,
swaying ecstatically to the vibrations, his followers arrayed like flowers
around his feet; and on the other by the YAC political leaders Ninti
and Malku, sitting two metres apart in their wheelchairs, each holding
one end of a white, purple and bright-red banner:

FREE ZABARIA
FREE the WORLD
FREE ASTRA ORDOTT

Una composed her own face into a rigid smile. 'I don't believe YAC
understands what a prize they have in that prisoner,' she muttered.

'She may be a useful martyr, but naturally they wish for her
release,' Marti retorted.

There was no time to argue. The car had stopped and the driver
was opening her door. She stepped out and faced the crowd, waving
and smiling. Journalists turned their Tablettes on her; Ninti and
Malku nodded their greetings. The music crescendoed and stopped.
At least YAC still knew who was the real leader here!

'My people,' she declared. 'I am moved to see you here, celebrating and protesting in equal force and style. Even for us, these are
dramatic times. Is-Land stands exposed, a Rogue State, its ruinous
plans for humanity revealed by one of its own leading scientists.
Yes, we have all seen the footage of ordinary Gaians rejecting the
genocidal policies of their government—' A growl rose from the
crowd, behind the banner, a growl that expressed cynicism, doubt,
acute awareness of Crystal Wyrdott's resistance to negotiations . . .
Una raised her palm. 'People, young and old people in Is-Land are
unhappy with their leadership and these images should give us all
hope. But while N-LA supports the return of democracy to Is-Land,

we also state, loud and clear, that we will never stop pressing for justice and freedom for our people! As the Prophecy states: when Istar arises, the placeless ones shall be in all places and all places shall sing glad hymns of welcome!'

She waited for the cheer, and it came, with a crash of Tiamet's tiny cymbals, in a sweet powerful rush to her ears. Her people were with her, and she was where she belonged: with her people. 'Non-Landers, I see you and I hear you. You are calling for the liberation of Zabaria and the closure of its toxic mine, and freedom for Zabaria stands at the very top of our agenda. Today, though, one of our own young scientists, a youth who has suffered and endured the worst of all we Non-Landers must face, is presenting his entry for a prestigious prize, a prize our great benefactor the Mujaddid has established in response to the message from our sister-in-chains, Astra Ordott: her urgent message that the human race must act quickly to end our dependence on poisonous metals. As Um Kadingir, the mother of our struggle and the bearer of Istar's light in Asfar and the world at large, I hereby enter this hallowed hall of learning, prepared to marvel once more at the ingenuity and leadership of our people!'

Humbly, she inclined her head to the crowd, then turned and sailed into the building. The doors shut behind them and the ushers gestured through the tall, dark foyer to a grand staircase. On the landing stood the Mujaddid himself, his incongruously slight figure robed in that plain hessian sack he had, in a masterstroke of PR that still annoyed her, recently taken to wearing.

'Water, Marti,' she whispered. 'I need water.'

'Are you all right, Una? Can you breathe?'

'Yes, I can breathe!'

The Mujaddid was welcoming her, his arms outspread. She stepped forwards, her face still rigid in a rictus grin. Did she have to explain everything to Marti? Surely it was obvious that before she embarked on what she would later proudly describe as a 'spiritual experience', she had to wash the taste of *that name* out of her mouth.

*

It was still almost three months before Earth's deadline, but Cyrus had heard that the Water Memory team was nearly ready to present their project to the Mujaddid. Plant IT had to cross the finish line first. After working flat out during the last month of the year, and with the help of bamboo Code to speed the growth of their experiments, Suen's team had decided to offer the Mujaddid two consecutive experiences in the psychosphere: a Living Library consultation followed by a group meeting.

The idea of a Living Library experience had occurred to Suen like a lightning bolt during his session in the community centre: if every plant or plant hybrid had its own spiritual fingerprint and created its own unique pathway through the tunnels of the psychosphere, shouldn't it be possible to store information in those tunnels that any voyager could access? Excited by the idea, he shared it with the team and Ñeštug, who'd set him and Cyrus the challenge of making it happen.

First, they'd cross-bred lantern leaf with Spanish flag, which, according to the library book, represented 'the thirst to learn', Chinese lavender for 'the thirst to understand' and, to establish a foundation for Suen's signature vibration, a rose. He had wanted a white one, reflecting his 'Integral love for the Divine', but Cyrus had insisted that he choose a pink one, representing 'Beauty in service of the Divine.' Suen had eaten the hybrid plant with Cyrus watching over him. It was a short trip, but a productive one. The bamboo turned out to speed up one's experiences in the psychosphere, a very useful discovery, and the Lantern Leaf Grandmother had been most forthcoming. She'd taught Suen how to cultivate intimate relationships with plant spirits, and respectfully ask them to become custodians of human memory and archivists of human knowledge. Over the next week, he and Cyrus worked on the base plant, further individuating it by adding plants that resonated with Suen's life experience: African daisy, for cheerful endeavour; wild iris, for inner vision; and Jericho Rose, for endurance. Suen had taken the resultant hybrid three times, each time encountering the plant spirits and leaving echo-records of his presence in their care. There wasn't much information stored there yet, but Cyrus and Mona had entered independently after his first visit, and each had been able to experience his brief account of his time in the IMBOD jail. Mona had cried a little afterwards. 'They tortured you and your family, and they took your sight,' she'd said, 'but you never hated them.'

He'd felt embarrassed. 'I was only six. I didn't have room in my mind to hate anyone. I had to figure out stuff, like how to eat without getting food everywhere, and how to get around by myself. Then we moved here and I had to learn Asfarian. And school started, and science was so cool. Also . . .' He struggled to express what was so obvious to him. 'I like listening. And touching. And inventing stuff. I don't really have time to think about the past.'

'Still, it must have been such a trauma – losing your father and uncle, too. And what your father did . . .' Her voice dipped to a whisper. 'Keeping silent and protecting Muzi even though he knew that the Gaians would hurt you in response. Have you really forgiven him for that?'

Even Cyrus had never asked him questions like this. Again, he'd thought hard about how to respond. 'There was nothing to forgive. My father told me to be strong, that the pain of the insect bites would pass. And it did. He didn't know the bites would take my sight, but if you could go blind to save your cousin's life, you would, wouldn't you?'

'I don't know,' Mona said slowly. 'Before I met you, I wouldn't have made a trade like that. But now I think I could. I mean, yes.' As she spoke, she made the decision, her voice firm and clear: 'Now I *definitely* would.'

'So my father made the right decision. Because of him, maybe, Muzi lived. Now he and I are the men of the family. I know I'm still young, but I have to be strong and focused for my family's future. My father told me I had to take revenge, but the best revenge is succeeding where the Gaians fail, in being wiser and more peaceful than they are. If I let the Gaians eat me alive from the inside, then they and their fire ants really have won.'

'Wow. That's just so amazing, Suen. I think you should go back into the Library and say all that,' Mona had urged. So he'd done it. Perhaps that would help other people, as she said.

The whole team worked on the other plant, which was designed especially for political meetings. The carnation's spiritual name was 'collaboration', climbing ylang ylang represented accurate perception, while the cork tree brought the energy of transformation to the participants. Again, the addition of bamboo ensured efficiency: now a journey into the psychosphere that felt as if it took hours in reality was over in fifteen minutes. Even so, the wait was agonising. To ensure neutral examination conditions, no member of the team was allowed to enter the psychosphere with the Mujaddid. Instead he had summoned Una Dayyani to share his meeting with the plant spirits, which was being overseen by a shaman especially brought in from Shiimti. Dayyani would also experience the Living Library. To ensure that taking both journeys in quick succession would not be physically upsetting or affect the quality of the meeting, the team had worked hard on the dosages, adding Alexandrian laurel, for physical peace, to minimise the gastric side effects of the lantern leaf. Still, watching the Mujaddid pour out the two glasses of plant juice was nerve-wracking. After being introduced and allowed to bow but not speak, the team were ushered into an antechamber and told to sit tight. As Něštug meditated, and the others worked on their Tablettes, Suen, Mona and Cyrus murmured together in the corner.

'The Mujaddid's a lot thinner than he looks in his pictures,' Mona said.

'He doesn't eat very much, I read,' Cyrus said. 'Not since he took the vow of poverty.'

'It's not exactly a vow of poverty,' Mona corrected him. 'He's just decided to live on the income of his poorest citizen.'

'Yeah, in a palace.'

'He sleeps on a mat, Cyrus! And by taking the vow, he's pushed his government into working on measures to lift everyone up to a decent standard of living.'

Suen was still glowing from being in the Mujaddid's presence. 'He's a man of light,' he whispered. 'He radiates peace.'

'Not like Una Dayyani.' Mona giggled. 'She radiates drama. She had that poor assistant running marathons for her.'

Una Dayyani was the Mother of Kadingir and the leader of the Non-Landers. Suen frowned. 'She has her dignity, Mona. We're asking some very important people to lie on the floor and take a drug that might make them throw up. I think if she wants a few more cushions, that's understandable.'

Cyrus chuckled. 'You didn't know Suen was such a Dayyani fan, did you, Mona? Insult her at your peril.'

Now Cyrus was teasing him. He'd learned not to jump for the bait, but still he flushed. 'I'm not her devotee, Cyrus. But she's achieved some great things for Non-Landers. The CONC compensation means none of us here in Asfar feel like beggars any more. If *she* took the Mujaddid's vow, she wouldn't lose weight.'

'I'm sorry, Suen,' Mona soothed. 'It's great she's here and can experience your story. Do you think she's Istar? Or that Astra Ordott is?'

He had spent a long time puzzling this one out. 'I think that everyone is a vessel for divine energy, and we can all channel all the gods if we're open to them. The Grandmother appears to everyone who takes lantern leaf, doesn't she? But because of the way we are made and how our bodies work, women are usually stronger channels for goddess energy, men for god energy and transpeople for a mixture of both. I believe that Dayyani and Astra channel different aspects of Istar's leadership. Dayyani represents Istar in the World Without, and Astra communicates with her in the World Within. They are complementary forces for good.'

'Yeah, I get that,' Mona said. 'It's strange, though, that Dayyani doesn't stand behind the Old Ones' messages. She's got all that money now from CONC, like you say, but she's not putting any-thing into non-metal tech. It's the Mujaddid who fronted the competition.'

'There's still some tension between her supporters and Ordott's left over from the old days of YAC.' He paused. His next idea was so big that he hardly dared to say it. 'Maybe,' he lowered his voice, 'if Dayyani can voyage to the World Within, her energy will fuse with Astra's and victory for One-Land will be certain.'

Suen was glowing brightly again. It didn't matter if they won the competition. All that mattered was that Una Dayyani experienced the truth of the World Within, and that the Non-Land leadership was united at last.

'Dayyani work with Astra Ordott?' Cyrus chuckled. 'Now that *would* be a transformation.'

Then Suen's stomach was turning. Dayyani was proud, everyone knew that. She had seen off all competition for her leadership for decades now. But surely she would accept equal billing with Astra Ordott if the future of the planet was at stake?

Una opened her eyes. Marti was kneeling at her side, flannel in hand.

'Are you all right, Una?' she whispered, dabbing her forehead with the cool cloth.

'I am . . . I am . . .' Her face was burning, her whole body tin-gling, her mind still spinning down those long green tunnels. For the first time in her life, words failed her.

'Here, let me help you sit up.' Marti supported her back, straight-ened her robe.

'Ooer,' she moaned.

'Una!'

'I'm *fine*. Just a little dizzy, that's all.' She grabbed Marti's arm, heaved herself to her feet. 'Fan me, Marti, fan me.'

The room swam into focus. Beside her on the stage, the Muja-ddid was already back on his seat, smiling that kind, serene smile of his. She returned it, gingerly, and settled herself in her chair. Her face was still hot, but Marti was fluttering the fan. With the cool air and her upright posture came some semblance of normality.

But could anything be normal again after *that*?

Suen brooded, unable to share his anxiety with the others, until a knock came at the door. 'The Mujaddid has asked for your return.'

They filed back into the hall. He turned his audio-description earbuds on. He needed every clue to Dayyani's state of mind. But the description was too general, didn't give him any information he needed.

'How does she look?' he whispered to Cyrus. 'Dayyani. Her expression, I mean.'

'Hard to say. Her assistant is fanning her. Solemn, I guess. Maybe a little dazed?'

She was being fanned? Was she too hot? But solemn. Dazed. That must be good. He'd never heard of Una Dayyani looking anything but supremely confident or blazing with righteous fury.

'Oh . . .' Mona gasped.

'What?'

'She looks ill now,' Cyrus said gloomily. 'She's gone all glass-eyed and clammy.'

'Una Dayyani is speaking with her personal assistant . . .' Even the audio describer sounded worried. 'Una Dayyani's personal assistant is sponging the N-LA leader's face with a cool towel.'

They'd made Una Dayyani sick. It was all over. They had failed. All that time wasted, a bunch of youths messing about with drugs, just like his mother had said. His own face was burning. He wanted to shrink, hide away, run off and join Muzi in the desert. The audio describer announced that the personal assistant had left the stage and Una Dayyani had signalled her readiness to continue, but he barely heard her. Then the Mujaddid was speaking, his soft voice buffing Suen's battered soul back into a shine.

'Thank you, team, for these fascinating experiences. I know I speak for all of us when I say we're all very grateful to visit the Living Library and learn of the spiritual journey of your Non-Lander member. This young man's fortitude, generosity and modesty are an example to us all, and I know my Honourable Colleague Una Dayyani was very moved by his story. Indeed, she still appears overcome by the emotion it provoked.'

Suen flushed furiously. But Cyrus was squeezing his hand, and Mona had slipped her arm into his. *Fascinating experiences. Overcome with emotion.* They hadn't completely bottomed out after all. They had offered their leaders something of value. How much, he couldn't say, but his soul soaked up the praise. He interlaced fingers with Cyrus, and together they awaited the next verdict.

'Equally,' the Mujaddid continued, 'our meeting in the psychosphere was most intriguing and fruitful. Might I even say, Lead Convenor Dayyani, that under the auspices of the lantern leaf, carnation, ylang ylang and cork tree spirits, something of a diplomatic breakthrough occurred?'

Suen realised he was holding his breath.

The Mujaddid was addressing her. An audience of professors, students, her entourage and select national and international journalists was waiting. She needed to speak. But how to do so? What to say? She blinked in the spotlight, the after-images and echoes of her time in that place, those tunnels and clearings, still pouring through her brain.

First there had been a bright light, far brighter than the stage lights, a light that had dazzled her, then seared her soul with its words: 'You are lion-hearted, Una Dayyani, and you have achieved much for your people. But you have not yet achieved greatness. To do that, you must learn humility. You are not Istar, I am. But if you serve me well, you may yet wear my mantle on Earth.'

The words had struck her to the core, frightened her, but also filled her with desire: a desire not only to be a great leader, but to grow. She had been her people's leader for so long, she realised with wonder as the light pulsed around her, that she had forgotten that the purpose of life was to grow. Then, when she could see again, there had been the boy. The boy with his story that rent her heart, the boy who had suffered the deepest wounds that her people could suffer, and yet had endured, survived, thrived; the boy who had led her to Istar.

And finally, there had been the tunnels, long green tunnels curling like vines, leading her to the meeting, that mysterious conclave with the spirits of the Mujaddid and the plants they had imbibed, cork, ylang ylang, carnation and the Lantern Leaf Grandmother, each sharing views, suggesting strategies, developing a plan, a way to serve all their interests – humanity's, Non-Land's, the plant world's – a plan so sound and so responsive to her own desires it had silenced all her objections, shrunk all her fears of losing her crown, sharing her power. The purpose of life was to grow, and to grow as a person, she realised as she awoke, meant to change . . .

'You might indeed, Your Eminence.' Her voice quavered. Had it all been a dream? Had she been given a drug that had addled her brain?

But the light. The light had spoken the truth. And then, somehow, the Mujaddid had been there. In the other world. The plant world.

She swallowed, spoke again. 'I confess that I thought I was coming here to, at best, experience a mild euphoria while in a light trance state induced by some harmless phytochemicals. Instead, I was taken on . . . an incredible voyage, a journey to which mere words cannot do justice.' Her face was wet. She realised she was weeping. Marti reached over with the flannel, dabbed her face again. Before, she would have brushed the cloth away, annoyed at the interruption to her speech. Now she smiled, patted Marti's wrist and said, 'Thank you, Marti. My dear, loyal Marti, whose patience and determination embody the spirit of my people.' Her voice was getting stronger, resuming its long-practised rhythms. She turned again to the audience. 'On my journey into the plant world, I met with the divine spirit of my people, with Istar. While I have been privileged to wear Istar's mantle these last years, She reminded me that all Non-Landers share Her brilliant light. In the plant world, I also met with that great, humble spirit, the Mujaddid, encountering his wisdom, and the wisdom of our plant teachers, in an experience that reminds me that all life is a shared dream. The Non-Land Alliance is proud that a youth from our land has helped to create this extraordinary development in what I can only call interspecies, perhaps even interstellar communication. I am humbled, truly humbled.' She drew herself up. 'But I am also invigorated: more determined than ever before to use all my strength in service of the vision of One-Land. As the Prophecy says, "Alone she will fly to the ashlands and bury herself in the Earth". From my journey with the plant spirits, burrowing deep in the tunnels of the earth, I arise now to claim our homeland at last!'

The applause was sweet. But sweeter still was the hug Marti gave her, and the *thank you* she whispered in Una's ear. Dear, long-suffering Marti who loved her, and deserved all Una's gratitude, and from now on would receive it.

Suen's fingers were squeezing Cyrus' so hard their hands were fusing; his soul was floating up in the dome of the hall. The plants had spoken to Dayyani. Spoken to the Mujaddid. A diplomatic break-through had occurred. Istar had used him, used his blindness, his brain, his family's suffering, to create change at the highest level possible in the material world. He didn't know what change it would be, if his team would win the prize: it didn't matter. Una Dayyani had been inducted into the World Within. He was filled with starlight. This was what it felt like to be in the service of the goddess.

'There are signs for us in all that the Oneness-of-the-Many has created.' The Mujaddid quoted from his Holy Book. 'I give thanks for these signs, and for all the hidden powers of creation. I thank all the young team for their work with us today. I am sorry to keep everyone waiting, but I must now discuss my experience with my own metaphysical engineering consultants, I will announce my decision tomorrow morning. I hope you will all be able to sleep tonight.'

You could hear the kindly crinkles in the great leader's voice. But sleep? There was work to do. Mountains of work. Love to make, oceans of love. And skies of wonder to float in. Suen would never sleep again.

Acid Green

Bracelet Valley
29.01.100

'Slow down, Brana. The polls are open for another sixteen hours.'

Esfadur was trudging behind her down the road at the pace of a geriatric hedgehog.

'I don't want to queue for ages in the cold, darling.'

'It's six o'clock in the morning! No one's going to be there yet. You're too excited, that's the problem.'

'Why shouldn't I be excited?' She opened her arms, pirouetted. 'We're standing at the dawn of real change, at last.'

'Or on the edge of a cliff-fall into catastrophe,' he grumbled. It was a new year, a whole new century, promising radical change for the country, but Esfadur had been doing nothing but grumble and doomsay all through the six-week election campaign. The Sec Gens would all vote for Riverine. The hicks in the steppes would all vote for Riverine. Crystal Wyrdott would lose and be placed under house arrest or forced into exile. Stonewayson would be arrested for his obvious role in Blesserson's defection. New Purism would be banned. Everything would be even worse than before.

'Oh, for goodness sake,' she puffed, her breath billowing in the milky morning light. 'Anyone would think you hadn't been on that demonstration! They came from *everywhere*, my husband. People all over this country bravely called for change, and change is what this election is going to deliver.'

'Not necessarily a good one!' he called gruffly after her.

She stalked on ahead. She knew all his arguments, word for word. Most of the marchers hadn't been calling for change, Esfadur had been telling her ever since the election was called. Most Is-Landers, he said, just wanted to prove to CONC and the world at large that they weren't psychotic mass murderers. For them, Riverine Farshordott's campaign manifesto, Is-Land Transcendent, was a defiant expression of national pride. Maintaining that Blesserson's story about the secret Vision Council subcommittee was a hoax, a cover for his and his lover's insane apocalyptic plot to kill off the human race and run Is-Land themselves, forever, thanks to Blesserson's longevity concoctions, Farshordott had promised, if elected, to try Blesserson *in absentia* for attempted genocide, and, if he and Odinson were found guilty, to free Stamen Magmason, their innocent victim. Her manifesto also promised the bare minimum of democratic reforms: just enough to reverse CONC's Rogue State designation and lift the sanctions crippling the economy, but otherwise keep the country hunkered behind the Boundary. Citing national security, she had promised to restart the Security Shots with a much-improved Serum, and only to induct one child per family unit. To the majority of Gaians, Esfadur had maintained, even those with damaged Sec Gen children, Riverine's concession sounded like a reasonable compromise.

But Brana couldn't let her grumpy husband have the last word. Not on this day of all days. She spun around, danced a finger under his nose.

'It *is* exciting, darling. Objectively exciting. Crystal and Riverine are neck-and-neck in the polls. In any other race, that's called a nail-biter.'

'Yes, but the polls exclude the Sec Gens. And the Sec Gens will all vote for Riverine's Spokes.'

Oh, the polls. They couldn't be trusted because IMBOD had banned pollsters from contacting Sec Gens. Being canvassed for their individual opinion would be too confusing for them, IMBOD doctors had claimed: Sec Gens thought as one and would feel anxious about giving a stranger an answer that might be different from their friends' or parents'. They were indeed lucky to have the vote at all. Is-Land national elections required one to choose seven local Spokes – most of whom had pledged allegiance to one of the Chief Convenor candidates – and there had been much debate in the mid-to-late RE seventies about the wisdom of allowing Sec Gens to participate in such a complicated process. Stamen Magmason, backed by high-ranking IMBOD officials, had argued strongly that the whole point of the Sec Gens was to eliminate the need for the imperfect mechanism of democracy. According to IMBOD, once the older generation of Is-Landers had died out and nearly everyone was, to some degree or other, Sec Gen, political decision-making in the country would be simply a matter of appointing a charismatic leader to inspire the hive mind and training competent bureaucrats to administer to the needs of the murmuration. But IMBOD, back in the seventies at least, was not the only powerful Ministry in the Wheel Meet, and a considerable number of Spokes had not felt quite so enthusiastic about endorsing the imminent obsolescence of their jobs. The question had been resolved at first by allowing Sec Gens to vote only for one Spoke, a Bioregional representative who would vote in Wheel Meet only on measures directly concerning Sec Gens. Then war had broken out in the Southern Belt and Magmason had declared his State of Emergency, a decision which meant that, to date, no Sec Gen in Is-Land had ever yet voted for anything more significant than whether to go for a swim or play another game of crickball.

But that didn't mean the youths couldn't make an informed decision. She fell in step with her husband, slipped her arm through the crook of his elbow. 'We don't know how the Sec Gens will vote. Halja's taking a great interest in both her candidates. And she certainly understands that a vote for Crystal's Spokes isn't a vote against Sec Gens.'

Crystal Wyrdott had in fact, Brana thought, carefully considered how she presented her own election promise to put the Sec Gen programme on hold, pending the results of Odinson and Magma-son's trial and a thorough independent investigation of the Vision Council. Early on in her campaign, standing before the IMBOD Shield and flanked by her own loyal Sec Gen guard, she had broad-cast a carefully pitched speech to reassure the electorate in general, and the Sec Gens in particular, that her proposal in no way meant that she didn't like Sec Gens. Quite the opposite. Sec Gens were very special people, with the wonderful qualities of loyalty, contentment, martial skill and strength; people who had been asked to do difficult things for their country, and who had done those things unquestion-ingly. But special people needed special care. With her proposal she was trying to ensure that, before we brought any more of these special people into the world, we should focus on helping the Sec Gens we already have to achieve all their dreams. Halja had watched the video over and over and then asked Brana: 'Am I allowed to have dreams?'

'Yes, well.' Esfadur sighed, his breath forming a cloud as large and soft as his beard. 'Our Halja's different from the average Sec Gen, isn't she?'

She squeezed his arm. 'And she's different from how she used to be, isn't she?'

The Lakeview Barn had come into view. There *was* a queue. Not a short one, and it would surely grow as people stopped off to vote on their way into town. She picked up her pace.

'Halja took the news about her sister better than I expected, yes,' he conceded. 'But that's the family loyalty gene asserting itself. And if every Sec Gen in the country just votes the way their parents want them to, that will skew the result towards Riverine.'

Oh, would he stop rabbiting on about statistics? Older Gaians and childless people leaned about 60–40 to Wyrdott's campaign manifesto while, by about the same percentage, parents of Sec Gens favoured Riverine. Brana was sick of the polls.

'The Sec Gens are adults,' she reminded her husband. 'Some of them are thirty years old. They might like the opportunity to make up their own minds for the first time in their lives.'

'Shh, darling.' Esfadur patted her hand. They were approaching the barn and an IMBOD officer was waiting to check their Tablettes. She dropped her arm and joined the queue. There were about a dozen people ahead of them, all older folk, three or four in green robes. Joy bubbled up in her chest. Just another twenty minutes or so to wait before casting her first vote in seventeen years.

Back at home, the day dragged, every minute feeling like an hour. Brana tidied up the Earthship, spent a couple of hours in the eco-tunnel, then decided to start another letter to Astra; she could finish it tomorrow, when she knew the results. She had settled at her desk with her homemade paper and quill pen when there was a knock at the door.

'Halja. Darling. Come in.' She raised herself on tiptoes to kiss her granddaughter's cheek. Even with her terrible posture, Halja still towered over her. 'Did you vote?'

'Yes, Omma.'

Halja slouched into the living room and slung her poncho over the back of the sofa. Apart from her hipbelt she was skyclad underneath: Sec Gens didn't feel the cold.

'Good girl.' Brana picked up the poncho, folded it and placed it on top of her wedding chest. 'And who did you decide on in the end?' She had tried hard not to pressure Halja into voting for Crystal's chosen Bioregional Sec Gen Spoke.

'The Crystal Wyrdott Spoke.' Halja's tone was flat as ever. 'She's going to help my dream come true.'

See, Esfadur! 'I thought Crystal's video had appealed to you, darling. Have you decided what your dream is, then?'

Halja was standing by her writing bureau, looking down at the parchment.

'I want to live with my sister.'

'Oh. Goodness. Well. I really hope that can happen one day. But Astra's in jail, isn't she?'

Halja knew very well that Astra was in prison: she asked endless questions about the conditions in Ashfields Max, wanting to know things that Brana couldn't possibly answer. In the end, Halja had done her own research online and written a report for Brana so she knew what Astra was likely to eat for breakfast, how large her cell was, even the wattage of her light bulbs. It was the first sustained piece of writing Brana had ever seen by Halja and, refraining from commenting on any of the spelling mistakes, she had printed it out and pinned it to the corkboard above her writing bureau, beside her photos of Astra, Halja and Eya.

Twisting her Bracelet Valley lake chain which, miraculously, she hadn't lost yet, Halja gazed at Astra's photo, taken from an old news article at the time of her deportation from Is-Land. 'I thought maybe Crystal Wyrdott could set her free.'

'Well.' Brana stood beside her granddaughter and straightened the photo. 'If Crystal wins, she might consider Astra's case, and I hope very much that she would understand that Astra wasn't to blame for everything that happened to her. But it's not one of her election promises, is it?'

'I want it to happen. I want to protect my sister.'

It was extraordinary, really, Halja's response to the news that Is-Land's greatest traitor was her older Birth-Code sibling. Brana had been afraid that she would reject her outright, or perhaps feel jealous of Astra for avoiding the Serum and not having to endure all the trials of National Service. But the opposite had occurred. In Astra's plight, Halja appeared to find a reason for her own inarticulate suffering: all she wanted to do was use her Sec Gen strength to protect her sister.

'She does need us. But even if she's set free, she might not come and live here. She has other family, in the dry forest. And because of everything that's happened, she might even be sent to live outside of the country.'

Halja clenched her fists. 'I'll go with her. I'll make sure no one hurts her again, ever.'

A little mouse of anxiety nibbled at the pit of Brana's stomach. It was all well and wonderful for Halja to fall in love with Astra, but Astra had never even met her half-sister.

'We'll just have to see what happens, won't we?'

Halja picked up the letter paper. 'I want to write to her. Like you do. With a feather pen.'

Well, goodness, Halja's surprises never ceased. 'Do you, darling?' She gathered up paper, quills, ink. 'I'm sure she'll like that. Why don't we sit at the kitchen table and write our letters together?'

Halja was still there when Esfadur came back from the orchard. She stayed for supper, and then decided she wanted to come with them to the Common Hall to watch the election results. The hall was full. Some people had brought their children and Gretel had made jugs of cocoa. At eleven o'clock, Esfadur turned the wallscreen sound on and people sat chatting quietly, awaiting the first result. Sif, Fasta and Vili, Brana noticed disapprovingly, were all seated apart. For the sake of the children, at least, that sulky Sif ought to try and patch things up with her husband and co-parent. But now was not the time to run a Parents' Counsel. Now the screen was taking them to the podium in Quartzton in the white desert, where fifteen candidates stood in a line behind the electioneer. Brana gripped Esfadur's hand.

It was an agonising result. Of Quartzton's seven newly elected Spokes, three were aligned with Riverine, three to Crystal and one was an Independent. The Quartzton Sec Gens had voted for their Bioregional Spoke, who would not be announced until all the white desert votes had been counted. Over the next hour, more Spokeseat results were announced, scattershot from all over the country, the total majority swinging back and forth between Riverine and Crystal, never more than four Spokes apart.

'I can't take a whole night of this.' Brana stood. 'I'm going to have a nap. I'll be back at half-past three.'

Other people were having the same idea: the hall was emptying out. Leaving Esfadur and Halja glued to the screen, and Sif, Vili and

Fasta still locked in their game of ignoring one another, Brana walked back to the Earthship, tucked herself into bed and set her alarm.

She was awoken by an earthquake.

'Omma! Omma!' Halja was shaking her so hard her teeth rattled. 'Omma, she won! Crystal Wyrdott won! You have to get up and finish your letter to Astra!'

Misted Silver

The Ashfields
01.03.100

Astra gobbled down her breakfast and turned to her stack of letters. Now that Crystal Wyrdott was in power and making diplomatic efforts to rebuild a working relationship with CONC, every day brought letters to the prison: long, only lightly redacted letters, not only from Jasper, Brana and Halja, her half-Code sister, but from people all over the world, strangers telling her not to give up, declaring that they had always believed in her and the Old Ones. Hang in here, these strangers urged. Your husband's cousin has helped solve the Tablette problem, CONC wants to take strict control of rare-earths mining and the Vernal Equinox brings the vote on universal disarmament: humanity is very close to breaking the pact with Metal. Soon not only you and both your countries, but the whole world will be free. Fervent Istarians wrote too. You have arisen, they declared. *We* have arisen. And soon, in our greatly strengthened global federation of nations, travel and trade will replace war and suspicion. People will move and live where they like, in a free exchange of culture and knowledge. The placeless ones will be in all places and a golden age of human harmony with the planet will begin!

With only three weeks to go before Earth's deadline, she needed such encouragement. The letter on the top of today's pile, however, she knew at once from the angular handwriting on the envelope, was not going to say anything remotely so hopeful. This letter was going to contain healthy dollops of anger and grief and a hosepipe full of emotional blackmail.

She set it aside and rifled through the other envelopes. There was a letter from Jasper: always top priority. She opened it to find a clipping, another of Photon's *Is-Land Watch* articles.

The Last Post: Is-Land Watch Goes Offline
by Photon Augenblick

Her heart contracted. Was Photon all right? Had his partner come back? Had he decided to give up the blog and go and live near his child in New Zonia? She couldn't blame him if so, but still she felt the pang of losing him, losing his words. Quickly, she scanned the article.

Is-Land Watch-ers are on red alert.

The good news from Is-Land continues. The new Wheel Meet Chief Convenor, moderate Crystal Wyrdott, is making good on her campaign promise to suspend the entire Sec Gen programme pending the trial of disgraced predecessor Stamen Magmason over the so-called 'Sex Gen' scandal. She and her slate of New Purist Wheel Meet Spokes are also pardoning convictions for protecting children from the Security Serum – everywhere else in the world banned under the Hudna as a Weapon of War – and she has ordered a full internal investigation into the alleged genocidal schemes of the secret 'Vision Council'.

But while the new regime's attempts to write Is-Land back into CONC's good books have been enough to rescind Is-Land's Rogue State designation and ease the sanctions that have been crippling the country's economy, they fall well short of open-hearted negotiations with the Non-Land Alliance.

Is-Land's foreign policy remains intransigent: the Boundary is still closed and Zabaria is still under Gaian occupation.

IMBOD, N-LA and CONC have all so far refused to comment on rumours that Astra Ordott, Is-Land's most famous political prisoner, is to be swapped for her Shelter brother, the former Sec Gen Peat Orson. Such a move would bolster belief in the controversial Non-Land 'Prophecy', which states that Istar will arise – just as Ordott already has risen in public consciousness over the last few weeks. But has the campaign to free her come too late?

With the Vernal Equinox just three weeks away, severe climate events continue to batter Earth. As forest fires rage over southern Neuropa, floods wash away entire New Himalayan villages and sinkholes consume small towns in New Zonia, Ordott's apocalyptic prophecies and messages allegedly passed on from the Old Ones are sounding ever more credible.

The recent Asfarian breakthrough in Plant IT, allowing people to meet in the psychosphere and consult plants as 'Living Libraries' of knowledge, has brought hope to many who believe these innovations will be enough to avert human extinction.

But Ordott herself has dashed those hopes. The week after the Mujaddid awarded the prestigious Institute of Metaphysical Engineering Prize to a team of young scientists which includes Suen Emeeš, Ordott's cousin-by-marriage, Ordott announced, 'Earth has asked me to convey the Old Ones' approval of humanity's renewed interest in plant messengers. But Earth also reminds us that the new technologies, while a step in the right direction, cannot be accessed while on the move. Even if just for a few minutes, one must be unconscious to experience the psychosphere. Until people everywhere forswear Tablettes, or develop non-metal-based mobile communications devices, the Old Ones remain unappeased.'

There is no need to remind readers that the Hudna ends this year on the Vernal Equinox. To meet the Old Ones' demands, humanity will also have to vote on that date to outlaw war as an archaic and barbaric mechanism of conflict resolution. But while CONC is finalising its draft of such a Commitment for its members to vote on, the Non-Land All Action Revolutionary Commandos (NAARC) have issued a statement threatening to liberate Zabaria by force. Should the Is-Land response include more secret weapons, it will likely force a military reaction from Asfar and CONC – or at least persuade delegates that universal disarmament is an unrealistic, even foolish goal. In that case, not even the invention of knitted woollen Tablettes will save us from the wrath of the Old Ones. Let us not forget that leading Istarian scholars have argued that the last word of the Prophecy could well be 'war'.

Comment

Photon Augenblick

In keeping with our philosophy, *Is-Land Watch* remains not hopeful but resolute. Although the Asfarian breakthrough does not yet go far enough to enable humanity to end once and for all our lethal pact with Metal, it is certainly true that if we all enthusiastically adopt the new Plant IT, that pact will be significantly weakened. From now on, therefore, *Is-Land Watch* is going offline and into the psychosphere. I have made myself available to the Plant IT team as a test subject and, as a result, I am pleased to announce that when I wish to communicate with the world, instead of writing on a Tablette, I will consume a unique cross-bred blend of lantern leaf, mountain sage and borage. During my time in 'trance-state' I will inscribe the plant's subtle DNA with an

echo-record of my thoughts on the current political situation.
Readers who wish to experience my analysis may purchase
the same plant leaves and seeds directly from the Asfarian
Institute for Metaphysical Engineering. Every two days,
between the hours of 4 p.m. and 6 p.m., NET, I will be available in trance-state, via the same plant channel, for discussion
with like-minded souls.

See you there, psychonauts!

She punched the air. Good on Photon – not just in the vanguard of
One-Land politics, but an early adopter of Plant IT. Jasper had
underlined the hours of his availability in the psychosphere, as if . . .
yes, it dawned on her, maybe she could join one of the *Is-Land
Watch* meetings! She'd have to ask the Old Ones, but surely they
couldn't object. Maybe Earth could dial her in on the plant's spiritual frequency.

That was a task for the evening. She set the article aside on the bed
for filing and checked Vultura. 07:40. The return of her privileges
had also meant the return of work duties, and she had ten minutes
before Lichena came to take her to the sewing room. She might as
well read that other letter now, then work off whatever frustration it
provoked on the treadle machine. She slid her finger under the envelope flap and removed two sheets of handmade paper.

Dear Astra,
I hope this finds you well and in good spirits. Forgive me for
my long silence. I am sorry to tell you that Nimma has not
been well for some months now. Her memory is slipping
and she caught an infection from her hip replacement –
alas, despite IMBOD's best efforts, there is still no sure-fire
cure for old age! – and caring for her has not left much time
for letter-writing. I hope you are keeping warm in this long
cold winter and taking heart from recent political changes.
Here in Or, we lost many crops in a freak blizzard last month,

and many people remain shaken by recent revelations, but since the election morale has been climbing, and I maintain hope that we will pull through, more united than ever.

For RE 99 was a very difficult year. It is my sad duty to inform you of the death, last spring, of your schoolmate Congruence, who took her own life after a long illness. Most difficult of all to accept was her suicide note, in which she confessed that she set that terrible fire in the dining hall: a moment of madness, intended only to frighten young Torrent and Stream, but which led to their deaths and Congruence's eventual descent into despair. She praised Ahn in her note for giving her strength but did not make it clear if he knew about her guilt, and I am afraid to say that many people, led by your old teacher Vishnu, accused him of shielding her from justice – a process which might have eased her stricken conscience – and even of exploiting her. Old suspicions surfaced again, about her age when their relationship began, suspicions that, since Ahn's arrest at Springhill – of which I am sure you are aware – have solidified for some members of the community. It began, I'm afraid to say, to feel like a witch-hunt and Ahn, who had already been spending much of his time in Atourne, left Or for good. Many people now feel a certain shame at having driven him away. Perhaps had we been more compassionate towards him, he would not have been drawn to that terrible place. Nimma and I tried not to take sides, and we naturally hope Ahn's trial will, if not demonstrate his innocence, then at least result in him getting some proper treatment for his own distress.

Astra's heart was running a marathon in her chest. *Congruence* had set the fire? Perfect, serene, self-disciplined Congruence? The horror of the fire struck her all over again, that furnace of anguish, the chaos and grief . . . and floating above it, Congruence's beautiful, expressionless face, the mask she had worn during Torrent and Stream's passionate relationship. Congruence, who had sought comfort from Ahn, who had protected him from Astra's attack . . . Astra's stomach turned, a bitter twist, but then it came, the lightness coursing through her, as she was relieved in a stroke of a burden she'd carried for so long it had become part of her: Lil had not been the arsonist. Lil was innocent.

She was also furious. Klor wrote like a master of diplomacy. 'Some members of the community', 'Many people', 'Old suspicions' . . . Why couldn't he just admit Ahn was a child abuser and that, until Wyrdott's election, Is-Land had been run by deranged paedophiles and brutal mass murderers?

Because of Nimma, that was why. Even if she remembered nothing else, Nimma would go to her grave declaring that Ahn was a sensitive, creative, misunderstood genius.

She stared back down at the spiky script, took a deep breath. At least Klor had written. And he hadn't written her off. With his love, though, came decades'-worth of emotional pressure. Bracing herself for her Shelter father's inevitable demands, she returned to the letter.

We also hope that, whatever the truth of Samrod Blesserson's testimony in Atourne, the current investigation into the Vision Council will prove a turning point towards better relations with the international community, and a return to unhindered trade and the possibility of occasional scientific collaborations. I am working on an all-seasons multigrain hybrid that would benefit from international investment, so I am hopeful that Crystal Wyrdott's negotiations with CONC will continue to go well. Many of us also hope, Astra, that Wyrdott's election will help bring to a close this long, painful chapter in your life. Every day, as I go about my tasks, I think of you languishing in that cell, and I ask Gaia for your freedom. And now, it seems, at last, an opportunity has come to make that dream a reality.

Astra, I believe you are aware that your Code grandmother Brana Yggdrasiladott visited us here in Or last week.
I say 'us', but we thought it prudent not to introduce her to
Nimma, who would likely have been confused by her presence. Vishnu came up from Sippur, though, and together
with Yoki and Meem and other Or adults, we heard what
Brana had to say. She is an intelligent woman, and much
concerned for your well-being. She brought us up to date
on her campaign for your freedom and discussed with us
the Asfarian Mujaddid's unexpected offer to trade Peat's
freedom for yours, an offer we had ourselves just learned of
from Peat's lawyers and his own letter to us: a letter in which
your brother stated that, if the suspension of the Sec Gen
programme is made permanent, he is willing at last to come
home. Our excitement, as you can imagine, was almost
dangerous to these old hearts! And yet it was doomed to
be short-lived. For from Brana, to our astonishment, we
learned that you have demanded that Cora Pollen be freed
with you, a condition Asfar has taken up but which IMBOD
has understandably rejected outright.

I cannot understand your decision, which grieves me
greatly. To see both you and Peat free would bring such joy
and peace to my winter years, and to Nimma's. She doesn't
yet know that you are the cause of the delay in bringing Peat
home, and I really do not want to have to tell her so. Please,
Astra, reconsider. Your legal situation is very different from
Cora's: you were a child, tricked into a life of political and
emotional deceit, and all of your regrettable actions have
stemmed from that initial betrayal of your innocence. Cora, in
contrast, was one of the people who created that trap for you.
She was your Birth mother's friend and I am sure that you will
have formed an attachment to her in prison, but please, consider your whole family, and your own health. Accept the
Mujaddid's offer and allow yourself and your brother to

rebuild your lives. I know that you would likely be exiled again
and I would not be permitted to see you, but it would lighten
my heart knowing that you were enjoying the sun and the
wind, and growing things in the earth, somewhere out beyond
these sad walls of history that confine us all.

Your loving Shelter Father,
Klor

Her blood racing, she set the letter aside and shoved her feet into
her sandals. Today, without doubt, she was going to break the
prison record for sewing hemp pillowcases.

The morning workshift flew by, and then it was lunch. She queued
for her ladleful of lentil mush then made her way with her tray
through the dining hall. Cora was already seated, her ramrod-
straight back to the world, her arm working mechanically, lifting her
spoon to her small cropped head. It was still strange to see her there
alone. But Crystal Wyrdott had acted swiftly, and Charm, Rosetta,
Pallas, Sunflower and all the other prisoners on Traitors' Wing, even
Fern, had been freed last week. That left a lot of empty chairs at Traitors' Table, and a massive ache in Astra's heart, one she had tried to
hide from the women as they celebrated their last meal in the jail.

The women's absence had also left a vacuum the guards were doing
their best to fill. As Astra took the seat opposite Cora, Lichena
approached. The guard leaned against a chair, fingering her diss-stick.

'Oooh. Look who we have here.' Lichena bared her teeth and
rolled a glance of filthy delight between Cora and Astra. 'Two little
traitor birds sitting on a wall. And should one of those traitor birds
accidentally . . . *fall*.' She rapped the diss-stick hard on the table,
right by Astra's elbow.

'Thank you for your concern, Lichena.' Cora patted her mouth
with her recycled napkin. 'But we're well accustomed to the height of

this wall. And if it hasn't escaped your notice, Astra's wings are getting stronger by the day. Some people, I hear, even say she's *arising*.'

'Ya, well.' Lichena leered at Astra. 'I wouldn't get too chirpy, Ornut. There's still plenty of folk out there in Is-Land *much* happier knowing you're safely locked up under my watchful eye.'

'I'm not going anywhere.' Astra dunked her heel of bread in her mush. 'Not unless Cora comes with me.'

'That's what you say now!' Lichena blinked her beady eyes. 'But Bircha and me got a bet on: fifty stones says that if Crystal Wyrdott rides up to the ashfields with the key to your cell door, we don't think you'd be so sad about leaving Aunty Cora behind to rot.'

The guard cackled and moved on. Astra stared after her with distaste.

'Don't let her goad you,' Cora said. 'She's panicking, like everyone in the old regime. And Astra, I'm telling you again: you must take up the Mujaddid's offer. You could be free in a matter of weeks.'

The bread was stale. Astra took a sip of water to soften it, finished chewing. 'I'm not leaving you here on your own.'

Without the others sitting around them, her voice was echoey in the hall. Without her here, Cora would eat all her meals alone. It would be tantamount to solitary confinement. She wasn't going to allow that to happen. If the Old Ones wreaked vengeance on the Equinox, it wouldn't matter where she was. And if humanity escaped annihilation, then she had plenty of time to negotiate freedom for both herself and Cora.

Cora pushed her bowl aside. 'Then you'll sit here until the pair of us rot, my girl. IMBOD isn't going to let us both go at once. Wyrdott needs to placate Riverine's supporters and releasing two arch-traitors simultaneously is precisely not the best way to do that. But if you accept the offer, and Peat returns home to great fanfare, then it will only be a matter of time before Wyrdott quietly lets me go, too.'

'Or she could just forget about you. I've got a case to be included

in the Sec Gen Amnesty. You don't. And I can't live with myself if I
know you're all alone here.'

'I won't be alone. Pallas will be visiting. And this lot need politi-
cising now.'

Cora jerked her head to indicate the rest of the dining hall. But
none of the other women in the jail had come and joined their near-
empty table. And although Pallas had applied for a conjugal ion
chamber visit with Cora, IMBOD had already refused the request,
forcing Cora's lawyers to lodge an appeal.

'Solidarity, you said.' Astra served Cora's words back at her.

'Solidarity means nothing without strategy! You have to get out
there, Astra! Thanks to the Mujaddid and a few freak snowstorms,
people are finally *believing* all your mumbo-jumbo. You've never
had such a high international profile. You need to be out on the
lecture trail; making yourself part of the One-Land negotiating
team. That's how I'll get my freedom: when One-Land is free.'

You just want to be the biggest martyr in the One-Land resistance,
she thought.

'I'm tired of your martyr complex,' Cora said.

'Me? Actually, *you*—'

'Listen to me.' The finger was wagging. 'Your political instincts
are right. You can't behave as though you're grateful for this offer.
You need to make a demand. But don't ask for freedom for me. Ask
for something for *yourself* for a change. That way we'll both get the
maximum advantage from this deal.' Cora stood, tray in one hand,
the other still chastising. 'Don't let yourself get institutionalised,
Astra. You've been locked up here for over a decade and your closest
relationships have been with voices in your head. Now you have a
chance to be free. Don't tell me you're afraid to take it.'

'I'm not afraid of freedom.' But Cora was walking away. The conversation, if talking to Cora was ever a conversation, was over. Astra
placed her spoon on the table. She'd only eaten half her bread and
mush, but suddenly she'd lost her appetite.

Bruise Purple

The Great Depression
05.03.100

'Oh you beautiful balls!' Sulima clapped her gloved hands, the muscled commander in her camouflage winter gear sounding, for an unexpectedly sexy moment, like a little girl at a party. 'You gorgeous diamond-dusted truffles. At last we're going to put you to use. If I don't eat you first!'

Enki grinned. 'I wouldn't like to hear you trying to take a shit afterwards.'

'Arse-wart.' Sulima made as if to swat his good arm and he raised his elbow to fend off the blow. Ñizal chuckled, his breath a cloudy spume that made Enki want to roll the cannons out of the tent and fire them until the air was thick with smoke. For he shouldn't tease Sulima: the quartz-coated projectiles were indeed a dazzling sight. And he too just couldn't get enough of the great guns: their glossy promise, boom and recoil, the sulphurous smell of burnt gunpowder with its hint of piss, he loved everything about them with an intensity that still surprised him. Even after a week of working with the weapons, his heart still swelled to bursting whenever he entered the heavy artillery tent, and realised anew: he had done it. Made his dream come true. Here he was, zooming between two columns of black cast-iron cannons, six of them, each with its own pyramid of Boundary-busting cannonballs: twelve hundred iron projectiles packed with explosives and coated with a thick layer of finely ground quartz crystal, enough for at least three separate assaults on the Boundary.

For though the idea of coated cannonballs had come to him in a dream, it was no fantasy; the technology was feasible, all the engineers he'd consulted had said so. While the exact composition of the Boundary cladding was a Gaian secret, if it worked the way IMBOD claimed it did, as an eddy current brake emitting a magnetic forcefield crazy powerful enough to repel iron and steel projectiles – bouncing them, according to the IMBOD video, back on the heads of their owners – then quartz crystal, with its remarkable ability to store energy, should absorb the forcefield and prevent it from detecting the missiles. Thus the cannonballs would bamboozle the brake and smash through the wall, where the explosives would do their job, igniting any wooden structures on the other side. The real joy of it was that the ground crystal was Is-Landic. It had been quarried in the white desert, within the Boundary, and bought – before the CONC sanctions hit – on the open market in Neuropa, then Zeppelined back to Asfar. Using the Gaians' stolen resources against them was a major coup: as every Non-Lander elder worth their salt told their grandchildren, clear quartz from the white desert was the most potent rock crystal in the world.

And possibly the sparkliest. Even so, these cannons and their glittering projectiles were just the confectionery. Rearing behind them at the back of the tent, mounted on its wooden chariot, a mammoth bronze bull, was the great weapon itself: the Şahi Topu, the super-sized Old World bombard Enki had remembered the morning he'd woken up from his quartz-crystal dream. He still had to pinch himself when he looked at it. The giant cannon had been a distant image on a website he'd visited long ago, back in the days of the gym tent in Kadingir, when his mentor, Abu Izruk, had urged a curious youth to educate himself about his people. Now, through dint of sheer bloody-mindedness, that youth had resurrected one of the world's greatest guns from the fathomless depths of the Dark Times and summoned it to the aid of the descendants of its creators.

As always, approaching the Şahi Topu, Enki felt not invincible, but humbled and awed.

Cast by a medieval Karkish engineer for his Sultan, measuring over five metres in length and weighing nearly seventeen tonnes, the Şahi Topu was so heavy it had to be transported in two pieces, a powder chamber and barrel that – with some difficulty – screwed together for firing. Each section was embellished with a grape-leaf relief Enki loved to trace with his fingers, and the bronze had turned a mottled jade grey over the centuries, the most beautiful colour – apart from Sulima's lemon-tea eyes – he had ever seen. But the gun was no ornament. The two sections ended in barred finials Enki had dubbed 'the four millwheels of fate' and engraved on the lip of the barrel's black maw was an ancient Asfarian inscription petitioning the Abrahamic god for help in vanquishing the Sultan's foes. In the era before the motor vehicle, forty oxen and three hundred men had been needed to haul the gun into battle. In action, it got so hot it had to be cooled down with gallons of olive oil and could only be fired seven times a day for fear it would crack. Yet the bombard had remained operational for centuries, resoundingly defeating an invading Yukay navy three hundred and forty years after it was made. As a youth, Enki had loved the story of the Şahi Topu. As the commanding officer of NAARC, he had committed himself to deploying it. That fateful morning, waking up from his dream, he'd remembered with a brilliant white flash of determination that the ancient gun used *huge marble cannonballs*. Against the Şahi Topu, the Gaians' precious forcefield would provide no defence whatsoever. Using the gun in combination with the smaller cannons and their explosive projectiles, NAARC would bring the Boundary down at last.

He was making history. He wanted the gun itself, not a replica. But how to get his hands on it? Returning to the internet, he'd discovered that, in a gesture of friendship, a later Karkish sultan had gifted the bombard to a great Queen of Yukay, who had placed it on display in a museum in a naval city on the coast of her realm. The city had been swallowed by the waves at the start of the Great Collapse – it would be impossible, Sulima had said, to retrieve the gun. But many drowned cities were now being dredged: surely, Enki had thought, one of NAARC's wealthy patrons would want to be known as the man or woman who rescued the Şahi Topu from the cold waters of Yukay and put it back in service of its homeland.

He had put the word out through his networks in Asfar. Tibir Ögüt, a young Karkish-Asfarian construction business titan whose father had died recently of a heart attack, leaving him to manage the family's billions, had responded. Although cautious by nature, Ögüt was drawn to the idea of financing the Non-Land resistance in his Karkish father's memory, and proved receptive to NAARC's view that, when diplomacy had stagnated, a short sharp dose of gunfire might be required to trigger new political breakthroughs. In any case, Enki had argued in one of their clandestine meetings before he had been banished from Asfar, liberating Zabaria was not an act of war. It was a long-overdue rescue mission. As for blasting a hole in the Boundary, *that* was a simple act of self-respect.

Through Ögüt's well-established maternal Asfarian family, private negotiations with CONC and the Yukay government had begun. At last it was agreed that, in exchange for the designation of the Şahi Topu as a cultural artefact, a decommissioned relic to be repatriated to its historical region of provenance, a team of Asfarian divers would conduct a full underwater excavation of the city's drowned museum. Two years ago, the ancient cannon had been raised from the seabed: an event that had made a media splash, but few ripples. A handful of journalists bemoaned the fact that this priceless treasure, which by rights should be displayed at CONC HQ, was passing into the private collection of the anonymous excavator; and then nothing more was heard of the gun. Zeppelined over to Asfar, it had been held in storage with other priceless treasures until Ögüt could be convinced that the time was right to release it. The smaller cannons, bought singly on the black market, and the ammunition, commissioned from a Karkish family with a noble Old World military lineage and desert factory, had been held separately in various locales scattered throughout Asfar and the Southern Belt.

It had taken so long for the young man's nerve to harden that Enki had nearly given up hope of ever seeing the weapons. Even the jailing of the Sec Gen and the subsequent crackdown in Zabaria had not moved Ögüt to action, and at times he even seemed to think that the upcoming Hudna vote would somehow benefit Non-Land. But now, at last, the election of Crystal Wyrdott, a supposed Gaian moderate who was refusing to withdraw from Zabaria, had convinced Ögüt that nothing would make Is-Land negotiate in good faith with Non-Landers. Two weeks ago, security at the billionaire's remote desert warehouse being surprisingly lax, a gang of knife-wielding robbers had arrived in a big truck, tied up the guards, and stolen the Şahi Topu. That part of the plan had gone exceptionally well. Ögüt had successfully claimed on his insurance, and his second cousin in the Asfarian government had immediately placed a media embargo on the theft. In light of the Hudna vote, there was no point in stoking international tensions by announcing that the world's biggest gun was suddenly in criminal hands; as the cousin had argued to his department, the thieves had also taken many bronze statues and would most likely be melting their entire haul down for its value as scrap metal.

The caravan of cannons had arrived at the camp a week later: four flatbed trucks winding through the scrublands, heaped with hay for the camels, though travelling slowly for such a light load. Also buried in the hay were the crates of ammunition and a host of lovingly-styled cannon accessories: powder bags to hold the explosives; wooden lanterns and rammers to load the bags into the cannons; friction primers to ignite the gunpowder; priming irons to clear the touch-holes of debris; sponge staffs to scour the cannons of any remaining live gunpowder; wad-screws to unload the used powder bags; and the quoin of mire, pieces of notched wood secured to the cannons for the gunners to grip while they aimed.

For Enki's money, though, after the Şahi Topu itself, the most beautiful thing in the arsenal was the super-sized bombard's pyramid of ammunition: twenty-one huge, white, spherical marble projectiles stacked at the base of the gun. He ran his hand over one, treasuring its smooth, cool surface: these gleaming balls were going to breach the Boundary and free his people.

Sulima stood reverently beside him. 'Enki's Blaster and its milky droplets.' She giggled, not so reverently.

'It's called the Şahi Topu,' he corrected her. For despite everything he had done to get it here, he could not take credit for this gun. Perhaps, he sometimes thought, gazing at the great bombard, he had been born to serve this ancient weapon; his life, the entire Non-Land cause, merely an excuse to resurrect its indomitable wall-smashing spirit, and fire it back into action.

Action that was fast approaching. After seven years of camel charges and rifle and revolver practice, every morning for the last week he, Ñizal and Sulima had been training cannon gunners: all three hundred and thirty-five warriors in the camp had been put through their paces, rolling the iron cannons out into the scrub-lands and firing shots with practice balls until everyone physically able to could load, fire, clean and reload the guns in under five minutes. Now the fastest teams had been picked and the time had come to set forth into battle. This was the final inspection.

'Are the camels ready?' he asked.

'Camels and riders have been commanded to be saddled and packed by nine p.m.,' Ñizal replied. 'Everyone else will spend all day striking camp.'

'And the horseboxes?'

'Already hitched,' Sulima confirmed.

It was three hundred and fifty kilometres to Zabaria. They had vehicles enough for the commanding officers, the heavy artillery and its crew, the tents and camp supplies, and the horses, which could not cope well with long journeys. The Great Depression had no roads, and given the danger of bandits it would be foolhardy to transport the weapons along the Upper Belt Road when they reached it, but the terrain was firm all the way to Šaganiri, the last oasis town before Zabaria. Travelling at night, off-road, at camels'-pace, it would take ten days to reach the outskirts of Šaganiri. There they would swing south, onto grazing land owned by a NAARC ally and, hidden in the hills, would rest before battle. Of course, anything could happen on the road, but give or take a day or two, the plan was to attack three days before the Vernal Equinox, the day CONC was voting on making the Hudna permanent.

Just thinking about the vote made Enki's blood boil. The so-called Global Peace Commitment was simply another step in the re-consolidation of economic and cultural power by the rich nations of the Northern hemisphere. Its vision of universal disarmament would leave the global oppressed no viable resistance to occupation and dispossession, and the world's only legal military arsenal in the hands of CONC, a bunch of jawing battle-shy committee junkies who could be counted on to do anything *but* intervene in regional conflicts. Fortunately, a lot of people felt the same way: according to all media reports, the Commitment was by no means guaranteed to pass. What was needed was not yet another philosophical debate, but a good strong outbreak of violent opposition, expressed in a language everyone understood. And violence, Enki knew, was con-tagious. The moment NAARC attacked, the Gaians, keen to restore their status as persecuted victims, would be sure to go run-ning to the world media, where images of cannon fire destroying the Boundary stood a good chance of triggering similar uprisings in trouble spots all over the globe. Timing, therefore, was everything. Attack too soon and any momentum would quickly be lost in the CONC echo chamber; too late and there would be no time to gen-erate a domino effect strong enough to scupper the vote. For with freedom fighting breaking out everywhere, the wealthy nations no doubt returning fire, and CONC in chaos, how could anyone with half a brain elect to 'abolish' war? Might as well abolish the need to eat when you were hungry. As for YAC's Istar followers, let them squawk: even if the Ordott ravings were in fact true, as far as Enki knew no one had come up with a viable non-metal Tablette yet. If the world was going to end, it should do so with a bloody great bang.

'What about the Claim of Responsibility?' Ñizal murmured.

Enki turned from the bombard. 'The Owleons are ready. They will fly from Zabaria.'

Operation Harsh Gemstone required secrecy if it was to succeed. But who knew what IMBOD had prepared in the event of a surprise attack? Even if all they did was send out a pack of Sec Gens, it was highly probable that most, if not all, front-line warriors would not survive. But, without doubt, the bombard would put at least one giant hole in that wall, and when it did his crack media team would be on it. Last night, Enki had pre-recorded NAARC's Official Statement, taking full responsibility for the first *real* breakthrough in years in Non-Land/Is-Land relations.

'We're all set.' Sulima put her hand on his shoulder. 'Let's get the cannons loaded up on the truck.'

'Along with Enki's sparkly balls.' Ñizal grinned.

Jokes could be made about the iron cannons. 'That's *fiery* balls to you, friend,' he smirked. 'Only Sulima gets to sprinkle glitter on them.'

'Enki!' She hit him again and he steered the electric chair out of her way, zigzagging back to the tent entrance to give the order: all hands on deck. The cannons would require wheeling and hoisting and lifting the bombard would generate much swearing and sweating, but once back on the flatbeds, the weapons would be ready to fire. Operation Harsh Gemstone was underway.

The tents were all folded and stacked in the vans, along with the bed mats, rugs, kitchen supplies, gym machines, portaloos and tools. The stallions had been led into their horsebox and the battle camels were packed and mounted. The roof of the Freedom Bus was loaded with barrels filled with boiled water from the river. Enki's six Black Blasters, his magnificent dream weapon, the Şahi Topu, and seven crates of cannonballs were strapped to the backs of four flatbed trucks, one of which was also transporting Enki and Sulima's chariot. A huge sprawling camp was now a shadowy cluster of vehicles and beasts growling and shuffling in the evening twilight. Muzi, on his camel, hung back from the cavalry. He had offered Enki his services as a scout, would travel to the side of the caravan and up ahead, keeping his eyes peeled for trouble and resources. As they passed by the Salt Chott, he would lead a small team out to the saltpetre deposits he knew about and collect more of the mineral for NAARC's gunpowder makers. And when they got to the scrublands, he would forage for plants.

Apart from that freedom to roam, he was under strict orders. 'You're not to fight at Zabaria,' Enki had said. The words still burnt in his chest.

'I'm a veteran of the Battle of Kadingir,' he'd reminded Enki. 'I still have my knife from Shiimti.'

'The Sec Gens eat knives for breakfast. And we don't have enough firearms to go around. You stay back and help the medics tend to the wounded. You can gather medicinal plants *en route*, too. We'll need sage and Solomon's Seal for poultices.'

He would do that, of course, gather as much food and medicine as he could. But he was a Non-Lander. Nothing could stop him from fighting the Gaians.

From the darkness, Enki's bullhorn sounded. Slowly, at the pace of the ancient caravans, axles oiled, electronic engine noise muted, camel bells muffled, the Non-Land All Action Revolutionary Commandos began their near-silent procession northeast. Muzi's beast shifted beneath him, a ship of the desert ready to sail. Whether his fate was to forage or fight, his Battle for Zabaria had begun. He said farewell to the hills, farewell to the mighty River Shugurra. Only the sky-god knew if he would ever swim its wild currents again.

Sour Gold

Occupied Zabaria
07.03.100

When he came home from football, Ama was dead. Dead on her bed mat. Her face was set as if sleeping, but she didn't wake as he ran into the room, and when he came closer and took her hand, though it was warm, she wasn't breathing. His heart pounding in his chest, he dropped her hand and backed off. That woman lying under the blanket with the gaping mouth and waxy skin wasn't Ama. Ama was gone.

It was four o'clock. He ran to Todo's house, but Todo wasn't there. So he ran to the park in the Gaian quarter. The park was the best park he'd ever been in. As well as swings and a sandpit with real sand, the climbing frame had a spiral chute slide, a climbing net and a superlong cableway that made an excellent slithery sound.

But today he couldn't play. Today he sat in the shady crawlspace underneath the cabin, shaking.

'My Ama wants to know if you're okay.' A little girl slid into the dirt beside him. She was wearing clothes: she was a Non-Lander, but he couldn't trust anyone.

'I'm waiting for my Ama,' he said. His lip trembled with the lie. Ama was gone. He could wait here forever and Ama wouldn't come back.

'You're crying.'

'No, I'm not.'

She toed a wooden car someone had lost or forgotten, rotating its red wheel. 'Do you want to bounce on the trampoline with me?'

'No thanks.'

She shrugged and heaved herself back out into the sun. For the hundredth time, he checked his Tablette. Four fifty-six. Tira would come and check the park at five minutes past five o'clock. That's what she'd said back in the spring in her office across the road, and that's what Ama reminded him weekly was 'the emergency plan'. Tira walked home through the park every day. If there was ever an emergency, he should come here and run out to meet her as she passed the playground, and they would go home together. Before, he didn't know why he and Ama couldn't just have Tira's phone number on their Tablettes, or even written down somewhere, but now he understood. His mother was a YAC Singular, and Tira was a people smuggler. Everything had to be top secret.

So he'd come to the park, dodging street fighting on the way – Non-Landers throwing stones at a trio of Gaians who raced at them with batons – but no one had noticed a boy dashing by. And now it was five minutes past five, and he had to scramble out of the crawl-space or stay here all night, and then he was back in the sandpit and there she was, Tira walking by, and he waved and she waved back, calling, 'Girin! Time to go home,' and for the sake of the mothers watching and the Gaians in the park, he called back, 'Coming, Ama,' and ran up to the gate of the playground as she opened it, bursting into tears as she enfolded him in bony arms that were nothing like Ama's.

Tira had a nice apartment. It was small, but much newer than his and Ama's, with shiny walls and furniture. She installed him on a bed mat with a game on her Tablette while she used his Tablette to call Todo and the neighbour and the doctor, conveying the news, expressing condolences, making the funeral arrangements and letting him speak to everyone so they knew he was safe. Then she cooked him dinner in her kitchenette.

'Just because I'm here doesn't mean I want to go to Asfar,' he said as she peeled an aubergine.

'Of course not. You can stay as long as you like and see how you feel.' She popped the skinned vegetable into a pot of boiling water and began washing a cucumber.

'Ama is my real mother,' he announced. 'She brought me up.'

Tira was chopping the cucumber into very small cubes, just the way he liked them in tabbouleh. 'The Gaians have different words for mother. They would call Ama your Shelter mother and Tiamet your Birth mother. Both of them are your real mothers. Like Girin and Ebebu are both your names.'

'I hate the Gaians. And my name's Girin,' he added for good measure, watching her slide the cucumber cubes into a bowl.

'I know it is, Girin.' She reached for a tomato. 'But your Birth name is Ebebu. It can be good to have two names. Then you can be a different person when you want to be.'

He thought about that for a while. 'Is Tira your only name?'

She laid the knife down then, sat on a kitchen chair and looked him in the eyes. 'No. It isn't. If you come to Asfar, I'll tell you my Birth name there. It's what Tiamet calls me. But in Zabaria you must keep calling me Tira, and you mustn't let anyone, anyone at all, know that I have a different Birth name. Promise?'

He promised, but she wasn't done yet. She reached out and gripped his wrist.

'Also, Girin – this is really important – you mustn't tell anyone that Tiamet is your Birth mother, not even my friend who is going to help us with the papers. If he knew I was sending you to join YAC Attack, he might not want to help us any more. It's our secret, okay, or I can't help you.'

He didn't even know yet if he wanted to go. 'Ama told me to keep it a secret,' he muttered. 'I already promised her.'

'Good,' Tira said, turning to the stove and sticking the aubergine with a knife to test it. 'I told my friend that your mother's name is Metti and she works as a cleaner.'

He watched her make baba ganoush with the aubergine and helped chop the coriander for the tabbouleh while she warmed up some flatbread. Tira just had a bit of the salad for dinner, but said he should eat as much as he liked. He ate nearly all the bread and aubergine, then said thanks, Tira, the dinner was good, but he wanted to go home. Tira wouldn't let him, though. The apartment was empty now, she said. The doctor and the priests had come, and his mother was awaiting burial.

He cried then, and tried to run out the door, but Tira grabbed him and wouldn't let him go. She held him for a long time, saying 'I know, I know' until he was exhausted from crying. The funeral would take place tomorrow, she said, and now he needed to sleep. He said okay, he would sleep at Todo's place, but he was yawning, and it was getting dark, and then there was a knock at the door.

Tira opened it a crack. 'Bud,' she hissed. 'Didn't you get my text?'

A man, a Gaian, pushed his way in and kissed Tira on the head. 'Babe. You said the little boy was here. Hey, this is family time.'

The man had a bunch of flowers. He laid them on the table. 'Hey, Girin. I'm Bud. Tira told me about your mother. I'm very sorry to hear that sad news. I'm here to say if there's anything at all that you need, you just ask me, okay, son?'

Girin backed into the chair, his heart hammering harder than even when he'd found Ama. No one had said anything about a Gaian. The man wasn't wearing anything except an armband and a hipbelt. He was old, and his thing dangled down. His chest was all hairy with white hair, and he was big as an ox. Gaians hurt children. That's what everyone said. And Gaians were looking for him. That was what *Ama* had said.

'You're frightening him, Bud!' Tira snapped. 'I haven't told him about you yet!'

'Well, tell him now, then. Introduce us!' Bud pulled up a stool and sat down, tucking his thing between his legs so it was hidden. 'Sorry, Girin, these old legs can't sit on bed mats any more.'

Tira hovered between them, clearly still angry but helpless to stop the Gaian from making himself at home. 'Girin, this is Bud. Bud's my friend who's going to help us. He's a Gaian, but he's not like the others, I promise you. He's a good Gaian. I've told him about you, and he wants to help you find your Birth mother.'

'We gotta keep that a secret, though, don't we, kid?' Bud tapped his hairy nose. 'Or Ole Bud could get into *big* trouble.'

Girin looked between them. Bud was old. He looked old enough to be Tira's grandfather. And he was *Gaian*.

'You said your friend worked for CONC.'

Tira winced. 'I know I did. I said that because I knew your Ama had a bad experience with Gaians, back before the takeover. But Bud wasn't here then; he's new in Zabaria. And he works *with* CONC sometimes.'

'Hey, Tira. The boy doesn't want to hear my CV.' Bud reached into a pocket of his hipbelt. 'His mother's just returned to Gaia.' He offered Girin a little paper bag. Girin looked at Tira and she nodded. He took the bag and opened it. Inside were some seeds.

'In my hometown,' Bud said, 'we plant roses when our mothers die. I'll help you germinate the seeds tomorrow, shall I, after the funeral?'

Ama would not have wanted a Gaian to plant roses for her. But as he refolded the bag and put it in his pocket, a possible solution to the unexpected puzzle of Bud occurred to him.

'Are you a One-Lander Gaian?' he asked. Some Is-Landers were One-Landers, he knew. Astra Ordott was one, and so were her lawyers.

Bud laughed. 'I wouldn't go that far! No, son. I just don't like to think of Tira's friend's little boy going lonely, that's all. Not when he has a Birth mother who's been looking for him all his life.' He stood up. 'C'mon, Tira, let's go. I'm double-parked and everything's ready at my place.'

Tira had lost all her fight. She looked like a different person all of a sudden. Smaller against Bud's bulk. She glanced at Girin almost apologetically.

'Bud's got a much bigger apartment, Girin. He's offered to let us both stay there. You could have your own room, and there's a great sound system. It's two buses to school, but I can take the first one with you.'

'And there's hot chocolate.' Bud grinned. 'Don't forget the hot chocolate.'

He could live with Todo if he wanted, his mother had said. Todo was coming to the funeral tomorrow. He could talk to him then. Right now, he was tired, and the streets were dark, and Tira clearly wanted him to say yes. Tira was Ama's friend. He wondered if Bud knew that Tira wasn't really called Tira. He had promised not to talk to anyone about that, though. And he mustn't tell Bud that his Birth mother was Tiamet, either. There was so much to remember. It would be so much easier to live with Todo.

But Tira was waiting for an answer. Bud, too. It was only for one night. He stood, avoiding the Gaian's gaze, clutching the bag of seeds in his hand.

Bruise Purple

The Southern Belt
16.03.100 – 17.03.100

'Our gods are great. Their will is One. We do their will, and with their will we will prevail.'

His army had made good time across the scrublands. Fed roast mutton and wild vegetable stew by their sympathetic landowner ally, they had rested for two full days off-road south of Šaganiri. Now most of that camp had been struck. Kneeling on her mat in the lee of the hill that had sheltered them, Sulima led the penultimate evening prayer of their battle march, and the last to include everyone. Though he did not join the chant, Enki prostrated himself in the front row to his wife's wisdom and surrendered again to the voice of his people. Around him, from over three hundred throats the droning incantation rose into the violet dome of the sky, a prayer to honour and summon all NAARC's gods: the ancient Somarian family of elemental deities; the Farashan fire spirits and Karkish Prophets; the Asfarian sacred principle of the Oneness-of-the-Many that some Non-Landers, like Sulima, had adopted; and She who presided over all: Istar, the morning and evening star, Queen of heaven and earth, love and war, Her journey in the sky a radiant harbinger of the Non-Landers' eventual return to their home. Not everyone believed that Astra Ordott channelled Istar's wisdom; some NAARC warriors called Sulima Istar now. She had tried to refuse the name, but like Enki, she could not, in the end, refuse the will of the people.

He did not believe in any of the gods. At the River Shugurra camp, he'd respected all religious observances, enforced none. But his warriors' determination to embrace their destiny, to commit their lives to his care, resonated at the core of his own dark faith in nothing but the necessity of *action*. He hadn't wanted NAARC to be a spiritual movement. The gods had abandoned humanity centuries ago, bored of the toys they'd created to amuse themselves. The only ones Enki had any sympathy for were the Old Ones: he understood Their fury, would be happy to just get his own revenge on the Gaians before Istar turned out the lights. His marriage to Sulima, though, had shown him the power of prayer. His wife prayed every morning, afternoon and evening, and he knew of no warrior more composed, courageous or even-tempered than she. In contrast, he knew, he was a hothead, a flamethrower, impatient and harsh, a leader more feared than loved, a demanding and uncompromising husband. It was the power of prayer, Sulima had once said, that enabled her to put up with him. Often she yielded, let him make his mistakes, never said 'I told you so'. But when she stood her ground, he'd learned to give way. Once the march to Zabaria had begun, Sulima had insisted on leading morning and evening devotions, ecumenical prayers for whoever wanted to join. From a small band of worshippers, as they'd travelled east through the Great Depression and saltlands, then, in parallel through the Southern Belt, the trucks on the road, the camels over the scrublands, the congregations had steadily grown. Now, just two nights' ride from Zabaria, the entire NAARC army had gathered together as one to express their devotion to their cause.

'Our gods are *great*.' Sulima's voice pierced the air, a shrill whistle that raised the hairs on his neck. 'We ride to meet them, on the *battle plain*.'

That was a sentiment he concurred with: though it ripped his voice into shreds, Enki led his army's answering roar.

The prayer ended. Muzi rose. A sense of enormous ceremony lingered in the air. Following Ñizal, three-quarters of the warriors silently filed through the dark to the camels and vans. The rest stood, waiting, with Enki and Sulima. It was now or never. Muzi slipped away from the back row, running wide around the departing line of warriors to the caravan of supply camels.

Ninda was tightening a beast's harness. 'What are you doing here?' she asked. 'I thought you'd been re-assigned to the horses.'

'I was. I just came to say goodbye to my camel.'

The supplies officer rolled her eyes. 'Better be quick about it.'

He found his beast, pressed his forehead to her rough jowl. 'Behave,' he transmitted. 'Don't step on Ninda's toes. Unless she beats you.' He moved back. 'She likes fresh grass, if there's any in the hills. But not too much or it upsets her stomach.'

'Don't worry, Muzi.' Ninda checked the buckles on the camel's girth strap. 'We'll take good care of her. She's our hospital camel.'

The beast was loaded down with sage, sheeth, Solomon's Seal, camomile, toothbrush twigs and other roots and herbs he'd gathered on the way. By rights, he ought to be leading her. But then last night, rattled by the long journey or spooked by the presence of the camels, one of the two black stallions had tried to bolt when it was let out of the horsebox for some exercise. He'd been nearby, had helped Kalkal, the horse-hand, subdue the beast, and when it was finally tied to the back of the pickup truck and had stopped kicking, he'd brought grass from his sacks, stroked the animal's sleek flank, whispered words of comfort and praise until it was eating from his hand. Afterwards, around the evening fire, Kalkal had approached him.

'You never said you were good with horses.'

He'd shrugged. 'I grew up with them. Near Kadingir.'

'Well, that's more than most of my stable-hands can say. Look, brother, I can't risk that beast rebelling tomorrow. I've talked to Sulima. You're coming with me.'

He'd fingered his hudhud feather. 'What about Enki? He told me to travel with the medical team.'

The big man had risen to go. 'If you want to ask for Enki's

permission, be my guest. But my orders come from Istar. I'll see you after prayers, at the pickup truck.'

It was the will of the gods. He gave his camel one last rub behind the ears, just how she liked it. Up ahead the cavalry were on the move, Enki and Sulima's gunners clapping Ñizal's warriors out into the night.

'Until the battle plain,' he said to Ninda.

Ninda raised her fist. 'Until we take Zabaria!'

Enki couldn't sleep. This was the hard part. Another full day and night ahead of restless rest, waiting behind with the trucks and the gunners as the lion's share of his warriors travelled on ahead. But it was the victory plan, hammered out over a solid week of strategy meetings, and Enki had to take full credit for it.

Once the date was set, when exactly to attack had been the first question. As Ñizal had argued, a night-time or dawn assault would stand the best chance of retaining the element of surprise. But the point of Operation Harsh Gemstone was to liberate Zabaria. Even if NAARC did blow an enormous hole in the Boundary, they would doubtless be fighting off Sec Gens; they couldn't exactly go knocking door-to-door in the Non-Land quarter, waking people up to inform them that the Freedom Bus was waiting to take them to Asfar. No, as Enki had declared, Sulima had agreed and Ñizal had finally accepted, NAARC had to attack in the day. Mid-morning was a good time to liberate a town: everyone would be awake and at their most energetic, still hoping that the day might bring some luck.

The second question then became how to avoid detection during their approach to Zabaria. The Boundary lookouts could doubtless see for kilometres south over the rolling scrublands and NAARC would be noticed long before they got into firing range. There was, however, Ñizal had pointed out on the map, a prominent hill range just southeast of Zabaria. If they reached these hills at night, and hunkered down behind them, they could launch an attack that, even in daylight, would give IMBOD next to no advance warning.

Except, Enki had objected, after Šaganiri the scrubland soil got softer. Especially if it was wet he wouldn't be able to ride a wheelchair through it, and they couldn't risk the possibility of the chariot or flatbed trucks getting stuck. In the end, the plan was his, a brazen one. The Belt Road was in good repair; Asfarian traders still served the oasis towns and, quite unbelievably, some even did business with the Gaians, driving their goods up to Zabaria's only checkpoint, East Gate. So NAARC would hide in plain sight. The cavalry would strike out southwest from their Šaganiri camp, then arc up to the hill range, arriving the night before the battle. The gunners would stay behind with the Freedom Bus, the horsebox and the four flatbed trucks, their lethal loads hidden inside fake containers knocked up from poles and canvas. On the morning of the battle they would hurtle to Zabaria along the Belt Road, stopping in prime position to fire. While the Şahi Topu could launch its marble shots from three kilometres away, the cast-iron cannons had to be closer, at fifteen hundred metres.

This plan also solved the question of where exactly to attack. No one knew how occupied Zabaria was organised and they couldn't risk blasting through the Boundary into a Non-Lander residential area. Non-Landers, though, were virtually never permitted to leave Zabaria, so shelling the checkpoint should result in only Gaian casualties. If any Asfarians got hit, well, that would teach them for trading with Is-Land. And there was, or at least had always been, a thriving livestock market near East Gate. If that hadn't been relocated, then punching a hole in the wall at the checkpoint would put hundreds of Non-Landers within reach of freedom.

The final question was who would lead the different assaults on the day. Enki had always imagined directing all three attacks simultaneously: wheeling in front of the troops in the chariot, Sulima at the reins, he would use his medallion radio to give the orders to fire the Şahi Topu. When the dust settled and a massive hole in the Boundary gaped ahead, he would command the iron cannon gunners, then charge down toward Zabaria, picking off Sec

Gens with his revolver as the dazzling quartz-coated cannonballs hurtled overhead, and the bombard gunners reloaded. Reluctantly, as the necessary logistics of the operation became clear, he had relinquished that vision. There was the problem of the soil, but also the gunner commander needed a clear view of the Boundary: he couldn't be racing over the field in the thick of the fray, at least not at first. Ñizal could lead the cavalry; Enki's place was with the cannons. Much as he wanted to light the bombard, though, as NAARC leader, he couldn't bring up the rear. He and Sulima would ride with the iron cannons, in convoy with the horsebox so they could move into the chariot when required. Depending on the battle conditions, he could charge into Zabaria.

For now, though, he was confined to the boardwalks he'd ordered to be laid down between his tent, the latrine and the bombard truck. He took morning prayers with Sulima and the gunners, then, on his wife's orders, went back to bed. After lunch he ordered a boy to tell Kalkal to get the chariot down from the pickup, harness the horses and bring it to his tent. Though the soil here was too soft for his wheelchair, it was fine for the chariot and he wanted to make sure it was in perfect condition.

When the chariot arrived, however, that ratbag Muzi Bargadala was holding the reins.

'What's he doing here?' he growled.

'He's assigned to the horses now.' Sulima slid the wheelchair ramp out from the back of the chariot and shunted it against the boardwalk. 'Kalkal said he was good with them.'

He drove up into the chariot. 'You're supposed to ask me before you make big decisions.'

'I appointed a horse-boy. It's not a big decision.' She heaved the ramp back into place, shut the gate and climbed into the driver's seat, taking the reins from Bargadala, who hopped down onto the ground, his eyes not meeting Enki's.

'Relax, Enki.' Sulima flicked the whip, striking the horses into motion. 'He's on our side.'

'Just about,' he grumbled as Bargadala slunk off.

But that mangy stray was soon forgotten in the day's preparations. Enki spoke with the drivers and mechanics, putting the drivers through their paces, practising sharp turns and reversing. Then he spent a couple of hours with the gunners, getting the cast-iron cannon crews to dismantle the false container walls on the flatbeds and fire practice shots. The trucks rocked with the recoil, but the cannon wheels rolled smoothly in the metal tracks the mechanics had laid down and the crews moved like clockwork, from truck-braking to firing in nine minutes. Afterwards, Enki drove up the rear truck ramp to spend time with the Şahi Topu. It hurt his heart, knowing he would not see the great gun being fired against the enemy, but Lugul was a strong warrior with a head for maths, and from the fatherly way the chief gunner polished the bombard with his soft cloth, the man, Enki thought, loved the weapon almost as much as he did. As he ran his own hand over the great cannon's bronze flank, he could almost feel all the shots it had fired over the centuries echoing in his bones.

Lugul lifted the wooden rammer. 'Listen,' he said. The older man struck the bombard with the staff. The bronze rang with a clear, deep tone, sending a quiver down Enki's spine.

'Reminds me of the Mikku,' Lugul said. 'The river parties. YAC. All the singing bowls and gongs. You leading the chant – "The pain is the path".' The older man rested the rammer staff between his knees, like a spear. 'Will there be a rhyme for tomorrow, then?'

Enki grunted. The singing bowl players had proved to be lightweights: none had made the trek out to the Shugurra. But the memory was an apt one: there'd been no dancing or beer drinking, but at times the atmosphere of the night marches, their steady rhythms and chanting beneath an ocean of stars, had come close to the hypnotic state of a Kadingir river rave.

Not close enough, though, to make him want to write poetry again.

'There's no rhyme as powerful as the Şahi Topu,' he said. 'She'll write the poem of history for us.'

'Oh, that she will do,' Lugul said. 'That she will do.'

Enki rested his voice after that, but although evening prayers were quiet and the meal a small one, with just thirty-six warriors to feed, the intimacy and the occasion demanded his full participation. He spoke a few words before they ate, then after the meal moved around the fire, stopping to talk, calling each warrior by name and praising them for their skills. Muzi, for once, was not eating alone, but breaking bread with Kalkal. 'Bargadala,' Enki rasped, his voice nearly shot. 'You've travelled a long way for NAARC and proved yourself a man of many talents. I wanted you on the medical team because you know all the herbs, but if Kalkal trusts you with the horses, so do I.'

Bargadala gave him one of his unnerving stares. 'The gods chose you, Enki Arakkia, to lead us to victory. Tomorrow all will go as the gods ordain it.'

Back in his tent, he waited for Sulima to finish her final prayers and get into bed. 'I know I shouldn't,' she said, draping her arm around him and laying her head on his chest. 'I know I should have compassion in my heart for all mortal creatures. But those people are an abomination. They make a mockery of god's teachings. I'm so glad my life brought me here with you to oppose them.'

Sulima had lost her whole family in the Battle of Kadingir – her father had died of a heart attack after her two brothers were killed by Sec Gens in the Hem, and her mother suffered a stroke and died during the long retreat to Asfar. In Asfar, Sulima had found religion. He didn't share her love of god. But he loved her hatred of the Gaians. 'They aren't people,' he replied. 'Not any more. When they turned their children into monsters the last of their humanity shrivelled up and blew away in the wind.'

She lifted her head and kissed him. As they had every night and every morning since their wedding, they joined again in their sacred union, their vow unto death. Like the sound of his warriors' voices raised in prayer, like the gonging reverberations of the bombard when Lugul struck it with the wooden staff, the movements of his wife's hips sent him deep into a trance – a battle trance, a sex trance, a spiritual trance, he didn't know which. All he knew was that his life was complete. His body may have been shorn of its limbs, his voice burnt from his throat, but his passion for justice had brought Sulima to him, and him, with her, to the boundary of something he had long ago decided was not possible – happiness. Her eyes shone like the stars above him, her smile curved like a thin silver moon, and for the first time ever he found himself laughing as they made love, laughing like an undammed river of pleasure and relief. He had done it: had brought his people to the very edge of reclaiming their land. The Gaians, CONC, the Asfarians, the Old Ones: it did not matter which forces rose in reaction to his, did not matter how tomorrow and the day after unfolded. Once he had tipped himself over that edge, he could die – die replete, his life's purpose fulfilled.

Sour Gold

Occupied Zabaria
18.03.100

'Put it down, Girin.' Tira filled the door to Bud's spare room. 'The permit says you're going to Asfar for medical treatment. We can bring a change of clothes, that's all.'

'But you're carrying the bag. I can take something. I want to take my *doumbek*.' He hugged the drum, its ceramic waist filling the crook of his arm.

'No one will believe you are sick if you're carrying a big drum. We talked about this before, Girin. There are world-famous *doumbek* makers in Asfar. You can get a new one there.'

He glared at her over the goatskin head. '*Ama* gave me this drum.'

'I know, *habibi*. But it's too dangerous to take it. Put it *down*.' She waited. He hugged the drum tighter. It was the only thing he wanted to keep. Ama had bought the *doumbek* for him with money she'd saved from working in the mine, exactly the one he wanted with the zigzag pattern, blue and white like his favourite New Zonian football team. And Todo had taught him to play it, made him practise his finger snaps and rolls and pops until the sound was crisp and consistent and people whistled and clapped after his solos at school. He was never going to see Todo again, hadn't even been allowed to say goodbye to him. He had nothing of Ama's except a few pieces of embroidered cloth. He was going to take the *doumbek*.

'We have to go *now*.' Tira could get angry, fast, he had discovered. But he wasn't afraid of her. 'We don't have time for this!'

'Hey.' Bud appeared behind Tira, blocking the light from the living room. 'What's going on?'

'He's holding us up! Make him put the drum down, Bud.'

Girin tensed. Bud, he was still afraid of. The Gaian had not touched him once in the two weeks he and Tira had been staying with the man. In fact, Bud had tried very hard to be nice, helping him plant the rose seeds for Ama in a shallow tray, making alt-eggs for breakfast every day and showing Girin how to look after the plants that lined all the windowsills of the large apartment on the sixth floor of the ziggurat. But Bud was a Gaian who walked around with his big veiny sword hanging out, and everyone knew you couldn't trust Gaians. He backed up against the bed as Bud entered the room.

'Hey. Don't worry, pal. I'm not going to hurt you.' The big man sat down on a wicker stool so his face was at Girin's level. 'That's a pretty special drum you've got there, isn't it?'

He set his jaw. Nodded. His eyes were wet, but he couldn't risk wiping the tears away in case Bud grabbed for the *doumbek*.

But Bud didn't move. 'Tira's right, though. The IMBOD officers will ask lots of questions if you're carrying a big drum. They might even take it away and smash it open in case you're trying to hide something inside it. You don't want that to happen, do you?'

A tear rolled down his cheek to his chin. He licked it away, stared with loathing at Bud's big flabby face. Gaians hated Non-Lander music. They had once even tried to shut down the pottery studio that produced the drums, but the potters had just started working at another ceramics workshop. Nothing would stop Zabarians playing the *doumbek*. Nothing.

'Tell you what,' Bud said, as if he hadn't noticed the tear. 'If you leave the drum here, I'll find a way to send it to you in Asfar when you've moved in with your mother. How's that for a deal?'

Homework, housework, trips to the park, Tablette game time, rides to school. Everything over the last two weeks had been negotiated on the basis of a deal. And so far, Girin had to admit, Bud had not reneged on anything he'd said he would do. Bud, in fact, Tira had said, wanted to help them so much that he'd got Girin's name placed on a special list of very sick children. Thanks to him, Girin now had a heart condition and needed to travel with his CONC chaperone to Asfar to have a life-saving operation.

'You can see inside it,' he said. 'I'll let the officers look.'

'You can offer. But it's dark in there, and hard to see in the corners.'

Circles didn't have corners. And the officers could use a torch. But the drum's waist was narrow, that was true. 'Then they can put their hands inside.'

'They won't do that, I can tell you for sure. They'll be afraid there's something inside that will hurt them. That's why IMBOD confiscates and destroys pretty much anything unusual people try to take out of Zabaria.'

In the doorway, Tira adjusted the straps of the bag on her back. 'He's telling the truth, Girin.'

His fingers traced the smooth rim of the drum. 'You promise you'll send it?'

'I promise,' Bud said. 'Just like Tira promised to plant your Ama's roses out in the garden at your school.'

He pattered the drumhead softly, one last finger roll, laid his cheek against the goatskin and kissed it goodbye. Then he pushed past Bud and Tira and, as Tira called 'Girin!', he carried the *doumbek* into the living room and set it down on the floor beneath the rose-seed tray on the sill.

Bud drew up outside a shop two blocks from the checkpoint.

'There you go. Not far to walk from here.'

'Aren't you coming with us, Bud?' Girin asked from the back seat, a note of worry in his voice. Perhaps because the boy mistrusted Bud, he got anxious if the man wasn't around.

'No, Girin,' Lil answered. 'Bud's done enough for us. We're on our own now. Just you and your CONC chaperone all the way to Asfar.'

Bud thought she was coming back. She had given up the lease on her own apartment, moved all her stuff into his. She pecked him on the cheek. 'Thank you, Bud. See you next week.'

'Hey, baby.' He patted her back. 'Anything to help a friend of yours.' She disentangled herself and he turned to address Girin. 'Goodbye, lad. I'll send your drum as soon as Tira gives me an address.'

'Goodbye, Bud.' Unexpectedly, Girin stretched through the front seats and gave Bud a fleeting almost-hug, grabbing the man's arm and pressing his forehead against it. 'Thank you.'

The embrace was over before Lil had the chance to feel fully heart-warmed, but after all the tensions of the last few weeks and the scene with the drum, she was relieved. Bud, she could tell, was touched.

'You don't have to thank me, boy. Just do what Tira says and look after your mother when you find her. All mothers embody the power of Gaia: they give us life and we need to look after them.'

Bud sounded pompous and the boy was squirming now. Her heart began pounding in her stomach. Equipped with all her savings and some money he had kicked in, Bud had arranged the Tablette work with a man in IMBOD's visa department, but the officer at the checkpoint was not part of the gang; indeed, would be trying to sniff out corruption in the ranks. Any irregularity in the visa or wrong move on her or Girin's part and they could be refused depart-ure, or worse, arrested.

'Remember, Girin – you're an orphan, and you've been living with me at my apartment since your mother died. If anyone asks about Bud, you've never heard of him.'

He cast her a sullen look. Another secret, his brooding eyes said. Another lie.

'I know.'

'Come on, then.' She grabbed the bag from the footwell and opened her door. 'We've got a bus to catch!'

*

The checkpoint waiting room was a ramshackle structure built against the wall beside the gate. A long, drab room with a smeary window, it had a door at each end: the one they'd entered through from the street, the other leading into the interview rooms and then out to the yard, where a bus was waiting to take this month's lucky few Non-Landers to Asfar. Since the election in Is-Land, more people were being allowed out for treatment, part of the new regime's paltry effort to redeem the Gaian state, and the room was half full. People sat on scuffed bioplastic seats, or in wheelchairs: a smartly dressed young man clutching a briefcase, perhaps someone with Asfarian relatives who might have scored a rare business visa; a family clustered around an old man with tubes up his nose; a mother tending a little girl with her head and neck in a brace.

Girin drummed against the seat with his fingers.

'Stop that. You're annoying people.'

'I'm not annoying people.'

The mother of the little girl in the wheelchair was smiling at them. 'You're annoying *me*.'

It was boring for him here, that was true. There wasn't anything for children to play with and the wallscreen just displayed an image of the IMBOD Shield; the only sound breaking the monotony was the infrequent summons over the loudspeaker to the interview room. She hadn't dared to bring Girin's Tablette in case the checkpoint officer confiscated it, searched it for phone numbers, anything that might contradict their story. But Girin was lucky to feel bored, she wanted to tell him. She was terrified. It was as if she were wearing her skin inside out, every square centimetre of it flinching at its contact with the air, her clothes, the seat. She hadn't known she could feel so afraid.

He stopped the drumming. 'I'm hungry.'

It was half past ten. They'd been sitting here for nearly two hours. She gave him an apple. He ate it with tiny bites, eking out the pleasure, then dropped the core in the compost bin in the corner.

'Tira Gúnida,' the loudspeaker crackled. At last. She jumped up, grabbed Girin's sticky hand, pulled him to his feet. The woman opposite cast her a bitter look, probably resentment, that they should be called first after arriving late. Or maybe it was disapproval for dragging Girin about. Remembering that he was supposed to be sick, she put her arm around his shoulders and led him to the interview door.

The room was small with a plain desk and several chairs. The one behind the desk was filled by the checkpoint officer, a thin man with oiled-back black hair. Beside him stood two Sec Gens, a young man and a young woman, impossibly tall and broad, their expressions impassive. The sight of them did nothing to calm her nerves.

The officer looked up from his Tablette. 'Ah.' He gave a pinched smile. 'Lilutu Beechnookdott. As our records have it. Welcome. We've been expecting you.'

Girin squeezed her hand, moved closer to her side. She froze. Then she whipped around, back to the door, yanking Girin with her. But the handle that had just turned easily as she shut the door behind them was now locked fast. Before she could swing back around and launch herself at the officer, the Sec Gens were behind her, pulling her and Girin apart, the male youth clamping her in his massive arms, lifting her off the ground.

'Let him go!' She fought for air. 'He's ill, let him go!'

'Ill? Oh, I don't think Ebebu is ill.' The officer smiled ruefully. 'Not according to the documents I've got here.'

'Tira!' Girin screamed. 'Tira! Her name is *Tira*. My name is *Girin*.'

She struggled and kicked. 'He's just a little boy! He should be with his mother!'

Then Girin went silent and the Sec Gen placed his hand over her mouth and nose, so that she could hardly breathe.

'Good work, Almond and Sunshine. Almond, take Lilutu to the holding cell.' The officer gestured to the room's second door. 'Sunshine, stay here. Ebebu is going to sit and have a conversation with me.'

Bruise Purple

The Scrublands
18.03.100

The morning dawned cold and quiet. People rose, dismantled their tents, rolled up their bedding, made fires, all with precision and economy, speaking little, joking not at all. Water, strictly rationed over the last two weeks, was heated for showers before morning prayers, one hose for men, one for women, behind two of the trucks.

'Are you going to wash?' Kalkal asked Muzi.

He shrugged. His gods did not demand daily washing.

The older man offered him a bar of soap and a scrap of towel. 'We might not be able to wash each other if we fall.'

Muzi considered it. If he died in the battle, who knew where his body might end up? At best, on one of the trucks, transported back to Asfar; most likely buried in a mass grave or burnt by the Gaians. But Somarian burial practices did involve a ritual washing of the corpse, and his mother, he knew, would want him to meet the gods clean. He took the soap, joined the queue, stripped and washed in the warm water; his body, shining in the steam, a strange thing to him – a gift he had not asked for, no longer felt particularly attached to, but could only return as a meaningful sacrifice to the gods he had served so long, in his own way. Washing was supposed to purify the body, he knew, but it also left him feeling vulnerable, exposed, already halfway gone from the world. Afterwards, he scooped up some of the mud from the ground at his feet and smeared it on his chest. If the earth-goddess was with him, he would go wherever she led.

Enki rose early, washed and clad himself in his battle gear: his comfortable old boots, specially made so long ago in Asfar for his long, slender feet, and a new leather jerkin and breeches. The armour was in the flatbed for later. Breakfast was a good one: hard bread and nut butter, porridge with raisins, cinnamon and pine nuts. Word went around at eight that the Rookowleon had flown in with the message that the cavalry had arrived safely. There would be no other contact with Ñizal until the battle. By half-past eight, the vehicles were moving; by nine the convoy was travelling northwest on the Belt Road. Enki and Sulima led the way in the first flatbed, their gunner crew hidden in its false container with two cast iron cannons, ammunition and the chariot. The pickup truck and horsebox and the Freedom Bus followed, then the other three flatbeds, Lugul and the bombard bringing up the rear. Apart from the occasional horse and cart, oasis dwellers who pulled over to let them pass, there were no other vehicles on the road. They travelled in silence, Sulima driving, Enki staring out through the windscreen.

Apart from a bank of dark grey cloud to the north, the sky was white, the morning light flat and cold, etching every detail of the featureless landscape, the hills, the leaves on the bushes, the potholes in the road, onto his brain as if with a magnifying glass. Ahead, for a long time, sky and land merged in a blurred grey horizon. And then it appeared ahead, the Boundary, a pale ribbon stretching endlessly to the east and the west. With his field binoculars, Enki could see the ramparts, the riveted seams of the cladding, the bulge where the wall reached out and closed its fist around Zabaria, imprisoning his people. He had almost forgotten how much he hated the Boundary. But now that he was speeding on his way to breach it, he could contemplate the loathed barrier with transcendent equanimity. In his day in Kadingir, the Gaians had screened violent black-and-white images on the Boundary: predatory animals designed to give children nightmares. Now that the plasma screens had been cladded and there weren't many Non-Landers left to frighten – just a few herders, straying out beyond the oasis towns to give their sheep better grazing grounds – he was hurling himself at nothing more menacing than a pale strip of light. The power of the truck rumbled up through his balls, and his revolver in its leather holster pressed against his hip. He raised his binoculars again: southwest of the checkpoint, the land rose in gentle waves; between those waves, Ñizal and the cavalry were waiting.

'Four kilometres,' Sulima announced. She was armed also, her rifle stashed above her head between two hooks in the roof of the cabin.

He reached to his neck and pressed the walkie-talkie button on the VoiceBox. The bit of gear was endlessly useful. So long as he stayed within the three-kilometre range of the CB radio in the truck, he could communicate with all his ground officers. 'Bombard,' he ordered. 'Prepare to halt.'

'Check.' The driver of the bombard flatbed responded, her voice thin and reedy and a bit too loud. Beside him, Sulima smiled. She still found it funny to hear other people talking through Enki's throat. They drove on for another minute.

'Three kilometres,' Sulima announced.

He gave the order. 'Bombard: *halt*.'

Through the wing mirror, he watched the bombard flatbed pull a U-turn onto the eastern verge of the road, the driver positioning the vehicle so that the gun could be fired from the back. It was an unusual parking job. Any half-awake Gaian lookout would question it. His heart began to beat faster and hot joy flooded his veins. The bombard flatbed shrank to the size of a toy truck as Sulima drove on.

'Two kilometres.' Sulima was sweating, her brow glistening as if anointed by dew.

He pressed the VoiceBox button again. 'Cannons: prepare to halt.'

And then Sulima was slowing down, wrenching the wheel to the left, and with a great shudder the truck veered off the road. She drove a good fifty metres before braking, perpendicular to the road, well out of the way of the bombard shot path. The other two flatbeds followed in line, Kalkal drove the pickup truck and horsebox behind the barricade, and the Freedom Bus sailed on up the road. Sulima turned off the engine, leaving the keys in the ignition, and reached for her rifle. Enki grabbed his helmet and plate armour from his footwell, pulled them on as she reached behind her seat to do the same with hers.

'Prepare the guns and the chariot,' he commanded.

The earth was shining: every grass blade glinting, every clod of soil gleaming. The truck rattled and shook as the crew dismantled the false container and lowered the ramp for the chariot. In the wing mirror, Kalkal and Bargadala were jumping out of the pickup and running round to open the horsebox. Enki trained the binoculars again on the checkpoint. Once the false containers were down, the Gaians would be able to see the guns, six black barrels pointing straight at the Boundary: if they hadn't already, they would surely now be raising an alarm. He strained forward, every muscle in his body aching for combat. He could see no movement, but that stillness, he knew, did not signal complacency. Whatever defence the Gaians were mounting, bring it on.

'Bombard ready.' Lugal's deep voice crackled from the medallion at his throat.

'Stand by, bombard.'

'Cannons One ready,' his own chief gunner reported, ten seconds before the next flatbed, and then the last.

'Stand by, all cannons.'

He unrolled his window, leaned out. The cold air burnt his lungs. Behind the truck the horses were hitched to the chariot, stamping the earth and shaking their manes. Kalkal was back behind the wheel of the pickup, ready to follow the chariot wherever the battle might take it, and Bargadala was at the reins. The man lifted the whip and the horses cantered up alongside the truck cabin. Enki opened his door, reached for the grab-bar and swung himself down with a thump into the back. Sulima followed. Bargadala clicked his tongue, flicked the reins and the stallions wheeled round to trot along behind the trucks for Enki's inspection of the cannon line.

The gunners were in position, their ladders dropped from the backs of the flatbeds, ready for the crew to clamber down and avoid the smoke. Right now, every breath was a crisp blast of fuel. Bargadala pulled up the horses at the end of the last truck. Enki gripped the VoiceBox. 'Bombard: *fire*.'

Everyone turned and looked back. A kilometre and a half away, to the naked eye the flatbed was tiny, the great gun virtually invisible against the dark back of the cabin. Through the binoculars Enki could see it in stunning detail: the sea-green belly of the gun, the black hole of the barrel lifted to the sky, the Şahi Topu raised at the precise angle Lugul had calculated necessary, the chief gunner and the crew crawling over the truck like flies on a cake. It was the longest minute of his life. At last it came. In staggered glory first the truck and the crew disappeared in a billow of smoke, then the boom of the gun shock the air. He ducked, they all did, but he could swear that he saw it, could *hear* the *whoosh* as the huge marble shot blasted over them, hurtling through the air like a stone moon on a collision course with all of space-time. His heart in his throat, he raised his binoculars again. Silence. And then, on the Boundary, another white cloud. A cloud of dust. Boundary dust.

A huge cheer rose from his crew, the warriors shouting and punching the air. Bargadala stuck his fingers in his mouth and whistled, the sound a rocket scream of triumph. Sulima hugged Enki hard then jumped up and down. The chariot shook. But there was no time to celebrate, no time even to let the dust settle. 'Cannons! *Fire*.'

And then it was fireworks, cracks and booms every three minutes, smoke blooming from the truck, the acrid scent of gunpowder, the earth shaking down to its molten core, Bargadala straining at the reins as the horses stamped and kicked in the harness to a volley of cannon fire: Enki's crystal balls blasting towards their target from six iron mouths, lashing the white sky with tongues of black smoke and flame, the tongues of the dead, screaming that vengeance had come.

Sour Gold

Occupied Zabaria
18.03.100

'Sunshine, stay here.' The horrible officer smirked. 'Ebebu is going to sit and have a conversation with me.'

He was kicking and wriggling, but the girl Sec Gen's arms were wrapped tightly round him and his heels flailing against her thighs made no impact on her grip. From the corner of his eye he could see Tira, also kicking and squirming, the boy Sec Gen's hand clamped to her mouth as he carried her through a door to a cell, taking her away from him, away from him forever. 'My name is Girin!' he screamed.

And then everything exploded. There was a thunderous crash like a mighty storm breaking right in the room or the biggest drum in the world cracking into pieces directly above his head, the blast hurling the chairs in the air and the Sec Gen back against the wall with a *whack*, a wall that was falling, like the Sec Gen, to the floor, bricks raining down all around as Girin landed, winded and shaking, on the Sec Gen's firm chest and rolled to the ground, his eyes and nose filled with dust.

The world had ended. For a moment, it wasn't shocking, it was just true. Just a fact. He was alone in a white cloud. His ears were plugged with silence. He couldn't breathe. Everyone else had disappeared. This was death. This was being dead.

Then his lungs grabbed at air, dusty air that made him cough, and his palms were stinging, and his knees hurt, and people were screaming everywhere. Screaming *Help. God help me.* Screaming *Ama.* Screaming names. Not his. No one was calling his name.

'*Tira*,' he yelled, struggling to his feet. Everything in the room – the desk, the chairs, the body of the officer sprawled on his desk, was covered with a layer of thick white brick dust. Through the dust floating in the air, he was conscious of light, daylight falling into the room from a hole, not in the ceiling, in the wall. He blinked. Behind the slumped officer he could see through the wall, out onto the land. There were sandy hills out there, beneath a blue sky. Again, he thought he must be dead.

'Girin.' Her voice was a rough whisper. He whirled, ran to her. She was sprawled on the floor, pinned beneath the body of the other Sec Gen, struggling to raise herself on her elbows, get free, get up.

'Tira!' he screamed.

She was staring into the light. She didn't look like Tira. She didn't look like anyone alive. Her hair was covered in dust. Her eyes were big, bloated fish eyes, and her head was all smashed up. There was a big gash on her forehead and blood was running down her face, black, sticky blood, all grimy with dust.

'Run,' she whispered. 'Run, Girin.'

The screams everywhere were getting louder. There were foot-steps, people running, and shouts now, deep voices not panicking, barking commands.

'No.' He crouched beside her, pushed at the Sec Gen, but the body was too heavy and he couldn't shift it. 'I have to stay with you.'

'Girin.' Her voice was an effort of gasps and he had to lean close to hear. 'There's a hole in the wall.' She was smiling, he realised, her eyes shining with a joy so pure and wrong it sent a corkscrew of cold right through him. She grabbed his wrist, shook it. 'Someone's come to rescue us. YAC, maybe. Or CONC. You have to go. You have to go to Asfar and find your mother. *Go now.*'

Her hand slipped from his wrist. Her eyes rolled back in her head, and then she slumped, face forward, into the brick dust.

He stood up, backed away. He couldn't stand it. His chest was burning. He wanted to explode, explode like the bomb or whatever it was that had hit them, but he couldn't move, couldn't make a sound. He was trembling and his vision blurred. Then there was a rattle at the door from the waiting room, someone shaking the handle, then a thud – a shoulder rammed hard against the door – and a man's voice, a Gaian's, calling for help. He swallowed, looked around. At the desk, the officer was groaning and twitching, the man's bony hand reaching up to rub at his head. Behind him, the girl Sec Gen moaned.

There was a hole in the wall. He ran, clambered through it, over the rubble and into the blinding white light of day.

Bruise Purple

The Southern Belt
18.03.100

'Bombard stand down. Cannons *halt.*' He gave the orders then trained his binoculars on Zabaria. Could he see it? . . . As the clouds of dust and smoke cleared . . . *Yes!* . . . They had done it! . . . There was a huge gap in the Boundary, a wedge-shaped breach, maybe ten metres wide at the top, spilling rubble onto the scrubland soil, the cladded wall on either side peppered with shot holes.

There was no time to stand around and rejoice. 'Chariot, *drive!*' He gave the VoiceBox order, then gripped the side of the chariot as Muzi whipped the horses forward, the nervy stallions needing no encouragement to gallop at full pace, but requiring all the man's strength to control. Sulima jumped forwards, took a set of reins, and together the two drivers steered the horses back to the road. Ahead, through the glasses, he could see the Freedom Bus, stopped on the road fifty metres or so away from the breach, its warrior team clambering onto the roof to set up the catapult, sending into Zabaria, as he watched, rubber balls stamped in three languages with NAARC's message: Non-Landers! Come out and take a seat on the Freedom Bus! He whipped his head east, to see, there, yes, a shadowy line streaking out from the hills: Ñizal and the camel cavalry arriving to defend the bus and its passengers.

The wind pelted his face, the chariot jolted his bones. He slipped the binoculars back inside his bulletproof vest, reached for his revolver and readied it in his hand. 'To the breach!' he yelled, the VoiceBox on megaphone setting now. 'To the breach!'

Sulima and Muzi whipped the horses on. The cavalry filled his vision, the camels galloping around the bus, kicking up dust, the riders stabbing the air with their rifles as the catapult flung its missives over the Boundary. Still, though, there was no counter-attack. No movement on the ramparts or through the breach. Had they really caught the Gaians napping? They could do it, his heart soared, *they could do it.* Then the chariot joined the swirl of the camels and he was roaring, pumping his arm, cheering with his men, waving them on towards the breach, the massive hole in the wall straight ahead – its ragged edge impossible to ride a chariot over, but an open invitation for ground troops. As he watched, a small figure stumbled out over the rubble: a child, who paused for a second, as if blinking in the light, then turned to run blindly east along the wall, away from the pounding milieu.

He fumbled at the VoiceBox, pressed Walkie-Talkie. 'Freedom Warriors: enter Zabaria. And someone rescue that child!'

Armoured with flak jackets, helmets and shields, armed with rifles or revolvers, the Freedom Bus warriors ran in a line to the Boundary, the cavalry forming a protective gauntlet on either side. Of the camel riders, only Ñizal had a VoiceBox, but he must have relayed the command, or given it himself, for a camel warrior peeled off, heading after the child. Enki leaned from the chariot, cheering and roaring.

Thwang. The arrow hit the breastplate right over his heart, the impact knocking him back against the rails of the chariot. Shocked but unhurt, he lunged between Sulima and Bargadala for the wooden shaft and snapped it in half as, right in front of him, a rider fell from his camel, an arrow sticking out of his neck. The camel pounded on for a moment and then there was a distant crack and the beast fell, too, writhing on the ground and waving its knobbly legs like some kind of huge hairy insect. Then Sulima was beside him, grabbing his shoulders, shouting in his face.

'Enki! Are you all right?'

'I'm fine!' He panted. 'Fetch the fallen man! Fetch him!' He activated the Walkie-Talkie. 'Cannons: *fire wide at ramparts.*'

And then the real battle began. A battle against an unseen foe, against death from the sky, against time. Arrows and bullets whizzing all around, the chariot wheeled back to the struck man. As they reached him, an explosion sounded. He craned back to see. *Yes.* A shot had hit the wall, high up to the side of the breach as ordered, then another, and another, aiming for the Gaians but allowing a pathway in and out of Zabaria. A ground warrior, Shulgu, was tending the wounded man. He stood as the chariot drew up, his face a grimace of anguish.

'He's gone.'

'Get on,' Enki roared, offering his good arm. Ahead, through the flying shapes of the cavalry, he could see his warriors entering the hole in the Boundary and then, as Shulgu clambered in beside him, someone running out of it, a slight figure pursued by a huge man, a Sec Gen trying to prevent the escape but hampered by the clinging presence of one of Enki's warriors on his back. It was almost comical – but where were the warriors' *guns*? – and then there was a crack and the Gaian crumpled to the ground, first to his knees, then flat on his face, and a camel rider was screaming with joy and the two foot-warriors were ransacking the body for weapons.

They had felled their first Sec Gen! 'Whhoar!' He, Muzi, Shulgu and Sulima roared, arrows thudding into the ground all around them.

'Forward!' he commanded. 'To the breach!'

The chariot thundered onwards. The bus was right up at the wall now, its armoured tyres safe from the arrows, and more people were emerging from the breach, some fighting with Sec Gens, others tugging children or running as hard as they could. His warriors ran with them, sheltering the Zabarians with their flak-jacketed bodies, with the camels. Some fell, arrows in their necks, bullets too still zooming down from the Boundary. The chariot was right at the heart of the battle now, Shulgu holding his shield up over Sulima and Bargadala, the smell of the smoking ramparts thick in the air. And the rescue operation was working: in front of him, a man was stepping onto the bus.

'We did it, Enki!' Sulima shouted. 'We did it!'

'*Free Zabaria!*' He raised his fist, pummelled the air.

This hit was soundless. Pain seared his chest. Sulima screamed. He fell to the chariot floor, his head cracking against the driver's seat, his vision a grey blur, his throat filling with blood.

Enki had been hit. Sulima and Shulgu were tending him. Muzi's leader was wounded and the horses were frothing. He pulled the beasts around, to the west, not knowing where to go.

'Where are you going!' Sulima yelled.

'Nowhere!'

Then Shulgu jumped off and ran towards the Freedom Bus and Sulima shouted, 'To the truck! Take us back to the truck.'

He cracked the horses on, seeking a route out through the chaos. Camels were charging in all directions, frightening the horses, and people were staggering in front of the chariot, in danger of being run over. Ahead, the cook Gorgan was crying in agony, trying to pull an arrow from his raw red calf. Muzi veered off in his direction: the man was still mobile, surely they could help him.

'What are you doing?' Sulima shouted. 'Straight ahead. To the truck! There's no time. No time!'

So he urged the horses on, past another man running in circles, trying desperately to catch the reins of a loose braying camel, past a beast on its back, its mouth foaming, eyes rolling, legs kicking in a spasm of terror and pain. Beyond it, Tugi, the best shot in the women's brigade, was dragging another woman by the armpits to the edge of the battlefield. The woman was holding her guts in her hands, tenderly as if cradling a baby. Bile rose in his throat and he looked down behind him. Blood was leaking from Enki's mouth. There was no time to stop, and rivers of sweat were already running off the horses: he was working them to their limit. He couldn't pick anyone else up.

At last, they were out of the battle zone, the stricken faces and gaping wounds of his comrades behind him, and the chariot was rattling over the scrub towards the smoking cannons on their flatbeds. The cannons were still shooting at the Boundary, Muzi realised, causing more damage, distracting the Gaians from the rescue operation, killing Sec Gens. Exhilaration and determination coursed through him. He had to get Enki to the trucks.

Sulima's hands were all over him, warm, feathery things loosening his plate armour, taking off his helmet, holding a water bottle to his lips.

'We're nearly there, Enki. Nearly there.' She pressed her face close to the VoiceBox, spoke into it. 'Cannon Gunners One. Wounded man on the way. Prepare the medical kit.'

The bullet was in his chest. He could feel the blood slowly flooding his lungs.

'To the bombard,' he croaked.

'The bombard?' Her lemon tea eyes filled his vision, merged into one weird, shining orb. 'No, Enki. That's another kilometre and a half away.'

His armpit was on fire. He couldn't move his good shoulder. He could barely speak; all he could see, a tiny shape reflected in Sulima's shining eye, was the Freedom Bus: a frail elderly man boarding the Freedom Bus.

'Call Lugul,' he rasped. 'Tell him . . . to bring me . . . the Sahi Topu.'

'Okay, Enki.' Her tears dripped on his face. 'Okay. But you're injured. I have to give the commands now.'

All he wanted was the bombard. He let her reach around his neck, unclasp the VoiceBox, heard her order, 'Bombard, come to the cannons. Bombard, to the cannons. Now.'

He closed his eyes, savoured her salt on his lips. She slapped his cheek. 'Open your eyes, Enki! Open your eyes! The bombard's coming. It's on its way. You've got to stay awake for the bombard.'

Her voice was an eagle's scream. Rattling and squeaking, the chariot rocked like a cradle over the land. Her face wobbled above him, framed by the darkening sky. *Ennnnki*. Faint on the wind, he heard his mother's voice, calling him. But he couldn't go to her yet. The bombard was coming.

'Faster,' Sulima screamed. 'To the cannons!'

Muzi urged the horses on, striping their backs with the whip until the blood foamed pink from their flanks and the chariot was jerking and swinging so fast he was afraid Enki would fly out of it. Then the flatbeds were right ahead to the left, still firing the cannons, and the horses' ears flattened, and it was all he could do to keep them from bolting west.

'Help me!' he screamed over his shoulder, and Sulima stood and grabbed the reins. Together they strained against the beasts' fear. 'Tell the gunners to stop firing!' he panted.

She had Enki's VoiceBox hanging on its rope around her neck, managed to keep the reins in one hand as she relayed the command. And then the only noise was the occasional faint crackle of the battle behind them, and he was wheeling round behind the trucks and Kalkal was waving a bunch of hay at the horses, and the beasts were galloping towards it, just as the bombard flatbed was rumbling towards them over the scrublands, Lugul leaping from the cabin as it arrived, and running to meet the chariot. Sulima hopped back down to tend to Enki, leaving Muzi, both sets of reins twisted around his arms, to pull the horses up as Kalkal and Lugul ran to grab the bridles, then disentangle himself, jump down and help Kalkal quiet the stallions, wiping their nostrils clear of foam, stroking their necks, feeding them hay, inhaling their fear, thanking them for working so hard when they were scared for their lives.

'*Lugal*,' Sulima shouted, and the bombard gunner ran around and climbed into the chariot.

Once the horses were quiet, Muzi followed, taking his place back at the reins, ready to transport Enki anywhere needed, or jump down again and dash to a truck for a medical kit, whatever Sulima ordered.

Enki was staring up at the sky. It was grey now, heavy and grey, the sky-god drawing a cold dark shroud over the land. Sulima was crying, choking out words. He couldn't understand what she was saying.

'What!' Lugul barked. The man's body jerked erect and his weathered face warped in disgust. '*No*, Sulima. No.'

'Yes,' she blazed. 'He's dying. It's his last wish!'

'It's insane!'

'Yes, because *he's* insane.' Sulima was laughing through her tears, a weird high, chattery laugh like a furious bird. 'That's why we *love* him!' Then Lugul was standing, towering over the woman, saying 'I'm sorry, I'm so sorry,' and reaching to embrace her, and Sulima was pushing him away, screaming, 'It's an *order*, Lugul, I *order* you to do it!' But Lugul was refusing, the old man leaving the chariot, brushing Muzi aside as he descended the ladder, and then Sulima had drawn Enki's revolver, was pointing it at Lugul screaming, 'You'll do it or I'll *shoot you*!' And Lugul was walking away with his back to Sulima, raising his arms, and Sulima was crying and shaking, and dropping the gun because she couldn't do it, couldn't shoot Lugul in the back for not doing something insane, and Muzi was leaping up to ask, 'What, what does he want?' And she was embracing him, and telling him what Enki wanted, her snot all over his shoulder, and he was saying, 'I'll help. I'll help. Just tell me what to do.'

She mastered herself. Her eyes shining like polished stones, she raised the VoiceBox to her mouth. 'Bombard Crew. Lugul has relinquished his command. I am now your Chief Gunner. Reverse the truck and prepare to fire!'

The bombard truck rolled forward, began to arc around so that the great gun was facing north. Sulima knelt again by Enki, forced water into his mouth. 'Take us to the Şahi Topu, Muzi. Now!'

He thought Lugul would try to stop them, but Lugul was still walking away, into the distance. He took the reins, waved Kalkal aside, clicked the horses forwards. Something hit his head, hard, and again, and again. There was a clattering sound from the chariot and everywhere small white specks dotted the earth. It was like nothing he had ever seen before. Small white balls of ice were falling from the sky. Hard and fast, in their thousands and thousands, tiny icy cannonballs plummeting all around, clacking and clattering, pinging and bouncing off wood, iron and bronze as he drove the chariot to the bombard truck, pulled up the horses and, using his knife on the leather straps, helped Sulima remove Enki's plate armour and carry him onto the flatbed, saw Enki open his mouth and taste the sky-god's little crystal balls, saw his glazed eyes light up in wonder as the cold shocks stung his tongue, heard Enki whisper hoarsely, 'Istar's tears . . .'

Then, as Sulima wept over his rapturous face, Enki rasped, 'Don't cry, Istar,' an order his wife tried but failed to obey as she and Muzi and the second bombard gunner lifted Enki Arakkia's torn body in its bloody jerkin and wet breeches up to the maw of the Şahi Topu and pushed it down, with their hands and arms, and the gunners' rammers, as far as it would go, down through the mighty Karkish Sultan's prayer to his god, through the great barred millwheels of fate, deep into the gun's black gullet, its massive bronze throat greasy with olive oil yet ringing like bright silver bells with the hard, fast music of ice.

Sulima stood back. '*Fire!*' she screamed.

'Stand down,' the second gunner shouted. Muzi jumped off the truck and ran backwards to the chariot, his eyes glued to the bombard, his face wet, teeth chattering with fear and awe, frozen shrapnel from a cold exploded star striking his chest as the gunner lit the powder chamber, the massive gun rocked back, smoke billowed from the truck and the lightning blur that was Enki Arakkia sailed over his head, over the scrublands, over Zabaria into the steppes, all the way into his homeland.

THE VERNAL EQUINOX
21.03.100

Misted Silver

Misted Silver

The Ashfields
21.03.100

You think you'll win.

The voice was cold. Bone-cold, as though her skeleton had become a cage of icicles. Crisp-cold, as though her skin were a lace-work of frost. She couldn't feel her toes or fingers and cold seared her lungs when she breathed. She tried to move but her body was entombed, in the burning-cold tankini, in an avalanche of snow. She tried to open her eyes but the lids were weighted down as if with lead seals. She tried to scream but her jaw was frozen shut. Her awareness, though, was as clear as ice, and she didn't need her mouth for soulspeech.

Metal, she replied.

You think humanity will renounce me today. You think that your species will cleave unto Earth and bury me in history; will dance with Fire and melt me down in the flames; will embrace Water and Air and leave me to rust. But you are wrong.

The voice was grindingly slow. It might have taken an ice age to speak. Her thoughts were heavy and slow, too, as though her mind had been numbed like her fingers.

I don't think anything, she replied. It was, she realised vaguely, as if remembering who she was from over a vast distance, true. Today was the Vernal Equinox. Earth's deadline. Amazigia was voting today on making the Hudna permanent, and on banning rare-earths mining unless conducted by CONC. Somewhere out there, a tiny silhouette at the wrong end of a telescope, was an Astra who desperately wanted to win those votes, who dared to hope that she might, but certainly didn't believe that she would. Global media images of NAARC's attack on Zabaria and the Gaians' armed response, the slaughter of the Non-Landers, followed by yesterday's miraculous arrival of the Freedom Bus into Asfar City, had sparked uprisings against hated rulers in four continents and thrown CONC into turmoil. More than the arguments, Astra recalled the emotions: she'd spent the last three days swinging between abject despair, wild hope and stoic acceptance. Thinking had not entered into it. The time for thinking was past.

That is true.

A chasm of cold ran through her. She wasn't sure, she realised, if Metal was reading her mind. If so, Metal wasn't particularly interested in its contents.

You are nothing but Istar's mouthpiece, and you speak only with the Old Ones she permits you to hear. But I am an Old One also, Fleshling, and you will hear me now. Trust me when I say that Earth is not your friend. Earth wants to keep living creatures trapped in the circle of decay. I offer you immortality.

The coldness, the numbness, the slow, hypnotic voice: the sensation of Metal was beginning to feel necessary, calming, like a deep, inevitable truth. She struggled to keep sight of that figure at the end of the telescope, that person she knew she was. *You bring us death,* she managed to respond. *You are swords and guns and tanks and bombs. You are hard and ruthless, and You trigger the worst in us.*

Death, too, yes. I give you violent, excessive death, mass destruction, and in exchange for this glorious sacrifice of the weak, the strongest of you will live forever, in me. That is the pact I offer humanity, and it is not one that is easily broken. You may win today. The weak may triumph briefly over the strong, and Earth may grant your species more time on this planet, but human beings will always gravitate to me. You are simply vehicles for consciousness, after all. Feeble, mortal vehicles, subject to decay. Some of you understand this, and in the end, human consciousness will migrate to me, and the universe will no longer have any need for your suppurating flesh.

The voice was getting heavier and heavier. Her chest was being slowly crushed beneath a freezing metal plate, squeezing the oxygen from her lungs. But it was fine, an almost comfortable feeling, for everything was happening the way it was supposed to. Her brain was not needed. Her body was superfluous. The tankini melted into her ribs, into her pelvis, and around her wrist she sensed a thin, cold fire, its burning clasp slowly searing the truth into her soul . . . Metal was stronger than she, and the weak should feed the strong, should gladly surrender, accept their fate, merge with Metal and live forever in its cold embrace . . .

Then, suddenly, a delicate warmth, verging on pain, tingled through her veins.

Astra. Are you there?

She gasped at the air, flexed her muscles, trembled and jerked. *Istar?*

Thank heaven. I'm sorry, Child. Metal is so angry about humanity's advances that it managed to break through the barriers I had set up to protect you. I have strengthened those defences now. Do not fear, Metal will not bother you again.

Her limbs felt drained, her head woozy. The tankini felt like it weighed a ton, and her wrist hurt, a burning, itching sensation. She had no idea what time or what day it was. *Have we won? Has humanity broken the pact?*

Not yet, Child. Not yet. But there is still every hope. The last word of the Prophecy is still unwritten.

There is one hope, one hope only!

Ow! The bed shook so hard she bit her tongue.

Earth, Istar chided. *Be careful with the Child.*

The Creatures of Clay are stronger than they appear, Earth grumbled. *She survived a visit from Metal, did she not?*

She is an evolved being, much practised now at speaking with the Old Ones. We must protect her. She shows Us how human consciousness could continue to evolve, without the need to migrate to Metal.

Humanity must meet My deadline first, or none of her foolish species will survive!

It was unnerving, listening to the Old Ones speak through her, and about her, as if she wasn't there. Unnerving, like the band of cold and heat her bracelet had become, and annoying, like the sharp pain in her tongue. But the presence of both Istar and Earth was also a rare opportunity. And she didn't need her tongue to soulspeak.

Istar. Earth. We're trying our best to meet the deadline, surely You can see that. We've developed plant tech, and I really think we have a chance today to ban war and restrict rare-earths mining to just a handful of sites. But Earth . . . She was hyperaware of the glowing bracelet around her wrist . . . *I can't ask people not to mine gold or silver or iron any more. People like precious metals too much, and iron is too useful. Please, I need to ask You to take pity on our foolishness. Can You amend that condition and give us more time to work on the Tablette replacement? If we figure that out, we won't need to mine rare-earths at all any more. If we outlaw war, too, wouldn't that be good enough?*

The bed trembled. Her body warmed. But Earth did not reply.

She speaks sense. Istar broke the silence. *Human fingers and eyes like smooth, shiny things, and their transportation and architecture technologies have benefited from steel. If You deny humanity all the pleasures of Metal, Earth, they will simply crave it all the more.*

Istar! The bed jolted beneath her. *You interfere!*

I am this planet's lodestar, Earth. I want it to reach its full potential, to take its rightful place in the constellium of consciousness. It will never do that if You destroy humanity.

Nor will it do so if Metal conquers the souls of these selfish creatures and between them they destroy all other life on the planet!

Humanity is moving in the right direction. And the more of them who learn how to meet in the psychosphere, the faster they will develop. Be kind to them, Earth. You used to be patient and generous, remember? Give them a few more years. Four or five more spins around the sun means nothing to You.

The bed hiccupped, then was still. *Plant tech is a step in the right direction,* Earth grumbled at last. *All right, Istarastra. If humanity votes today to ban war and control rare-earths mining, I will give you a three-year extension to end all metal-based Tablette technology and ban rare-earths mining for good. If the vote fails, then the Old Ones will rise before midnight and reclaim this planet for the sake of all Life!*

The bed shook once more, then ceased moving. Her forehead tingled, as though the goddess had planted a kiss on her brow. And then Istar, too, was gone.

She opened her eyes. The cell was the grey of predawn. She squinted at Vultura. 21.3.100· 05:32:15. The vote on giving CONC control of all rare-earths mines was being held at ten a.m. in Amazigia, three hours behind Is-Land, followed in the afternoon by the vote on universal disarmament. Her email privileges were still suspended, and assuming Earth hadn't devoured the jail by then, she wouldn't know the result until the six o'clock news. Jasper, though, had managed to schedule an ion chamber visit for four o'clock. Just eleven hours to wait . . . unless it was all over right after lunch. The week's cocktail of fear, anguish and longing began to fizz again in her veins.

There was no work on a Vernal Equinox. Instead Vultura screened documentaries all morning on Gaian advances in vermicomposting and humane slug control. Astra went to the dining hall at noon but couldn't eat. Her stomach was in knots. She could barely speak, either; she just stared down at her plate, pushed her food around, her lip trembling.

'Look, I know it's tense,' Cora said, 'but you have to eat. Today's result could have tremendous consequences for Non-Land, and for both of us. If CONC votes to take control of the rare-earths mines, that will put massive pressure on Wyrdott to withdraw from Zabaria and start serious negotiations with N-LA. We have to keep our strength up.'

She knew all that. She mashed a grey carrot into her lentils, set the fork down.

'Come on, Astra. Buck up. Things are going well. That child's been reunited with his mother, hasn't he? The YAC percussionist and her little drummer boy. You couldn't ask for a better symbol of freedom for Zabaria than that. The drums of peace are booming, Astra. All around.'

The incredible news had broken last night. Not on Gaian Tablettes, of course, but Jasper had called to tell her: Tiamet had been reunited with her son. It wasn't clear yet exactly what had happened, but somehow – possibly with CONC help – Ebebu had made it on to the Freedom Bus on his own, determined to find his Birth mother. Astra hoped Tiamet was giddy with happiness.

'Today's Earth's deadline.' Her face felt bloodless. 'If just one of the votes goes against us, nothing will matter any more.'

Cora sighed. 'Astra. I wish I could help you. I really do. Sometimes I think maybe you *should* ask for some medical assistance for your mental health problems. Maybe your grandmother could find a decent therapist who'd be willing to make ion chamber visits.'

'I don't have *mental health problems*!' she shouted. 'Fucking *humanity* has a mental health problem, all right? Fucking humanity is totally off its fucking rocker!'

Heads turned. Lichena and Bircha were staring daggers at her from across the hall.

'*Quiet at the back,*' Bircha yelled.

Cora sucked her teeth. 'That's one way of looking at things. Humanity has certainly been slipping about all over the place lately. But perhaps it will climb back on its rocker today. We just have to wait and see, and not lose morale.'

Astra's face was hot now. She felt awful. This might be the last time she ever saw Cora, and she'd raged at her. Tears pricked her eyes.

'I'm sorry. I didn't mean to shout. I'm wound up, that's all.' She reached across the table and placed her hand on Cora's. She couldn't remember ever having held Cora's hand before. That was because it was the gnarled claw of a fierce bird of prey, a knobbly, liver-spotted gauntlet thrown down daily at Astra, its forefinger raised at every opportunity to lecture her, impart vital knowledge, harry her into action.

Which was how Cora showed love. 'Thank you for being my friend,' she said. 'And for being Eya's friend and sending her to Hokma to give birth to me. Without you, I would have been a Sec Gen. I don't regret anything that's happened to me. And I'm so glad I've got to know you.'

Eya's bracelet shone between them. Cora clasped Astra's hand firmly and squeezed tight. 'I'm honoured to be your friend, Astra. Now get some rest this afternoon and let's hope we have something to celebrate this evening.'

The afternoon had passed without incident. But that didn't mean anything. The CONC votes could have gone badly and the Old Ones might just be biding Their time before wreaking revenge. Any moment now, the ground could crack open and a black abyss yawn beneath the prison, red-hot lava welling up from the bowels of the Earth as basalt bricks thundered down on their heads and acid rain fell like spears from the sky. Her nerves on fire, Astra did yoga in her cell, recited pre-Abrahamic poetry to herself, tidied her files. At three forty-five, Lichena banged on the door to handcuff her through the meal slot, then swung the door open, hard.

'C'mon, Dottyface. Move it.' Lichena jabbed her in the back. Astra stepped out into the corridor, still grateful for Lichena's minimal attentions these days. Since the change of prison Governor and Wyrdott's election, the guard had more or less left her alone. Perhaps she'd been ordered not to break any CONC rules, or maybe it was just the continuing cold. Waiting for the elevator, watching the guard scowl and rub her hands together, a dewdrop at the tip of her nose, Astra's stomach panged.

Earth could swallow them up at the next breath they took, bury them in the rubble of the prison. Lichena might be the last human being she ever saw. The person she died with. Suddenly, she couldn't bear it. Couldn't stand the idea of dying with someone who hated her. Of dying filled with hate.

'Did the prison order you that extra layer of clothing yet?' she asked.

Lichena pinched the dewdrop away, wiped her fingers on her thin fleece. 'What? IMBOD keep the lowly guards at Ashfields Max warm on their rounds? I think not.'

The words floated out of Astra's mouth before she could stop them. 'I could ask my grandmother to send you some thermals.'

Lichena face's distorted with a look of horror and derision so extreme it was comical. 'You are really out there, aren't you, Ordott? Out there where the solar buses don't go.'

The elevator doors opened. She grimaced. 'That's what everyone says.'

'Yeah, well, don't go dragging me into your weird mental world.' Lichena gave her a shove. 'This job might be shit, but the last thing I need is to lose it for fraternising with the traitors.'

The elevator began its descent. She knew next to nothing about Lichena, she realised.

'Aren't there any other jobs you could get?'

'With a month holidays and proper sick leave, in the ashfields? You must be joking.'

'You could move. Go to the steppes.'

The guard sniffed. 'Some of us, Ordott, got a sense of family responsibilities. Some of us don't go deserting our parents and grandparents just because we feel like kicking up trouble and making a name for ourselves out there in the big wide world.'

She was silent. It was a dig. But it didn't hurt. It was interesting, she realised, to see the world from Lichena's point of view. Maybe, she thought, for the first time ever, Lichena was a bit jealous of her. Perhaps Lichena had a yen for travel, really wanted to see the world beyond the Boundary. If she wanted to change Is-Land, it occurred to her for the first time, she had to try and change Is-Landers like Lichena. People who hated her. She had to try and understand that hate. If she lived, she vowed, she would try to do that.

If she lived. The elevator stopped and the doors opened. 'Did you hear about the votes?' she asked, on an impulse. Lichena had a wallscreen in her office, she would surely have access to a rolling news service.

'What votes?'

'The CONC votes.'

'For frack's sake. You lot and your *votes*. Haven't we had enough votes here to last a lifetime?'

They had reached the ion chamber. Astra sat and Lichena secured her cuffs to the table. 'An hour max. And no talking about anything you shouldn't.'

The guard left, shutting the door behind her. For a moment, she was alone in the chamber with Vultura and the stopwatch. A disempowered Vultura, though. Astra's visits with Jasper were conducted under CONC security settings, which – altered at IMBOD's demand – ran a verbal pattern-recognition program that would alert the prison officers to any mention of Muzi or his family but was otherwise unable to transmit their conversation. Jasper's familiar bronze ion form emerged into view, his plump translucent face beaming at her from his seat opposite.

He gave a thumbs-up. Her heart leapt. Then, behind him, two more forms appeared. The glimmering silvermist outline of a robed elderwoman, holding hands with a hulking, skyclad young woman.

'Brana!' She gasped as her grandmother waved at her. 'Jasper, how did you—'

'Shhh.' He put his finger to his lips. She trailed off, bewildered. Behind Brana and the young woman a fuzzier image was emerging, a tall, thin, smudgy-grey figure, its outlines hazy but clearly a man, dressed in a T-shirt and trousers, stooping slightly, with a shock of thinning hair . . . Was it? Yes, it was, unbelievably, *Photon*, smiling his same old shy, crooked smile as there, in the other corner of the chamber, two more ion visitors appeared, the pellucid bronze forms of a man and a woman with familiar faces . . . They were broader and older and wearing smart suits, but it was Rudo and Sandrine, ghosts from her past and ghosts in the chamber, their semi-opaque forms mingling and overlapping with the silver-pearl, bronze and storm-grey shapes of the others. *Photon. Rudo* and *Sandrine*. And who was that young woman . . . she was so huge she could only be a Sec Gen . . .

'Surprise,' Jasper whispered.

Surprise, Brana mouthed. The others said the word noiselessly, too, grinning and beaming and waving. She didn't get it. Wasn't their audio working?

'What's going on? Where are you all?' The pit of her stomach twinged. Why was everyone here? Had they come to say goodbye? Had . . . She blinked back tears as a devastating thought ran through her like a sword . . . Had everyone *died* already? Was this what being dead was like?

'Jasper.' Her voice quavered. 'Did the votes—'

'You betcha!' Jasper punched the air. 'You met Earth's deadline, Istarastra. Both votes passed with flying colours. Seems like the recent outbreak of hostilities has reminded everyone that we can't afford to go backwards now. Nations are queueing up to relinquish their rockets, and from now on CONC's taking control of all rare-earths mines *and* all weapons of war. I don't know about you, but I thought a little party was in order!'

It was like being rinsed in a shower of light. Everything shone. Everyone was silently cheering, their glowing forms merging and swaying like lanterns in the wind. Sandrine and Rudo were embracing and jumping up and down. Photon was waving his hands in the air like a maniac. Brana was clapping and the unknown young woman was sticking her fingers in her mouth, whistling without making a sound. She wasn't dead in a room full of ghosts. And she wasn't going to be buried alive with Lichena in a basalt tomb. She was breathing and weeping and, although chained to the table, she was soul-dancing with her family and friends. Tears glazing her eyes, she glanced down at her bracelet, its thin loops a blurry gleam on her wrist. *We love you and we need you but we're not your slaves*, she transmitted to Metal, wherever It was.

'Hey, are you okay?' Jasper asked. 'Your face looks wet.'

'Yeah.' Shackled to the table, she couldn't wipe the tears away. 'I thought we were all going to die.'

'We are all going to die.' He grinned. 'But not today.'

Not today, no. Today the prison floor would remain the floor, flat and rough beneath her feet, and the walls around her would stay standing. Earth's red-hot bowels would keep on roiling deep inside its crust; Air's winds would refrain from blowing down buildings; Fire would not burn whole cities to the ground; Water's scorching rain would evaporate from the clouds before it fell; the seas would splash against the shores up to the long tidemarks of straggly seaweed, weathered wood and tumbled shells they had left behind the day before, and then retreat. Astra could have floated out of her shackles and tankini to bump against the ceiling like a balloon, except . . . She peered through the dancing forms to the looming wallscreen just about still visible behind them.

'But what's everyone doing here? Can they hear me? And what about . . .' She mouthed, *Vultura?*

The party calmed down a little. Rudo placed his finger on his lips.

'Hey, a little natural cunning goes a long way.' Jasper twirled an imaginary moustache. 'I told you these CONC machines have their advantages. I got my IT gals to tinker with the settings so anyone else transmitting into your chamber will be speaking on my vocal frequency, then I organised a Group Visit at my end and hey, here we are!'

She flicked a glance over her shoulder, expecting Lichena to barge in. 'Will that really work?'

'We don't know till we try it. Like I said, guys, just don't everyone talk at once, and don't say anything I told you not to!'

'Hello, darling,' Brana said. Or at least the Brana form's mouth
moved: it was Jasper's voice that sounded in the chamber. Everyone
smiled. 'Astra, this is Halja. Jasper arranged for us to visit from the
CONC office in Atourne.'

Halja. Of course. Her half-Code sister and a Sec Gen, she had
been writing to Astra, sending demands for lists of obscure factual
information about her health and daily routine at Ashfields Max,
requests Astra complied with, though she suspected most of the
details would not pass the prison censors.

'Hi, Halja,' she said. 'Thank you for your letters.'

Halja raised her wrist and shook her bracelet, a twin of Astra's
own. Astra couldn't reciprocate, but she lifted her fingers as much
as she could for a wave.

'Hello, my sister,' Halja said solemnly, also in Jasper's voice, then
turned shyly to Brana, who put her arm around her.

'It's strange talking in another person's voice, isn't it, darling?'
Brana said, as though the young woman were a child.

'She's got the same hands as me,' Halja announced, holding hers
out. And though Halja's were bigger, it was true.

'Thank you for coming, Halja,' she said. 'I'll hold your hand
one day.'

'Rudo and I are here in Amazigia, Astra. We came for the vote.'
Sandrine's eyes were sparkling as if she, too, were fighting back
tears, but her broad smile was as warm as ever. Beside her, Rudo had
definitely put on some weight. Mainly muscle, Astra realised as she
took in his solid neck and chest.

'It's crazy town here, Astra.' Rudo tuned in next on the Jasper
frequency. 'Humanity's on a Himalayan high. Wouldn't miss it for
the world, so ta speak.'

'Rudo and I were catching up in the bar,' Sandrine said. 'We
were *just* talking about you when Jasper found us.'

'Well, what else would we be talking about? Except our life goal of gatecrashing an IMBOD ion chamber party, of course!'

'It's so amazing to see you guys.' Her face ached from smiling. She turned to Photon, whose fuzzy form hadn't gained in definition. 'Hey,' she teased. 'I thought you were just using plant tech now, Phot. I tried to join you but the Old Ones weren't being co-operative. Are you in a lantern leaf dream chamber, then?'

'Close.' Photon's voice was on the same frequency as the others but slightly faint and fuzzy, like his form. 'I am in an Ion Shroom Room. Not a psychosphere chamber, but a new mycelium technology developed by CONC bioengineers here in Björkånland. The first non-metal ion chamber in existence, it will be launched next month alongside a new range of fungus-based Tablettes. One of the developers is a big reader of *Is-Land Watch* and so I am invited to test drive the device today!'

'Whoah!' Rudo cheered. 'Trust the Phot! You're driving a magic mushroom, dude?'

'Not yet. But fusion technologies are in the planning stages.' And then they were all straining to understand, letting Photon explain how fungi, through their thread-like spores – mycelium – transmitted signal molecules that triggered reactions not only within the fungus, but also in the cells of other organisms. By clinging to the roots of trees and plants, spreading underground and transmitting messages about the health of their hosts, mycelium, in fact, facilitated a system of communication so advanced, Old World biologists had called it the underground internet, or – Photon giggled – the Wood Wide Web. Old World innovators had exploited mycelium's dense mat-like structure to create incredibly strong and fully biodegradable packaging and building material. Now, at last, CONC bioengineers had learned how to amplify the power of fungi signal molecules and program them to behave like electronic circuitry: run by mycelium microchips, the Ion Shroom

Room was a living computer fuelled by water and nutrients. Some functions were still a little clunky, but the advantages were obvious: the Tablettes only needed an eyedropper of liquid food every day and were completely compostable.

'That's incredible!' Astra erupted. 'If we can use plant tech for gaming and meetings and Living Libraries, and mycelium tech for instant messaging and mobile communications, we won't need to mine rare-earths any more. That means we've really done it. We've met *all* Earth's demands.' Bouncing on her seat, Photon's fuzzy orb of a head beaming down at her, she tried to explain. 'Don't you see? This is the breakthrough we've been waiting for. Ditching metal comms tech means we can spiritually evolve at last. We can learn from the biosphere and the Old Ones. We can reach our full potential as a species, become star travellers, cosmic voyagers! Who knows where we'll go next?'

Everyone had fallen quiet. She trailed off. No one believed her, she knew.

'First, though, we gotta finish off the rare-earths industry,' Jasper said. 'IREMCO's done, but the other companies are going to appeal today's ruling. I hate to be a party pooper, Astra, but rare-earths and metal Tablettes are the status quo for a reason: they do have their advantages.'

'Plant tech is slow, no doubt about it,' Photon conceded. 'And so far, mycelium interface is monochrome and low definition, not very glamorous. That's a good thing, in my view – it makes the virtual world less addictive – but most people . . .' He paused. 'Most people will need a little *persuading* to give up their hi-rez screens and chambers.'

'We're not quite there yet, Astra,' Brana said firmly. 'What we need is you.'

She sat back, puzzled. 'You have me. I'll keep sending messages as long as the Old Ones want me to.'

Jasper shot a glance at Photon. 'Astra,' Photon continued, 'I speak as your friend, and as the editor of *Is-Land Watch*. You have a loyal international following, and now that the world has heeded Earth's message, your profile will grow in strength. But to reach as many people as possible, your story needs an update.'

She frowned. 'I'm not a piece of hardware, Photon. That's the whole *point*.'

'Never mind the metaphor,' Jasper cut in. 'He's saying that you need to get out of prison, Astra. To make the headlines again, and use the attention to fight for the planet, and for One-Land. As your lawyer, I'm telling you again that you need to drop your challenge to the prisoner exchange. We all want you to ask the Mujaddid's team to revert to the original conditions, a straight swap for you and Peat, and then come out into the world and spread your message in person.'

'Yeah, Astra,' Rudo chimed in. 'You've got a ton of global groupies, from mystics to eco-developers. Folks need to meet you in person now. I'm stationed out in Southern NuAfrica these days, could arrange a tour for you here, no problem.'

'I Zeppelin back to New Zonia tomorrow,' Sandrine said. 'It's a relaxing flight, and oh my gosh, people there would so love to meet you!'

'And don't forget Is-Landers, Astra,' Brana said. 'We need you and Peat freed, too, all of us. Wyrdott's election has emboldened so many of us. Every day, more young people are revealing that they are not really Sec Gens, and more parents are demanding the reversal treatment for their children who had the shot. If Peat comes home, he could be the figurehead of this movement. And even if you can't stay in the country, my darling, you need to be out in the world, speaking freely, trying to reach Gaians as well with your messages. I want to see you out of this place, healthy and happy, and calling for peace with our neighbours.'

'You don't have to worry about IMBOD,' Halja said. 'I'm going to be your bodyguard. Brana says I can't leave Is-Land, but I'm going to ask Crystal Wyrdott to let me.'

Brana squeezed Halja's waist. 'That's a lovely idea, darling, and I'm sure Astra appreciates the offer. You'd make a smashing team.'

She stared at her grandmother. 'I don't just want peace with Non-Land, Brana. I want the Boundary to fall, and for Is-Land to evolve into One-Land.'

'I know.' Brana clasped Halja's hand again, so that their bracelets were touching. 'Astra, since my visit to Or to meet your family there, I've been thinking very hard about what you've said regarding Non-Land. When I consider what your own country has done to you – your suffering in the neurohospice, the hardships you've endured here in jail – well, it's been very humbling to realise that it was your time with the Non-Landers that gave you your remarkable strength. I perfectly understand why they consider you a goddess. And goodness me, visiting you makes me hate walls! I've changed my mind, darling. I think we should give the Non-Landers a chance to live with us. As soon as you're freed, I'm going to start a campaign to invite a Non-Land family to come and stay with us in Yggdrasila. That's what Una Dayyani is calling for, isn't it? Well, after what the Vision Council was going to do in our name, I think all Is-Landers ought to try and be generous.'

Astra was lost for words. As she stared at her grandmother, Jasper cocked his head. 'How about it, Ordott? Time for me to start renegotiating the prisoner swap?'

Everyone was waiting. No one had said she was nuts. No one had offered to find her a therapist.

But did they believe her? She was afraid to ask.

Then, as she looked between Brana and Halja and their proud, smiling faces, to Rudo and Sandrine, Jasper and Photon, their glowing bronze, silvermist and raincloud-grey forms merged into the radiant shape of love, and she understood that it didn't matter. Her family and friends believed *in* her, and that was what counted.

'The last word of the Prophecy is missing,' she said slowly. 'Some scholars claim it is "war". But today, humanity decided that all places should sing glad hymns of welcome and of peace. That's just a dream, still, though. To make it happen, I know I've got work to do out in the world. I'm coming, I promise. And Peat can come home, too. But I just have one demand.'

'Darling!' Brana's tone was Jasper at his sharpest. 'Didn't you hear Photon? You have to drop that demand. IMBOD won't let Cora go!'

'Not Cora. She's fine here. What I want is an Is-Land passport. I want to be able to travel freely now. To be in all places. To go to Asfar if I want, or Amazigia, and always be able to get back home. Is that a reasonable demand, Jasper, to allow me to spend time with my family here? Wouldn't granting it help put Wyrdott back in CONC's good graces?'

Jasper grinned. 'Sounds doable to me.'

And then they were all chatting, catching up, doing their best to talk one at a time, Rudo giving her the low-down on Southern Nu-African politics, Sandrine sharing a peanut brittle recipe with Brana, Halja pelting her with questions about the exact dimensions of her ion chamber and the caloric content of her meals, and Jasper grinning and turning in his seat to give two fingers to Vultura, the hoodwinked Vultura who couldn't tell that Is-Land Enemy Number One, Astra Ordott, was having a party. A party to celebrate the end of war and the beginning of her freedom. A party of ghosts, cherished ghosts, present and absent, as, in the lustrous mingling forms, she caught glowing glimpses of others who should be here, too ... Hokma, Uttu, Zizi ... Her dead, whose absence had once felt like a choke-chain around her neck, now flowing and chiming, their shapes moving like wind in the chamber, echoing the joy. There were other faint traces visible in the intermingling, too: Lil, Klor, Nimma, Peat and Sheba ... And there, over Brana's shoulder, a bright sapphire wink ... But it hurt to sense Muzi, a sharp pain in her heart.

'Are you all right, darling?' Brana asked.

'I was just wishing ...' She couldn't say his name or the party would vanish. 'You know ...'

Brana smiled. 'We have much to thank him for, don't we?'

Rudo nodded. 'I reckon he was thinking a few moves ahead, Astra. Smart guy.'

Then Photon and Jasper and Sandrine were nodding, too. And

suddenly she understood. An effervescent warmth spread through her chest. If Muzi had freed Peat in the Asfarian court, Non-Land would have nothing to trade her for and she wouldn't now be on the verge of release. She didn't know her husband any more, had never known him well; he was a mystery and maybe would always remain so, but when she thought of him now, it would be with gladness and gratitude.

'Now, if only we could get Blesserson behind bars.' Rudo mashed his fist in his palm. 'Any chance of making *that* swap, Jasper?'

'Just tell me where he lives.' Halja pulled back her arm as if aiming a bow and arrow. 'I'll get him for you, Astra.'

Through the fine mist of her amazement, Hokma's words came floating back to her: It would be better, Astra, if you could forgive Samrod . . . or you will never be free of him, even if you walk out of this prison, all the way to Asfar.

Forgive Blesserson? She didn't know if that was possible, but for the first time since she was a child, she didn't hate him. And more than that, she realised, a tiny part of her was grateful to him, too, for the momentous move he had made in Amazigia, the tarnished whistle he had blown to get the game of justice moving again. Maybe she could never fully forgive Samrod Blesserson, but at least now, when he intruded on her thoughts, she had a choice about how to feel.

'Thank you, Halja. But no.' She shook her head. 'Let him camp in the ruins of his life. We've got more important battles to fight.'

All too soon, the party was over, everyone reaching out their arms to say farewell, their luminous forms popping like soap bubbles, leaving just Jasper to say goodbye. Then he faded, too, and the ion chamber was empty again, empty except for her and Vultura and, beneath Vultura's grimace, the clock. Except, she realised, the chamber wasn't empty. She was in it, and she was brimming, overflowing like a starry fountain of light with the peaceful awareness of how much she was loved and how much she had to give.

Then Lichena was opening the door, grumbling about the cold. A conclave of rooks had flown by unnoticed, like an Owleon in the night. A golden flame of an hour had flickered past, as glorious and fleeting as a hoopoe on the wing.

But that was all right. She let the guard unlock her wrists, stood and stretched her legs. She had all the time in the world.

Acknowledgements

Without the dedicated work of my medical teams at the Park Centre for Breast Care and the Sussex Cancer Centre, The Gaia Chronicles would have been left unfinished. Thanks to them, and to all my family, friends and colleagues who supported me during that challenging and transformative time, this book was at last written, a year later than planned, but shaped as it could not have been otherwise by a profound belief in our human desire and ability to heal one another.

After my diagnosis in 2016, the Royal Literary Fund awarded me a generous grant that enabled me to focus on my recovery, and this book. Emma-Jane Hughes and Richard Joyce gifted me time at Creoso Cottage in Ciliau Aeron, Ceredigion, in which mythic landscape I first returned to the novel after my treatment. A subsequent grant from the Francis W Reckitt Arts Trust allowed me to continue to work on the book at writing retreats at Hawkwood College, Gloucestershire and Monica Suswin's Cabin on the Hill, Forest Row. Piet Devos, Hugh Dunkerley, Rob Hamberger, Sarah Hymas, Joanna Lowry and Bryan Wigmore all gave encouraging and insightful comments on early drafts. A million thanks go to Louise Reiser for her forensic attention to the final drafts of the book and her loving concern over Muzi's state of mind, all of which so enhanced the music and meaning of the text and alleviated my lonely hurtles to the deadlines. Once more I owe John Luke Chapman a crate of gratitude for his careful help – plus a beer for his thoughts on the fire at Or. The late, much-missed Fionn Brady gave me shelter at a deep discount for sixteen years, a landlordly magnanimity maintained by his siblings Deirdre Brady and Darragh Brady.

Thanks to a research development award from the University of Chichester I was able to travel to the West Bank in 2016, where I volunteered at Marda Permaculture Farm and the Palestine Museum of Natural History. As a member of InterPal's Bearing Witness Women's Delegation to Lebanon I also – albeit briefly – experienced conditions in Palestinian and Syrian refugee camps that winter. I remain humbled, informed and inspired by the spirit of resistance and sheer determination to thrive that I encountered on these travels. Here in the UK, Ziauddin Sardar of *Critical Muslim* and Yasmin Khan of *Sindbad Sci-Fi* have supported The Gaia Chronicles since their inception, and I thank them and all my friends at the Muslim Institute for encouraging me to travel ever deeper into the field of Islamicate SFF. 'Jews on Quests!', a talk by Farah Mendlesohn on Jewish narratives in fantasy, influenced the final draft, and gave me hope that some of the philosophical aims of the quartet might indeed also resonate with aspects of that faith and culture. As my idiosyncratic dance around the Abrahamic Shamanic fires continues, time spent with Lee Whitaker, Susie Lobb and my beloved aunt Mary Griffiths deepens my appreciation of the Christian faith I was brought up in. I am indebted also to Bryan Wigmore for introducing me to the term 'psychosphere', Les Paul, for links to online articles that refined my understanding of mycelium technologies, and Karen Griffiths for sharing her knowledge of medieval weaponry with me. The quote from Hafiz, Ghazal 29, is my translation. Suen's knowledge of the plant world derives from *Flowers: Their Spiritual Significance* by The Mother (Sri Aurobindo Society: Pondicherry, 1998). The Şahi Topu can be visited at Fort Nelson, Hampshire, where it sits in a light-filled atrium beneath a banner displaying a verse from the poem 'The Voice of the Guns' by Gilbert Frankau (1884–1952).

Chapeau as always to Jo Fletcher, who's had my back at every turn of the saga, and to her crack team of Molly Powell, Olivia Mead and Lisa Rogers, who between them have so professionally nurtured this book and, along with my agent John Berlyne of Zeno Agency, staunchly supported the entire quartet. My final thanks go to all those working for peace, justice, equality and environmental sustainability in our volatile, beautiful world.